Silver Linings

VIOLET PAGE

Copyright © 2025 by Violet Page

All rights reserved.

No part of this publication may be reproduced, distributed, or transmitted in any form or by any means, including photocopying, recording, or other electronic or mechanical methods, without the prior written permission of the publisher, except as permitted by U.S. copyright law.

The story, all names, characters, and incidents portrayed in this production are fictitious. No identification with actual persons (living or deceased), places, buildings, and products is intended or should be inferred.

Editing by Alexa of The Fiction Fix

Cover Design by Brenna Jones Design

Author Photo by Lavender Sage Photo

Content Warning

Hello dear reader. Thank you so much for choosing Silver Linings as your next read. While Silver Linings is very much a book filled with humor and spine tingling romance, it does contain sensitive materials that I hope I handled with care. If any of the following topics make you uncomfortable, I urge you to take your mental health into consideration before proceeding.

Silver Linings contains the following: mentions of child abandonment, familial death, strained parental relationships.

For anyone who tells themselves they can't do what they dream—
you can. You contain multitudes. Let your magic out.

And for Miley—who sat my side, nudging my hand off the keyboard
for the years I spent writing this.
I love you.

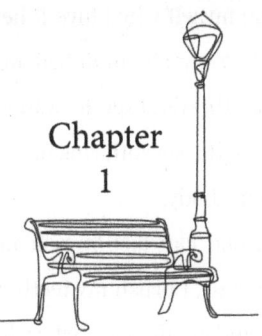

Chapter 1

Silver

It's my own personal belief that having to roll yourself out of bed when you are *most definitely* hungover from the night before should award you with some small semblance of mercy from the universe.

Apparently, the universe is a bitch.

Being woken up before the good lord intended—also known as the third time the snooze alarm goes off—by jackhammering pounding into pavement outside the window is certainly *not* my idea of a post-celebratory night out wake up call. It's actually making me feel vaguely murder-y, if I'm being honest.

And yet, here I am, suffocating my head with my pillow, cutting off much-needed oxygen in an attempt to drown out the sound of the construction blaring five floors below. They might as well have placed their jackhammer directly on my skull with the way my head is throbbing, fueled by last night's one too many gin and tonics.

But after another agonizing ten minutes of cursing the city for being punctual in repairing something for once—while simultaneously asking myself why I love it here so much—I finally find the strength to drag myself out of bed and army crawl my way into the bathroom for a shower. I set the water dial to a temperature that would put shame to the seventh ring of hell and start scrubbing last night's sins from my body.

Once I'm clean and can face myself in the mirror without screeching away in horror, I brush my teeth, not caring enough to bother with makeup, and get dressed before heading downstairs to go to work…to the shift I'm running late for.

The elevator doors ping open to reveal the lobby of my building and the short, stocky doorman standing just behind the welcome desk. He turns to face me with an animated smile stretching wide across his ruddy face.

"Good morning," Tony bellows with enthusiasm, making me wince as the headache on the edge of my brain flairs to life.

I grunt out an unintelligible reply.

"Yeah, I heard you got in really late last night," he chuckles.

"You and Randall need to stop whispering about the tenants during shift change." Randall is our overnight doorman, and he and Tony are worse than little old ladies gossiping at a town hall bingo night. I rub at my forehead, hoping to ease some of the tension still lurking there.

"But then who would update you on the latest building news?" His inflection is conspiratorial, and *news* is just a nice word for gossip.

"Oh?" I sidle a bit closer to his desk, tucking my hair behind my ear, as if that will help me listen better while feigning disinterest. "Something happened yesterday?"

He leans in conspiratorially. "Mrs. Evans on four threatened to sue Mr. Sanders' daughter."

I furrow my brow in confusion. "Mr. Sanders' daughter? Isn't Isla five?"

Tony starts cackling. "Yes! I told Isla she should hire Caroline on seven as her defense attorney." He takes a sip of coffee from the mug behind the counter, the scent traveling over, making my stomach cramp in need. "Oh, and Sal is retiring."

That shocked me out of my thoughts. Sal is, or I guess *was*, our building's maintenance man. He has been keeping this building running for over fifty years without fail, and he's very much like the building he's tirelessly looked after for the last five decades—old, a little rough around the edges, and probably the most likely to survive the apocalypse by sheer force of will.

"Damn, I thought he would never retire. Have they found his replacement yet?" I glance down at my phone and note the time, knowing I still need to stop and get coffee on the way if I'm going to survive the day.

"I think they've got their eye on someone, but I haven't met him yet."

"I don't want to cut this bonding moment short, but Holly's going to kill me if I don't get to the store soon." My coworker, Holly—also known as an angel amongst mortals—already opened the store for me due to my previously-catatonic state. I make my way towards the door. "But tell Isla I'll be a character witness in the case against Mrs. Evans!"

I press out onto the street, immediately assaulted by a wall of heat and humidity.

One thing no one realizes when they think about New York City is how insufferable the summers are here. There's a reason most of the movies and tv shows seem to take place during fall and winter—it's a much more romantic setting when you can't smell steaming garbage as you walk literally anywhere. As it stands, it's currently the end of July, and I can feel sweat building on the nape of my neck.

Reaching into my purse, I shuffle around until I find my handheld electric fan, turn it on and blast my face with a tepid breeze. I have no shame when it comes to heat, and if this is what I have to do to stay even moderately comfortable, I'd do it.

Hot weather and I do not a couple make.

My feet drag me toward my favorite coffee shop as I dodge people swirling around me. It may be a Monday, but the city is always buzzing with an electric sort of vibrancy. Walking down the street in your neighborhood is like reliving a scene in a movie you've seen a million times—familiar, comforting, and you can time everything down to the second. There's the symphony of pigeons taking flight because a child gave chase, cabbies honking at other drivers, business men feverishly talking into their phones, and my personal favorite: the neighborhood watch dog judging all of us from his windowsill throne.

Even after years passing by and trying to earn his trust, he's never warmed to me. I must be suffering a moment of insanity, because even in my *withering* state, I decide to try my luck.

I hedge close to the window where Bob holds vigil, lips starting to recede from his canines and a comically large bow tie around his small neck. "Good morning, Bob. Are you on step four of world domination today?"

Robert, the seven pound mini poodle, stares at me quizzically before devolving into a fit of barking that sounds suspiciously like: *back away from my window, bitch.*

He really doesn't like it when I call him Bob.

I step away, hands up in surrender. "One day, I'll get you to love me."

The only response I get back is a snarl, and my head throbs in reply.

God, I need coffee, perhaps a three gallon IV drip intravenously injected for maximum potency if I'm going to get this ache to finally abate.

Respect the Drip is my favorite coffee shop in the entire city—stepping into their haven is like being enveloped in a hug. The scent is warm and comforting, everyone is smiling and caffeinated, and the barista *absolutely* knows your coffee order because you are a creature of habit who refuses to try anything else. My best friend, Makena, would argue I need to broaden my horizons—step out of my comfort zone—but why mess with something that's already perfect?

I drag myself inside, letting the air conditioning wash over my sun-fevered skin in a cooling caress.

"I wondered when I'd see you in," Dax calls out from behind the counter as he makes someone's macchiato.

Dax, the owner, became our friend after I painstakingly wore him down over many early morning visits with an unwavering determination to make nice with someone who could always keep me caffeinated. He was there last night celebrating Makena's promotion, but he left early since he had to be here at five for morning prep work.

Stepping up to the counter, I lean dramatically against the concrete slab. "It was touch-and-go there for a while, I won't lie." The Grim Reaper, in all his dark robed glory, made an appearance in my booze induced dreams. When I jolted out of bed this morning,

I may have thought I'd been sent straight to hell, but no—that was just construction, so metaphorical hell then.

"You want your usual?" He knows without me having to say anything—I want a toffee nut cold brew with sweet foam on top.

"Please, and a flat white for Holly."

I pay and step aside, dropping a couple extra bills in their tip jar and waiting for Dax to work his magic on the only hope I have left to cure me.

"What happened with that guy at the bar last night?" Dax asks as he whips up my drink. "It looked like things were escalating when I headed out."

He's referring to the corporate analyst I met and then spent the rest of the night kissing. I almost forgot that happened—I *would* have forgotten, without the reminder.

I open my mouth to tell him as much before I'm interrupted.

"She left that poor sap high and dry before he could even learn her name. Don't you know by now, Dax? Our Silver doesn't *do* commitment," my best friend since grade school, Makena, says from behind me.

What the hell?

I didn't even see him come in. Why does he look so good? We both went out last night, and we both drank our body weight in G&Ts. So why the hell does his deep brown skin look luminous and hydrated while I look like a bridge troll?

"First off—" I look from Kena to Dax, "—that is absolutely true. I am a hump and dump kind of lady. Secondly—" I round on Kena "—how in the actual hell do you look so good right now? Did you do some kind of ritual sacrifice before you went to bed to look so full of vitality?" Meanwhile, *I* look like a reanimated corpse.

Kena barks out a laugh, a wide smile stretching across his face. "No, honey. I just washed my makeup off and did my skincare before I fell asleep. You should try it some time." He rolls his eyes with a hint of chastisement.

I want to retort that I *did* wash my face, but then I remember it wasn't until this morning, and I definitely woke up with mascara flakes all over my cheekbones.

"Are you nervous about today?" We both grab our coffee, waving goodbye to Dax, and head out arm in arm towards our destinations—him to catch the train and me towards the bookshop.

Kena and I grew up together in the city, living at The Langham until Nan moved down to Florida and his parents went upstate. Our whole college experience, we lived in my nan's rent-controlled apartment. It will be a cold day in hell when I leave.

It's the perfect location, just on the border of West Village and Tribeca, and it's disgustingly cheap. New Yorkers know when you find a place in a great neighborhood with a good layout and efficient building management, you're more likely to die there than you are to move.

"I'm pretty anxious," he admits, pausing before I nudge him to continue. "I guess I just don't want to mess it up. Maison Atelier has been on the vision board since high school." His ebony eyes take on a dream-like quality as he smiles softly to himself. "I can still hardly believe it."

I halt our steps with a hand on his arm. "You are Makena Williams. You have been mixing textiles and patterns since your mom took you to the garment district at age three, and you got lost in a sea of brocade and silk. You have given countless clients their dream home. Hell, you made our apartment a palace when we lived there—not to mention the magic you can work on a flea market flip."

"I do love a good flea market flip."

"Everyone does, babe. That's not the point." I loop my arm through his, steering us forward and back on to the topic at hand. "You are the most talented designer I know—"

"I'm the only designer you know."

I give him a playful shove. "You're the most talented designer in the *world*—" I wave my arms with an exaggerated flourish, "—and clearly, Maison Atelier saw something in you that made them break all their rigid rules for hiring. Be yourself. You shine brightest when you don't hide."

We reach the steps into the train station, and I pull him into a hug. "You're going to crush it. There isn't a single doubt in my mind."

When we pull apart, he gives the lapel of his maroon jacket a tug, nodding his head at me in confidence.

"Atta boy!" I balance my tray of coffee in one hand and slap his ass right before he takes off down the stairs.

He whips around, spearing me with a look. "You're incorrigible."

I beam wide and trill my fingers at him in goodbye.

There's still ten minutes on my walk to work, and I'm lucky that three of them are spent on the phone to Nan. It's impossible to get a hold of her these days because the over-sixty community she lives in keeps her booked and busy with a better social life than mine. She deserves it after having to put up with the trials and tribulations of raising me, but our call ends just as quickly as it began, and I'm left missing her with a persistent ache in my chest.

The sun beaming down on me slowly aids my recovery, but the light is making my already-sensitive eyes burn as sweat collects on my back.

Typically, I can handle my drink well enough to rally the next morning and make it through a work day. Last night was a rare case. One look into Kena's pleading eyes, and I was agreeing to whatever his stupid cherubic face wanted. Which, as it turned out, was for everyone involved to get shit faced off Sambuca shots (vile) and stay out celebrating what he dubbed, *"the last night of relative freedom before I become too busy to even remember who any of you are".*

Charming.

Taking a sip of my cold brew, I'm about to round Christopher Street in the West Village, heading closer to Brownstone Books, holding the coffee I'm still finishing and the one I got for Holly. I start rifling through my canvas bag, looking for my sunglasses, not needing to pay attention to a walk that's muscle memory after a decade of commuting.

I'm treading a fairly brisk pace to at least *attempt* to arrive on time, digging through the black hole that is my bag, shoving twenty receipts, my wallet, and a minimum of seven lipsticks aside so I can find my sunglasses and—HA! There they are. My eyes can finally get some relief from–

"Omph!"

Pain lances through my body at the abrupt collision. Did I just walk into a wall?

"Damnit!" I cry, glancing down at all the coffee I just spilled. "Well, that's not ideal." At least the rats will be caffeinated.

"No, it certainly isn't," a deep voice grumbles from above my head.

The resonance of the voice vibrates through my body, making me go still. I didn't walk into a wall—no, I walked into a person. A very *hard* person. Practically built from granite. And yup...that is my precious toffee nut cold brew puddling around and all over his shoes. I slowly drag my eyes up from his cognac-colored boots, over strong thighs encased in dark denim, and further up to a dark green henley hugging a trim, muscled waist and a broad chest.

My interest builds the longer I let my eyes roam up this stranger's form. Who needs to arrive to work on time? Holly has it covered, right?

Continuing my perusal, I'm struck speechless as I feast my eyes on the most attractive man I have ever seen in my life—tanned golden skin, dark stubble neatly hugging his jaw, dark chestnut hair with a slight wave you just want to run your hands through, bright hazel eyes that remind me of the sun spearing through pine trees in a forest. And his mouth is full, sinful... and moving?

I snap out of my daze and obvious perusal to see him scowling down at me. "I'm sorry, what did you say?"

"I was asking if you were okay, but I see you've gone into some sort of—" he gestures at me with his hands, "—catatonic state, mumbling to yourself about pine trees."

I smirk, continuing my not so subtle perusal of him, noting the tattoos peeking out from beneath the sleeve of his shirt and the lack of any sort of ring on his left hand. There's no doubt a deranged gleam in my eyes.

"You're staring. Are you concussed or something?" There's a vague note of concerned irritation in his tone, his eyes darting behind me.

"Oh yeah, I'm fine! I'm so sorry about your shoes. Here, I think

I have a napkin." I sift through my bag but come up empty. I do, however, have all twenty receipts that will do the trick in a pinch. I grab the wad of them, smiling as I bring them up to his face for him to see. He flinches back from my sudden movement.

"No napkins, but these will work." I kneel on the sidewalk to clean up the mess I made.

"What the hell are you doing?" he asks incredulously.

I pat at the liquid coating his shoes with the physical proof of my love for a sweet treat. "I know it's not ideal; the absorption of these is just *not* on par with a napkin or paper towel, but it's all I have." I look up at him from the ground, pasting on my best flirty smile. "If you want to give me your phone number, I can call you to get these cleaned properly." It's not exactly the most subtle come on.

He clenches his jaw, his whole body rigid. "Please get up."

Okay...maybe I'm off my game today. Normally, I'm more charming than this, but I did spill coffee all over his shoes and look like a swamp creature.

I slowly stand, looking up at him. He looks like he stepped straight out of the crystal blue waters of the Mediterranean, in one of those cologne ads that *never* make any sense, all rugged lines and intense stares.

"So, like I said, I can get those cleaned for you when you aren't currently wearing them and have them returned to you ASAP." I reach to grab my phone so I can hand it to him to put in his number.

"No, thanks. They'll be fine." He's still looking past me.

"Are you sure? It's really no prob—"

I can't even finish my sentence before he looks at his watch anxiously. "I've gotta go." He leaves no room for argument before he takes off in the direction I just came from, and I watch him as he goes.

I don't make it to work on time.

Instead, I alert Holly of my arrival by barreling through the front door, the bell ringing in my wake, and I'm instantly put at ease. Every time I step inside Brownstone Books I feel like I've come home again after being away too long. Like I *belong* here.

Kena likes to joke that the store is my one true love because it's the longest relationship I've ever had. He's wrong—it's the *only* relationship I've had. It's just always been easier for me to not do the *romance thing*. I've never particularly had the urge, and the way I figure it, the closer you get to someone, the greater risk you take of them leaving you. So, I keep it simple and keep my circle small—like count it on one hand small. My constants are Nan, Kena, and this shop, just the way I want it.

Holly steps out from the back room, shoulders easing when she sees it's just me.

"I know, I know. I'm sorry. I'm later than I said I would be. Forgive me?" I curl my fists against my chest and give her my best pouty face.

A bout of fear claws at my chest thinking I might have inconvenienced her. The anxiety that seeps in through carefully held together cracks if anyone is upset with me, or if they don't like me, is a feeling I've grown familiar with over the years. I know it's impossible to please everyone, but I'm programmed to try. If they're happy, maybe they'll stay.

"I didn't expect you to be on time, Silver." Holly huffs a laugh.

"Not after last night's phone call."

"God, I'm so sorry. Did I say anything mortifying? I can't be held responsible. Everything is Kena and liquor's fault." I hold up my hands in placation, a surrender for mercy.

"Nothing out of the ordinary. You did propose to my wife *again,* but that's fairly commonplace for you," Holly says.

"Yes, well, she is an actual goddess. What else was I supposed to do?"

"I can't even blame you." Holly's eyes take on a dreamy quality.

Her wife Serafina is a baker with a famous cooking blog called Mental Bake Down. They met years ago in their twenties, and they realized pretty quickly that what they felt for each other was different. Holly always said she was lucky to be in Serafina's orbit, that it was pure happenstance that landed her in the café where Sera was the head baker...but I see the way Sera looks at Holly. She looks at Holly like she's the lucky one, bettered just by knowing her, let alone loving her. It's pure, their love, two souls who compliment *and* challenge each other, for better or worse. It makes my heart hurt sometimes to witness, knowing I'm not made for that.

I snap myself back into the present. "Full disclosure, I did have a coffee for you...but then I ran into a wall of a man and dropped it on the ground."

"A wall of a man?" Holly repeats back to me.

"Yup," I say, popping the *p*. "He was so tall, broad, and grumpy."

"Stop drooling," Holly calls me out of my reverie. "Did you get his number?"

"No. I tried, but he didn't seem interested," I pout.

"That's...unusual for you."

"He's the one that got away," I sigh dramatically.

"Okay, well, that's a bit intense. Do you even know his name?"

"That is beside the point and completely irrelevant, Hols. He was the hottest man I've ever seen. Now, I'll always wonder what could have been. I'll be eighty in a nursing home, ranting to Kena about the walking sex symbol I spilled coffee on and how he could have been my best lay ever until Kena gets so tired of my rambling, he beats me to death with his badminton racket." I suck in a breath of air. "The point is, I'll never know, and the lack of knowledge will haunt me until the end of my days, because I will never see him again." I slump against an age-worn bookshelf that creaks precariously under the pressure.

"Are you done?"

"I think so." I pop up to stand.

"Great. We have some new releases to put out on the shelves." Holly points at a shipment we must have gotten in this morning. "But you're going to get me a coffee first."

I start laughing as I grab my wallet.

"Flat white?" I ask as I back out of the shop, on my way to a different coffee house a block over.

"The biggest one they've got. Try not to spill this one on any other hot men!" She calls before I'm out of earshot.

"No promises!"

Chapter 2

Silver

I'm elbows deep in our newest shipment, prepping it to go on shelves by logging the UPC numbers, inputting the quantity on hand, and actively trying not to go cross-eyed from the mind numbing task.

I love my job, and I'm distinctly aware a lot of people can't say that. The first time I walked into Brownstone Books as a freshman in college, an unenthusiastic Kena in tow, I knew in my bones that I wanted to work here. I walked right up to Pat, not knowing she was the owner, and asked to interview. I needed a job, and as it turned out, she needed a part timer. It was the closest I've come to love at first sight. I didn't even have to regale Pat with my extensive knowledge of books. She claimed she had a feeling about me, and she always followed her gut. I guess she was right, since I've worked here for the better part of a decade.

With Holly gone for the day, I'm left logging the new releases into the system on my own when our part-timer, Carmen, comes out from the stockroom, caramel curls bouncing with each step.

"Okay, I organized the romance backstock by sub-genre so it's easier for all of us to find things. We have—" she pauses and takes a deep breath, counting them off on her fingers, "—rom-coms, rom-*sads*, mafia romance, regency romance, and last but not least, highlander romance." I'm about to comment something along the lines of, *is that all*, when she pipes up again. "Oh, and they are all organized alphabetically by author, and labeled with stickers for easy visibility. I'll tackle thrillers tomorrow."

"You're honestly terrifying sometimes."

"You know label makers are like aphrodisiacs to me."

Carmen joined our team last year after she moved from Arizona to attend Columbia. She is currently pre-law and terrifyingly smart. Plus, her compulsive need to organize everything here works to my benefit, so I don't complain.

"We need more variety," she continues, unable to sit in silence for too long.

"What do you mean?"

"The store... It needs more variety. The way it stands now, it's kind of a dinosaur. Oh, don't give me that face." She must read my expression, but she perseveres. "I *love* this place. You know this is like the family I never had. That's why I care so much, and I know you do too. Silver, this place has been a part of you for *so* long, but it needs a facelift and a better business model that will bring in customers. I've heard you and Holly talk about it before. You need to talk to Pat."

I look around the store, the place I've called my second home for a decade.

Ten years ago, it used to be charming and worn in. Now, though...even I admit, it's looking a little ramshackle. It could use a good clean out, fresh fixtures, and a good coat of paint. At a *minimum*.

She was right, I have thought about it, but I never wanted to rock the boat. If Pat was happy with her shop, who was I to suggest changes? But the fact that Carmen is noticing our slowdown in business is alarming. Maybe she's right, and this is the wake up call we need to do something, fix the place up a little and curate a collection of books that will sell, not just a few obvious bestsellers while the rest collect dust.

"You're right. I'll talk to Holly and get a game plan together for the next time Pat is in. We can talk to her about it together with ideas already in place. You know how particular she can be." I take a sip of my cold brew resting on the counter.

"Monster smut!" Carmen shouts, jumping up and down and clapping her hands.

"Uh—" I'm not even sure what to say, but she doesn't give me the chance before launching into her bid for horny monsters.

"Don't knock it till you try it, Silver. I know you're a *freak*." She wiggles her eyebrows. "It's really taken off on TikTok the past couple years, and there are *so* many good monster romance books out now. Plus, I know you like those fantasy books, the ones where the men have wings. This isn't really that far off. I have so many recommendations for you already. There's a particularly delicious one, a mashup of an Indiana Jones-type quest with shapeshifters." She beams at me.

Admittedly, that does pique my curiosity quite a bit.

"I'm not sure monster romance is the way to get Pat on board, but let's start a list of potential genres we're missing out on. I know we can use more fantasy romance and more thrillers from this decade. Oh! Hockey!" I exclaim.

"Hockey?" Carmen parrots.

I groan just thinking about it. "God, yes. Hockey romances are the pinnacle of a wet dream."

"Don't hockey players have missing teeth?"

"Not the fictional ones." I sigh dreamily. "The men are beefcake sex gods who dominate on the ice and in bed." Now it's my turn to waggle my eyebrows.

"I don't like sports, but I'm titillated enough to ask for a recommendation."

A smile stretches across my face. "I'm actually getting really excited by this."

"Well yeah, beefcake sex gods get my engines going too, but we're at work, so..."

"No, not that—well yes, *always* that—but I meant the idea of fixing this place up and curating our stock." But the more I thought about it, the more nervous I got that Pat would think me foolish and say no.

Carmen pulls out a piece of printer paper, and we start taking notes on anything and everything we can think of—updates to be made to the shop, genres we're missing, things we could house by the cash wrap for easy add-ons. The list grows longer and longer the more we volley ideas back and forth.

A feeling of purpose swells in my chest. It's a feeling I haven't felt in a while—maybe ever. I can't actually remember the last time I had a goal to focus on. Have I been going through life so aimlessly for that long?

Something about that thought doesn't sit right with me, but I shove it to the back of my mind and refocus on the list at hand.

The day progresses in an endless stream of tourists coming in, looking around, and buying nothing before leaving, interspersed with a couple regulars popping in to see what's new on the shelves. I'm setting aside a couple books someone called to put on hold when a particularly disgruntled man comes up to the counter, looking visibly put out.

"Hi. Can I help you?" I try to imbue my voice with cheeriness, even though judging by the scowl settled over his mouth, that same respect is not about to be reciprocated.

"I want to return this book." He slams it down on the counter, shoving it towards me.

I glance down at the book that has *clearly* been read cover to cover, because the spine is cracked in multiple spots, the corners are bent, and I can vaguely see—yeah, those are coffee rings on the cover.

I shove the book back towards him and give him a simple "No" with the same cheery smile I know men *love*.

He scoffs. "Get your manager, girl I want to speak with him."

"Sure thing." I imbue my voice with false saccharine sweetness and do a slow one-eighty, turning to a stop with a flourish. "Brownstone Books manager at your service, sir." I tip an invisible hat to him. "Now that the formality is over, the answer is still no."

He huffs. "You clearly don't understand. This book was *terrible*. It was predictable, derivative, and a complete waste of my money." His fists are balled now, and he bangs them on the counter, thinking if he gets angry enough, I'll cave to his whims out of fear.

"I actually do understand that you didn't enjoy this book." I lean forward, as if I'm about to share a secret with him. "Believe it or not, I've been known to crack a book open from time to time, and while I am sorry you were disappointed in the plot, that isn't an acceptable reason for return." I'm trying to be respectful, but I'm reaching the end of my patience.

From the corner of my eye, I can see Carmen standing next to a shelf of thrillers, ready to throw hands if needed. I stop her with my right hand, gesturing for her to stand down for now.

"This is unacceptable!" Spit flies out of his mouth, and I step back from the splash zone. He looks me over from head to toe, taking in my pale blonde hair and pale yellow sundress. It's about to get ugly. "What kind of establishment would hire *you* to run this place? You look like a vapid airhead who doesn't know how to balance a checkbook."

There it is, the thing men do when they realize they can't bulldoze a woman into giving them what they want. They attack their looks. Unfortunately for my new friend here, Nan raised me with a healthy dose of self-confidence and I'm not easily cowed.

Her steady voice floats through my mind now, strong and sure.

There are people in this life, buttercup, who are going to try to dull your shine. They will do whatever they can to shred your self-worth and your identity, especially if you're unapologetic about it. That's a reflection on them, not on you. Shine bright for all to see.

With her words ringing in my memory, I turn my focus back onto this man. I've hit my limit.

"What a *weird* insult. No one knows how to balance a checkbook. It's an antiquated way to budget, you fossil." I hear a snort from the corner of the room where Carmen lurks. "I don't know who pissed in your oatmeal this morning, but what we aren't going to do here is continue arguing. It's embarrassing for you and annoying for me. I will not be returning your money because you read the book front to back, which is apparent by the copious amount of visible damage. Check your receipt for the return policy if you don't believe me."

He tries to interrupt me, but I'm on a roll and can't be stopped at this point.

"I tried to be nice, but you clearly didn't want to extend that same courtesy. Therefore I'll give you the same respect you've given me. Not every book is going to be a winner, and that won't be solved by you coming in here and trying to demean and bully me." I push the book back towards him, and his face flushes with anger. "There's a little free library around the corner if you'd like to donate it on your way out." It's the nicest way I can possibly say *get out*.

"This is absolutely preposterous," he spits out.

"She asked you nicely to leave, so leave." I swing towards the door at the sound of that voice. All five foot one of Pat's tiny, imposing frame stands in the entrance, ready to rain down hellfire.

"Who the hell are you to tell me to leave?" he spits.

"Well, Jim, I'm glad you asked." Here we go.

"My name isn't—"

Pat cuts him off. "I don't give a bumble fuck of a care, *Jim*." She tips her head in my direction. "My girl here was being nice because she's trying to be professional at work, but as the *owner*, I have no such compunction when you treat my staff as if they're below you." She walks over to the cash wrap. "Take your copy of..." she grabs the book he's been trying to return off the counter and shoves it at his chest, "*Eat, Pray, Love*, and get the hell out of my store." She yanks his arms, turns his body around, and gives him a light push in the direction of the door.

"Absolute legend," Carmen whispers, awestruck.

Pat doesn't visit the store often. She usually just leaves us to run it because she trusts us to get things done the way she likes. The unexpected visit puts me a bit on edge. Well, that, and because I just promised Carmen I would talk to Pat about renovating the store the next time I saw her. I just didn't expect that day to be *today*.

Carmen sidles up next to me as Pat walks around the store a bit.

"Now's your chance! Go talk to her about all our plans." She turns me toward the matriarch of Brownstone Books and gives me an encouraging slap on the ass. I don't even make it two steps forward before Pat faces us.

"Girls, we need to talk."

"What do you mean, you're selling the store?" I shout.

"I'm sorry, kid. I just don't want to do it anymore. I'm tired, and if I'm being honest, there are months we aren't breaking even. I want to sell and use the money to retire somewhere warmer." Her voice has gone uncharacteristically gentle.

I've been stunned into silence. I never expected *this*...though I'm not sure why I didn't. Pat is in her early seventies. Of course, she would eventually want to live a quieter life. I just don't think I ever thought she would. She's such a force, someone who likes to be busy.

Oh God, I'm starting to spiral. What am I going to do? This place is like home to me, and now, it was going to be sold and turned into something else—probably a bagel shop or a Dunkin. As if we don't have one every couple of blocks already. I shudder at the thought.

"I know this place means a lot to you, but I've got more wild oats to sow...in Bermuda."

I drop my head, trying to remember to breathe, when Carmen puts a hand on my back, rubbing in soothing circles. I feel like I should be comforting her. She really needs this job; it's what pays her bills, but more importantly, it gives her extra time she needs to study when we have downtime. She wouldn't get that additional time working at most other places.

I can't let this happen.

"I've arranged severance packages for the three of you. I'm planning on putting the space up for sale soon, but I wanted to give you guys time to make other plans—"

"I'll buy it." I rip my head up, making it go a little light.

Nothing has ever sounded as quiet as the store does right now.

"What?" Pat asks calmly just before Carmen screams, "WHAT?"

"I want to buy the bookstore from you," I say resolutely.

With every second, I feel more and more confident that this is the right decision—albeit a reckless one.

"Silver...that's kind of a big decision, and a costly one at that. I'm not sure you could afford it on what I've been paying you." There's a look of pity in her eyes, the kind a person gives you when they wish something wasn't true but they know they can't do anything to change it.

"What are you, a secret Rockefeller? Ay dios mio, all this time we've been working together, and I never knew you're loaded. To think, every time I brought crap coffee from the bodega, I could've asked you to bring me the good stuff from your fancy spot." Carmen sighs dramatically.

"I *do* bring you coffee—quite frequently."

"Yes, well...Now I know I could've pimped you out for muffins too." She sighs wistfully. "It's always the missed opportunities in life that hurt the most."

I'm belly laughing now, twisting to look over at Pat. I sober immediately under her assessing gaze. She looks confused as she stares at me, and I realize I just got momentarily distracted from the fact that I offered to buy the bookstore two minutes ago. Holy shit, I must be certifiably insane.

"What are you talking about, Silver?" The tone in her voice is soft, quizzical.

Here goes nothing. I straighten my spine and imbue my voice with a confidence I don't quite feel yet.

"When my dad passed away, I got a pretty sizable life insurance sum." I can tell I have their attention now, and even though I hate talking about this, I take a deep breath and continue. "He had arranged for it to be transferred to a trust in my name to accrue interest and become accessible to me upon my twenty-first birthday. Because I was privileged enough to receive scholarships for college and was living in my nan's apartment, I haven't had a reason to cash out."

I can feel my throat getting a little tight, and I clear it with a cough to force my emotions back down, not wanting them to see my soft underbelly. Darting my eyes to the right, I see Carmen looking at me with softness lining her eyes before looking away.

"Anyway, I've built up a lot and haven't had anything to use it on. I want to use it on this. Let me buy the store. I *love* this place." I look around the shop, taking in the too-close-together shelves, the broken stairs leading to the long-unused second level, and the hundreds of books spanning all genres. I bring my hand to my heart. "I was going to talk to you about making changes to the store anyway—giving it a fresh look, cultivating our inventory, and building community here. I think I can do it, Pat. I *know* I can do it."

She's quiet for what feels like an eternity. She just stares and stares at me until I feel like I'm going to melt into the floor from mortification. Did I really think she would just sell me her shop because I made a heartfelt speech? This is her life's work; she probably wants someone who is a safer bet, not a twenty-eight year old she's known since she was a teenager. Fuck, I'm sweating *everywhere* from this extended silence and scrutiny. A river is forming under my ti–

"Okay," Pat says succinctly.

"Okay?" I parrot. "Like okay, I'll sell you the bookstore, or okay, you've lost your mind, and I'm calling psych for an eval?"

"Don't be so melodramatic, Silver." Her eyes are narrowed, but there's a fondness in her voice she's working to mask. "Let's set up a meeting this week to talk about it and go through the financial aspect. I'd rather sell to you than some half-wit who will turn it into some sort of mini gallery dedicated to erotic sculptures."

"Let's not be too hasty. That sounds fun too," Carmen interjects.

Pat snorts and looks over at me. "Does Wednesday morning sound good to go over things?"

"Yes, perfect."

With that settled, Pat gives us a nod and walks out the door, leaving me absolutely stunned.

"Oh my God," Carmen squeals, jumping up and down.

"Oh my God," I mimic while trying not to throw up.

Later that night, long after the initial shock wore off, I'm walking into my building, thinking about all the documents I'll need to gather before my meeting in a couple days.

"You alright, sweetheart?"

I look over to see Tony by the mailroom, organizing some of the packages that haven't been picked up yet. I give him a tired smile. "I'm alright, Tony. It was just a long, bizarre day. Nothing that a glass of wine the size of my bathtub won't fix."

"Just let me know if there's anything you need."

"Such a mother hen." I cluck my tongue.

I hit the call button and wait for the car to descend from one of the higher floors. As I'm waiting, I hear a shuffle to my left and look down the hallway leading to some offices and the emergency stairwell. I catch the last second of someone walking through a door. I could have sworn it was *him*, but there's no way. It's just my mind conjuring up an incredibly tall, incredibly sexy man to soothe my anxiety over the day's excitement.

Later, when I'm freshly showered and in bed, my mind oscillates between three things:

Holy shit, I'm about to own my own bookstore.

I have got to find my mystery man again and get him out of my system.

Has that spot on my ceiling always been there, and why does it look puffy?

Chapter 3

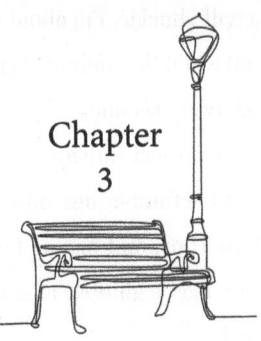

Silver

I'm turning onto the corner of my block when I notice the fire hydrant in front of my building has exploded. *Exploded*. Who even knew that was possible? Water gushes from every direction in a deluge so fierce, it's flooding the storm drains and rapidly filling the streets. Neighbors watch from their windows; kids try to play in it while their guardians attempt to keep them from the torrential spray. At the helm of all the chaos, Tony is on the phone, screaming out our cross streets to first responders.

I amble closer to the building while skirting away from rising tides.

"Tony!" I wave him down. "What happened?"

"Couple of teens thought it would be fun to try and do kick flips off the hydrant." He scratches at the back of his neck, visibly stressed.

"You're telling me that *this*," I point to the river running down the street, "isn't for everyone to quench their undeniable thirst for you?"

That earns me a half chuckle. I'm about to say something else to try and ease his mind when the wailing of sirens careens towards us, growing louder with every second.

The firetruck pulls up just outside of the building, and the firemen from Ladder 18 scramble out into action. One of them hustles over to speak to Tony, and just as I'm about to get out of the way and head inside, I get a glimpse of someone familiar. I do a double take, then a third.

Oh my God.

He's here. *The one that got away*.

And apparently, he's a firefighter. He definitely has the frame for it—all muscle and thick corded forearms that would even make a nun consider damnation.

Shit. Am I drooling again?

I'm definitely being a creep, just standing here watching him assess the situation with his squad, but I can't seem to look away. What are the odds he'd be here?

I get lost in my thoughts, and I startle when I notice he's starting to take off his shirt. Somewhere in the back of my mind, I've registered that this is odd behavior for a fireman. But he's standing there, hedging closer to the hydrant in his uniform, *sans* shirt, suspenders bracketing his shoulders straining to hold up his soaked pants, and I can't find it in me to care that this is *really* bizarre. The sight of him underneath the spray is tantalizing to say the least. This man has been sculpted by Michelangelo himself, and he's standing under that rainfall like he is Neptune at the Trevi fountain.

I'm about to toss a quarter into the flooded street and make a wish for him.

But oh no, my wish is already coming true. As bizarre as his mini strip tease is, I can see every drop of water sluicing a path between his well-defined abs, cutting down and dripping below the waist of his bunker pants.

I am in a daze. A nuclear bomb could not tear my gaze away.

He slowly takes the right suspender in his hand and lowers it over his shoulder. *Drip.* I don't know what is warranting the free peep show, but beggars can't be choosers, and I am most certainly begging. He reaches for the left suspender and starts to pull it down over his shoulder. *Drip.* His pants start to fall from the weight, no longer held up by his shoulders. The vee at his waist becomes more and more narrow with each second of descent.

Drip.

Drip.

Drip.

I startle awake. You have got to be kidding me. The single best dream of my life, and I had to wake up right before I got to see the fireman's hose?

Drip.

Am I still dreaming? I reach up to my forehead, and my hand comes away wet.

What the hell is that? It's still dark out, and my eyes are bleary from sleep, making it impossible to see anything. I reach over to turn on my bedside lamp as another drop of liquid hits the side of my face. I settle on my back, rubbing the sleep from my eyes.

Drip. Drip. Drip.

The dripping has increased to a steady stream when I notice my pillow is soaked. Has this been happening all night? I must have been sleeping off to the other side of the pillow, rolled over during my dream, and woke up when the water started pelting my face.

I groan, knowing I'll have to get maintenance involved. I haven't met the new guy yet, but the building manager sent an email out to all the tenants last week giving us the name, H. Wells, and contact info for work order requests.

I sit up and look for my phone so I can get in contact with him.

I'm riffling around under my *dry* pillows when I hear the distinct sound of creaking right above my head.

Everything happens in slow motion. I look toward the ceiling and see the bubble has swelled to a staggering degree. I have no time to process that I should really, *really* move right about now when the bubble ruptures from the pressure, and a deluge of liquid comes crashing down over my head.

I sit frozen in a puddle of regret and what I hope to fuck is water.

Turning around, I frantically shove my hands under pillows to find my phone wedged between the two largest at the back, grateful for their thick stuffing protecting it from getting waterboarded.

I haul myself out of bed and pad over to my bathroom to grab every towel I own and start cleaning up. I'm stamping the bed, trying to absorb the liquid before it seeps too far into my mattress, and eventually just leave them in a heap under the ceiling damage while I look for something to collect the still-falling water.

It's just after six in the morning now, and I know Tony will be downstairs already, so I walk into my bathroom to grab my robe, slip my arms in, and tie it at my waist. At the front door, I slide my feet into a pair of slippers, and step out into the hallway. It isn't until I'm almost at the ground floor that I realize my soaked pajamas are starting to seep through my thin robe. Hopefully, since it's still early, no one will be around to witness this.

The elevator dings open, and I haven't even fully stepped out before I hear—

"God only knows what kind of sexual deviance you've been up to all night to look like a sodden street walker at half past six in the morning." Mrs. Evans' voice is laced with disdain. It's been years since she moved into the building, and she still hates me with the fire of a thousand suns. I have never been able to figure out why. To be fair, she hates pretty much everyone, so I try not to take it personally.

"Just some light bondage, a flogger or two, nothing too wild. It was a very *casual* evening." I shrug past her. She stomps off, unamused, toward the elevator in a cloud of Shalimar that has me holding my breath.

"Antagonizing Mrs. Evans this early in the morning? You're brave, kid."

"Tony..." I draw out his name in a sickly sweet tone. "Look at me. Do I look like I want to be antagonized this morning? Mother Gothel over there is always the one to start it."

"Okay, okay. But," he clears his throat, "she's not exactly wrong. Why do you look like 7B's Pomeranian after it's been caught in the rain?"

"It would seem that cruel bitch fate has decided today was to be my day of reckoning."

"Less cryptic, doll."

"Water damage. I woke up from the best dream of my life to water flooding down from the ceiling in a way that felt borderline apocalyptic." Now I'm thinking about the dream again, the sculpted abs, the water slicing its way down each ridge of abdomen, green eyes the color of—

"Pine trees?" Confusion laces Tony's voice.

"Never mind. I want to go shower, but when the new maintenance guy gets in today, can you send him up? I'll be home for a while before work."

"Sure thing. I'll fill out the request for you. He should be here around eight."

I quickly thank him before making my way back onto the elevator to the pond of doom residing on my bed.

Around a half hour later, I'm still in the shower when there's a loud rap on my front door.

I thought I had more time. I wasn't expecting the maintenance man until closer to eight, and a glance at my phone sitting on the bathroom sink tells me it's only a quarter past seven in the morning. I scramble to finish rinsing the conditioner out of my hair, running my hands through my pale blonde strands to make sure I don't leave any residue behind.

I'm twisting the excess water out of my hair when I hear another, much louder, knock on the door.

"I'll be there in a minute!" I shuffle around my bathroom floor, looking for my robe that has mysteriously disappeared.

I can't possibly answer the door in just a towel and meet the new guy half-naked. That would not make a good first impression, and I *need* to make a good impression.

The thing about maintenance technicians is, you really, *really* want to get on their good side. They can make or break if you have an easy time living in your building. They are the one lone soldier you have between yourself and any issue that comes your way. If they don't like you, you are *fucked* in any non-emergency situation. Leaky faucet? It'll get fixed in three to six months. A light's gone out in the fixture you can't reach on the ceiling? I hope you enjoy living in darkness. *Forever.*

They are season six, episode nine, Jon Snow during the Battle of the Bastards scene standing down an army horde of rats waiting to eat your face off in the middle of the night. That's not dramatic, it's just a fact. Maintenance techs are the end all, be all of easy living.

The knocking has progressed to a curt bang, I have not found my robe, and I am out of time.

I jog over to the door, water dripping from my hair down onto my neck as I clutch my towel to my chest. I rip open the door before he can knock again, or worse—leave.

"I'm so sor-" All the words fly out of my mouth as I stare up, mouth gaping like a fish at *the one that got away*.

He's staring down at me in what seems to be abject horror. Silent. So silent. His gaze slowly coasts over my face, down to where my hand clutches the towel closed over my chest. His gaze snaps back up to my face quickly, and he seems... I'm not sure. Irritated, maybe? Shit. I can't get on his bad side. I already ruined his shoes. I'm at a disadvantage.

"You." His voice drips with definitive displeasure.

"You." My voice is laced with a flirtation that's second nature.

We're in a standoff, staring at each other in disbelief. I'm just about to invite him in when he brusquely clears his throat. "Can you show me the problem?"

"Problem?" I'm still in disbelief that he's in front of me. The universe has dropped this delectable morsel into my lap for a second time, and I intend to do something about it.

He stares behind me into my apartment like there's a hidden mine field to navigate.

"Of course! Come in." I step aside to let him pass. "I'm sorry it took so long for me to answer the door. I wasn't expecting you this early, so I hopped in the shower," I gesture to my towel, "and didn't hear you knocking."

He remains silent and just gives me a nod.

I lead us into my bedroom, and he stops dead in the doorway when he surveys the damage. "I'm just going to go put some clothes on while you start looking into all of...that." I gesture to the bed, the heap of towels covered in ceiling debris and the trash can catching stray drops.

I walk to my dresser to grab a pair of pink denim shorts covered in watermelons and a white tank top before popping into the bathroom to change. I'm towel drying my hair when I hear him talking to himself.

"You have got to be kidding me," followed by, *"this is not good,"* and a few expletives thrown in for extra flavor.

I chuckle. "Are you alright?"

I get no response, so I brush out my hair, giving it a scrunch with the towel before I step back into the bedroom. He's standing there with his hands clasped behind his neck, looking not at the damage, but at my armchair to the left of the bed. It's clear he hasn't heard me, because his gaze is zeroed in on the corner of my room, his jaw clenching. Following his line of sight, I realized that in my derailed morning, I didn't think to pick up my apartment before he came by.

My new maintenance man is staring directly at my bright red, *very* scandalous panties draped over the arm of my reading chair.

I make no move to hide them from his view, taking sick delight in the fact that he's getting a little flustered. "Mr. Wells?"

He flicks his gaze toward me. "It's Hendrix."

"So that's what the 'H' stands for. I was wondering when Fairbanks sent out your information. I'm not going to lie, I was definitely hoping it was something cooler than that. Hamish, perhaps. Havershim would've been good too." There's a teasing lilt to my voice, and I can see that the corner of his mouth wants to quirk up, but he won't allow it.

"I'll tell my parents they chose poorly."

"Please do." I smile wide. At least he's speaking now.

"I'm just going to assess the situation for a bit. I'll need to move your bed. Is that alright?" He's pointedly looking anywhere but my face or the armchair.

"No problem. I hide my contraband in the nightstand, not under my bed." I give him a devilish grin. He stares at me silently, and I know he's going to be tough to crack. "Do you want any help?"

"No, I've got it."

I head into the kitchen to make myself some much needed coffee, and as I'm waiting for it to brew, I think about how serendipitous this second chance meeting is. I'm loath to admit that since I ran into him, I've thought about him on more than one occasion—something I never do. My bread and butter for dating, if you could even call it that, is to get in and get out. I never dwell on the guy afterwards. It's always a simple, mutual exchange of pleasure, and that's what works for me.

So why was I so hung up on Hendrix the past couple days? Unrequited infatuation? I'm not used to that, and therefore I now want him more? What kind of psychological mind-fuckery is that?

The coffee machine beeps, signaling it's done brewing, and I fill a cup for him along with mine, taking the two steaming mugs into my room.

"Coffee?" I extend a mug out to him.

"Don't you think I've had enough coffee where you're concerned?" The words almost sound teasing, but when I look at him, his face is stony.

"This is New York. There's no such thing as too much coffee." I hold the mug out further, and he takes it, careful to avoid touching my hand and nods his thanks.

"You really didn't notice water damage on your ceiling? A hole that size would be kind of hard to miss." He lifts the mug to his mouth, taking a sip and grimacing. There's an air of judgment and disbelief coating his tone, making my hackles rise slightly.

"I wish I could tell you I have good spatial awareness, but I don't. I noticed a small bubble a week or so ago and forgot about it. Kind of wish I didn't, though, or else I wouldn't have met a watery grave this morning," I say with a bite in my voice.

He doesn't apologize. "This is going to take a few weeks to take care of. Water damage isn't a quick fix."

"My schedule is pretty flexible, and if I can't be here, then you're fine to come in and do whatever you need to. Just make sure to let me know you're coming by so I can...hide my unmentionables." I nod towards my panties, and his ears flush while his face gives away nothing. The irritated tension from before eases slightly.

He coughs. "Right, well," he scratches the back of his neck, "it looks like the water has come to slow crawl. I think you're okay for now, but I'm going to turn off the water valve on that line and investigate where the leak is coming from. I'll be back soon to tear some of this damaged ceiling out so the foundation can dry." He starts heading towards my front door.

"You have my number, so you can let me know when you're coming by."

We're standing in the doorframe, staring at each other now, not saying anything.

"Thank you for the coffee–" He pauses, realizing he hasn't asked for my name and I haven't given it.

"Silver. And you're welcome. Happy to keep you caffeinated whenever you need it."

"Silver," he tests out my name, his voice a low timber, and God help me, but I like the way it sounds rolling off his tongue, like molten metal. "What, your parents couldn't think of something cooler?" He smirks.

I laugh as he sets his mug down on my entry table, stepping out into the hallway and closing the door behind him.

Distantly, my brain registers he's very different from the men I'm used to, but I stuff the feeling down.

I'm about to turn away from the door to get ready for the day when I hear him on the other side of the door, a faint but there exclamation.

"Shit."

Chapter 4

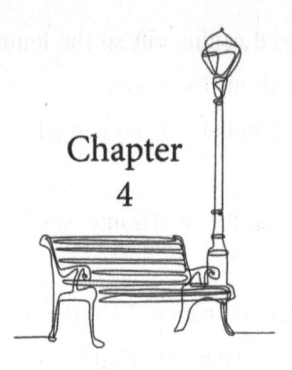

Hendrix

"Shit."

That is the single resounding thought filtering through my head as I tear myself away from Silver's doorstep and walk to the hardware store a few blocks from the apartment building.

I checked through the maintenance supply room in the basement, found it to be severely lacking in materials, and decided to duck out for some fresh air after my encounter with the enigmatic woman upstairs.

Am I using a supply run as an excuse to get out of the building and touch some grass? Who's to say?

Get Nailed isn't what I was expecting when I asked Tony where the closest hardware store was, and I'm starting to suspect he wanted it that way. Typical hardware stores in the city are usually so small, you can hardly move around in them without knocking something over, but this is a mecca in comparison to those tiny neighborhood shops. It's filled floor to ceiling with anything you could imagine, from screws and hammers to kitchen utensils and dog toys. There is not a square inch of visible wall to be seen.

I'm trying to decide where to start when my mind begins to wander back to this morning. This is not good. Now the woman who made my shoes eternally smell like a coffee shop has a name, and she lives where I work. It was easy to soldier on that day knowing I'd never see her again, but by some hilarious trick of the universe, here she is again, magnetic and effervescent and completely off limits from what Mr. Fairbanks, my new boss, told me the day of my final interview.

No personal relations with the tenants. The statement was leveled at me with the weight of a two-ton anvil, his intent and assumptions of me very clear. Dating is the last thing on my mind, though. I'm just trying to settle into my new life here. I don't need or want any complications, especially not ones in the form of short blondes with charismatic personalities.

"Can I help you find something?"

I look to my left to see an older woman with lined olive skin, white hair cropped close to her head, wearing an all-denim ensemble, staring at me. She has a name tag that reads Marjorie and a no bullshit look on her face. She looks pointedly between me and the wall, and I realize I've just been standing in an aisle staring at four hundred different types of screws for who knows how long.

"Hey, I'm Hendrix," I extend my hand out to her. "I just started as The Langham's new maintenance technician." I try my best to paste on a smile that feels foreign to me now.

"Ah, so you're the poor schmuck who got saddled with Sal's job." It's a statement, not a question.

Marjorie sizes me up with an inscrutable expression on her face. I'm starting to get a little uncertain about my next move when her eyes start to crinkle at the corners, and a wide smile breaks across her face. She finally clasps my hand firmly and gives it one abrupt shake before letting go.

"Well, kid, I'll be keeping you in my prayers."

That's comforting.

"Oh, I'm just kidding. Well, sort of, but you should've seen the look on your face!" She starts to walk away, signaling me with her hand. "I only meant that Sal was here weekly to get materials. That building is going to keep you busy."

She stops walking in the front of the store by the door.

"I'm going to give you a quick tour of the shop, so keep your wits about you, because this place will get you more twisted than a bowline knot. I once found a guy in the cleaning products section clutching a Scrub Daddy, rocking in the fetal position, because he couldn't find his way out." She throws her head back and guffaws. "He said he'd been walking around for forty-five minutes and couldn't get out. Dave's a bit of a legend here now. He's never come back, though."

I'm shocked into silence.

"Was his name really Dave?" I ask, only half believing her tale.

She waves her hand through the air, as if she's swatting at a gnat. "Oh, who knows! Now, pay attention to the tour so you don't meet the same fate as Scrub Daddy Dave."

I follow. "Wouldn't dream of becoming a story of hardware lore to future customers. Hacksaw Hendrix just doesn't have the same emotional impact."

That earns me a snort as she motions me throughout the store that it is, in fact, a labyrinth of products stacked and hung all over aisles so narrow that I have to angle my body so my shoulders don't knock things over. At one point, I even see trail mix, so if I do ever get lost, at least I won't immediately starve.

She stops abruptly once we're towards the back of the store, and the sudden shift in movement has me smacking my head against a pack of gloves hanging low off the top shelf.

"So what is it that you need today?" Marjorie has a unique talent of looking down at me even though she's looking *up* at me.

"A few things. One of the tenants," a tenant who smells like apricots and—*stop,* I can't go there and don't deserve to, "has pretty extensive water damage on her ceiling. I'll need drywall, a putty knife, compound, drywall screws, and joint tape. Probably new pipes too once I get in there and figure out which joints need replacing."

Marjorie whistles. "What an inauguration to the position."

She walks me through the store, helping me grab all the materials except for the sheets of drywall, which she promises to have delivered to the building for me in the next few days. As we head over to the register to check out the other supplies, my mind lures itself back to Silver.

That's going to be inconvenient.

When I ran into her the first time on the street, I felt like I couldn't catch my breath. I just stood there like an idiot. She was the most beautiful woman I had ever seen. I almost thought she wasn't real, that she was a mirage conjured straight from the depths of my fantasies—hair like sheets of pale spun silk, eyes the most unique shade of pale green that verged on blue, and full pink lips that looked as soft as clouds.

Seeing her today was a shock to my system. Suddenly, there she was, in a *very* small towel, glowing with pink flushed skin, water dropping down her golden skin and smelling fresh and sweet. I *hadn't* made her up in my mind, and she was even more beautiful the second time around, standing in the doorway of a home that somehow *felt* like her, bright, light and bursting with color.

Like red lace—*no. Not going there.*

She was off limits, which was for the best anyway. With the state of my head these days, it's not like I'm in any sort of position to date.

I shut down thoughts of her and pay Marjorie with the building credit card Fairbanks left for me. I have to stay focused and not get distracted. I'll fix her ceiling and then keep a very *safe* distance from her and her unmentionables, as she called them.

Grabbing the bag of supplies from the checkout counter, I thank Marjorie and head back to work, trying not to think of platinum hair and eyes like chips of sea glass the whole way back.

I spend most of the day organizing my office. Which, as it turned out, took longer than I expected because the last guy was a bit of a hoarder. I've found everything from newspapers dating back thirty years to a stockpile of ramen so large, even a doomsday prepper would be impressed.

There's an hour left of my shift when I get a knock on the door and open it to find Tony leaning against the frame, a note pinched between his thumb and forefinger.

"Got a job for ya, dreamboat. Can you squeeze it in?" He extends the note out to me to read.

It's a simple fix to the kitchen faucet in an apartment on the seventh floor. "Yeah I got time."

Tony nods, gives the door frame of my office a tap, and heads back to his desk.

I grab my tool belt, a few parts I may need to fix the faucet, and go to catch the elevator up to the seventh floor. I'm waiting for the car to descend to the lobby floor when the front door to the building opens.

"You're home earlier than usual," Tony calls out.

"Well, you know what they say: the early bird gets waterboarded by the vengeful spirits that no doubt reside in these pre-war walls."

I hold in a groan, knowing exactly who that voice belongs to: the one person I'd like to avoid.

Why the hell is this elevator taking so long?

"I don't think anyone says that."

Silver continues talking to Tony, but I can feel her stare on my back. "I went into the store early today since I was up. There are a lot of changes going on over there right now, so I figured if I was awake, I might as well go and get stuff done."

How is it possible the elevator still has five floors to go?

"Holly shoved me out the door, though. She said I was being too bitchy to customers because I was tired and cranky. Personally, I think she's a filthy liar. I'm a goddamn delight. Do you think Caroline would take on a defamation case?"

Three floors.

"Everything okay with the store? You know I like to take my nieces there when I can get them to hang out with me instead of their friends."

Two Floors.

"Yeah, everything's fine, it's just a...change of ownership."

One floor.

"Pat's leaving? Seems to be a lot of that going around."

The elevator doors pop open, and a little girl with red curls bounces out, her visibly harried father chasing after her while she giggles and gallops towards the front desk.

Stepping onto the elevator, I hear Tony say hi to the kid named Isla then turn around, leaning into the wall of the car as the doors start to close *too* slowly. I'm almost home free, and I distantly think that maybe I'm just being irrational about this whole thing. I barely know Silver; she might be attached to someone, and I'm over here trying to avoid her because...well, I don't even know why.

I take a steadying breath when a delicate arm shoots through the almost-closed doors and stops it in its tracks.

"Hey, Hugo," Silver says as she steps on the elevator.

"It's Hendrix." Ill humor coats my tongue as I correct her.

"Mmmm, I don't know—I'm trying out a few different names for you. I'm not sure Hendrix suits you." I slow blink, stare flat. "You should probably hit the button for the floor you need."

Right. I reach for the panel of buttons on the wall, bringing me closer to Silver in the process, but she doesn't concede an inch. She stays firmly planted as I hit the number seven, noticing she hasn't selected her floor. I press the five and readjust my body to stand away from her again.

Civil avoidance, that's what I'm going for. I don't want to be an asshole, but I shouldn't engage more than necessary. Professionalism is what I need to be thinking about, not how beautiful she is, or that fresh fruit is now choking my airwaves, making me dizzy with her scent.

The elevator finally starts to climb, and I see Silver turn to face me in the reflection off the steel doors as I staunchly stare forward.

"So," Silver starts, "you never answered me last week when I offered to have your shoes cleaned after my clumsiness."

I turn my head slightly to look at her now. She's not flirting, but there's definitely a glimmer in her eye that spells trouble.

"It's alright. I couldn't get the smell out of them, so I tossed them out."

Her face goes slack. "Oh my God, I'm so sorry. I'll get you another pair. Just send me a link!"

"I'm teasing you. They're my favorite pair of shoes." They weren't before, but they are now. She doesn't need to know that, though. "I didn't throw them out."

A bell dings, and the doors open to her floor.

And then I see it, her shift back into this confident indomitable force as she *saunters* out of the elevator.

Just when I think she's not going to respond, she flicks her gaze over her left shoulder. "Good. Now you can think of me every time you put them on."

Then, the elevator doors close, and she disappears from my sight. Which is a good thing...so why do I feel a ridiculous tightening in my chest?

"Honey, I'm home!" Jae calls out from our apartment hallway.

"I'm in the kitchen."

"Exactly where you should be." He walks in and slaps my ass while I'm standing at the stove.

"How was work?" I ask him.

Jae has been my best friend since freshman year of college when we first became roommates. After we graduated, I moved back to Seattle, and Jae became a tattoo apprentice here in the city.

Now, he's a full-fledged resident artist at Anarchy, one of New York's most elite studios, booked out for months in advance.

"I got to do this sick photo-realistic landscape of my client's hometown in South Korea. We made it look like it was inside a stamp. It's one of my favorite pieces I've done this year."

We used to sit on a ratty couch in our dorm, tv playing in the background while he would ignore his coursework to draw, and I would be doing mine because failure wasn't an option for me. My dad had only agreed to let me go out of state for college on the condition that I come home after with a business degree to prep me for running the family business.

Most days, that was okay with me. I had always liked our business of custom furniture, loved the process of sketching and designing and would shirk off studying from time to time to draw with Jae. Sam and Faye, the other two of our group, would inevitably join at some point, and the night would descend into chaos. I loved it. Leaving home gave me the small taste of freedom I craved away from my dad and his expectations, but I went back as agreed and I stayed, training under him and my uncle to take over—that is, until our world shattered two years ago. The very air in Seattle became so stifling that I finally had enough, packed my bag a few weeks ago, and ran back to the only place that ever felt like home: New York.

I pull myself from morose thoughts. "Let me see a picture of it." I motion to the salmon I'm frying in a pan. "Do you want some of this?"

"Have you ever known me to turn down a meal?" He turns to grab a couple beers from the fridge, depositing one next to me and popping the top off with the silver ring he always wears on his index finger.

"Good point. Thanks." I reach into the cabinet for dishes to plate up our dinner.

He fishes his tattooed hand in his pocket to grab his phone. "You would be able to see my work without asking if you would just get on social media. Even my halmeoni has Instagram now."

I grunt in a non-committal response. I deleted social media after the accident, unable to stomach the surface-level messages from too many people who didn't really understand. I like it better this way, cut off from the bullshit. Anyone who needs to reach me has my phone number, and that's all I need.

We settle on the couch, and I set our plates on the coffee table before flicking on the Rangers game that started a half hour ago. Jae hands me his phone and the image on the screen is so crisp it's like looking at a photograph.

"Dude, this is some of your best work." I zoom in with my thumb and index finger to see the lush green mountain-scape surrounded by a flat open field. It's hard to wrap my head around how he fits so much detail into a six inch piece.

"When are you going to let me tattoo you? It's embarrassing my best friend won't let me draw on him. I swear I won't put a dick on you." He holds up three fingers in the universal scouts honor signal.

I only have one large piece—a series of vines that twine from my wrists, up my forearms and biceps, curl under my arm onto my chest, and sweep over my shoulders to connect to a root in the center of my back. One vine for my sister, Laurel, and one for my brother, Maddox. He and I had it planned for months, and we went in on his twenty-fifth birthday—I got my vines, and he got a scape of Mount Rainier.

I haven't been able to bring myself to get anything new since, feeling like if I do, I'm moving on in some way.

"Maybe one day." I can feel my best friend scrutinizing me.

He snatches his phone back. "Enough about me. How was your first day?"

I pause, taking a sip of my beer. "It was fine."

"That feels loaded"

He sees too much, knows me too well.

"Seriously, it was fine. I got there early this morning, and there was already an issue in this woman's apartment. Collapsed ceiling from water damage. It's gonna take me a while to fix it." I lean forward to take a bite of my fish, staring at the game, trying to give him nothing.

"She's hot, isn't she?"

"*What?* Why would you say that?" How could he possibly know that? What is he, a fucking psychic?

"Because you wouldn't look at me when you started talking about her, and you kept the details very...clinical. You always do that when you're hiding something." He's so smug as he takes a sip of his beer. "So, how hot is she?"

I groan and throw my head back on the couch.

He whistles. "That bad, huh?"

"She is unreal and off limits." I go into detail, telling him about how I met her the day of my final interview and how surprised I was to see her this morning. When I finish, he sets down his plate and beer and turns to face me fully.

He grabs my face in both hands. "Fuck the rules, Hen." He lets go, reaching forward to palm his beer.

On the screen, grown men pummel each other into baseboards, and it feels weirdly indicative of how the inside of my brain feels.

"I can't risk this job. You know I can't go back home."

"I'd float you for however long you need."

It's an offhand comment, one born out of a desire to see me happy again, but my feeble pride would never allow that. It was bad enough that I let him handle my share of rent until I was able to get a job. To entertain it again... No, I couldn't and wouldn't do that to him. This is my burden to bear, they were always my burdens to bear.

He truly is the best person I know, a brother by all accounts except birth, and one of the only people I've leaned on these past couple years, even in the limited way I was able to. When everything felt bleak, Jae never gave up on me and checked in on me constantly, as if distance and a time difference didn't matter. But something always prohibited me from being entirely forthcoming, an attempt to keep the knowledge of how bleak it felt—feels—from him.

He asked eventually, of course, why I abruptly showed up at his door out of the blue, but he never pressed for answers when I didn't give them.

"I know you would, but it won't come to that, because I'm going to remain professional."

"I'm going to be blunt with you."

"When have you been anything *but* blunt with me—or anyone, for that matter? You have no internal filter."

"Stop deflecting, dick. The last couple years have been shit for you. If she would help bring you some happiness, I think it's worth the risk. You deserve to be happy. Maddox would *want* you to be happy."

I'm white knuckling my fork, and the bite of salmon I just ate turns to ash on my tongue.

Fuck, my chest hurts. Everything hurts when I think about my baby brother. But just like I have for the past thirty-one years, I bury the feeling, unwilling to show weakness.

"I'm okay with how things are. I'm back in New York and around my friends. That's all I need right now." He starts to object, but I continue. "I won't risk my job now that I have one. It's enough."

I think he can sense I'm starting to shut down, so he doesn't press it further.

"What's her name?"

I arch a brow at him skeptically. "Why?"

"Call it curiosity."

"I just know her first name is Silver."

I think he's finally dropped the subject, because we go back to the game. A few minutes later, I can see him fiddling on his phone right before a wide, Cheshire Cat smile spreads across his face, crinkling his dark eyes.

Turning the phone to me, I see he has Instagram pulled up to an account called @SilverLinings. Silver's face beams back at me from her profile picture, and it stuns me stupid yet again.

"Is this her?" I suspect he already knows, so I only give a non-verbal nod to confirm. I stand and head into the kitchen for another beer and hear him chuckling. "Dude, you are *so* fucked."

Chapter 5

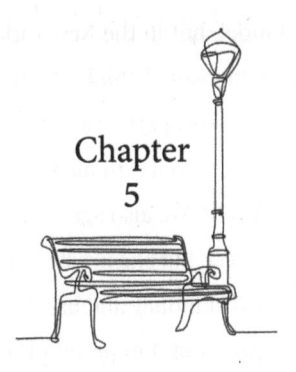

Silver

"Wait a minute." Holly stares at me like I've sprouted three heads right before her eyes. "You're telling me I was off work for a couple days...and now you *own* the store?"

Well, when she says it like that, I guess the decision to buy Brownstone Books did come out of nowhere.

"I expect my 'Sexiest Boss Ever' mug to arrive within five to seven business days," I say with a nonchalance the moment *absolutely* doesn't call for.

"That's a violation, and I'm calling HR." There's mirth in her gaze before she wipes it off her face and levels me with a no bullshit stare. "What's going on? How did this happen?"

I understand her shock and hesitation. It's exactly how I felt for days after I heard the words "I'll buy it" come out of my mouth a week ago. Since then, I have felt apprehension, excitement, nausea, certainty, and *a lot* of fear.

I had my meeting with Pat a few days ago to crunch numbers, and it's going to be really tight. The money from my dad's life insurance was substantial, but in the New York real estate market, it doesn't go as far as one would think. Pat bought the store back in the late seventies, when property was a lot more affordable, and because of that, she's able to sell it to me for under current market value and still make a profit. We also agreed I would make monthly payments to pay off the rest, but she insisted on far too small a sum, telling me to take the extra money and use it to turn the store into something I could be proud of. I'm proud of it now, but there's no denying it needs some updates.

"To be honest, I sort of...blacked out and offered to buy the store. I don't know, Hols. It seems crazy, but it *feels* right. I can't explain it."

"Carmen has been freaking out, going on about how you must be affiliated with the mafia."

"I think I'm going to start using that theory. That sounds much cooler than the 'my dad died and I got a lot of money' story I've been operating off of." I finger the necklace settled around the base of my throat, the one I've worn every day for over twenty years.

"Oh," she exhales. "You've never mentioned... I mean you never talk about your parents. I didn't realize. I'm so sorry." The pity in her gaze is one of the reasons I never brought it up.

Only Kena and Nan know my whole sordid past. It's not something worth dwelling on or talking about, and I'm not going to start now. The day I lost my dad—and by proxy, my mom too, is a wound that's still raw, even twenty years later.

Shaking myself out of my morose thoughts, I paste on a forced smile. "Sorry! I didn't mean to make it all doom and gloom there," I chuckle, but I can tell from Holly's face that it sounds fake to her ears too.

Before she can try to pull me into her comforting embrace, I deflect. "So, basically, I run this shit now, and we're bringing in monster smut, updating everything from the look of the store to the inventory. It's too dark in here and too outdated. We need to liven this place up, start hosting events, and tailoring to more people. I want to build a community."

"Monster smut?" She gives me a quizzical look.

"You know, aliens, gargoyles, dragons, krakens—"

She cuts me off before I can continue. "What the hell can krakens do?"

I smirk. "What *can't* they do is the better question. Multiple tentacles and unlimited sucky things, Hols. Think about it."

She gives me a horrified look that morphs into intrigue the longer she thinks about it.

"So, will you stay with me now that I own this place?" I have a knot of anxiety in my chest that she might say no. It's not like working at a bookstore pays a premium salary. I don't want to assume that just because we're friends, she'll want to stay around as everything changes. She has to look out for her own best interests, and the people around me do have a tendency to leave eventually anyway. It's for the best that I never get too attached or expect too much from anyone.

"If I stay—" she leaves the question open, and my anxiety expands like a balloon— "do I have to read the monster smut?"

The anxiety ebbs, and a smile stretches across my face. "It's not required, but it is *very* much encouraged."

"I'm in," she says right before pulling me in for a tight hug. "This might be the stupidest thing you've ever done." She pulls away and surveys the shop. "Where do we start?"

I tell her about the plans I've been making in my head for the last week. "Clearly, this place needs a facelift." She nods in agreement.

"It has its charm, but it could definitely use an overhaul if we want to compete with the big box bookstores in town."

"Exactly. We still have some time while all the papers are finalized before I can start on anything that's cosmetic, so I think the first thing we need to assess is our inventory. We've been barely surviving on selling cult classics and new bestsellers, but we're sitting on a lot of old inventory, things that have been in this shop longer than I have. We need to clean up the stock and donate a lot to libraries, shelters, and schools."

She looks at me contemplatively. "I've gotta say, it's pretty hot when you go into boss lady mode. So confident and assertive."

"Stop it. I'm saving myself for your wife." I laugh. "I'm going to pull reports of our inventory so we can go through and see what we can relocate to a new home. That way, we can clear space to bring in new titles and appeal to a wider demographic."

Holly nods. "That's where the monster books come in, I presume."

I walk over to the computer system at the cash wrap and start punching in dates from the past two years, pulling reports, from our bestsellers to our slowest sellers.

"Amongst other things, yes." As the list prints, I admit, "I've been diving into the numbers now that I have full access to them and," I hesitate, "it's pretty bad. Pat never said anything, but as a whole, the store was barely breaking even. It seems miraculous she only decided to sell now."

"Shit."

"Yeah." I step out from behind the register. "We need to really expand our selection, bring in more genres, host events and mixers for authors and our community. We *need* to set ourselves apart."

My mind is whirling a million miles a minute, and Holly doesn't even have a moment to contribute before I'm rattling off more things and pacing the length of the store.

"Author signings, launch parties, trivia nights." I stop my pacing and turn to Holly. "Are you getting this down?"

She jumps into action and murmurs what sounds like *yes, master* to the tune of Igor, but I don't have a moment to entertain it before I'm on to the next thought.

"Monthly book clubs. Oh! It can be interactive. We'll hold polls on Instagram for people to vote on the book for the next month. Oh my God—A SINGLES MIXER!" My abrupt shout scares the bejesus out of Holly, but she nods and continues writing down everything I'm saying. "What would be better than hosting a singles mixer for book lovers when ninety percent of this city is aggressively horny all the time?"

"It's probably all the monster erotica," she deadpans.

"Definitely a contributing factor for sure."

Holly surveys the shop with her hands on her hips. "So, inventory first. What comes after?"

That is something I've been thinking about for days. How exactly do I want to make this place look and feel? Brownstone Books definitely has a rustic sort of *charm* to it, though some would describe it as dilapidated. It definitely needs upgrades. About half of the shelves are in need of repair or total replacement, cracked or sagging in the middle. The stairs leading to the top loft have been roped off and out of commission for *years*. Those will need to be fixed so we can use the second floor again.

There's a lot I want to do. I didn't realize how many ideas I have been storing in my mind for what this place could become—what it *would* become.

"While we wait until I get everything finalized with Pat and the property lawyers, we'll take care of all the excess titles. After that, I'll start looking into DIY-ing versus hiring a contractor."

"You're thinking of doing this on your own?" Skepticism is clear in her tone.

"If the cost of a contractor is out of budget, yes."

"I really don't think you should attempt this alone without some sort of...supervision."

"I cannot *believe* what I'm hearing. What kind of feminist are you? Women didn't endure the suffrage movement for me to hire a *man* to do what I can do myself," I scoff in mock outrage.

"You are one hundred percent going to break something."

"Yeah, probably, but emergency room visits are all a part of the adventure!"

She rolls her eyes. "I'm telling Makena."

"Go ahead. I'm not scared of him." I absolutely am.

"You absolutely are."

"Don't be a narc. I'll tell him myself; he's going to ask when I get his advice on styling for the store anyway."

She chuckles. "Good, because you need adult supervision for this."

I level her with a stare that conveys I am not amused as I walk back around the cash wrap and grab the report I printed. I split them in the middle of the stack, handing half the pages to Holly.

"Help me go through these so we can figure out what we should and should not donate."

We work in companionable silence, only the sounds of *Folklore* floating from the speakers of the store. We start by referencing the list and grabbing the books off shelves or out of the stockroom when my phone pings with a text notification.

> **Unknown**
> It's Hendrix the maintenance tech. Will you be home tomorrow for me to start repairs on your ceiling?

Flutters erupt in my stomach. That's...new.

I don't know what to do. Do I text back right away? Play it cool for a while? What is wrong with me? I've never been unsure of what to do when getting a text from a man. He's just the maintenance guy; of course, you don't wait to text back.

God, what is wrong with me?

I must be zoned in on my phone, because I don't hear Holly when she asks me what I'm looking at, and I don't see her when she comes up behind me, snatching the phone out of my hand.

"Who's Hendrix?"

I try to snatch my phone back, but she evades me around a table stacked with paperback bestsellers.

"If you read the text, you nosy gremlin, you'll see he's the apartment's new maintenance man," I huff, trying to come around the table to take my phone from her grasp.

"Why, exactly, do you seem like you don't want me to know about this *maintenance man*?" She says the job title with air quotes, like she doesn't believe me. "*Oh*, is maintenance man a euphemism for sex? Is it a role play thing?"

Why am I feeling shy about this? This really isn't like me, and I need to shake myself out of it. There's no reason I can't tell her Hendrix is the same man I ran into on the street that day.

I tear my phone out of her hand. "No, you thief. He's my building's new tech."

"Okay? What's the big deal?"

"He's also...*him*."

"Him?" I give her a look that pleads with her to remember. She looks at me, puzzled for a moment, and then I can see the moment it clicks for her. "Oh, him! The one that got away is what I believe you called him. So, his name is Hendrix."

"Yes."

She's staring at me, giving me a 'bitch really' look and waiting for me to divulge more. There's no reason why I shouldn't. I just got the second chance with Hendrix I wanted a week ago when I didn't even know his name. I'm having a momentary lapse of sense by getting nervous, and I shake myself out of it. I am Silver James. First of her name. Queen of sex positivity. Mother of vibrators and ruler of my own mind. I will not let one man—one disturbingly gorgeous man—have me acting like a cowering maiden. No, I wanted Hendrix then, and I still want him now, and something tells me by the way he was staring at my...*armchair* the other day, he may be interested too.

It's game on.

Holly shakes me out of my internal pep talk. "So, you're getting your second chance." A statement, not a question. She knows my style, how I approach dating: decidedly non-committal.

"It would appear so." I'm certain there's a gleam in my eye that probably makes me look like a rabid raccoon that just found its next meal.

"What's the plan?" This is why I love Holly. She encourages my delusions and feeds my feral nature without second guessing if it's wise.

"Well, I found out he works in the building because I had a massive water leak burst through my ceiling and onto my face at six in the morning." Holly gasps in acute horror. "Color me surprised when I open my door an hour later, *in a towel*, to find Hendrix on the other side." She's repressing laughter now, I can see it all over her face.

"That was him," I say, motioning to my phone, "texting to see if I'll be home tomorrow so he can start working on repairs."

"You work tomorrow."

"Not if you switch shifts with me." I bat my eyelashes, pleading with her to do me this favor.

"Fine! But you and Kena have to come to Sera's trial run workshop for her new course. She wants to make sure her curriculum and timing runs smoothly before starting the class with paying students."

"Done. Any excuse to see Sera looking all cute and bossy in an apron." I throw her a wink and then run out of the way when she sends a book from our donation pile soaring through the air at me.

Once I've survived a flying book assault, I step around a bookshelf and out of sight, pausing to look down at my phone and open my messages. I don't second guess. I just type.

Silver

> I'll be home, and I'll...clean up before you arrive.

I shoot off the text, put my phone away, and get back to work, vowing to put Hendrix out of my mind for the rest of the day, just like I would with anyone else.

"Yes, Nan, I know what pickleball is."

I've just left the shop, walking towards the East Village to meet Kena and Julien for a drink at this bar they walked past last weekend. They like to find random and obscure places to visit, and I like to join them because Julien usually foots the bill. That might make me a mooch, but I just bought a fucking store, so I feel like it's at least a bit more acceptable now.

"Not a single pickle involved. It's absolute bullshit," she huffs dramatically.

"Nan, it's followed by the word *ball*. What did you think you were getting into?"

"Hell if I know. I thought there would be food involved, or that maybe it was a double entendre, if you know what I mean." I absolutely know what she means. "But no, I show up, and everyone's batting around *holey* balls with ping pong paddles, nary a pickle in sight! Absolutely absurd. Just play tennis, for fuck's sake!" She shouts so loudly, I have to pull my phone away from my ear.

"Quite the passionate reaction, Nan," I battle a laugh.

"I'm sorry, I'm hangry. I didn't eat lunch because I thought there would be food, and I'm on my way to meet Babs for dinner at Chilis. Did you call for something specific, or just to chat?"

"I'm calling to share some news with you." Despite us being close, I still haven't told her about the store. I've been telling myself it was because I wanted to wait until everything was finalized, but really, I was nervous she would tell me it was a bad idea, that I shouldn't put all my eggs in one basket. Spending my entire savings on one endeavor definitely falls under that category.

"Spill it, Bear." *Bear*. Nan gave me that nickname when I first started living with her. She said I kept everything warm because

I always wanted to cuddle like I was hibernating. But eventually, that stopped. The incident was a lot for an eight year old to take in, but after some time, I was able to understand what happened, the reason why I was living with her now. That's when the cuddles stopped. The nickname stayed, though, and so did Nan.

"Shit. I'm just going to rip the Band-Aid off. Pat was gonna sell Brownstone Books, so she and I worked out a deal, and I bought it with Dad's life insurance money." All the breath whooshes out of me.

"Oh, thank fuck!" That's not the reaction I was expecting. "I thought you were going to tell me you were pregnant or dying."

"I see we're back to being dramatic."

"It's called *PICKLEBALL*. I think the dramatics are warranted."

"That's all you have to say, though? No foreboding warnings? No sage words of wisdom?"

"Yes, actually," she says, taking on a solemn tone. "I don't care if you shake your ass on OnlyFans to make money. So long as you keep up the apartment's annual fees, I'm happy."

"I'll keep that in mind as a backup," I chuckle. "I guess I worried about telling you for nothing."

"Silver, I trust your judgment to decide what's right for your life unequivocally. If buying the store is what's right for you and your needs, then I'm proud of you."

Shit. Don't cry. Don't cry. Don't cry.

I settle for a simple, "I miss you."

"I miss you too, Bear. We'll work out who's going where for the holidays soon, but I just got to Chilis, and the triple dipper is calling my name. I love you."

"I love you too." There was a time I wouldn't say those words. I still find it impossible to say to anyone besides Nan and Kena.

We hang up, and I round the corner onto the block the bar is on. The call with Nan distracted me enough on my walk that I hardly even noticed I had already gotten to the East Village, very nearly at my destination.

I double check that I'm on the right side of the street and walk just a little further until I see the iron and wood blade sign sitting above the door, reading The Blackbird.

I pull open the door and immediately have to squint in the dim lighting. I look around for a nano second before I see Kena and Julien sitting at a corner table towards the front of the bar. I walk over and give them both a hug before setting my bag on the empty seat.

"I'm gonna go grab a drink. Do either of you need a refill while I'm over there?"

"I'll take another Cab Sav," Julien says. I look to Kena to see if he wants anything, but he just shakes his head no. I reach in my bag to grab my wallet, but Julien stops me with his hand, "Don't be silly. I already have a tab open."

I smile sweetly. "If you insist, Daddy Warbucks."

Kena nearly spits out his drink. "Only I call him Daddy," he says, giving Julien a heated look.

I leave them to their glances and head over to the bar, where a taller man with a husky build is chatting up a girl sitting on a barstool. When he notices me waiting, he walks over with a massive, infectious smile on his face.

"Hey, gorgeous. What can I get for you?" His tone holds a flirty quality to it that I find endearing and amusing in equal measure.

"I'll take a Cab Sav and a Dark & Stormy. Add it to Julien's tab, please."

"Got it." He slaps the bar top with his hand and backs away to make our drinks. Suddenly, a loud crash sounds from the back of the bar, and I hear the barkeep mumble under his breath, "Fucking finance bros."

He hasn't even had a second to get out from behind the bar when I hear a deep, familiar rumble two feet to my right. "Sam, hand me a towel. The table of douches next to us shattered a bottle. I'll help you clean it up."

I turn toward the voice that sends a shiver skating down my spine, and a smile breaks across my face. There before me, looking like the mirror image of himself when I opened my apartment door, is Hendrix Wells.

Neither of us say anything for a minute, and I don't miss the way his eyes quickly flick down my body, lingering briefly on the sliver of exposed skin between the top of my jeans and my cropped red baby tee before fixing his gaze back on my face.

I'm very aware of Sam staring at the two of us staring at each other.

"Well, Huxley, it would seem the universe keeps our paths crossing. Three times is a pattern." I have a cheeky smile on my face.

"Purely coincidental. Sam, the towel?"

"Oh, absolutely not," Sam says with that megawatt grin stretched across his face. "You stay right here, Henny. I'll take care of the mess." And with that, Sam leaves me and Hendrix staring at each other. A smile stretches across on my face, and he seems decidedly put out.

"Do you come here often?" I ask before realizing that is the quintessential cheesy pick up line.

Hendrix's mouth gives a tiny quirk, like he's actively trying not to emote. "Practically lived here in college."

He doesn't give me much to keep the conversation going, and I suspect that is highly intentional, so the idea of throwing him off a little off axis is too good to pass up. I drag my gaze down his body, taking in the simple t-shirt stretching over broad shoulders and displaying the tattooed vines wrapping around his muscled arms as they spiral from his wrists all the way up corded forearms until they disappear under the cotton of his sleeves. The dark ink pulls and flexes across his skin now, distracting me far more than I care to admit. I drag my gaze back up and settle on his face, not even attempting to hide my admiration.

"Right, well, I'll just—" I signal over to my table with Julien and Kena and start to turn around.

"Do *you* come here often?"

I smile to myself before facing towards him again. "First time. My best friend Kena and his boyfriend Julien passed by it on their way home from the farmers market. I should probably get back to them now."

"Yeah, I should get back to mine." He signals towards his friends at one of the back tables, and when we turn to look, we catch them all peeking out of the booth, staring directly at us. They all duck quickly, but the damage is done. "For fucks sake," Hendrix murmurs.

Sam makes his way over to the bar, telling me he'll bring over our drinks in a couple minutes once he's sorted out the issues with the rowdy table.

"Thanks, Sam." I smile, reorienting back toward Hendrix. "I'll see you tomorrow, *Henny*."

I can feel eyes on me as I'm walking away. I'm not saying that

I intentionally add a little extra swing to my walk...but I'm not *not* saying that either.

I'm halfway back to the table when I hear Sam. "Do you come here often?" It's followed by a grunt from Hendrix and a barrel laugh from his friend.

Chapter 6

Hendrix

I'm walking to work, Hozier crooning through my earbuds, when I feel my phone buzzing in my back pocket.

Mom.

I stop in my tracks and stare at my mother's face beaming back at me from the caller I.D.

I've been dodging my family's calls since I moved back to New York, and I don't break that habit now as I stare at the screen, waiting for the call to go to voicemail. A knot forms in my throat, making my mouth feel thick. It's official—I'm the world's shittiest son. It makes me the worst sort of coward, to move across the country without giving them a reason and then not answer their calls. I just can't stand to hear their disappointment. It's selfish, but I can't face them yet.

I pocket my phone once the call drops and finish the last few blocks to work while trying to shake the lingering feeling of anxiety I always get when I'm faced with the reality of my family. How fractured I left it.

I run down to the basement to my office to grab the supplies to start on Silver's ceiling damage. I turned off the water pipe the leak was coming from so the water wouldn't continue to drip through and onto her bed. Luckily for both of us, it was a pipe connected to an apartment that was having work done. No one knew there was a leak, so the outside contractors were running water pretty frequently for a couple weeks. That leak was right above Silver's apartment, soaking into the wood and drywall until it all came bursting down.

As I make my way up to the fifth floor, I solidify my resolve and pray to the universe that this time when she answers the door, she has on more than a towel. I knock on the door to her apartment and take a step back while I wait for her to answer.

"Just a minute," she shouts just before a loud thudding and, "SON OF A B–"

The door flies off its hinges, and then she's standing before me, looking wild and beautiful and *very* out of breath.

"Are you okay?" She is thankfully dressed, though today's outfit of painted on workout leggings that hug her hips in a way that should be illegal and a cropped band tee is *almost* as bad as the towel.

"Yes, perfect. Just tripped over my dignity on the way to the door."

I stare at her, unsure of what to say. Her wild hair is piled on top of her head in a haphazard bun with what looks like a...paintbrush sticking out of it?

"You have something in your hair." I point to her platinum nest.

"What?" She pats around her head until she feels the brush. "Oh, that's just my eyeshadow brush. I was doing my makeup when you knocked."

We're staring at each other, me on one side of the door and her on the other.

"Can I come in?"

She snaps back to herself and shoots me a smile. "Sorry, I got lost in thought for a minute. Come in." She motions me forward while stepping out of the way. I take an exaggerated step over the threshold, and she cocks her head to the side, giving me a questioning look.

"I didn't want to step on your dignity." I smirk and walk further into her apartment. Much like it was the first time I was here, the space feels warm and inviting, with its intricate crown molding, colorful rug, pink couch, and bookshelves lining the walls.

"I need to spend some time in the affected area. Is that okay? I don't want to be in your way while you go about your day." There, that sounded professional.

"I'm working from home today, so I can just stay in the living room while you work."

That would be preferable. Out of sight out of mind.

"I'm going to get started. Is it okay if I head into your bedroom?"

"Yeah, of course. I'm just going to finish getting ready in the bathroom, and then I'll get out of your hair."

I trail after her into her bedroom and survey the landscape like I'm looking for bombs in the form of red lace. I'm equal parts relieved and disappointed. I'm not sure what's going on in my head, why it feels so jumbled when she's around, but all I need to do is finish this job, and then I won't have to see her so often. I tell myself it's just because it's been *awhile*, my body reacting to being attracted to someone for the first time in years, and it's sending very mixed signals to my brain.

I head over to the far part of her bedroom and set my tools down on the oak floors. Looking around, I see Silver leaning over her bathroom sink, her paintbrush in hand, and a look of extreme concentration on her face.

She looks up, and our eyes lock through the mirror's reflection. She shoots me a smile, one full of implications. *I caught you looking. Do you like what you see?*

I clear my throat and look back towards the ceiling. "I'm gonna move your bed so I can strip the ceiling to dry it out. Is there anything you need to get from over here," I motion to the section of her bedroom that looks like it occasionally doubles as an office, "before I block your path?"

"Just my iPad." She sticks the brush back in her bun and sways over to her corner desk to grab the device. "I'll be out in the living room if you need anything."

I nod.

She leaves me in her bedroom, and I shift her furniture before getting to work, stripping back layers of paint and sheetrock so beyond salvaging, it's better to gut it all and replace it with fresh material.

If I look deeply enough, I know there's a parallel between the damaged ceiling and the last two years of my life. *I'm* the one who needs to be gutted and have my insides replaced to become a different version of myself, a shiny new edition that doesn't taint everything and everyone around him. A version that doesn't feel like it's been through multiple rounds of a meat grinder.

I cut into the wall and tear a piece out, dropping it in a ruined heap on the floor.

It's around lunch time, and I've almost fully gutted the section of the ceiling containing the damage. It was a hell of a lot worse than I thought, and I'm drenched in sweat and debris as I climb down the ladder to grab the bottle of water Silver brought me a half hour into starting. I guzzle it down as I raise my shirt to wipe off the sweat coating my entire face.

"Hey, do you want something to ea—*wow*." Silver halts her steps as she walks through the doorway to her bedroom, mouth gaping like a cute fish. I smirk because, while I didn't mean for her to see me lift my shirt, her reaction certainly gives me a bit of an ego boost.

"Mouth closed, Sunshine. You're starting to drool." She snaps her mouth shut and looks up at me with a challenge in her verdant eyes, arms crossed over her chest.

"Well, I don't know what else you expect from me. I'm a warm blooded woman with twenty-twenty vision, Harvey. It's like putting a slab of steak in front of a lion." I swear to God, I hear her whimper, and a tingly sensation shoots straight south.

"I apologize. I didn't realize my bare stomach would cause such an uproar."

"I'll be alerting the church elders as soon as you leave. Expect a riot of pitchforks at your door in no more than two hours."

I can't help the light laugh that bubbles out. It takes a second to register that it came from me, the sound as foreign to my own ears as it must be to her. From the look on her face, you would think she won the lottery. But whatever glee was on her face a minute ago fades once she looks towards her mangled ceiling.

Silver takes a step closer to the damage, and I have to fight the urge not to pull her away from it in case any loose debris falls. I lock my arms firmly behind my back.

"I'm going to cover it up while it dries so you don't have to worry about any material falling."

She just nods, top knot bouncing with the movement.

"I made lunch." It's such a complete one-eighty to what we were talking about that I'm caught off guard before I realize she means *for me.* She made lunch for me.

"You shouldn't have done that."

"It's not a big deal. I was making food for myself, and I tend to make more than I ever need. Come on, it's ready."

Logically, I know I should turn her generosity away and leave for the day, but I find myself following her to the main living area and into her small galley kitchen, where I notice two baguette sandwiches. She reaches over into the refrigerator, grabs two bottles of water, and hands one to me.

"Thank you, for lunch and the water."

"Don't mention it." She hands me a plate before hopping up to sit on the counter and digging into her own meal.

I take a bite then throw my head back and stifle a groan. *"Jesus."*

Yeah, this is definitely better than the decade-old ramen packets I was going to eat.

She giggles to herself, the sound fizzy and light like bubbling champagne. "I know. It's my Nan's legendary chopped sandwich. She taught me how to make it when I was a teenager."

"Chopped sandwich?"

She swallows a bite. "You put all the ingredients on a cutting board and start whacking away like a woman who's ended up on an episode of *Snapped."*

"Graphic," I grimace.

She continues without hesitation. "Then, once everything is chopped and mixed thoroughly, you put it on your bread of choice. But Nan is adamant it's always best on a fresh baguette, and I never argue with her."

She speaks of her grandma with such fondness, it makes my chest ache a little bit.

"Are you close with her? Your nan," I ask, knowing I shouldn't.

A soft smile brightens her face. "She's my best friend. Well, her and Kena. I miss her every day."

"I'm sorry for your loss." I've stepped in it; me of all people should know the delicacy around familial loss. It's been all I've known the last two years.

"Oh, she's not dead! She's just living a promiscuous life in Florida now, so I don't get to see her often anymore. She raised me for most of my life." There's a brief sadness that flits across her features before it's gone. There's a story there, one I have no business being curious about. "When I started college, she decided to retire down south, and I lived here."

"Well, please tell her hats off to the chef."

"Why? I'm the one who made it while she gets sunburned on her ass today at the beach."

I snort around another bite.

"Did you just move to the city?" She hops up on the counter as she takes a sip of her water, legs swinging back and forth.

I track their movement as they swing like a metronome, hypnotizing me, and then catch myself. "I went to college here but moved back home to the Seattle area after. I've been back for just over a month now." That says enough without saying much of anything at all.

"How mysterious." She eyes me skeptically, like she can sense there's something I'm hiding. "Let me guess. You walked in on your lover slathering honey all over your boss, and you were so devastated, you had to change your name and skip town."

"My boss was my sixty year old father."

"Ooooh, age gap. *Nice*." She waggles her eyebrows suggestively, and heat creeps up my neck. She notices the flush spreading over my skin and smiles like the cat who got the cream. I think she likes making me flustered.

"Do you usually say everything that comes to your mind?" I think I like that about her. People tend to hold everything close to their chest, like the slightest bit of vulnerability is equal to embarrassment or shame, myself included. My father taught me well. Since my brother's accident, I don't open up at all. What right would I have, seeking comfort or absolution after what I did?

Most people in this world wouldn't open up to you unless you gave them something in return. Not Silver. She seems to be an open book, unaware or unaffected by people's perception of her.

It's refreshing, like the first dip into the ocean after lying in the sun all day.

"Almost always." She looks extremely pleased with herself, smiling over at me while she sits on her kitchen counter, swinging her feet back and forth. The sight is so cute, my mouth involuntarily twitches up, which is exactly a thought I do not need to be entertaining. "So, was I right?" I must look confused, because she clarifies a second later. "Were you jilted, and that's why you're back in New York?"

I clear my throat, throwing up my guard. "No."

This is veering towards territory I do *not* want to talk about or expand on. I start fumbling around her in the tiny kitchen, desperate to avoid this topic and her stare. I set my cleared plate in the sink after rinsing it off and look everywhere but her earnest eyes, knowing somehow, it will be hard to look in them and have to lie. There are things I can't talk about, things I haven't been able to broach for two years now. So, I do what I've learned is the easiest course of action when uncomfortable. I run.

"I'm going to tarp your ceiling so nothing will fall on you while everything dries up."

Silver looks like she wants to say something, but I turn on my heels and walk back toward her bedroom, finish today's work, and high tail it out of there without so much as a backward glance.

Chapter 7

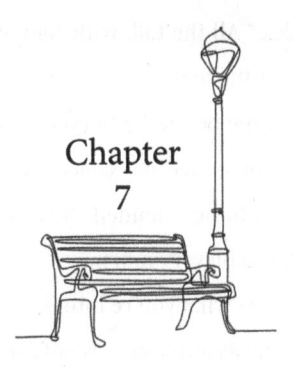

Silver

"Why do you have zucchini in your basket? Are you feeling alright?" Kena searches my eyes, putting his stupidly soft hands on my forehead, checking for a fever.

"Stop being so dramatic." I swat him away.

He looks affronted. "Oh, I'm the dramatic one? Silver, I have not seen you touch a vegetable since the time you mistook an artichoke for a paperweight."

"Well, who the hell uses vegetables as decor!"

"It was a *staged* autumn-themed cornucopia for a Thanksgiving table spread! It was for Home & Garden, for fuck's sake."

Looking around, I notice a few people have stopped to stare at us, so I smile, loop my arm through Kena's and steer him towards the snack aisle of the grocery store.

"Seriously Sil, what's up with the zucchini?"

I pause and look at him, trying to decide if I'm really about to admit this out loud.

"I thought it was a cucumber," I frown. "I was going to try to make my own pickles." All the talk with Nan about pickleball gave me a weird craving for the food.

He just stares at me before he bursts out laughing. "Oh thank God, I thought it was for something salacious."

Now it's my turn to be offended. "Excuse me! I do not need produce for *that*, thank you very much."

"Well, I never know what you're into nowadays."

"Okay, well, let me assure you, it is not now, nor will it ever be, phallic produce."

We loop around the store for around twenty more minutes, grabbing random things we both need for the week. This is a ritual of ours that we do at least twice a month when we have the time. With his new position at Maison Atelier and me deciding to lean into the delusion that led me to buy a bookstore, we've had less time than normal to see each other.

"What is going on in your romantic life? You haven't mentioned anything lately."

"Ew, don't call it my *romantic* life. You know how commitment gives me a stress rash."

"Stop deflecting. What's going on with your hot maintenance guy?"

I groan. Absolutely nothing is going on with Hendrix, and I would very much like it to be. I'm not really sure where I went wrong when we were eating lunch together a few days ago, but the mood shifted, fast. I must have said something wrong, or pried too much and upset him. I'm usually good at reading signals, and I thought we were getting to know each other. I was attempting some light charm, and I thought it was going well...until it wasn't. I haven't stopped thinking about it.

I can't place what it is, but I can't stop thinking about *him*, and it's freaking me out. Is it the thrill of the chase? I'll admit, that's a bit of a novelty for me. Men are...simple creatures, after all. But something about Hendrix has me stumped.

"Nothing."

"Nothing? You?" Kena is shocked. He's never known me to back down. I tend to be singularly focused when I set my sights on someone. It's been the same song and dance since college—we have fun for the night, and then I'm gone before they think to ask for my number. Easy. Satisfactory. No messy feelings involved.

"I don't think he's interested."

"Really?" A large, bright smile stretches wide across Kena's ebony face, and suspicious glee lights up his eyes.

I slap his arm. "Don't look so happy about it, asshole!"

"I feel for you." I cast a scowl his way. "I do! That man is..." He whistles and fans himself. "He's probably the hottest man I've ever seen you go after. I mean, his tattooed arms alone—"

You should see his abs.

"Do you have a point?"

"I just think the pining is good for you. It'll build character." He pats my arm.

"I am *not* pining."

"Tell that to your face. You're pouting."

"Well, you can wipe the smug look off your face. He's not interested. I've all but climbed into his lap, and he's not taking the bait. I think he might be hung up on someone back home." I think about the look on his face when I started to pry.

Makena looks contemplative. After over twenty years of friendship, I can always count on him to help me see a situation clearly. After my dad died and my mom left me with Nan, I learned leaning on people would only end in heartbreak. Nan was all I had until Kena's family moved into the building. As kids, we ran around the building together, had park play dates, and went to the same school. As teenagers, we ravaged bodegas and used our fake I.D.s to get into bars. As college students, we were still ravaging bodegas after a night spent going to those same bars, only *legally* now. He wore me down over *years* of persistence, so I let him in, and it became a party of three. Him, Nan, and me. That was all I needed. All I wanted.

"Why don't you try being his friend first?"

I slow blink. That's certainly a novel idea. "Friends..." I repeat slowly, as if he asked me to explain quantum physics to him.

He places his hands on my shoulders and crouches down a little to meet me at eye level. "I know it's not what you're used to, but if he *is* hung up on someone else, you don't want to get in the middle of that mess. Maybe he just needs friends right now. Invite him to hang out with us soon and get to know him—as *friends*. If something is going to happen between you two, it will."

"You have to stop watching those 'trust the universe' TikToks. They're rotting your brain and making you use logic."

"One of us has to be the voice of reason, and we both know it won't be you."

I groan. "I hate how fair that is." I take a deep breath and push it back out. "Okay, you're right. I'm going to let it go."

He grabs my free hand in his and holds it up between our chests, affectionate to a fault as he stares in my eyes. "You are Silver *fucking* James, you don't chase after men. You are *always* the prize."

I stare into the deep espresso eyes of my best friend in the entire world, one of the only people on this planet who knows me beyond surface level niceties. I nod so he knows I understand what he's trying to tell me. It's what he's been trying to tell me for two decades. I'm worth sticking around for, I'm worth loving. But hearing and understanding are two different things.

So, I deflect.

"You have got to tell me what hand lotion you're using."

Half an hour later, I'm getting out of a taxi with a billion bags of groceries because I overbought while at the store like I always do and couldn't lug it all home on my own. Thanking the driver, I hoist a few bags on each shoulder and then grab the rest in my hands, making my way into the building. I go to grab one of the doors when Tony runs over, looking flustered as he shoulders the door open to help me get through with my bags. And then I hear it. The raised voices.

"Keep your gremlin in line!"

"Don't call her that," a voice growls back.

"If it walks like a duck and quacks like a duck..."

Mrs. Evans and Simon are yelling back and forth at each other in the lobby while the rest of us watch on in horror.

"What's going on?" I ask Tony as I set my groceries down.

"Mrs. Evans is on a tirade because she claims she can hear Isla running around their apartment late at night, and it's disturbing her, since she's in the unit below them."

"She's not doing anything wrong! She's five years old, she's in bed by eight p.m., and you're delusional and bitter."

Mrs. Evans squares up to Simon with all the fury of an agitated badger. "I know what I hear."

I see sweet Isla over in the corner by the mailroom on the verge of tears, and I make my way over to her to comfort or distract until this argument blows over.

But I don't make it even halfway across the room before Mrs. Evans gets me in her sights and decides I'm the new target of her ire.

"And you." Her lip pulls away from her lined mouth in a snarl.

"Here we go." Out of the corner of my eye, I see Hendrix standing in the doorway that leads to the hallway his office is down. I steel my spine for whatever vitriol she's about to spew my way.

"I am so sick and tired of the revolving door of men you have coming in and out of this building."

My face flames, and I have to work to not glance over at Hendrix. "Slut shaming is very two thousand and two of you, Joyce."

"Mrs. Evans," Tony tries to interject and diffuse the tension in the room, but nothing is going to work. She is primed and ready to explode like Mount Vesuvius, and I am Pompeii in the way on her path of destruction.

"Constant strange men–"

"It's not *constant*," I grumble.

"–in and out of here like I'm living in a brothel! It's indecent and immoral. They're probably all criminals, and you're letting them into this building and endangering us all!"

My eyes finally connect with Hendrix's, and a muscle ticks in his jaw as he leans against the door frame, taking in the scene and watching me be scolded. I need to end this quickly. I look over at Simon and motion to Isla in the corner.

"Get her out of here." I turn to Mrs. Evans as Simon gathers up his distraught daughter and leaves. "I don't think this is the best time to—" She cuts me off before I can get another word out.

"I. Don't. Care. You parade around here in your *skanky* clothing—"

"That's enough." Lethal calm is the only way to describe Hendrix's tone. I look over at him in surprise, and he looks exactly as he did a few minutes ago: arms crossed over his broad chest and seemingly unaffected, minus the muscle feathering in his jaw. But there's a fire in his eyes now as he looks over at Mrs. Evans, and you could hear a pin drop as they face off against each other from opposite sides of the room.

She glances at me and rolls her eyes. "You sleeping with him too?" She glances back to Hendrix. "Word to the wise: don't get involved with this one." She hooks her thumb and indicates to me.

"I didn't ask for your opinion, and I think we're all done hearing it tonight." Damnit, he's so sexy when he's defending my honor. Is it anti-feminist to be so turned on by this?

"How dare you! I'll have you fired for speaking to me like that," she huffs in outrage.

"Joyce," Tony interjects, voice like syrup. "Do you remember that time you came home from that gala trashed off pinot and you broke into Mr. Fairbanks' office and opened that four hundred dollar bottle of bourbon?"

Mrs. Evans face goes pale. "How did you know about that?"

He spreads his arms wide. "I'm Tony. I know everything that happens here at The Langham." He looks distinctly smug. "Keep your opinions to yourself, and I won't have to show George any footage I discreetly disposed of."

She stomps off toward the elevator, and I step out of her

way and hold my hands up in supplication. As she steps onto the elevator, she turns around and levels us all with a withering stare. "You'll regret crossing me."

I turn to thank Hendrix for stepping in, for coming to my rescue and shutting down the vicious attack on my character. But as I look over, I see he's walking out the door without a word of goodbye.

It's been a few days since the incident in the lobby, and I've not seen Hendrix since. I've assured Tony nothing was going on between me and the new maintenance man so he could start reiterating that to anyone in the building who thinks otherwise. I'm fairly certain he's avoiding me, though he can't avoid me much longer. He's coming by today to check on my ceiling and hopefully patch it up. Just as I've had the thought, there's a knock at my door, and I race over to answer it.

Hendrix is standing there in a pair of worn-in jeans that hug his thighs beautifully and a sage t-shirt, long sleeves pushed up his arms, showing off the tattooed vines that wrap around his forearms. There's scruff dusting his cut jaw, and his hair looks slightly mussed, like he just ran his hands through it.

"Morning."

That's all I get?

"Let me grab a jacket, because with that frigid attitude, it's a little Baltic in here," I retort sarcastically.

He doesn't say anything, and I'm getting more frustrated by the second. Kena told me to try and be friends with him, but that's a little impossible when the guy won't even talk to me. I don't know what I did to warrant this reaction. Did I pry too much the last time he was here? Was it what Mrs. Evans said? My fingers are starting to go numb from the anxiety of somehow unknowingly upsetting him. I can fix this. I'll give him some space for now and then broach the conversation later after he's warmed up.

"The room's ready for you."

"Thanks." Seriously, it's Lapland in here.

He steps into the hallway and drags in a few panels of sheetrock, propping them against the available wall, careful to avoid the ornate molding. Letting him do his thing, I head into my living room and sit down on my pink velvet couch. I attempt to read for a while, but I keep getting distracted by all the noise coming from my bedroom and all the silence between us.

A few hours pass as I distract myself as best as I can. I pick up my iPad to work on content for events we're planning when Hendrix steps out of my bedroom, a thin sheen of sweat over his face and neck. It is borderline pornographic—and a little insane that my eyes even catch on such a minute detail.

I stand up and trot into the kitchen to grab him a bottle of water to distance myself. He takes it without hesitation and downs half the bottle in one swig.

"I'm sorry. I should have grabbed that for you earlier."

"I should remember to bring my own."

God, this small talk is awkward. I'm just going to bite the bullet and—

"Thank you," I blurt out before he can leave.

"For what?"

"For standing up to Mrs. Evans for me. It's not easy to shut her down when she gets going on a rant, but you didn't back down."

"What she said to you was wrong," he says, like we've been

friends for ages and he's an expert on me and my character.

"You don't know me."

"No, I don't," he agrees, taking a step toward me subconsciously before he realizes and retreats again. "But I know she's wrong. I could see it on your face. What she said hurt you, and I couldn't stand by and let it happen."

I'm stunned he perceived me so well. My poker face is one of my best hidden talents. People never know when something bothers me, I've perfected the art of apathy and adopted a *shake it off* mentality.

One time in middle school, rumors spread that I gave Billy Jensen an STD because he told everyone I went down on him in the auditorium. I'd never so much as looked at the little twerp, but no one believed me, and from that moment on, I built up skin as thick as dragon hide.

Something about Hendrix hearing Mrs. Evan's barbs made my stomach drop, though. I didn't want him to see me the way she did.

"I'm fine."

"I know, you don't have to be though." His words stun me, and my eyes bounce around his face. We're just sort of staring at each other, not saying anything, when he seems to snap back to himself. "Everything is patched up in your ceiling. I moved your bed back, but the compound needs to set fully before I can paint over it."

So, he'll be back at least one more time, and who knows when? Now is the moment to follow Kena's advice and invite him out. *As friends.*

"Great. So listen, a couple of us are going to karaoke on Friday night at this place in Midtown. Do you want to come?"

"Oh, I don't think that's a good idea." He scratches the back of his neck, inked vines undulating as if they're dancing on his skin. "There's a strict no fraternization rule between building staff and tenants."

"As friends!" I shout at him. "Bring your friends. My best friend Kena and his boyfriend will be there. It's a totally casual *friend* thing. I just thought it might be nice to help you resettle into the city if you met some new people around your age."

Maybe if I said the word friend enough, I would start to believe it. The invitation sounded casual enough—not at all like I was still picturing licking the sweat off his neck.

"Uhhh..." He trails off, scratching the back of his neck in clear discomfort.

"No pressure. The offer is open if you want to bring someone with you." This couldn't feel more awkward.

He nods before gathering up his tools and materials, and I follow him to the door. He steps out into the hallway and slings his tool bag over his shoulder in a way that is so inherently masculine, it makes my thighs clench.

I wave goodbye as he heads towards the elevator, and then I shut the door after him, immediately banging my head against it. I have no idea who I'm becoming in the wake of meeting this man, but I've never felt so flustered and nervous around a guy before.

And that confuses the shit out of me.

Chapter 8

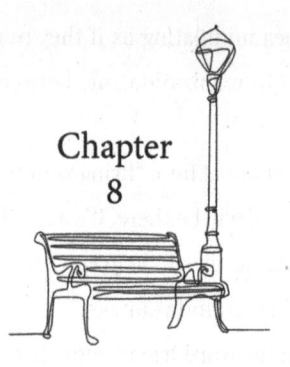

Silver

It's been a busy day at the store, and it gets even busier when our delivery driver drops off ten large boxes. Where am I going to put all of this?

Why did I order so much new stock when I still need to renovate this place?

We only just finished going through old stock and donating a lot of what we didn't want to keep in an effort to clear the space out before updates. But even with the donations, there is a distinct lack of storage and I'll have to leave the new books in their boxes before I can find shelf space for them.

Carmen comes bounding out from behind an end cap. "Is this our new stock? Did my monster books come in?" She sounds so excited and hopeful, I *almost* want to let her go ahead and start opening the boxes, but I throw out my arm and halt her grabby hands.

"The monster erotica is off limits for now."

Carmen pouts at me and then stares longingly at the boxes.

"That's not very progressive of you."

I stifle a giggle. "I promise, I'll let you have it soon, but I gotta get some of the renovations done around here before I start pulling out new stock."

"I still can't believe you bought this place with drug money."

"The cartel didn't need it. They'll bounce back quickly." I wave her off, sorting through invoices as she goes to help someone who just came in.

Ignoring the stacks of boxes that need my attention, I start working on a list of all the things I need to do to turn this place into my dream. Closing while I renovate would make things easier, but I can't do that without losing significant revenue. A little over a week into this endeavor and money is already tight. Between the large down payment, orders placed, materials needed for the renovation, and dwindling foot traffic—I suspect I'm going to have to make some cuts to my plans to make things work. It's just a matter of what.

At the top of the to-do list is painting. This place needs to be stripped and completely repainted. I'm talking walls, banisters, and bookshelves, not to mention fixing the things that are broken, namely the staircase leading to the second floor. I've reached out to at least a dozen contractors, but most of them laughed at my budget for the project. Only one person said he could make it work, promising to get back to me with final numbers soon.

Who knew running a business would be so expensive?

Everyone. Literally everyone.

I'm adding a few more plans to my ever growing list of repairs when a throat clears in front of me. I look up and startle to find a man standing in front of me at the counter.

He's cute. Really cute. Dirty blond hair that falls perfectly around his brows, giving him a boy next door vibe. He's tall, has a solid frame, and is dressed impeccably. He's exactly the kind of guy I'd go for normally.

Hazel eyes and strong broad shoulders flash through my mind's eye.

Stop it. You are not thinking about him right now.

"Do you have a second to help me?" I banish thoughts of Hendrix to the far reaches of Long Island where they can't find me without a minimum of four train transfers.

"Yeah, of course. What can I help you with?"

He scratches the back of his neck while looking sheepish. "My sister's birthday is tonight, and I need a gift. She likes books, but uh...I don't know what girls like to read."

"Cutting it down to the wire, aren't you?"

"Yeah a bit," he chuckles, making a dimple pop on his right cheek.

"Tell me a bit about her. That way, I can get a feel for who she is and maybe pare down the selection."

His eyes soften. "She's a communications major at NYU, but she's so goofy, just always game for a laugh. She and her girlfriend like to throw pottery on the weekends, and she loves to hate bad reality tv shows." It's obvious how much he adores her, and I'm hit with a rush of longing. I used to wish I had a sibling, someone to stand with me in solidarity against the world—a built-in best friend when things got bad. In hindsight, I guess it's good I didn't.

I take him over to our Pride section and show him a release from a few months ago about a sapphic influencer who starts her own web series and falls for the camera woman she hired.

"It's hilarious and irreverent and painfully romantic. I think she'll love it." I walk him back towards the register around all the tables and boxes to ring him up.

"Thank you, I wouldn't have known where to start."

He pays for the book, and I place a complimentary bookmark inside the cover.

"Tell her to come by and let me know what she thinks after she finishes. We're going to be starting some events here shortly, including a book club. In case she and her girlfriend want to join." It's a bit of an elevator pitch, and I hope it comes out natural, but I've got to get word out about these events somehow.

"Can I come too?" I slowly blink as I look up at the shy grin stretched across his face.

I think of Hendrix again. Which is ridiculous, because we're barely friends—acquaintances at most—so there's no feasible reason for me to turn this guy away.

"Of course you can." I smile back.

He's turning to leave but stops. "Can I be honest with you?"

Apprehension fills my chest. "Sure thing, person I met five minutes ago. Tell me what's pressing on your mind."

He huffs out a laugh. "I didn't need to come in."

"Is it not your sister's birthday?" I ask, confused. "Does she not exist? Did you eat her in the womb?"

A smile crinkles the corners of his blue eyes. "No it is, but I wasn't going to get her a book." He sheepishly scratches the back of his neck. "I know this is kind of forward of me, but I saw you through the shop window, and you're really beautiful. I'd like to take you out sometime." He extends his business card out to me.

I take the card from him and see his name is John and he works in finance. Finance bros are notorious fuck boys, and honestly, that's been my bread and butter in the past. They never want or expect anything from me beyond a physical connection. It's easy and uncomplicated. But it feels different this time. I don't feel that flirtatious pull towards him that I expected to despite the fact that he's inhumanly attractive.

"Finance bro, huh?"

"We're not all bad, I swear."

I laugh and wave his card in the air. "I'll think about it."

He nods in understanding and thanks me again for helping him find a gift for his sister before heading out.

I look over to where Carmen helps a couple, and she's looking at me like I've sprouted a tail. I definitely don't turn down dates with cute guys, *ever*.

Yeah, I don't know what's wrong with me either.

It's late in the day, and I've sent Carmen home so she can finish studying for an exam she has later this week. Now that I'm alone, I can take off the mask I've been wearing all day—the one I put on so no one knows how anxious I am, how scared. I feel unsettled, but I have to act like everything is perfect, I chose this. It's just more overwhelming than I thought it would be. I jumped into this head first without any thought, and I know it was reckless but I don't regret it. It feels right. This place has always felt like home to me, and it's *mine* now—mine to ruin if I'm not careful.

I'm standing in the middle of the store, surveying like a captain at the helm of their ship when my phone starts ringing. I jog over to grab it, assuming it's Kena, since he's the only one who calls me. I don't even check the caller I.D. before I answer.

"Thank you for calling McDick's, would you like a foot-long with a side of fries?"

"Silver?"

My blood turns to ice in my veins as pinpricks shoot across my skin like wildfire before my skin goes numb altogether.

Why is she calling me?

I haven't spoken to Carol James in *years*. She made her choice long ago to not be in my life when she said it was too hard to look at me and not see *him,* to not see my dad. Years of waiting—of hoping she would come back, passed before I realized it wasn't going to happen. I lost my dad, and then I lost my mom too—except she's still alive and just chose to not want me anymore.

She resurfaces every now and then, usually to fulfill some kind of *I checked in on my kid so I'm not a bad person* quota. But it's been longer since the last time, and I stopped expecting her to try years ago. I stopped caring—or at least trying not to care.

I've let the line go silent long enough that she calls out for me again.

"Silver, honey, are you there?"

"I'm here." My voice sounds lifeless, even to me. A byproduct of the effect my mom leaves me with. She blows back into my life when it's convenient for her, and I'm left feeling cold and numb. The worst part is, she never seems to notice or care.

"Oh good. I'm glad I caught you." She says it like she calls me all the time and not once every few years. "Look, I'm going to be in town soon and I want to see you."

Not a chance in hell.

"Oh, I don't know. I've been really busy lately, and getting time off has been a struggle." Not technically a lie. I have been super busy between the apartment getting fixed and buying this place.

"Oh, come on. I haven't seen you in years, Silly," *Silly*. My dad gave me that nickname when I was a baby. He said it was because I was his silly girl because I was always happy and giggling. He always knew how to make me feel special. Hearing it coming out of her mouth sounds like nails scraping down a chalkboard, shrill and wrong.

"Who's fault is that?" I snap.

"Silly—" she starts before I interrupt her.

"You don't get to call me that, not anymore." There is a distinct pause of silence that heightens the tension, and I'm glad no one is around to witness me like this. I pinch my brows between my thumb and forefinger, anxiety flooding my whole body thinking about why she's calling. Does she somehow know about the store and wants to chastise me for spending the life insurance money like this? Better to ask and get off the phone as quickly as possible, minimize the damage. "What do you need? I'm swamped."

A deep sigh resonates through the other end of the line. "Like I said, I'll be in New York, and I want to see you. There's things we should discuss." Well, that sounds ominous, and therefore, I want nothing to do with it.

"Now's not a good time. Maybe next visit, though." I need a get out of jail free card, so I fake greeting a customer to make it seem like I'm busy in the store. "Sorry, I'm by myself, and I just had a group come in. I'll talk to you later." I hang up before she can protest.

I spend the rest of my shift feeling off kilter. My mom calling never fails to leave me feeling the same way I did when I was a little girl, when I realized she was never coming back for me. I know I'm immeasurably lucky because I had Nan, but I don't think the pain of your mother abandoning you in the wake of your father's death ever actually leaves you. The number of birthday candles you blow out with a phantom wish that your mother will walk through the door never leaves you. The nights you wish you had your mom to talk to after a boy at school broke your heart, before you learned not to let them, will never leave you, as much as I want it to.

As a result, I've spent years cultivating my unbothered, confident façade, and all it took was one out of the blue phone call for it to all come crumbling down.

It's around six in the evening when I make my way home. I can't seem to shake the heaviness that makes it feel like there's an oily residue coating my body, so I put on some nineties British punk music and head home to get ready for karaoke later. Hopefully, a night out with my friends will help me brush off this afternoon.

I'm nearly to the building when I see Tony standing outside, talking to one of the other neighborhood doormen. I wave hello to him but make my way inside to the elevator bank to avoid any chit chat, I'm not in the mood. I just want to get inside, have a glass of wine, and slowly get ready for the fun night out I desperately need. I'm shuffling through my bag, looking for my keys, when the elevator opens. I step on only to hit a wall—no, a chest—and look up to find Hendrix stoically staring down at me.

"We have to stop meeting like this," I quip, trying to lighten my mood.

He doesn't say anything, just looks sort of pained, so I step out of his way to let him off the elevator. He nods at me in thanks and starts to walk away, but I stop him with a hand to his forearm.

"Are you going to come to Spotlight for karaoke tonight?"

He looks down where I'm still holding onto his arm, and his

jaw flexes.

"Probably not a good idea. Thanks, though." He stalks off. He's so hot and cold. One minute, he seems to want to be friendly, and then the next, he's aloof and distant. I don't get it, or him. But the picture is loud and clear: he's not interested in me. That's fine. I've never felt the need to let my thoughts linger on a man before, and I've given Hendrix far too much space in my brain already. After the day I've had, I'm ready to let all the bullshit go and move on.

Putting my bag down on my kitchen counter, I move over to the fridge, pull out a bottle of wine, and pour a healthy glass. The drink flows down my throat, warming me from the inside and setting my resolve. To really put everything out of my mind, I need to get back to the old me. The me of a month ago wouldn't be giving a grumpy, stoic, admittedly sexy man a second thought.

I reach into my back pocket and pull out the card John gave me earlier when he asked me out. I stare at it, take another sip of my wine, and pick up my phone.

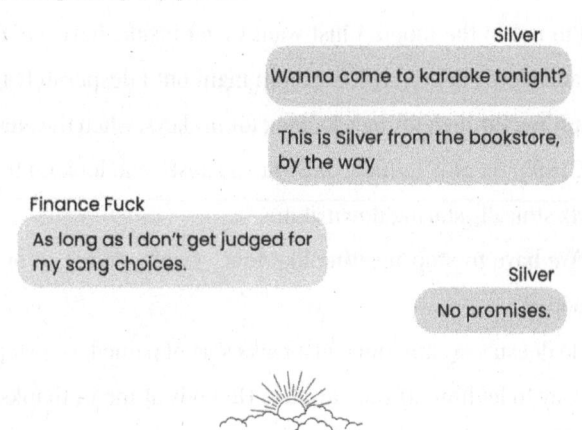

> Silver
> Wanna come to karaoke tonight?
>
> This is Silver from the bookstore, by the way

> Finance Fuck
> As long as I don't get judged for my song choices.

> Silver
> No promises.

Kena is smiling a mile wide as he walks off the stage following his *fourth* Celine Dion performance. If you've never seen Makena

Williams receive an encore in a small karaoke bar line up, you haven't truly lived. He struts his way over to where we sit, accepting adoration and accolades from every table he passes with a megawatt smile and mini bows, bathing in the praise.

"He seems to be enjoying all the attention." John leans further into me, neon lights reflecting off the tumbler of scotch he's holding. He was already waiting outside of Spotlight when we arrived, rapidly talking to someone on the phone about investments and stocks.

I nod my head while taking a sip of my drink. "He's a blackhole vortex for praise. This is just round one of his nightly performances."

"You always ease them in with Celine before you dazzle them with Mariah." Kena plops down between me and his boyfriend, Julien, who was sitting on my other side talking to Holly and her wife, Sera. In the background, the venue MC calls up the next person to the stage, and they start singing Careless Whisper *incredibly* off key.

I'm about halfway out of my funk. The second French 75 of the evening definitely has something to do with that. But the fog of the afternoon still feels like it's looming over my head, waiting to descend again.

John sets his drink down on the table in front of us and turns his body more towards me. Crossing my left thigh over my right, I lean more fully into him and try to forget the first half of my day.

"You look beautiful." His eyes dart quickly down my body and back up.

Nan always made sure I grew up with a healthy dose of self-love, and while it's not always been easy—especially during my more formative years—it's given me a soft sort of confidence that comes naturally to me now. But with the men I've hooked up with in the past, the words have always felt hollow. Do I believe they find me attractive? Yes, but in the fleeting, surface level way.

It's never bothered me before—until now.

I can't parse out what's changed, so I just take another sip of my cocktail. "Thank you." I hope he doesn't notice my uneasiness. "So, what's your go to karaoke song, Wall Street?"

"Mr. Brightside." He places his arm on the booth and around my back in a covert but confident gesture.

I grimace into my cocktail. "I'm afraid that's the most frat boy answer you could have supplied."

"Hey, don't judge me. It's a good song."

"I remember saying judgment was a very real possibility."

He holds his hands in a supplicate gesture. "Okay, I concede. What song should I choose?"

"Oh, sweet summer child...you're going to wish you hadn't asked me that." I pat his cheek in mock comfort. "They should be calling us up to the stage any minute."

"I'm feeling a bit scared now."

I grin fiendishly, and all my friends behind me, who had *apparently* been listening to our conversation, speak in unison, "You should be."

Not a moment later, the MC calls us to the stage, and I lean in to whisper the song selection in their ear.

"You're not even going to tell me what it is before we start?"

"It's all a part of the experience, Wall Street. Consider it a hazing ritual of sorts."

I grab our microphones, hand him his, and drag him out to center stage. The opening notes start to filter through the speakers, but the tv displaying the lyrics for us to follow hasn't caught up yet, so he still doesn't know what song I've chosen.

"Keep your wits about you. Your part is coming first." I nod to the screen, where the title page reads "Lay All Your Love on Me" from the life changing 2008 classic, Mamma Mia!

He stumbles at first but catches his footing, and the crowd starts to sing along and cheer. I stand to his right, dancing coyly and getting into character, while I wait for my part to start. I'm wearing a cropped fuchsia lamé top with a plunging cowl neckline that leaves my back exposed, and every time the light catches the metallic fabric, it shoots a pink glimmer across the room. It is the ultimate karaoke top and sinfully sexy.

I turn and give the audience my back right before my part comes in so I can do a dramatic turn into the song. Kena isn't the only one with stage presence, thank you very much. I take a deep breath and whip around right as my opening line starts, locking eyes with the last audience member I expected to see.

Hendrix Wells.

He looks disgustingly good in dark jeans and a fitted white t-shirt topped with a vintage leather bomber jacket. *That's just not fair.*

I miss my opening line, and John places a hand on my back to get my attention. It's hard to tell in the dim lighting of the bar, but it looks like Hendrix's gaze narrows on that minute touch.

"Are you okay?"

Shit.

I don't answer him with words, but I give him a nod, pasting on a smile and performing like I'm on stage at the Winter Garden Theatre. I prowl toward John, circling him as I sing into my microphone and trail my hand across his chest. I commit to the role no matter who's watching, even going as far as to crawl across the stage like Sophie did on the beach in Greece. By the end of the song, the audience is hollering, and I'm laughing as I climb off the stage with John in tow. We make our way to the back booth where my friends are.

"I'll be right back. A friend came in while we were performing."

"Sure. Do you want another drink?" *God, he really is nice.*

"That would be great, thanks."

I walk towards Hendrix, my heart rate picking up speed the closer I get to him. Someone to his right claps him on the shoulder and I realize he brought a friend with him. He sees me approaching and tracks my movement the whole way, his intense stare scorching my body as his gaze scores over me from head to toe.

"So you came after all." I stop in front of him and stare up into his hazel gaze.

"He wanted to come." He gestures to his friend.

"And who might you be, handsome?" I ask with a coquettish tone.

"Since this asshole isn't going to introduce me like a civilized gentleman," Hendrix rolls his eyes, "I'll do it myself. Jae Song. I'm this surly bastard's best friend and live in boy toy."

Oh, I like him. Jae is tall with dark eyes, perfectly coiffed but somehow tousled hair, a humor-filled stare, and tattoos all over his arms that extend up his neck. He has that effortlessly cool style, wearing a baggy t-shirt, with loose black pants and a silver ring on every finger.

"Hi, Jae." I extend my hand, which he grabs with both of his, pulling them to his mouth to place a kiss on the back of mine. *Let's add charming to his list of attributes.* "I'm Silver James. I'm this surly bastard's building tenant and all around thorn in his side."

"Oh, I know who you are." I cock my head at him in confusion.

"That's enough of that," Hendrix interrupts, looking at Jae in irritation while Jae looks back with challenge.

"Hey, here's your drink." John is suddenly by my side, handing me another cocktail while settling his palm against my bare back. Hendrix takes notice, and, yep, his gaze is narrowing. I *didn't* imagine it earlier, and I'm suddenly feeling very self-conscious about the hand on my back, but I don't step out of his hold.

"John, this is my...friend, Hendrix, and his best friend, Jae. Guys, this is my date, John."

Jae looks at Hendrix, and I follow his stare to see his jaw flexing minutely. There and gone in a flash.

The guys exchange hellos and handshakes, and an air of awkwardness settles around us. We need more buffers...other people to flip the energy into something less tense. I usher the guys back to the booth where the rest of our party is drinking and laughing. Everyone else *except* Kena, who has made it up to the stage again to start part two of his extensive set list. I introduce Hendrix and Jae to the rest of our group, and they settle into the chairs opposite us.

Holly leans over to whisper to me. "I get it now."

"That is *so* not helpful right now."

She chuckles and leans back into Sera, who wraps her arms around her and rests her chin on her shoulder. The gesture is so familiar, so affectionate, it makes something deep within me ache. I sneak a glance over at Hendrix, who is already staring at me with a look bordering on intense before he looks away. It makes me flush with warmth. It makes me uncomfortable. *Since when am I uncomfortable with the male gaze?*

Clearing my throat, I look to my right and smile at my date.

John has been nothing but nice, and I'm being rude by staring too long at my maintenance man who wants nothing to do with me. *Right?*

An hour goes by, and in that time, I've done a solo to 'Lose Yourself' by Eminem, Jae has surprised everyone, except Hendrix, by performing 'All Too Well (10 Minute Version) (Taylor's Version)' with so much gusto that even Kena was impressed, and Hendrix has surprised no one by singing nothing. Whenever I've dared to glance at him in between conversations, he's been white-knuckling his beer, no doubt regretting the decision to come out tonight.

I refocus on my date, who is telling me about his vacation to Mykonos last summer and a story about a particularly sordid night involving *a lot* of Ouzo, a priest, and a traveling circus. It's so outlandish, it can't be real, but it has me in tears laughing. He leans toward me, the strobe lights of the bar reflecting across his face, and places a hand on my thigh. The warmth of his hand seeps through my black jeans, and I swear I can feel eyes glaring from my left at the contact.

Hendrix stands abruptly and heads toward the bar. I track his movement the whole way there, and he flags down the bartender before sitting on a stool.

"That guy seems intense. He's your friend?"

I have no clue.

Chapter 9

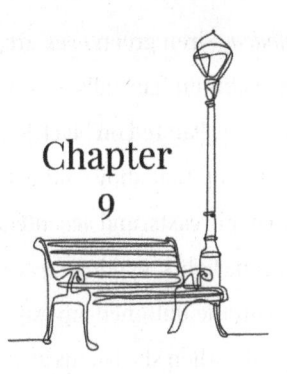

Hendrix

The pit in my stomach hasn't left since I secluded myself to the bar. Seeing Silver's date put his hand on her thigh elicited a very *primal* reaction in me. Which is stupid—I have zero claim to her, and she isn't mine to feel possessive over, I know that. But seeing the polished up frat boy touch her with brazen familiarity sets my teeth on edge. She didn't push him away. Why would she? She's single and he's attractive, nice, and isn't weighed down by the rules of his job or traumatic past.

No fraternization with the tenants.

A rule that when informed of, held zero weight over me. But day by day, it becomes harder to abide by, even as it serves to remind me that as much as I may like Silver, I'm not allowed to go there. Seeing her with a date tonight was a surprise, but it's something I'll have to get used to. I can't avoid her completely since I work where she lives.

But *fuck*, if it doesn't grate.

She looks...*devastating* tonight. Every day, she looks perfect— bright and colorful and full of life. But tonight? She looks sinful and sexy and...*forbidden*. Siren green eyes are lined with a smokey black liner, and her platinum hair falls around her bare shoulders in soft, voluminous waves. Painted on black jeans hug her round ass and offset a shiny pink top that shows off a sliver of her stomach, dipping low between her breasts, and accented with a gold necklace glinting under the strobe lights, making *every* part of my body ache.

Watching her with the buttoned-up guy to her right feels like a slow torture, especially when she laughs at something he says, her eyes scrunching at the corners and her lips curving upward. I *want* that light, *need* that light, *can't have* that light.

She's like the sun, and I'm the cloud threatening to cover her rays.

Irritated at myself, I throw back the rest of my beer and signal for the bartender to bring me another, hoping it will help me forget the sight of Silver crawling across the stage. I glance around, aptly avoiding Silver and her date, and see that Jae is no longer chatting to Holly and Sera but is now flirting with a bachelorette party on the opposite side of the room. Yes, the whole party.

The barkeep stops over with a fresh beer for me, and I thank her and turn to face the room. As much as I don't want to, my eyes keep drifting back towards Silver, like her mere presence in the room demands my attention. The strobe lights are arching across the room and dancing over her skin in a kaleidoscope of endless possibilities, drawing my eyes to her on a never-ending loop.

I try not to make it obvious as I watch them. John has his hand rested on her thigh, and it makes me want to break something, but at least she's not touching him back. She's smiling and laughing, but there's something about her body language that feels...off, like something is bothering her. I know what her real smiles look like, have been an undeserving receiver of them. She always burns brightly, but right now, that fire feels dimmed. Is it him? Or something else? Am I just imagining it because I don't want her to be into him?

As if she can sense my eyes on her, she looks up, catching my gaze. Neither of us backs down. We stare at each other for what feels like an eternity. It's bliss—it's agony. Everyone and everything else fading away, and we're the only ones left in the room. Then I see it, just there, behind the eyes: a sense of something that isn't right, something she's trying *really* hard to cover up with smiles and laughter. I want to ask her about it, dive into her head and extract all the bad out so she doesn't have to remember it, so nothing will mar her happiness and dull her shine. But that's not my place. I break our eye contact first and turn back around to face the hundreds of bottles lining against the wall.

I should leave. Irish goodbye my way out of here.

I'm about to ask to pay my tab when someone sits down next to me. I think it's going to be Jae, but it turns out to be Kena.

He drags his chair closer to me and takes a seat. "June, my love!" He calls out to the bartender, who comes gliding over at his call.

"Baby, you are four sheets to the wind. Don't tell me you're about to order another drink," June says in a thick Southern accent.

Mock affronted, Kena grasps at his chest and then reaches out his other hand to grasp mine. "Junie, I am perfectly sober enough to have a shot with my new brother wife here." He pats my chest as I choke down the sip of beer I had just taken.

"Alright, fine. But I'm getting Julien if you get too wild. You remember what happened last time."

"That was one tiny, *minuscule,* some might say, fire. I put it out and replaced the drapes. You can't hold it against me forever," he harrumphs at her pouting.

"I can and I will. Now, what do you want?"

"Two Slippery Nipples." He flashes me a bright wide smile as I cough into my fist.

June leaves to go to make our shots.

"Brother wife?" I ask, curious as to what exactly he means.

"Mhmmm," he hums, not bothering to elaborate. I see him glance back to Silver, and I follow his gaze. She's bumping shoulders with Julien, singing along to the song the person on stage is wailing while her date is on his phone. Ridiculous that he could focus on anything *but* her.

Kena notices me and where my gaze has wandered.

"She likes you, you know."

"She can't."

"But she does, and she doesn't *ever* like men." I look at John, and he catches me clocking the movement. "Don't get me wrong, she has...*friends*, but only ever for a night. She doesn't let it go farther than that."

The thought of John being one of those *friends* makes me grind my teeth and white-knuckle my beer bottle.

I deflect and nod towards her and John, trying not to let a vague tint of bitterness color my tone. "They seem to be getting along."

"Oh, please. I don't know why he's here, but I *know* Silver. He's only here because she doesn't think you're interested."

I whip my head to him. "She said that?"

He grins, knowing he's caught me in some quasi admission. "She didn't have to. You, however, have come up in casual conversation multiple times now, and I don't think she even realized she mentioned you."

"That doesn't mean anything, and it doesn't matter because I can't go there. So if she does feel something, she'll have to get over it."

He shakes his head. "You're both so stubborn, unwilling to admit to any sort of feeling."

"There are no feelings." My molars grind against each other. There can't be any feelings, and someone like her deserves better than me.

He studies the side of my face. "Right. Of course, I must have misread every time I saw you staring at her tonight."

I remain quiet. Resolute.

June comes barreling back over. "Sorry! Got a little swamped at the end there, but here you go." She sets two tall shot glasses down in front of us filled with a tan, creamy liquid. "Two Slippery Nipples to wet your whistle." She walks away to help other customers before I can thank her.

"What's in this?" I lift the glass, eyeing the concoction with skepticism.

"It's better you don't know. Okay! Time to cheers." Kena picks up his shot, holding it out towards mine. "To new beginnings and stepping out of comfort zones."

He's more on the nose than he could ever possibly imagine. I nod my head and smile before clinking my glass against his, tapping it on the bar, and then tossing back the drink.

"Fuck," I choke. "That was vile."

Kena swallows his shot and throws his arms in the air while dancing in his seat.

"Kena! You're up again," the MC calls him over, and he hops off the stool.

He holds his hand out to me. "Let's go, brother wife."

"No. No way." He can't force me to do this. I won't go up there and embarrass myself in front of Silver and her stupid date. No way in hell.

"Nope. Not an option. Get that delectable ass off the stool, stop moping, and let's go have some fun." He grabs my hand with surprising strength and drags me off my seat towards the stage against my will.

"Kena, I don't want to do this." He's not listening to me.

I'm starting to panic a little, knowing I'm about to make a fool of myself.

When we get up there, he turns to me, deadly serious. "Tell me, brother wife, are you familiar with Disney Channel Original Movies?"

I roll my eyes, trying for a shred of false bravado to bolster my nerves. "I grew up with a sister who made us watch them constantly."

"Don't act like you didn't love them."

He turns and shows the venue MC his song of choice before leading us out to the center of the stage and hands me a mic.

"Alright, Spotlight! We've got a virgin here, so be gentle with him." He winks at the crowd and then nods to the man to start the music and video feed.

"I'm Isabella, and you can be Lizzie. I'll offer background vocals for support. Time to shine for our girl." I'm momentarily confused before the opening notes of the song starts playing, and I realize he's selected 'What Dreams Are Made Of' from *The Lizzie McGuire Movie*. It was one of Laurel's favorites growing up...and mine because I had a crush on Lizzie. She used to make Maddox and I watch it constantly. A pang of sadness hits me over missing my sister before I realize it's my part to come in, and the opening notes chase away the feeling, replacing it with reluctant but genuine fun.

I start singing, voice shaking slightly as I try not to think about all the people watching me or the nausea churning in my gut. It's not bad, but it's not good either. I look over to Kena, and he's nodding encouragingly while dancing off to the side, just like Isabella does for Lizzie.

So, I embrace my inner pop star and this new group of friends I've made tonight, looking out into the crowd because I don't need the lyric monitor. I'll probably be embarrassed about that fact later.

Kena and I are perfectly in sync, even if I'm not in tune, and as we get to the part of the chorus where we sing *"this is what dreams are made of"*, I look out into the crowd and find Silver dancing with abandon, the light back in her eyes with full force, staring right at me with a laugh falling off her full lips.

And for the first time in the last two years—I feel lighter.

Kena's words bounced around in my mind like a pinball machine for the rest of the weekend. They're still bouncing around in my head now as I finish up the last bit of work on Silver's ceiling. It didn't need much work today. Now that the compound is dried, I just need to sand it down till it's smooth and paint over it. It'll be like the Niagara Falls of pipe bursts never happened.

She likes you, you know.

She's smart and funny and beautiful; how could I *not* like her too? I can't seem to stop thinking about her, about how she looked at Spotlight—ethereal, sultry and addictive. I'm dreading the fact that this is the last day I'll need to work on her apartment but also relieved knowing it's for the best to get some distance. She brought a date to karaoke; she's moved on from whatever flirtation she was trying to start with me.

I can't even act on my feelings anyway, not without risking my position at The Langham. If I lose my job, then the threat of having to move back to Seattle becomes very real. I know Jae wouldn't kick me out, but I am a product of my father, and I'm confident my ego would get in the way of allowing his charity a second time. Then there's the harsh truth that I'm too much of a coward to face all that I left back home. I don't want to be confronted by my mom's sadness, Laurel's disassociation, or Dad's bitter resentment.

I left Seattle when I realized I would never not be haunted by the loss of my brother. After two years, we had all moved on in the only way a family can after weathering that kind of suffering. Dad dove further into work, his anger always on a short fuse, Mom focused on the kids still alive, Laurel started to party more, and I—well, I retreated into myself. Slowly, we all stopped talking about it, about him. I couldn't take it anymore. There was always an inexpressible balloon in the room swelling with all the words left unspoken, and I was constantly on pins and needles waiting for it to pop.

I wouldn't force anyone to talk about it and relive the singular, all-consuming torture of those memories, but I no longer wanted to be suffocated by the silence, by all the avoidance. So, I came back to the only other place that has ever felt like home: New York.

I didn't give my family much time to adjust to the news of me leaving before I was gone. Next thing I knew, I was on Jae's doorstep with a large duffle thrown over my shoulder. He had no idea I was showing up, and he didn't ask questions as he took my bag to his spare room and then grabbed me a beer from the fridge while ordering takeout for us.

I made the right move, even though it hurts to think about my family, who no doubt feel betrayed by my swift departure.

"No, that can't be right. You quoted me fifteen grand when we spoke last week."

Silver's voice pulls me out of my daze, and I realize I'd been painting over the same spot so much, it left streaks. I grab the roller brush to give it another coat and smooth it out.

"What do you mean, it's going to cost *fifty thousand dollars*?" Silver's voice rings out, rising in octaves with every word.

I step off the ladder and move closer to the door leading into the living room, where her footsteps are wearing a path through her floor.

"You've got to be kidding me." She sounds like she's pulling at her hair, making it wild and messy. "No, I can't proceed!" A pause, more pacing. "Because you're price gouging me, you cretin. You wouldn't be doing this if I was a man. It's despicable, you're despicable."

Cold fury washes over her tone. I've never heard her so angry, and hearing her sound so upset has me on edge as I step into the doorway.

Just to check on her, I tell myself.

She's pacing through her living room, skirting a path between the packed bookshelves that line the back wall and her pink velvet couch. She moves around her side tables and in front of a coffee table that houses even *more* books, then back to the bookshelves again. She's created an F1 racetrack in her own living room, all the while listening to whatever the person on the other line is saying. She's shaking her head, and a scoff slips from her full rosebud lips right before she starts punching the air like there's a Century Bob in front of her. Her form is surprisingly good, even as she holds the phone between her shoulder and ear.

She stops abruptly and goes eerily quiet. "You're going to *rue* the day you crossed me, Phil." More silence follows. "Yes, people do say that in real life! You're fired." She hangs up the phone, lets out a silent scream, and then turns to toss her phone onto the couch. When she spots me leaning in the doorway, she jumps.

"What the hell, you creeper!" She's clutching at her chest, trying to catch her breath. "You can't just eavesdrop on someone's conversation like a real life Joe Goldberg."

"Who?"

"*You?*"

"Me?"

"No, it's a show called *You*—never mind!" She settles her hands on her hips. She's dressed in a pair of cut off denim shorts and an oversized Rangers tee. The sight is so casual but still makes my insides twist and pull like they're on a taffy stretcher.

"You have a lot of books in here." I nod around the room at all the books lining the walls, on the coffee table, lining the window sills.

"It kind of comes with the territory."

"What, do you work at a bookstore?"

"I own one, actually. It's falling apart," she huffs a harried laugh, "but it's mine."

I walk toward one of the shelves now, pulling off a title and looking over the cover as I think about how much the occupation suits her. She seems exactly like someone who's spent her life jumping through different worlds, like the one she lived in couldn't contain all her wonder or satiate her endless curiosity.

"Is that what the phone call was about?" I glance toward her discarded phone.

She groans and plops down on the plush, rosy cushions of her couch. Tucking her smooth legs underneath her, she reaches behind her for a throw pillow that she clutches to her chest while motioning for me to sit down next to her.

I place the book back on the shelf, hesitantly taking a seat, unsure of what to do. Do I face her and relax? That feels too familiar. But sitting here as if I have a rod shoved up my ass like a marionette puppet isn't much better.

"You can relax. Your virtue is safe here." She chuckles at my hesitation.

"I'm not worried about that," I grumble as I adjust myself to fit more comfortably on the couch, it's small size bringing us closer than is wise.

I clear my throat. "Is something wrong at your store?"

"So, here's the thing...I sort of impulsively bought the bookstore I worked at around a month ago with blood money."

"What do—" She cuts me off before I can finish asking my obvious question with a finger to my lips.

"*Shhh,* don't interrupt." Her eyes flick down to where her digit rests against my mouth. I'm so tempted to bite the pad of her finger, but before my intrusive thoughts can win out, she yanks it away and sits on her hand.

"I've worked at Brownstone Books since I was in college, and the owner, Pat, decided she wanted to sell. I just couldn't stand to see the place turned into another Dunkin Donuts or something. And I *love* donuts, so that's really saying something."

I grimace.

"Don't tell me you don't like donuts," she trails off.

"It's a sugar coma made of air."

"What's next? Are you going to say you don't like puppies? This fake situation we're having in my head is never going to work if you don't like donuts *and* puppies."

"I love puppies. I'm not a psychopath." I'm pointedly going to ignore that she thinks about us in a fake romance scenario.

"That remains to be seen. I guess it makes sense you don't like donuts. You do look like *that*." She gestures to my physique, and a small part of me—okay, a big part of me—preens at her attention.

I love how she says whatever thought comes to mind. Silver is completely uninhibited, and it's so damn refreshing after years of everyone around me holding back everything they're feeling.

"So, I gave Pat a down payment for the store and have worked out a monthly payment plan to pay off the remainder, specifically so that I can renovate the store. It's a bit worse for wear."

"How bad is it?" I'm genuinely curious and amazed that she jumped into something like this with no fear.

"It's not great. The bookshelves are pretty dilapidated because they haven't been updated since the eighties when Pat opened the place. The upstairs area has been totally out of commission since I started working there a decade ago. That, combined with new paint, updating our point of sale system, overhauling our inventory, and bringing our online presence into this century—I'm a bit overwhelmed."

"What was the phone call about then?" I ask.

She takes a deep, steadying breath. "That was Phil, the contractor I hired to help me renovate the things I didn't think I could DIY on my own, calling to tell me that the fifteen grand he quoted me originally was somehow miraculously going to cost fifty thousand dollars now."

"Fucking hell." I resist the urge to shout.

"I know it's a bit of a job, but fifty grand seems like he's trying to take advantage of me. So, I fired him."

"Good girl."

Oh, shit. I did *not* mean to say that. God, I can actually feel the tips of my ears heating, and I've somehow stunned Silver into silence. I didn't think it was possible, and thank God she takes mercy on me and chooses to ignore it, even though…yup, her eyes look a little glazed. Shit.

She clears her throat. "Right, so…I'm a little stressed about what to do. I guess I'll be watching a lot of reno videos off YouTube."

Don't do it. Don't do it. Don't do it.

"I'll help you with the renovations."

And there it is, the singular moment I can point to later on down the road and say, *and* that *was when I lost my mind.*

"What?" She's blinking at me, clearly confused as well.

Fuck it all. If I'm going to offer, then I'm going to commit to it. I *want* to help her, and I'm not going to let a small thing like my inconvenient and unnecessary feelings get in the way.

"I don't know if you've noticed, but I'm a bit handy with my tools." The second it's out of my mouth, I realize how suggestive it sounded.

She smirks. "Oh, I've noticed."

I level her with a glare. "What I mean is…before I moved back to New York, I worked at my family's carpentry shop, building furniture, cabinets, *bookshelves*...custom work for homes and businesses. I'm kind of exactly what you need. For the bookstore," I clarify quickly.

"You would you really help me?" A rare glimmer of vulnerability clouds her features.

"Yes," I say, no reluctance in my tone. I have a strange feeling that she doesn't ask for things often, and if I were to hesitate, she wouldn't accept my help.

"But you don't even like me."

"I like you just fine." Her eyes flare with soft light.

"I can't pay you much, but I *will* pay you." She seems adamant, so if it gets her to let me help, then I'll acquiesce.

"We can figure that out later." Maybe it will help keep the lines from blurring.

She looks at me with a slight skepticism but also a sliver of hope.

"What do you get out of this?" Foolish. This was so foolish, and now I have to bluff my next words.

"It'll help build my portfolio for the business I'm planning to start eventually." I have no intention of starting a business here. I haven't even picked up a pencil to draw in two years. I used to love it as a way to escape. To create a piece in my head, put it on paper, and then build it with my hands was supremely rewarding work. But I haven't drawn for business or pleasure since that day at the gorge. The inspiration dried up.

"It'll be really long days for you since we'll have to work on it after the store closes."

"You won't scare me away, Sunshine. Let me help you." We

stare into each other's eyes, and I don't know if she realizes it, but I could do this all day with her, study the dozen different variations of green and blue in her irises.

I really need to get myself in check, remember she's not mine, and that I can help her with this but it doesn't mean anything beyond what it is.

It's not happening, Hendrix. Point blank.

Silver stretches her hand out to me, and I don't wait to grasp it as an electric shock fizzles up my wrist from the touch. Does she feel it too? From the way she's staring at our joined hands, I think she might.

"Let's do it." Determination strengthens her gaze.

I know I'm well and truly fucked when I realize I'd do just about anything to keep that look on her face.

Chapter 10

Silver

> **Silver**
> Are you ready to get down and dirty tonight?

> **Hot Handyman**
> ?

> **Silver**
> The bookstore. Why what were you thinking?

> **Hot Handyman**
> So we aren't fighting crime in the subway tunnels with the Ninja Turtles? Bummer.

> **Silver**
> That's after we start on the bookstore. If I don't get this place fixed, I'll be living in the subway tunnels.

> **Hot Handyman**
> Can't have that. You and Raphael would level Grand Central. 6 PM okay?

> **Silver**
> I don't know. Raphael's kinda cute…

> **Hot Handyman**
> Goodbye.

> **Silver**
> See you tonight!

"What's got you smiling like that?"

I look up from my phone and see Holly staring at me from behind a table of stacked bestsellers, a knowing smirk on her freckled face.

I didn't even realize I had been grinning down at my phone like a maniac. I couldn't seem to help it. But whatever this emotion roiling around in my gut is, I need to lock it down. I still can't get a read on him. One second, he's avoiding me, and the next, he's offering to help me renovate my store. It's confusing, and this is starting to feel like it's breaching territory I've worked my whole life to avoid. Still, I can't deny that there is a persistent pull, tugging me closer even as I try to pull away.

"In the state of Missouri, it's illegal to worry a squirrel." I smile sweetly. We both know I'm lying.

"Liar."

"It's true! You can look it up."

"You know that's not what I'm asking." She levels me with a *don't bullshit me* glare. I don't respond and start to sort through a stack of books I'm prepping for a local author to come in and sign when she decides she isn't going to let it go. "Hendrix was really nice. Jae, too."

I take a long pull from the iced coffee I picked up from Respect the Drip before coming in today. "Mhmm." I bob my head neutrally at her statement, neither confirming nor denying how I feel. That's my strategy. Another sip of delicious cold brew.

"From where I was sitting, he couldn't seem to take his eyes off you."

I sputter a little, taken aback. What is she talking about? He barely looked at me the entire night, and he certainly didn't speak to me.

He talked to everyone else, though.

"Oh, well...you know—a sparkly top makes it hard to not grab attention," I reply, brushing off her earlier words.

"Interesting."

"What?" I'm getting flustered now.

"It's just peculiar that you would be so nonchalant about this, considering you couldn't stop staring at him too."

"Did you know it's also illegal to wrestle a bear in Missouri?"

Deflect. Deflect. Deflect.

"Silver James, what is wrong with you?" Holly throws up her arms in exasperation. "A few weeks ago, you were being dramatic and calling this man *the one that got away*, and now, you're acting like there isn't something between you two. Explain yourself."

"There *is* nothing between us." She settles her hands on her hips, cocking her head to the side while waiting for me to elaborate. "Look, he's hot. Really, *really* hot. But anytime I've tried to flirt with him, he doesn't seem into it. Sometimes, I think we might be having a moment, but then the next, he's being stoic again. I can't get a read on him. Most guys are pretty direct about what they want from me, but he's all over the place, and it's messing with my head."

She takes that all in and marinates over what I said.

"He also doesn't seem like the casual hook-up type," I add. No, Hendrix definitely doesn't seem like a casual kind of guy at all from what I've gathered about him. I'm confident he would be singularly focused on whoever he was with. He would give her all his focused attention. He would listen to her when she speaks—not because he has to, but because he genuinely cares what she has to say. He would be kind and compassionate and—

"And that's all you want?" There's a challenge in her tone.

"Obviously." I turn away, suddenly uncomfortable with the attention she's giving me in conjunction with the mental gymnastics my brain is doing conjuring up Hendrix as a boyfriend.

I have to change the subject.

"So, the sign up for our first book club is live, and already, a couple spots are filled. We should have a great turnout for the first meeting in a few weeks."

She and I both know I'm changing the conversation, but she doesn't push me on it. Holly has always been good at knowing when to challenge me and when to leave me to my thoughts.

"So posting about it in local coffee shops has been working?" Holly shifts around some books in our non-fiction section.

"It would seem sending Carmen around to the neighborhood cafés armed with fliers and the spirit of a honey badger will do the trick."

"She's really going to go places," Holly says fondly as I chuckle in agreement.

I've never met anyone more fearless than Carmen. Those honey badger tendencies will come in handy when she's kicking opposing counsel's ass as an attorney.

"Do you mind just unpacking those boxes?" I point at the shipment of new stationery we received this morning in the corner of the store. "I have to call the web designer because they're dragging their feet, but I need those boxes cleared for the contractor coming tonight."

"It's so cute when you boss me around." Holly winks before walking towards the boxes.

"How many times do I have to tell you? I'm saving myself for your wife."

Apprehension settles over me like a fog when I think about Hendrix coming to the store tonight. Something about him offering to help me feels different. He doesn't *have* to do this, and honestly, he shouldn't want to, considering he seems inclined to avoid me half the time.

Unless you ask Holly, who thinks he's got a thing for me. She's wrong. I can always get a read on a man, but Hendrix is a closed book. Sometimes, he's relaxed and seems content, but then he almost realizes he's let his guard down and throws up his walls again. It's confusing.

I need to put it out of my mind before he gets here, focus on organizing our plan of attack on this reno. There is so much to do, and I'm a little nervous that once he arrives, he's going to look around, see how much work he blindly agreed to, and hightail it out of here.

I'm paying some supply invoices when the door opens, and in walks Hendrix...early. As in, early enough that Holly is still here and I haven't told her who my newfound contractor is, just that Phil no longer has the job. Which is going to make it seem like I was hiding it—which I wasn't. I wasn't.

"You're early," I say through clenched teeth. *Very astute observation, Silver.*

"What a friendly welcome," he deadpans and then signals to the tray of coffees in his hands. "I was off already and just decided to head over. I thought it would take me longer to walk here."

Holly, as if summoned by his voice and any chance to say I told you so, pops out from behind one of the standalone shelves with a downright delighted smile gracing her face.

"What are you doing here?" From her tone, Holly knows exactly why, but she wants one of us to admit it out loud.

"Coming in here is like a warm hug." Sarcasm drips from his mouth. "I'm here to help with the renovations. I was a little early and stopped to grab coffee for everyone. I thought we might need it."

Holly whips her head in my direction but addresses Hendrix. "You're the new contractor?"

He scratches the back of his neck, clear confusion written across his handsome face. "Yes?"

"Interesting..." She draws the last syllable out.

"Holly, can I talk to you in the back?"

"About what?" She is enjoying this far too much.

"The migration pattern of monarch butterflies." I grit my teeth, glaring at her with a look so harrowing, I hope it conveys, *come to the back now before I karate chop you in the throat.*

"Sounds fascinating." She turns a beaming smile towards Hendrix. "We'll be right back. Make yourself at home."

I roll my eyes, turning to walk toward the stockroom—if you can even call it that, since it's a glorified broom closet. Close on my heels, Holly follows me into the room and immediately starts a rapid-fire interrogation.

"Oh my God. Why didn't you tell me about this? Did you ask him to help? Is he even qualified for this beyond his sumptuous biceps? You're *totally* going to fall in love. This is basically kindling for a Hallmark rom-com!"

"Are you done?" I huff while leaning against a rickety metal shelving unit housing a lot of our stock. She nods, clearly eager for me to answer her questions.

"Okay one, I didn't tell you because I knew you'd react like *this*. Two, he offered to help after overhearing my conversation with the original contractor. Three, yes, he is qualified, and no, I will not be commenting on his *sumptuous biceps* and give you more ammo against me. And four, and most importantly," I make sure I have her full attention for this next part, "do you really think *I* would ever be in a story appropriate enough to air on the Hallmark Channel?"

"You're TV-MA for sure. So what's the deal then? He's just helping you out of the kindness of his brooding heart?" She leans towards the doorway to spy him walking around the store, one hand holding the tray of coffees and the other holding a book reading the synopsis on the back. It is *infuriatingly* sexy.

"The deal is, he helps me fix the store, and I help him build his portfolio for the business he's wanting to start here," she's staring at me skeptically, so I quickly tack on, "and I'm paying him."

"In blow jobs?"

"Well, if I thought he'd be into it..." I murmur.

"What was that?" She asks.

"Are you planning on staying now?" It wouldn't be surprising if she decided to extend her shift to "help" just to be nosy and rile me up.

"As much as I want to witness what is no doubt going to be a painfully awkward night, I promised Sera I would help her with planning her course."

"Small mercies." Sardonic ire laces my tone as I motion for us to leave the stockroom.

We make our way out onto the main floor and back towards Hendrix, who is now leaning against the cash wrap with the tray of drinks next to him.

He changed from his normal workday uniform of work pants and a henley to a pair of worn-in denim and a black short sleeve shirt that fits him in a way that makes my skin tighten. As if all of that wasn't sexy enough, he has a faded Rangers hat on backwards. *Backwards*. He is clearly trying to torture me. How am I supposed to keep my thoughts pure as the driven snow when he's hammering around looking like *that*?

"Okay, well, this has been fun, but I've got a hot date with my wife and the questionable use of a pastry bag." I stifle a burst of laughter before she bounds over to Hendrix and grabs one of the coffees. "Is this for me?" He nods as she takes a sip and presses up on her toes to pop a friendly kiss to his cheek.

Lucky bitch.

"You kids have fun." She laces her tone with innuendo, and it's then I decide shoving her out the door is probably the safest course of action for everyone.

"Goodnight, Holly." I lightly press on her back, and right as she's out the door, she turns back and mouths *use protection* before I slam the door in her face.

I take a moment to steel myself and flip the open sign to 'closed' and lock the door. The tumble of the mechanism locking into place sends a jolt of awareness through me. We are now alone, with no buffer or threat of interruption.

I turn around and face Hendrix, who is burning a hole through the deadbolt of the door.

"Regretting your decision to help?" I ask in an attempt to ease us back into normal territory.

"No." He clears his throat.

Maybe he's unbothered, but I'm crawling out of my skin knowing I'm about to spend the next several hours alone with him. How is it possible to be so drawn to someone while simultaneously wanting to put as much distance between us as possible? Every time I'm around him I get more and more confused, and I have no idea what he's thinking.

"Earlier today, I started compiling a list of things I want to fix or update. You can let me know what's realistic and what you're willing to spend your time on," I say to break the tension.

"Nothing is off the table." I meet his gaze and see steel resolve behind his golden eyes.

"Even still, I know this is your spare time, so if there's ever a day you can't come in or something about the project that isn't working for you, just let me know."

He nods his head in agreement. "Let's see this list."

"As you can see," I gesture throughout the store at all the age-worn bookcases, "the store is stuck in the eighties, and not in an *ironic but still cool* kind of way."

Hendrix huffs out something between a laugh and a grunt as I step around him to a row of bookcases lining the walls.

"I think the main things to be done are building new bookcases. I don't think these are salvageable, but you can tell me. I think my other big thing is this." I point to the staircase leading up to the unused second floor. "Pat never bothered to fix the staircase, so it's been broken the whole time I've worked here. I don't even know what's up there, but I'd love to convert it into a cozy reading space that doubles as a place to hold events." He's being disturbingly quiet, which hastens me to add, "Of course, all of that can come later, but if we could at least fix it to have access to eventually do something, that would be great." He nods his understanding and motions for me to keep going, to get all my thoughts out at once, giving me the space to work through my ideas without interruption.

I continue with his encouragement. "I definitely want to repaint everything. I keep reading that a fresh coat of paint is the perfect way to make a big impact quickly. I think the last important thing would be the floors. I don't think there's money in the budget to gut and replace them, but maybe we could buff them down and stain them with something more in line with the direction we're going. I just want everything to feel fresh and light and happy, somewhere people seek out and feel welcome, at home. You know, like they're being enveloped in a *warm hug.*"

He snorts. "Should be easy enough to do." He says it so simply, as if we're talking about making break-and-bake cookies and not a renovation.

"Where should we start?" I crane my neck back to look up at him and, damn, I really don't need to notice this height difference right now.

He looks down at me to answer and is about to say something when he pulls up short and just stares down at me, transfixed. I don't say anything, unwilling to break the moment we're having, but fate has other plans. An ambulance rushes past outside with its siren whirring, snapping us back into the present moment.

His eyes flit around my face. "Let's go look at paint swatches."

"Yeah, okay," I gulp out, just a tiny bit breathless. "I'll look up somewhere to go."

"Actually, I know just the place."

Chapter 11

Hendrix

"I can't believe I didn't know this place existed!"

Standing on the threshold of Get Nailed, Silver's eyes dart all around, unable to settle on a single place to land because there's too much to take in. We're in that cave where Aladdin finds the genie's lamp, except filled with screwdrivers and nails instead of treasure, jammed full floor to ceiling with materials that could fall with one ill-timed sneeze.

"This place must be like porn for you."

I choke around a laugh. "Sometimes, thoughts are meant to stay inside your head, you know."

She beams up at me and *Christ*, she's beautiful, but also whip smart and mischievous and passionate. I could see the determination in her eyes as she looked around her store, explaining what needed to be fixed to bring her vision to life. There was a drive firing her speech, even as trepidation nipped at her heels.

"And deprive you of the wonders of my mind palace? That would be cruel." That does pull a laugh out of me.

She steps further into the store, staring around in wonderment with me following closely behind, hands in the pockets of my jeans so I don't do something stupid like touch her. We're closer to The Langham now and anyone could walk in and see us together. We're not doing anything wrong, but it wouldn't look good.

"The paint is towards the back right corner." I press a hand to her lower back, urging her forward, the desire to keep my hand on her courses through me before I force myself to drop it.

We walk through long narrow aisles, turning right and left then right again, passing rows of door knobs and sink faucets to gummy bears and a hundred different types of lightbulbs stacked from floor to ceiling.

Silver is on her second inappropriate joke—the first was something to do with screws, and the second about "laying pipe". She's doing it to rile me up, I can tell, because each time, she looks over at me in anticipation to see if I caught the innuendo. It's equal parts charming and frustrating.

She twists around to see my reaction to her most recent joke, not realizing there are bags of concrete powder stacked in the aisle in front of her. I open my mouth to tell her to be careful, but it's too late. Her shins collide with the stacked bags; she twists her body, and in an effort to catch herself, she reaches out to grab onto a shelf, only to realize there isn't one. Instead, Silver smacks her hand into a bundle of rakes that crash to the ground with a rattling bang.

She's in the process of falling over when I shoot out my hand to latch onto her elbow, tugging her towards me to right the trajectory of her fall. But I overcompensate and tug her harder than necessary, and she crashes into me. I wrap my hands around her waist to steady her as her own come to rest on my chest. Our eyes catch, and we're both breathing hard. Something tells me by the way her cheeks flush, it isn't from the near fall.

"Who even needs a rake in New York?" Her breath coasts over my mouth from the proximity, and my heart starts to beat faster. We're still holding each other, and it feels so nice that I ignore the voice in my head telling me to let go, to stop touching her immediately.

"Maybe Raphael and the Turtles use them to clean up the garbage in the subway tunnels," I quip.

We're smiling at each other, only pulling away when Marjorie rounds the corner into the aisle we're standing in.

She settles her wrinkled hands onto her hips. "What the ever loving hell are you doing back here?"

"We'll clean it up, don't worry."

"I wasn't talking about the mess. I was referring to the way you guys jumped apart like horny teenagers when I got here." She smirks, and I look over at Silver, who is grinning like a fiend.

"Oh, I like you."

"We need paint." I turn on my heels and head in the direction of the paint section, hoping Silver follows.

"Would you rather be a walrus or an armadillo?"

After what felt like five hours of paint swatch deliberation, Silver settled on a pistachio green for the walls and a simple white for the bookshelves and table fixtures. We've been painting for the last five minutes after spending some time clearing the counter, taping the edges, and laying down drop cloths. We *were* working in companionable silence until now.

"Excuse me?"

"Walrus or armadillo, Hudson?" There's a look of exasperation lining her features, like she's telling me to keep up, like it wasn't the most random question she could have come up with out of absolute thin air.

"Walrus, I suppose."

"Interesting. Defend your position, please?"

What is happening right now?

"We're playing twenty questions."

Apparently I said that last part out loud. "I guess because they live in colder climates and aren't riddled with diseases."

"Fair play." She nods her head, accepting my answer. This is the most bizarre conversation I've ever had. I watch her as she dips the bristled brush into the quart-sized paint bucket in her opposite hand. A fierce look of concentration settles over her features as she skirts the edges of the wall in a thin layer. She meets the junction of a corner and bites her plump bottom lip as she fills in the space without it dripping.

God, why am I staring at her painting a wall like it's the most fascinating thing in the world?

Because she looks hot doing it.

My subconscious mind is an asshole and keeps reminding me of Silver in the most mundane moments, but being in her presence is worse. There's no escaping my wild thoughts when she's around, especially because she changed into a pair of pink overall shorts and a strapless banded top that shows just the tiniest sliver of skin on her waist. With floral chucks and her hair half pulled back with a clip, she's just about the cutest person I've ever seen.

I need to get a grip.

"What about you? Walrus or armadillo?" I'm desperately trying to move my mind to anything other than that sliver of skin and the wisps of icy hair falling around her face.

"Definitely a walrus. Armadillos are basically roadkill, and I'm not trying to become some rando's dinner." I'm saved from having to respond when she asks a follow up question. "What do you do for fun?"

I open my mouth to respond but the words catch in my throat. I—I can't think of anything, and thinking back on recent years only dredges up memories of long hours working for my dad. But Silver is staring at me with expectant eyes, and the thought of telling her the truth—that I don't know what fun is anymore—isn't something I want to do.

"Usually wind up at The Blackbird." I focus on painting my section of the wall while thinking up a question of my own before she can ask me any more. "Did you always want to work around books?"

She hesitates. "You're supposed to ease into the intensity of the questions, Hal." Her intonation reads like she's joking, but I can see a slight shuttering behind her eyes.

"If you aren't comfortable—" She waves me off, focusing intently on the spot she's working on.

"My dad used to take me to the bookstore every Saturday when he wasn't on a work trip. It became sort of a tradition. He loved books and always said he wanted me to have worlds I could escape into when I needed it." She takes a deep, steadying breath. "I guess I wanted to keep the tradition alive even though he isn't. When you work in a bookstore, every day can be Saturday."

She looks over to me then, and I can see a deep pain cascade over her whole being before she catches it and forces a smile.

"Favorite ice cream?" I ask, wanting to turn the fake smile into a real one.

"Chocolate hazelnut crunch. You?" She grabs the roller out of the tray and points it at me menacingly. "I swear on Ben and Jerry, if you say you don't like ice cream too, I'll never speak to you again. I can't handle you not liking donuts *and* ice cream."

I laugh, big and hearty and real. She keeps doing this to me.

"I like ice cream, and I guess butter pecan is my favorite."

She scoffs. "Okay, grandpa."

I don't think, I react, taking the paintbrush in my hand and swiping it down her cheek. She's frozen, delight and shock written clear across her face like the stripe of pale green that now adorns it. Slowly, she nods her head, pursing her lips and clearly plotting my demise.

She looks up, and the fire is back in her eyes. She slowly steps toward me, a hunter stalking its prey and a wicked gleam in her eye. I take a step back, hands up in surrender, but quickly hit the corner of the cabinet.

"Listen, Savannah, I think we can talk this through like rational adults." I finally take part in her game of names to try and placate her, but all it does is bring a dark sort of glee to her stunning face.

She prowls closer, within arm's reach now. "The thing is, Hector...I'm not a very rational person."

With revenge burning in her gaze, she brings up the paint roller and starts a path from the edge of my jaw, down my neck, and onto my arm, covering half my tattoos.

I deserve this fate and have nowhere to go—she has me caged in.

But then, she makes a move to do the same to my other side. I grab hold of her wrist to try and wrangle the roller out of her hand. Her grip is firm when she turns on her heel, swinging herself under my arm and fighting for control. In the process of the maneuver, she ends up in front of me, her back flush to my chest, my arm wrapped around her waist.

She tugs, and it pulls me closer and—shit. That fact she fits against me perfectly is not something I need to know. This close, I can feel the softness of her skin, feel her hair tickling my chin, smell her apricot-scented shampoo, bright and fresh. If I don't get out of this position soon, it's going to get awkward for her and embarrassing for me.

But something in me aches to hold on, to allow myself this one thing, whether I deserve it or not.

"Give up, Harlan," she pants.

"Not a chance, Skylar," I echo, my breath ruffling the loose strands of hair framing her face.

She rotates her head to the side to look up at me, mouth mere inches from my own. There's a hunger in her stare I'm certain is mirrored in my own.

I look down at her, gaze darting to her parted mouth. My breath puffs in and out in rapid succession, a silent question in my eyes.

A line that *shouldn't* be crossed.

A line I've been *thinking* about crossing for weeks.

A line we both *want* to cross.

She gives me a "it's about time" look, along with the slightest nod of her head, tilting her mouth up to me just a fraction closer in invitation.

I begin to lean down infinitesimally, giving her time to change her mind—or maybe giving me the time to talk myself out of a selfish decision. But the combination of her scent mingling with the feel of her body on mine is making me dizzy and stupid.

Our mouths are nearly touching, and—

BUZZ!

The loud vibration of her phone against the counter rattles us out of the moment, and frustration and relief war against each other.

We've pulled apart by a couple inches, no longer in the danger zone, when I reach for her phone behind me.

> **Finance Fuck**
> Hey! I had a great time with you the other night. I'd love to take you out again. Are you free this weekend?

I straighten to my full height and hand her the phone, pretending I didn't see the message. She starts to type out a reply. Is she accepting the date? Suggesting a place for them to go? I can't read the look on her face from the corner of my eye, trying not to make it obvious I'm snooping.

What the fuck am I doing?

How did I conveniently forget she was seeing someone? Kissing her when she's still involved with John would be a mistake, and one of the many reasons I've been trying to keep my feelings under lock. The last thing we both need is for this to get complicated because I couldn't keep my hands to myself and then have to see her all the time at The Langham. Fairbanks' no fraternization rule was starting to make more sense. Things already feel awkward, and we didn't even kiss.

She fiddles around on her phone while I resume painting my

section.

Twenty minutes pass by in awkward silence and ignoring the almost kiss. Night has fully descended, and it's edging close to ten at night when Silver finally breaks our silence.

"What's your favorite movie? Don't say *Die Hard*."

"*Die Hard 2*."

"Okay...what would you take with you to an abandoned island?"

"Flint."

"What is your deal?"

"I don't know what you mean." I avoid her gaze.

"Yes, you do. Half an hour ago, we almost kissed, and now you're completely shut down." We're still standing behind the register counter when she faces me head on, hands on her hips and paint forgotten. "Look, if you changed your mind, that's fine, but don't be a dick."

Fuck.

"I...I saw that John texted you, and he seemed like a nice guy, so I thought...I thought I should back off if you were already taken, not complicate things further."

"Taken? This isn't the fifties. No one is staking their claim on me. Maybe you should ask before jumping to conclusions."

"I-I—" I stutter out before she cuts me off.

"If you had just *talked* to me about it, I would have told you that yes, John is a nice guy, but it won't work out between me and him in the long run." She's definitely edging on angry. "But instead, you made an assumption based on one night out. A night where you barely spoke to me, by the way."

I don't know what to say, everything I've said already was just digging me deeper.

"Look, it's fine. We can just call it. You've been running hot and cold since I met you, and it's been giving me whiplash. If this was something you wanted, you would have made a move, because I made it more than clear I was interested."

Was.

"Let's clean up for the night. I won't let this make things awkward. Like you said earlier, we're adults, and this store is important to me, and nothing is getting in the way of that."

Panic claws at my chest. She turns to walk out from behind the counter, away from me, when, for the second time tonight, I don't think—I react, unable to let her walk away.

I reach out my hand and hook my finger into the belt loop on her overalls before she can get too far away from me. With a sharp tug, I pull her back and use my opposite hand on her hip to spin her towards me. She looks up at me with confusion.

"I don't want to call it."

Without thought or hesitation, I crash my lips down onto hers.

Shock quickly melts into enthusiasm as she leans into me, fingers digging into the tops of my jeans, brushing bare skin to tug me closer. I groan into her mouth from the slight graze as my lips move against hers in a fervent rhythm. Running my tongue against the seam of her mouth, I beg for an entry she grants in earnest, and I delve in deep and fast.

I've never tasted anything as sweet as Silver James, and it makes me dizzy. Every moment since I met her has been a powerline of our collective currents, building and buzzing, bringing us to this moment, drawing us closer together until we lit up with electricity.

I slip my hand up through her silken tresses, tilting her head back with my thumb under her chin to deepen the kiss. I nip on her lower lip to test and tease, and she lets out a soft moan that makes me half-hard in an instant.

Stroke for stroke, she meets me in challenge, rolling her body against mine in a need to be closer, and it's a desire I'm more than happy to assuage. I hook her arms up around my neck and reach underneath her thighs to hoist her up around my waist before depositing her onto the counter behind us.

She lets out a soft squeal at the sudden movement, but I swallow it with another bruising kiss, stepping into the space between her legs and resting my hands possessively on the tops of her thighs, squeezing and stroking. I kiss a path down her jaw and onto her neck, lavishing the pulse point at the base, feeling it thunder against my attention. Silver rolls her body against my hardening length in retaliation, forcing me to grunt out against her neck.

"You'll be the death of me," I growl, breathing rapidly.

I hear her chuckle in my ear right before she bites down on my lobe, nearly buckling my knees, and I pepper drugging kisses on a path back toward her mouth. Our hands leave paint marks on each other's bodies, clothes—the counters.

I've spent weeks trying to push her away, and I can't remember why. The taste of her mouth, the feeling of her skin burning against my palm, it feels like we were always meant to end up here. Like a moth to a flame—unavoidable. I want to *burn* in her light.

With the most monumental effort of my life, I take one last, long pull from her mouth, and she whimpers at my retreat. Forehead flush against hers, we try to catch our breath and fail. I'm smiling softly like an idiot as I lean forward, unable to help myself, and steal one more long kiss.

After a moment, Silver breaks the silence. "What's your guilty pleasure?" Her fingers play with the ends of my hair in a maddening rhythm.

You, I think. "*Great British Bake Off.*"

She pulls back and looks at me with amusement.

"Such a mystery, Mr. Wells." Mirth lines her gaze. "Though I do suppose Paul Hollywood is kinda foxy."

I toss my head back, laughing loudly, and when I look back, she's smiling at me with a sort of wonder.

I think I'd do anything to keep her looking at me like that.

Chapter 12

Silver

I don't want to call it.

Those gruff words and Hendrix's rough hands on my body have been playing on a loop in my head since last night. My skin tightens at the memory of his lips moving against mine, and I find myself zoning out far more than I'd care to admit.

This is going to be a problem.

I can't remember a time when a kiss distracted me well into the next day—scratch that, *ever*. With past hookups, it's been an in the moment feeling, we say our goodbyes, and I don't think of it again. But with Hendrix, I can't seem to *stop* thinking about it.

I had thought I just needed to get him out of my system, but one fleeting moment has turned into an all-consuming derailment of my day. It's alarming how I'm feeling today post hot-as-hell make out against the very counter I'm leaning on.

I recall in visceral detail the way his mouth felt slanted over mine. How his palms felt running up my thighs, callused and confident. The sounds he elicited that I've never heard myself make, with *anyone*. Desperate and wanting, like if I didn't get more of him, closer to him, I would regret it.

I'm feeling what I can only assume are butterflies, smiling down at wood stain swatches for the floors and stair banister, when the shop phone trills out a loud ring that makes me jump out of my skin. The fact that no one ever calls here should have been my first indicator that the store was in the red and reminds me that I need to call the phone company and get the account transferred under my name and update our devices.

"Brownstone Books, how can I help?" I chirp into the phone.

"Hi, honey." All the blood drains from my face, and a pulsing drumbeat starts up in my head.

This is the second time my mom's called me in just a few weeks, and her persistence is starting to put me on edge. I can't even begin to fathom what she could want outside of money—hopping from town to town and never settling in one place can get expensive, after all. But she always went to Nan with that sort of request. It seemed to be the one thing she wasn't interested in burdening me with. Child abandonment and its subsequent trauma was okay, though.

"Yeah?" My voice comes out low and hollow.

How easy it is to revert to the eight-year-old version of me when she's around. For feelings of intense sadness at having lost not one parent, but two, to drag me down. Losing my father was too much for *her* to deal with while having a kid. Her solution: ship me off to grandma's house forever.

Memories resurface of me standing outside The Langham, otter stuffy dangling from one hand while I waved goodbye, thinking she would be back for me soon. But soon turned into a week, that turned into a month, and that turned into forever.

"You never got back to me after our last talk," she admonishes.

"I didn't realize we were on a call back basis. I must have missed all of yours growing up." It's impossible to keep the bitterness out of my tone.

"Don't be like that. I just want to see my daughter when I'm in town in a few weeks." Always on her schedule, only when *she* wants or needs it.

"Now's not a good time. Maybe next time you're visiting." Also not likely, but anything to end this phone call and the chill that's crept over my body like a fog.

"Silly, please, we should really talk—"

"Sorry—what–I…hear–phone's cutt—" I wince. Hanging up the phone was definitely not the mature approach, but panic started to sink its claws in.

A sticky feeling coats my skin whenever I'm confronted by the hurt my mother's actions caused. I didn't date, kept nearly everyone at a distance, never chose a career path because commitments didn't mean anything in my world. Nothing was permanent, and anyone could change their mind in an instant. Even a mother could leave her daughter.

I frantically grab a sticky note and write a new task to get done: change the shop phone number.

Maybe I'm lucky to get this second call, to get this reminder of why I don't like committing to anything or anyone. It's too hard, and people always end up hurt in the end. It's easy to get swept up in a moment and let it nearly knock down your carefully constructed walls.

I have to end this.

Whatever is going on with Hendrix, I have to end it now, or I'm going to find myself swimming through capsizing waters I vowed to myself long ago I would never drown in.

I can't be like my mom. I won't.

I won't let my world get so wrapped up in a person that I can't function without them. It's easier to stay detached in the long run. If I don't let myself want it to begin with, I can't be disappointed when it doesn't pan out the way I'd hoped.

And I could see myself getting attached to Hendrix.

I allow myself a few moments of longing, one moment to reminisce on the heat of last night's kiss before I let it go.

I'm going to end it. *I am.*

I have to.

"Are you okay?" Holly knocks me out of my tortured reverie.

Snapping back to reality, I straighten from the counter—the one I was just laying on horizontally, as if I could infuse myself into the wood grains and stay in the memory of kissing Hendrix just a little longer.

"Yeah, why?" I infuse my voice with levity so she doesn't suspect something's wrong.

"It's just that you were staring off into the distance, and it looked like you were trying to hump the counter."

"What goes on between me and the cash wrap is no one's business but ours."

"How was last night?" Holly's tone is just a little too casual to not be suspicious.

"It was fine." Cool as a cucumber.

"Mmmm." I know she's not buying it. "The store already looks better. I like the color you chose." She points to the wall behind me. "It livens up the place, but it's not so bright that it distracts from everything else going on."

Grabbing my iced coffee from the counter, I step out and walk the floor to where she stands, surveying the work we got done the previous night.

"I'm really happy with it too. We're going to fix and paint the shelves white to offset the flooring, and I'll grab some colorful rugs to put under the tables."

"Have you thought about changing the name of the store?"

It has crossed my mind, but when I tried to come up with another name, the commitment and permanence of that decision started to make me feel panicky. So, I threw it to the back of the filing cabinet in my mind to be looked at another day.

"A little. But there's just too much else to focus on. Hendrix and I spent four hours working last night, and this is all we got done." I point to the wall we finished.

"Speaking of Hendrix..." She trails off, raising her eyebrows and looking to me to spill any kind of dirt on the previous night.

I consider telling her, would have in the past, but something stills my tongue. It's a weird sense of wanting to keep that moment with Hendrix between just me and him, like if I don't put the moment we had into words, I can pretend it didn't happen and it'll make ending it with him easier.

"We're just friends, Hols."

"That's not what it looked like from where I was standing. I was practically being hotboxed with sexual tension. It made me a little horny myself, actually," she pouts.

"You're ridiculous." I laugh. "Can we get to the task at hand, though?"

She squints her eyes at me. "Fine. Let's talk about events."

"Perfect! So for now, we can have events here on the main floor by shifting these tables off to the sides and setting up chairs. When we fix the second floor, we can do them up there so we won't have to disturb the main floor."

"What other events are you thinking about other than the book club we're starting next week?"

"I was thinking we could host writing socials. Once a month, we offer a free space where writers can come together in a safe space and just get out of their head for a bit." I can see the happiness in her eyes. Holly may work here, but writing is her first love.

"Silver–"

I cut her off. "I was also thinking we could do author events eventually, book release parties, signings, that kind of thing. Maybe a localized mini market once a month to give artists a place to sell their work on weekends. Dating mixers could be fun—"

"You know who could benefit from a dating mixer?" She points a direct look at me.

"I don't date." Holly opens her mouth to continue, but I cut her off. "I'd love any and all sorts of ideas from you and Carmen, though."

"Craft events would be fun—like a make your own bookmark station. Maybe we can partner with that craft store over on Mulberry and help drive business to them too."

We bounce ideas back and forth throughout the day while helping shoppers and shifting around stock to make room for the newer titles released this week, trying not to think about Hendrix every time I see the new paint color adorning the left wall.

"You have to *knead* the dough, Silver," Seraphina shouts at me from the kitchen of her and Holly's home in Brooklyn.

I am fulfilling my bargain to be a test dummy for Sera's baking workshop. That way, she can work out any kinks in her curriculum before she takes the announcement live to her blog, Mental Bake Down, and starts booking regular classes.

"I do need the dough. I *need* it in my mouth," I quip while Kena snorts next to me.

"I told you bringing her here would be a disaster."

"Hey!" I huff out in a grumble and settle my flour-coated hands on my hips in indignation.

"Sweetie, I love you," I smile at his words, "but we both know anything to do with cooking or baking is not your strong suit."

"And that's what makes her the perfect student," Sera says, walking back into the dining room where we're at. "Knead," she directs with a tilt of her head toward my slab of lumpy dough.

"Will you come show me how? Like we're Patrick and Demi in Ghost at the potter's wheel?"

"Stop hitting on my wife!" Holly shouts from their bedroom, where she's working on her current manuscript.

We settle into our work with gentle but firm instruction from Sera as needed. When we're done forming the dough into balls and placing them in a greased bowl to rise, Sera says she's going to make us all something to eat, leaving me and Kena to rest with a glass of wine each.

"How's everything at the Atelier now that you've been there for a bit?"

He heaves out a deep sigh, worry lines bracketing his mouth. "The work itself is amazing. I'm getting a lot of great client referrals and working in the most insane homes..." He lets the sentence drop off.

"But?" I coax.

"But I think there's some jealousy from other designers. Sometimes, I feel like I'm on the design world's version of Selling Sunset."

"Are they bullying you?" My hackles start to rise. Kena dealt with enough bullying when we were growing up that just the thought of it happening in our adult life makes me borderline homicidal.

"Calm down," he laughs. "No one is bullying me. Just petty glances and sharp tongues. It's a little stressful but also flattering."

"Okay, but if they—"

"Bring the intensity down. You're channeling Bob again, and it's a little scary."

He always says this when I get defensive of anything. When I argued that Summer is the worst of the four seasons, he likened me to that six pound hell demon. But I stand by my controversial statement. Summer in the city is a sweltering cesspool of humidity, the scent of steaming trash, and under-boob sweat creating a slip-n-slide under your shirt. Sure, the daylight hours are nice, and seasonal depression takes a hike once the sun comes out, but I, for one, am glad it's the end of September.

"How's it going at the store?"

"It's slow progress since we can only do small sections at a time. We painted the left wall behind the register last night, and it already looks so much better."

"What's next on the plans?"

"Probably the bookshelves. I think they're going to take the longest. They're in bad shape, and a lot of the shelves have to be replaced and painted. They're bowing under the weight."

"Are you sure you don't just want to close down the store for a couple weeks so you can do everything quickly?"

"I can't afford to." I look away, knowing he was worried about this very thing happening. "After paying Pat, all my spare cash is going towards the renovation, and I can't close the store down and still have money to pay Holly and Carmen when the store is barely breaking even on a good day."

"Is it really that bad?"

"It's not great. That's why I need this to succeed. I didn't realize how bad the store was doing before I took over. Pat never hinted at or wanted us to do anything to increase sales. She always said getting a book in a person's hand was all that mattered, but the store has been in a deficit more months than not. God," I drop my head and stare down at my lap, "maybe I was too rash."

I turn to look at my best friend of over a decade and see compassion lining his features.

"You know how steadfastly you believe I can do anything I want to do? How frequently you've told me that over the years?"

"Yeah..."

He grabs my hand and tucks our joined hands against his heart, like whatever he's about to say, he *needs* me to hear, to understand but isn't sure that I will. "There is not a single thing you can't do, Silver. The world is *limitless* for you and your potential. All you have to do is reach out and take it...and when you have it—don't let go."

I want to say I'm scared—scared that I've gotten in too deep, that I've taken on a project so big, there's no possible way I could finish it. That even if I did, it's destined to fail no matter what. That the anxiety I've been hiding from him and everyone else sometimes feels so paralyzing, so isolating, it's like I'm on the Zero Gravity ride at the fair and it won't stop spinning. It'll just go round and round, scrambling my brain until I'm just a husk. I'll never feel the solid ground again or take a steady breath.

But I don't.

I do what I always do when someone feels too close to seeing the version of me I want to hide away, even Kena after all these years. Don't let anyone see how much you may need them, don't worry the ones who *are* close enough to you to notice. This carefully constructed version of me I give to the world is all for show. I'm so good at it now, I even trick myself.

"You've been listening to too many motivational podcasts." I paste a smile to my face as I pull my hand from his grip and run it through my hair.

Sera comes back into the room carrying a plate of focaccia bread topped with rosemary and a few bowls of her homemade Bolognese.

I reach out with grabby hands like a starving toddler, but before I can grab a bowl, she swats me away like an Italian Nona.

"I'm going to serve my wife first. She's been working hard on her manuscript all day."

I harumph and settle back in my seat. "I guess, if you want to be romantic or whatever."

When she comes back into the room, I sit up again and take one of the steaming bowls of piping hot tagliatelle and meat sauce. Nothing makes me happier than carbs...except maybe sweets.

I'm taking a bite larger than my fist when she asks, "So, Silver, tell me about the sexual tension between you and the handyman."

I start choking on my dinner while Kena pats my back with too much enthusiasm.

"There is no sexual tension," I cough out. *Yeah, and I'm the pope.*

"You could have cut it with a knife the other day at the store!" Holly shouts from her office.

"You were basically eye fucking him at karaoke," Kena adds.

I scoff, but it comes out high pitched and reeking of denial.

"First off, you are not even in the room, so you don't get an opinion," I lob back at Holly. "And second, of course I was. The man looks like he stepped out of a GQ cover shoot."

"He's a nice guy, so what's the problem?" Always count on Sera to get straight to the point as she tears into her piece of focaccia.

"There isn't a problem. It's just not like that between us." It is, but if I had to end it, then there was no point in bringing them into it.

By the looks on their faces, no one believes me. I've never been one to back down from a guy I'm interested in, and they know that, but I don't exactly want to explain. *We kissed last night, and it was so Earth-shattering that it scared me shitless, and now I must disassociate, or I'll end up like my mother.*

I don't think I could even explain it if I wanted to. So, I don't.

"It's okay if you like him, sweetie," Kena remarks *too* gently, as if he's trying not to spook a skittish animal.

"I know." I fight for nonchalance and take another bite while I think of something convincing to say. "He's obviously attractive, but I don't want to risk making things complicated when I have so much riding on the store." That's not even a lie, just another convenient reason why I have to keep things platonic from now on.

My explanation seems to appease them, because they all nod

and settle into a conversation about a new gallery that just opened where the artist uses various body parts to paint his pieces, and that's honestly enough to make me want to go.

"Even his di—" I start before Kena cuts me off.

"Every. Usable. Appendage." He over-enunciates every word.

"Let's go this weekend."

We all agree on a day and time, and I realize my anxiety has settled from the stress of the day just by being in the presence of my people. I don't need to shake things up further by risking an unknown variable like Hendrix. No, it's best to keep things platonic. But my mind keeps going back to that kiss, his forest rich eyes boring down into mine with intensity and a need to explore—me, us, whatever this connection is.

This might be harder than I thought.

Chapter 13

Hendrix

My feet pound against the pavement as I sprint a path around Washington Square Park, trying to clear my mind for the day ahead. The sun is hiding behind the cover of clouds, and there's a soft, cool breeze floating in the air, hinting at the first signs of early autumn.

It's a task that's proving to be more difficult by the minute with Silver invading my every thought. A cab almost took me out earlier while at a crosswalk. I was distracted thinking about what I could ask during our next round of twenty questions, and didn't notice the yellow blob in my peripherals barreling toward me, blaring its horn. I jumped back in barely enough time to not get mowed down, but I *did* get a colorful string of expletives thrown out the window in my direction.

It's early on Sunday morning, and the city that never sleeps is as quiet as it will ever be—which is to say, still really fucking noisy, something it now has in common with my head.

I got up around five, wide awake with frenetic energy and the strong desire to pick up my long neglected sketchpad and pencil for the first time in years. I drew in bed without thinking, my mind replaying the kiss with Silver on a never-ending highlight reel while I mindlessly doodled. My brain helpfully supplied reminders of each gasp and moan she made to a near-torturous melody, building into a crescendo until I set down my drawing supplies and sprang out of bed to go on this run, afraid if I didn't, I might take matters into my own hands—literally.

But it wasn't just the lingering taste of her on my tongue that had me fidgeting in bed until the sheets tangled around my legs like a boa constrictor. It was just her...and the sense of awareness my body has when I'm thinking about her or near her. I thought I would go in there, help her paint, and then be done with it. But then, she started that damn twenty questions game, and fuck, it was so charming and...*disarming*. It made me want to tell her things, unearth hidden truths and desires.

It's too soon for that.

We agreed when we parted that we would keep renovations to weeknights so we could both rest on our weekends. That's probably for the best in hindsight—to give me a chance to get my ever-loving shit together. I told myself repeatedly to keep my distance, but I kept getting sucked into her gravitational pull, unable to wrench myself free.

Do I even want to be free?

No, I don't, but I should. This consuming need to be near Silver has been joined with a feeling of guilt that's persistently knocking at the back of my mind, demanding to be let in. How could I enjoy myself, feel light and free and alive, when Maddox is dead? My brain has been doing mental gymnastics since Friday night, trying to reconcile the two things, compartmentalize them in separate files so I don't feel like I'm betraying my younger brother.

Because denying feelings for Silver—trying to put her out of my mind—is getting harder by the day. I'm not sure the connection I feel to her is something I will be able to let go of easily.

She makes me feel...everything.

And it's been a long time since I've felt *anything*.

Silver is the human embodiment of sunshine. No matter who you are, she makes it a point to make you feel welcome and at home. That's what walking into her store felt like, even before we started making changes, and I realize now it's because *she* was there. Nothing else. Just her presence brightening up any room she's in.

She reminds me of Maddox.

The thought jolts me back to reality with the force of a lightning strike, and my shame renews as I pick up my pace, weighing the pros and cons.

Cons: losing my job is a very real threat, and that can't happen for multiple reasons. This city is expensive, and I won't rely on my friends to bail me out of a hard situation if things go south. Then, there's the fact that I don't *want* to move back to Seattle. Call it cowardice, but I don't want to face my family after the way I left. I can't bear the look in Mom's eyes or the vitriol my dad would spew my way. And then there's the niggling feeling of betraying Maddox that won't go away.

Pros: Silver's eyes lighting up every time she makes a crude joke. Her laugh ringing out over a crowd of noise, making me feel grounded. The soft moans she makes when I kiss under her ear. The way she looks out for the people around her. How utterly brilliant and brave she is despite her fear. How I crave apricots every day. The razor sharp wit she flings out like grenades, making me laugh for the first time in years. The way her nose scrunched up in distaste when I told her I don't like donuts. How she's burrowed so deeply under my skin, I can feel her energy thrumming through my veins, her unfiltered thoughts flowing freely and uninhibited out of her petal-soft mouth.

Silver. Silver. Silver.

I slow from a run into a slight jog when I come up to the coffee shop I stopped at the other day. I check the watch on my wrist, it's half past seven in the morning, and I've been running for an hour and a half without realizing.

It's not something I do for fun, more of a habit I picked up to clear my head after Maddox died and things between me and my father strained past a boiling point. The first run came after one particularly aggressive blow out. Dad blamed me for a client's unhappiness with their finished build, and he made sure I knew it was my fault. The words he flung at me that day still singe across my memory like acid. *"It's all your fault! Everything is your fault and now I have to pay double the cost of materials."* The intent in the word *everything* was not subtle, I knew exactly what he meant, and it had nothing to do with cabinets. After that, I couldn't contain my tumultuous feelings or my anger over everything, so I took it out on my body in punishing workouts. It's a pattern that has stuck since and morphed over time into something more routine.

I push my way into the coffee shop, the blast of air conditioning immediately cooling my flushed skin, and get in line to order.

It's pretty packed in here for being so early—people on their morning commutes grabbing the coffee that will get them through the day, laptops being set up for work that will be done from the table they've staked a claim to. The sound of beans grinding and steamers hissing creates a cacophony of music that makes up New York City.

Breaking through it all from the front of the line is a boisterous laugh that feels like warmth. I look to where the sound came from, knowing who will be there, and spot a familiar head of sleek platinum hair tossed up in an impossibly cute messy bun.

Silver James has her head tossed back, laughing at whatever the barista just said, and I feel a pit of jealousy in my stomach that I'm not the one who put it there.

I'm greedy. I want all her smiles now. I want to feel them on my skin—taste them on my tongue.

I stand in line and wait as she steps to the side with the group of people waiting for their drinks. She hasn't noticed me yet, and I cross my arms against my chest, watching her as she talks to a woman she just met, who's rocking a stroller back and forth. When the baby starts to get fussy, she hikes up her lavender sweatpants to crouch down to eye level with the child and starts singing a little song while clapping her hands to create a beat. The child instantly calms, and the mother looks at her from above with wonder. Apparently, she has this effect on everyone, not just me.

I move to the front of the queue and place my order around the same time the woman with the stroller leaves. Silver still hasn't noticed me when I slip up behind her in the group waiting for orders.

I lean into her, getting a whiff of her subtle apricot scent. "I'm starting to think maybe you should be a popstar instead of a business woman with how much you like to sing in public."

Her body stiffens in surprise before slowly turning towards me. There's a subtle tinge of pink high on her cheekbones and wisps of blonde hair framing her face.

I have the urge to tuck an errant strand behind her ear.

"The world is my stage." She tilts her head back, and there's a challenge in her eyes.

I meet her stare. "I'd buy a ticket."

She's blushing harder than she was a minute ago. I like that color on her face—I like that something I said invoked it.

"You couldn't afford me."

"No, you'd be priceless, but I'd still be there, front row."

She's struck speechless. I'm no stranger to flirting, but it's been a long time since I felt the urge. Dating always came naturally to me. I had a couple of girlfriends post college, but nothing ever felt *right*. I was always too focused on work or family, and any relationship fizzled off before it could really go anywhere. Then, my brother passed, and it started to feel like enjoying any part of life was an insult to his memory. After that, dating never really crossed my mind.

Until now. Until *her*.

We're staring at each other, seafoam green eyes to my hazel, silent and waiting for the other to say something.

"Silver!"

We both turn to see the barista who made Silver laugh earlier set down her drink. She moves to grab it from the counter and turns to face me again. Barely a second later, my name is also being called out, and I lean forward into her space to grab mine. My chest brushes her arm, and she inhales quietly.

I go out on a limb. "Do you want to sit with me?"

Her mouth pops open, and she hesitates. Fuck—did she have a different reaction to Friday night than me?

I mean, I thought that kiss was...good doesn't even scratch the surface. From her reception of it, I would've thought she did too, but I've been out of the dating game long enough to doubt myself now.

"Actually..."

My stomach sinks. I don't know how, but I must have misinterpreted everything wrong, and I'm suddenly feeling very stupid.

The front door opens. "*Hello*, brother wife." Kena saunters into Respect the Drip with the confidence of a king, dressed head to toe in vibrant floral brocade.

A smile spreads across my face at the sight of Silver's best friend.

"Could you, *for once*, not make me look like a bum in this coffee shop?" Silver throws up her arms in exasperation before looking at me. "He always comes in here looking like a Disney prince when I look like this." She points from her messy top knot down to her sweatpants and cropped tee.

"I think you look beautiful." I sip my coffee.

Kena's head whips to me with a smile that can only be described as maniacal.

"Oh?" There's a lilt to his voice as it raises several octaves, and he looks between Silver and me.

"And on that note," Silver grabs Kena by his shoulder and twists him towards the door, "we're going to Drag brunch in a bit."

"Unhand me, you goblin," Kena says while I chuckle from where I'm standing. They're basically siblings, and it makes me think of mine and how we used to act the same way.

She starts walking towards the door, dragging Kena with her as she goes. "I'll see you tomorrow night though?"

She's almost fully out the door when I nod my head in their

direction and salute them with my coffee. "See you then."

Something changed, I can see it in her face, hear it in her voice. I just don't know what.

"I'm telling you, the koala population in Australia is in danger because they're *all* getting chlamydia. It's an epidemic, and you all should really care more."

The three of us stare blankly at Sam as he takes an irritated pull from his IPA, indignant that we didn't know about the burgeoning threat to marsupials in the farthest reaches of the eastern hemisphere.

"How did we get here?" Jae's eyes dart around, looking at each of us in confusion.

"I asked where the new beer on draft was imported from." Faye rubs circles into her temples. "Apparently, it's from Australia, and now, I'm full of regret."

"This is a serious problem. Depending on the region of the country, up to ninety percent of the koala population is affected." You would think he's on trial with how serious he is.

I take a bite of the wings I ordered as I sit and watch the chaos of my friend group unfold.

Faye is telling Sam he should get fixed until his frontal lobe develops, Sam is looking at Faye with hearts in his eyes, and Jae is singing along to the song playing over the speakers—loudly.

This is pretty much what all our nights consisted of when we were all in school together. We spent our days running around the city, going to different classes for different majors, but we always found our way back here by nightfall, at The Blackbird, together.

Some nights, we drank ourselves under the table playing whatever drinking game the others had come up with that made absolutely no sense, and some nights, we covered our table in textbooks with notes and highlighters everywhere.

It was the memory of these nights that I missed the most, that I longed for once I moved back to Seattle. I wanted to stay here, open my own business with the degree I earned from NYU. But when I shared that with my dad, even showing him business plans I had drafted, he said it was time to come back home and work under him like I had agreed before I left for college. There was no room left to argue.

When I left for school, it didn't seem like such a bad compromise—a small price for four years of freedom from his constant scrutiny. I loved the work at the shop, especially when I was designing my own pieces, but I didn't expect to feel so at home in New York. After my four years were up, my pride saw me back on a flight to Seattle. It had been drilled into me from adolescence that a man was only as good as his word. For a while that kept me in line.

Until a few weeks ago.

Ever since, I've been avoiding my family's calls—well, Mom and Laurel's calls. Dad stopped speaking to me altogether, but that silence started long before I left.

I need to stop being a coward and face the music of their disappointment. I'm just not sure what good the argument will do when I don't want to leave New York again. I shouldn't have the first time, but a niggling voice in the back of my head says if I hadn't, I would've missed those last few years with my brother. That alone was worth it all.

My friends are now in a heated argument about who would

survive the longest in the Australian outback, and I'm going to have to settle this for them the rational way.

"Jae would be out the second he saw a Huntsman spider, and Sam would probably get too friendly with a kangaroo, and it would beat the shit out of him. Obviously, Faye would last the longest."

Both guys look affronted while Faye does a happy shimmy in her seat.

"I'm gonna go get another drink. Does anyone want anything?" I look around the table.

"I'll take anything that *isn't* from Australia," Jae requests at the same time the others request refills of their current drinks.

I slide out of the booth and head over to the bar to put in an order for another round when I feel my phone vibrating in my back pocket. I pull it out, and it's like my subconscious summoned this call.

Laurel.

It's do or die. I can't keep putting off my family forever, and it's probably better to do it now when I have a plausible reason to hang up if things go south quickly. The buzz from the alcohol helps too.

"Hey, Laur."

"*What the fuck,* dickweed? Mom's called you like…a billion times, and you won't answer her, but you answer me?"

"Mom's called me twice…"

"That's basically a billion times for a mom. She asked me if I thought you'd already joined a gang yesterday."

"I did. Questionable job description, but really good benefits."

I can hear her huff on the other end of the line. She may be mad, but she's also a secret softy.

"She's worried, and so am I. When are you going to come

home?"

I scratch a hand down my face in frustration as I turn my back to the bar. I see Jae from our booth giving me an *are you okay* look. I nod and signal I'm going to slip outside.

I step out into the cool early October air, passing through a group of people and a cloud of cigarette smoke to sit on the stoop of the building next to the bar.

"I *am* home, Laurel." There's a pang in my chest at the resulting silence, loud and thick and suffocating despite the noise of the city surrounding me.

"You're never coming back?" She's shell shocked, I can hear it lacing her tone.

"I don't know... I'm sure Dad's happy I'm gone."

"He was just hurt. He didn't mean what he said when you told us you were leaving."

"He did, and we both know it."

Vicious, ugly words were thrown around that night. They haunt me before I close my eyes, like a specter waiting until I'm asleep to descend and feast on my misery.

It's your fault he's gone. You might as well leave too.

Laurel sighs deep. "Are you happy there?"

"I–" I want to say yes and immediately ease her worries, but I go for honesty, or at least as honest as I can be. "I'm getting there. I like my job, and I've made some new friends you would like."

I think of Silver and how quickly she and Laurel would take to each other.

"Well, anything's better than the riffraff you already call friends," she sneers in sarcasm.

At that exact moment, Jae steps out to check on me, mouthing to ask who's on the phone. When I mouth back that it's Laurel, a look of unfiltered glee fills his eyes, and his smile beams from ear to ear.

He launches himself over the railing of the stoop to sit next to me and grabs the phone out of my hand while I'm distracted by the fact that he parkoured over a stone fence like he was an Olympic pole vaulter.

"Hey, baby, have you missed me?" His voice is deep and seductive.

I can't hear anything happening on the other end of the line, but I would put money on Laurel laying into him. But Jae takes everything in stride, and his grin never wanes while he hangs on her every word.

There were years Laurel would come to visit while I was in school, and the one off year Jae came to Seattle to visit for the summer while apprenticing with an artist based out of Capitol Hill. Jae took to Laurel's prickly nature quickly, but the same can't be said for her taking to his happy-go-lucky disposition, but even knowing this, he's never backed down.

"I hear what you're saying, beautiful, I do. I just don't believe you."

"Must you always hit on my sister in front of me?" I groan.

"Plug your ears then." He pats my knee like one would to comfort an irrational child.

He listens raptly to whatever she's saying. "Nah, you just both haven't come to accept that you and I are endgame. It's okay, I'm a patient man."

A few purring mhmms and deep chuckles from his end and what sounds like violent sarcasm coming from the other. "Alright, love, whatever you need to tell yourself. Do you want to talk to Hen before we hang up?"

He pulls the phone away from his ear, and I hear what sounds like *ofcourseIdoassholeIcalledtotalktohimnotyou* through the speaker, and through it all, Jae remains unphased.

"She wants to speak to you." He holds the phone out to me.

"How benevolent of you."

I put the phone to my ear and can't even get a word out. "Your friend's a fucking idiot."

"Yeah." I hear Jae murmur *I'm your fucking idiot* next to me.

"I gotta go, but we're not done with this talk. I'll call you back. Make sure you answer."

"Hey Laur?"

"Yeah?" she snaps, a lot frustrated and a little impatient.

"I love you." A small weight lifts off my shoulders..

A brief pause before she exhales her anger. "I love you too, dickface. Call Mom."

We both hang up, and I feel not necessarily lighter, because there's still a lot that needs to be said, but there's a relief in hearing my sister's voice for the first time in weeks.

Jae puts his tattooed arm around my shoulders. "You good, man?"

I nod. "Yeah, I'm good."

"Great, because I think we've left Faye and Sam alone together for too long, and she's either killed him or has talked him into investing in Koalas for a Kure while we were gone."

Chapter 14

Silver

I've worn a hole in the already battered shop floor from the pacing I've been doing all afternoon. The kiss was *days* ago, and I can still feel a phantom touch of his lips on mine. It has me twisted up in knots, and he's set to arrive any minute now.

Not that I've thought about it a lot.

Why am I nervous?

I have the distinct feeling that being alone with him is a very bad idea if I'm trying to be platonic. Not because I don't trust him to not cross that line; I somehow know he wouldn't if I asked. I just don't think I can trust *myself* around *him*.

"Hols?" I call out to Holly, who is in the back room of the store, grabbing stock.

She pops out from behind the walnut door, looking harried and out of breath. "Yeah?"

"I know you're almost off for the day, but would you mind staying after to help us start on the shelves?"

That sounded casual, right? Cause Holly can smell bullshit like a bloodhound, and she'll call me out and try to extract the truth like an evil dentist.

Last year, Carmen started acting a little cagey over everything, no matter how big or small. I thought she was just really stressed out from school and finals, but Holly sensed it was something else and convinced me to stage a quasi-interrogation. In hindsight, it was probably a little invasive, but also effective. Within minutes of Holly flipping off the lights to the store and shining a flashlight in her eyes, Carmen admitted she started seeing her toxic ex again.

To put it delicately—I fucking *hate* that douche canoe.

She left him to apartment sit for her, with the purpose of him taking care of her plants. When she came home on an earlier flight, she found him in *her* bed with someone else and all the plants dead. She was heartbroken for weeks—mostly over the plants.

When asked why the hell she would ever get back with him, she said she was *dickmatized* and couldn't see clearly until that moment when she had to admit it to us. She's been on the straight and narrow since, and he's been terrorizing every sorority princess he can get to fall for his charms.

"I wish I could, but I promised Chloe I would go to a yoga class with her." Chloe, Holly's lifestyle influencer half-sister, is always going somewhere or trying something new. There isn't a single restaurant in lower Manhattan she hasn't tried and reviewed thoroughly to her hoard of followers.

"You're going to yoga?" The very idea was ludicrous, since Holly abhorred physical activity of any kind. Every time I asked her to go to a class with me, she changed the subject suspiciously quickly.

"Ugh, I know." She flails her arms around above her head as if to say, *I don't know what I was thinking agreeing to this*. "She lured me in under false pretenses by telling me it was puppy yoga. She didn't fess up until this morning that she's a big fat liar. There will be no puppies. The *hot* yoga class is non-refundable under twenty-four hours, so I can't cancel."

"That's actually a brilliant way to manipulate you." I bob my head, impressed at Chloe's scheming.

"She's the creepy man in a white van asking if I want any candy, but instead of a van, it's a yoga class, and instead of candy, it's puppies." She's thoroughly pouting now as she aggressively restocks our bestseller shelf. "I've now been enlightened that my once-cherubic little sister is actually a lying sociopath."

"Now there's a headline for your Christmas newsletter," I quip, moving my way around the front feature table.

I've barely made it behind the checkout counter to review my half-thought out renovation Post It notes—totaling close to a hundred now, and scattered across the tabletop along with invoices I want to ignore—when Hendrix comes in. He's in a distressed band tee that stretches over the dips and valleys of his arms and chest, faded Rangers hat on backwards, and the most devastating smile I've ever seen in my life—and I've seen Michael B Jordan in the flesh.

"Hey." Warmth I want to sink into like a Snuggie infuses his tone as he slowly glides towards me. Or maybe he's walking at a normal pace, and I can't tell because I'm so hyper aware of his movements that it feels like he's slow-mo Baywatching me right now.

"Hi," I sputter out when he stops in front of me on the opposite side of the counter.

"*Hey*," Holly says slyly.

Fuck. I forgot she was here.

Thankfully, Hendrix doesn't draw attention to Holly's

innuendo-tinted greeting and pulls out one of the fliers to our event tomorrow.

"Unhinged Book Club?" His eyes pinball between me, Holly, and the page in his hands that advertises our new monthly event.

"It's a club for very...specific readers." It doesn't explain anything, but I also don't want to tell him exactly what that means either, and give him a reason to be curious.

"You should totally come to the meeting, Hendrix. It's next Friday night," Holly offers, and man oh man, I've never wanted to strangle her faster. Logically, I know she doesn't know about the kiss or that I'm trying to avoid this weird feeling in my gut that feels unfathomably like butterflies. The verdict is still out on that though, having no prior experience with the sensation, it could be indigestion for all I know.

"Oh, he doesn't want to do that..." I sneak a glance over at him, only to find him already looking at me closely.

"I don't?" Never taking his eyes off me, he crosses his arms over his chest and cocks his head in a challenge. Even having him look at me like *that* sends a series of shivers skirting up and down my spine, like a colony of ants is walking a path from my lower back into my hair and making me squirm.

"You haven't even read the book, and it wouldn't be easy to jump into the conversation. I wouldn't want to make you uncomfortable."

"So thoughtful of you," he deadpans.

"He could just sit in and observe," Holly offers.

I narrow my eyes at her, but she just stares at me with an angelic look on her face.

"Didn't you say you had somewhere to go after work?" I tilt my head at her in accusation. "Pilates with the Antichrist, was it?"

A minute ago, I was practically begging her to stay and act as a buffer, and now, I want to get her out of here before she has the chance to invite Hendrix to future events.

She checks her watch. "Shit, yes." She grabs her bag from behind the counter and speed walks to the door. "Have fun repairing the dilapidated shelves. The one towards the back right broke earlier from a kid treating it like his personal jungle gym!"

The front door bell signals her departure and the imminent, death-by-embarrassment I'm sure to endure after what I have to do.

I reinforce my spine, readying myself to tell Hendrix we can't have a repeat of Friday night and that things need to remain friendly and professional. But when I've finally worked up the nerve, I turn to find him leaving.

"Where are you going?" I stutter out.

He pauses on the threshold of the store. "I'm just grabbing the tools I left outside. I didn't want to have them on the floor while you might have customers still browsing."

Oh. Well, that was thoughtful.

He steps through the door and starts hauling in planks, electrical sanders, paint, and a large bag of tools. Christ, I really would've been lost if I had tried to do this all on my own.

"When—" I clear my throat as he stands from dragging the last of the materials in. "When did you order all of this?"

He stands to full height, pulls the hat off his head, pushes his hair back, and repositions his cap in one bizarrely, shouldn't be sexy move. "After the first visit," he says sheepishly.

"Oh." I suddenly feel queasy.

"Should we get started?" he asks tentatively, as if sensing the shift in my tone. "Maybe with the shelf the kid was climbing on?"

I nod and head over that way, and, yup, there it is, a row that's collapsed in the middle of the shelf. I start pulling the books off that one first and set them on the table behind me so we can clear it for repairs.

Hendrix wordlessly follows my lead and pulls titles off the shelf next to mine, occasionally pausing to read a synopsis or flip through the pages. It's...disarming, seeing him look so comfortable here while I feel anything but. There's a tension in the air, a rubber band pulled taut, waiting to snap. I can feel him glance over at me every few minutes as we continue to work in silence—and I ignore it each time he does. Even as I struggle to pull titles off the highest shelf, and he reaches over to help me, crowding my senses with his woodsy scent, I keep my gaze downcast and murmur my thanks.

Book after book is removed until we have two, floor-to-ceiling shelves removed of stock to repair broken or bowed wood, fill any dings, so we can sand down and paint them until they're gleaming. Then, we'll repeat that on the other twenty that fill the room, not including the tables, floorboards, staircase and second floor.

I feel Hendrix's eyes shift to me again, and I know I can't keep putting this off. Time to put on my big girl pants and rip off the proverbial band-aid.

"We need to talk...about Friday," I blurt out.

"Will you be looking at me during this conversation?"

I face him, slightly chagrined.

"Great. Okay, great," I stutter over my words, unsure of myself. "I'm just going to come out and say it. While that kiss was super hot...like *really* hot..." I chance looking up at him and feel the full weight of his stare, heavy and inescapable. For a second, I forget why

I even wanted to do this, but I power through. "I think it's best if we keep things professional from here on out."

I don't know what I expect to see in his eyes after I deliver my speech, but it certainly wasn't the look he's directing at me now. He looks resolute. Determined. A little pained.

"Can I ask why?"

I'm nodding my head, even though I want to run out the door and jump into the Hudson River. "I just think this," I point between him and me, "could get too complicated very quickly."

"Are you sure this is what you want?" The look on his face is impossible to decipher.

No. "Yes."

"Sure thing, Sunshine." He holds his hand out to me to shake, and when my skin touches his, he tugs me forward and leans down towards my ear, warm breath ghosting across my skin, making me suppress a shiver. "I'll be the best damn *friend* you ever had."

Every inch of my body coils tight in anticipation .

"Great. So, uh," I step out of his hold, "now that the shelves are empty, where should we start?" I ask, desperate to erase the previous topic from the forefront of my mind.

"Let's remove the broken planks, and then we'll each grab a sander and start stripping off the old wood stain."

He motions for me to follow him to grab the tools we left by the door. There's a lingering awkwardness in the air, but I must be the only one who feels it, because Hendrix carries on, unperturbed. I don't know if I should be relieved or disappointed, but if he can carry on as if nothing happened, then so can I.

We make our way back to the shelves, equipment in tow, and I'm about to start sanding when he stops me with a hand on my wrist.

Slowly, he pulls the device out of my hand and sets it on the ground. When I give him a questioning stare, he responds by pulling something out of his back pocket.

When I look down, I see he's holding a protection mask and glasses. He hands me the mask to put on, and before I can grab the glasses from him, he leans forward and slips them over my ears to rest on my face, unintentionally tucking my hair.

"Safety first." His eyes glitter with amusement. What is this, psychological warfare?

He hands me back the electric sander after he removes the broken pieces from the two built-ins we're focusing on today.

Grabbing his own, he looks at me. "If you could go to any place, real or fictional, where would it be?"

And just like that, the tension I was feeling is broken, and he puts me completely at ease, yet again.

The two weeks leading up to book club passes in a blur of eighty grit sandpaper, paint rollers, and a never-ending round of twenty questions.

Hendrix has shown up every day, ten minutes early, coffee and tools in hand.

I don't know what I thought would happen. Maybe for him to decide this project wasn't worth it? That *I* wasn't worth it if he wasn't getting something more out of it? Isn't that what I've come to expect after twenty years of lived experience?

There were a few years after Dad died and Mom left that I was still too young to fully grasp the magnitude of what I had endured.

I just knew the world was duller and my parents were gone. Then, I met Kena, and he never backed down from my quiet demeanor. He was larger than life to me, even then. Every time I saw him, he chipped away at my grief until he could finally see *me* underneath the wreckage, and he pulled me out.

For a long time after that, I didn't care to give anyone else the time of day. It was better to keep my circle small. But along with growing up comes hormones and recklessness, and I found myself letting down my guard again when I was in high school with a boy.

Jeremy Rollins was perfect—at least I thought so at the time. He was attractive, cocky, and he could play guitar. Basically, an early 00s wet dream. Everyone wanted him, but he wanted *me*. It made me feel special for the first time in a long time, and I got swept up in that rush. Being wanted when you spent the most formative years of your life feeling the opposite, felt akin to winning the lottery. I couldn't believe it was happening to me—that this person was *choosing me*. Every word out of his mouth was honey, and I found myself opening up to him. He repaid me a few weeks later by sticking his tongue down Melanie Virochec's throat at a party. When I asked him why, he said, *"You were fun for a minute but I need someone less complicated, less damaged."*

It just served to confirm what I already knew—it's easier to keep things casual. No one wants the messy bits, keep it fun. That fail-safe has worked for me my whole life since.

Until now.

"What's your death row meal?"

I smile. Hendrix took the twenty questions game I started on our first night and turned it into two hundred. The queries vary from completely ridiculous to borderline philosophical.

Yesterday, he asked me what my favorite midnight snack was (pizza rolls), and immediately after, he asked me what song I thought best described me ('The Bolter' by Taylor Swift). Then, to my mortification, he played the song, *out loud*, with me right next to him. When it finished, he put his phone back in his pocket, said "I like it", and then resumed his project like nothing was out of the ordinary.

I like it. *What does that even mean?* Does he like the song or me?

"You're going to laugh."

"That seems likely, knowing you."

I smack him with the towel I carry around to wipe up stray paint drops, but he ducks away, chuckling.

"I'd start with a fat stack of pancakes that have been waterlogged with syrup." He grimaces at my lack of restraint when it comes to sugar. "Don't judge! Then, I'd get a pizza from this place on Bleeker. It has pancetta, three different cheeses, and a spicy peach jam on it." I pause to look at him, but he just urges me to continue, knowing I'm not finished yet. "For dessert, I'd have a funnel cake and wash it all down with a cold brew."

"I'm concerned for your arteries." He runs his hands down his face in exasperation.

"What's yours then?"

He thinks on it for a while. "Steak and fries."

"God, that's—I need to corrupt you asap if you're to survive the mean streets of New York."

I look over at him, and he's already looking at me with a glazed look lining his stunning eyes. The sun's just setting, and the light is streaming in through the front bay windows, gilding his features in a halo of golden light.

"Corrupt me then." His voice sounds husky, and my body flushes, suddenly remembering the feel of his stubble-lined mouth grazing my neck, scratching and creating the most delicious friction while he worked me into a frenzy.

I cough and resume painting the shelf in front of me. "What's Seattle like?"

There's a long, pregnant pause before he answers. "Beautiful. The city is nestled between Lake Washington and Elliot Bay, so it's three-sixty views everywhere. And you're near some of the best trails for hiking, with the most stunning mountains you'll ever see. It's pretty incredible." Admiration and sorrow war for dominance in his tone.

"Why'd you leave?" I hesitate to ask, sensing there's a story here he might not want to tell.

"Needed some fresh air." He paints his shelf in vertical strokes, the ink on his tattooed forearms coming alive with each movement.

"And you came to New York for that? We basically ingest a cocktail of carbon monoxide and oxygen on a daily basis."

He shoots me a grin, but his tone feels loaded. "And yet my head has never felt clearer."

There's obviously something he's not saying, a story he isn't ready to divulge to me—maybe to himself. If he wants to keep something to himself, I respect that, even if I want to crack him open like a piñata, and watch all his thoughts spill out before me. But something tells me from the tense look on his face, even this small admission was a lot for him. I have the urge to reach out and rub my thumb against his furrowed brow, make it disappear and soften the frown settled on his flawless mouth, eradicating the sadness shading his gold flecked eyes. But I keep my hand clutching my paint roller.

"Favorite animal?" I ask with a nonchalance that deserves an Oscar.

Hendrix huffs out a breath. "Not a fucking koala, that's for sure."

I tilt my head at him in complete bafflement. "I don't blame you. They're *ripe* with chlamydia."

He looks at me with a bewildered expression before he lets out a hearty laugh, a real laugh with eyes alight and shoulders shaking. Gone is the heaviness hanging over his head like a cloud.

And dammit, if it doesn't set me beaming.

Chapter 15

Hendrix

This may be the most idiotic thing I've ever done.

Silver asked me to keep things platonic—and I have. For the most part, at least. I swear, friendship is all I'm thinking about as I pause outside the threshold of Brownstone Books, thinking over this decision before I go in.

When I asked her earlier this week if she planned on keeping the name of the store the same, a fleeting panic crossed her features before she wiped it away with a smile before she noncommittally shrugged and said she hadn't decided yet. I pretended not to notice, but I haven't stopped thinking of that look since. My brain started concocting ways to keep that look from ever sneaking onto her lovely face ever again, before chastising myself for not being able to keep her off my mind for long. I'm trying to honor her wishes but our evenings spent sanding, painting, and *talking* are my favorite part of the day. *She* is my favorite part of the day.

I felt like a different person around her. My shoulder felt looser, smiles came easier. Over the past two years, I had become accustomed to living without Maddox, and I was slowly starting to realize it wasn't living at all—it was surviving. And now that I've had a taste of what life could be like, I want more, and now, she doesn't.

When she told me we needed to stay just friends, it felt like a punch to the gut, a bone-deep disappointment I worked overtime to not show on my face. I suspected her need to keep things amicable was out of self-preservation. Despite the fact that there was something inherently *unfriendly* about the way I would catch her looking at me over the last week. If all she wants from me is friendship, that's what she'll get. I'll be the best damn friend she's ever had, and friends show up to their friend's book clubs.

Taking a deep breath, I step inside to the sound of raucous laughter, Silver's bright voice ringing out over the crowd.

Everyone is enthralled with her—or maybe I'm projecting, but every eye seems laser-focused on what she's saying. There's around thirty people here all crammed into the small space. They pushed the tables that line the center of the store off to the sides to make room for chairs.

Luck is on my side, because it's standing room only by the time I arrive, so she hasn't noticed I've slipped inside yet.

Silver is striking in a hot pink satin skirt that reaches her mid-calf and a multi-colored stripe sweater molded to her torso. The combination is loud and demands your attention, just like she does. She captivates the audience with no fear, totally in her element, hands gesticulating as she speaks animatedly about whatever book they read.

She is the most beautiful person I have ever seen.

I shift over to the right, where there's a small table with refreshments, and grab myself a cup of coffee supplied by Respect the Drip.

I lean with my back against the entrance door frame, content to watch Silver monopolize everyone's attention, magnetic and engaging. She works the room after each question, listening while people provide their thoughts on what sounds like a romance. But swords were mentioned so, maybe a fantasy?

She checks her notes, and addresses the crowd, "Okay, there were a lot of different themes throughout *Forged by Fire*, but my favorite by far was the slow burn. It felt like I was slowly being tortured. Every time I was about to set the book down and go to bed, I got roped back in thinking they were about to finally break the tension. I literally started screaming at the book at one point, begging them to kiss, fight or fuck." The crowd laughs at her fervor, but I can see a slight flush creep onto her cheeks. "But I'm curious to know what your favorite themes or tropes were?"

I take a long pull from my coffee, belatedly hoping it's decaf, as someone to my left responds to Silver's prompt.

"Personally, I loved that Finn had two dicks."

Several people are murmuring their assent as I start choking on my drink.

I'm fighting for my life, aggressively coughing around my shocked sputters, when everyone in the room turns to look in my direction.

My eyes connect with ones of aquamarine, and a slow, mischievous smile engulfs Silver's face.

"Are you okay, Harrington?" She challenges.

I work hard to catch my breath. "Perfect, thank you, Saffron."

Her eyes glint, and we hold each other's stare, completely unaware of the tension filling the room as several eyes bounce back and forth between the two of us.

"Carmen," continuing to hold my gaze, she calls out to the young woman who just borderline killed me, "can you elaborate on what you said?"

She's teasing me on purpose.

"Absolutely. I could filibuster this particular topic." She stands and makes her way to the front next to Silver and Holly. The latter introduces her as the shop's part-time bookseller and in-house monster smut expert. "First, I think we need to address the fact that he is the Orc village's blacksmith. That may not be relevant to the double peen situation, but it *is* hot. Metaphorically and literally."

The audience collectively bursts into laughter, with several people hollering in agreement.

Joy emanates around the room for the rest of the evening. Everyone is making new friends, laughing together, forgetting their troubles, and it's all because Silver had an idea. She brought all these people together. She had a part in the story of the friendships formed tonight. This thing that has brought her anxiety and fear has also brought community.

I don't think she even realizes it.

So, I take it all in for her. I listen to every question and answer.

I have no idea what the hell they're talking about the whole night, but I know in my bones that I'll read every book from here on out.

For her.

I hang back at the entrance to the store while Silver, Holly, and Carmen all chat with various members of the book club at the back.

There's a signup sheet for the next meeting, and nearly everyone who attended today has signed up to come again next month. One thing is undeniable: each person left feeling lighter than when they came in, myself included.

When the last person shuffles out, Silver makes her way towards me, and damn, if my heartbeat doesn't pick up just a little.

The satin of her skirt swishes against her hips with each step in my direction, and I try my damndest to not stare for too long. I fail miserably, and she definitely notices, if the smirk on her face is anything to go by.

"What did you think of *Forged by Fire*?" A wicked glint dances through her eyes knowing I was completely blindsided by the subject material.

"I'm considering a career change. It would seem metalsmiths are more popular than maintenance techs, based on everyone's reaction tonight."

"I don't know… I can think of one maintenance tech I kinda like." She holds my stare, not backing down. Always bold. Always sure of herself and what she wants.

"Yeah?" I swallow.

"Yeah." She smiles. "I *really* miss Sal."

A laugh explodes out of me, and her resounding giggle does me in further.

"How are you feeling about tonight?" I nod to the empty seats scattered everywhere. Cups and napkins litter the floor from where Silver told people to leave them for her to pick up later.

"It's actually incredible." She beams. "I knew we had some signups, but I didn't expect that many. Could you tell I was nervous?" She glances down at her shoes shyly.

I shake my head. "You were a natural," I reassure her.

"Yeah?"

"Yeah," I parrot softly back to her.

It's insane to me that someone who exudes such effortless confidence is doubting herself after an objectively successful night. It makes me wonder how much of what she projects to the world is real and what's for show.

"I was a little apprehensive that all the unfinished projects would put some people off, but no one seemed to mind." She gives a contented little sigh as she scans her eyes around the room.

We've made good progress over the last week, but we're only a third of the way done with repairing all the shelves, which means two thirds of the furniture throughout the store is well-worn and walnut brown while the third we've repaired this week are pristine and a crisp white. Finishing the bookshelves in addition to some repairs to the tables, floors, and the staircase leading up to the second floor will keep us busy for a while. I'm assuming it'll take another few weeks of work to get this place exactly how she wants it.

And I'm perfectly content with extending that timeframe if it means more time with Silver.

"Why did you come?" she blurts out after a prolonged silence while fiddling with the gold pendant hanging off her neck.

How honest should I be?

I came because I can't stop thinking about you.

I came because I wanted to hear your laugh and see you smile.

I came because even though I tried to push you away, you burrowed into my bloodstream, and I can't excise you. I don't want to.

"We're friends. I wanted to make sure you had a good turnout. It would seem I didn't need to come at all." I reach my hand to scratch the back of my neck.

She's looking pointedly away from me but has a slight tinge of pink at the top of her cheekbones.

"Let me help you clean up," I offer.

She stiffens a little. Barely perceptible, but I caught it.

"Oh...that's okay. There isn't much to do, and you've already done so much to help me this week." She tries to brush off the rejection with a nonchalant wave of her hand and a smile plastered to her face.

"I don't mind," I attempt to assure her without making her feel pressured.

She plays with the gold chain hanging off her neck, zipping the small pendant back and forth. "I appreciate the offer, but it's not necessary. You've done so much for the store already. You should enjoy the rest of your weekend, free of this place." I can see the walls going up around her body like a concrete fence. Part of me wants to poke and prod, force her to let me in, but I don't.

Friends. I'm starting to resent the word.

"Well then, thank you for an...illuminating evening." She chuckles under her breath and looks up at me from beneath lowered lashes.

"I'll see you on Monday, Susanna."

"See you Monday, Hank."

I say a quick goodbye to Holly and Carmen and step out into the cool night air, even though all I want to do is stay.

I'm a few blocks away from the store when I realize it's after ten at night, and I've left Silver to walk home alone. I'm not an idiot;

I know she grew up in New York and knows these streets better than anyone. But something is niggling me in my stomach to turn around and go back, to see her home safely.

Another part of me is screaming that I'm being a territorial brute who needs to back off. She made it clear she wants to be alone, but the voice in my head is persistent, yelling at me to double back and walk her home.

The city is pulsing around me, completely unaware of the internal battle I'm fighting. People stumble in and out of bars, the bass from the music blasting out of cars zooming by, friends arm in arm, laughing with each other as they walk around me.

I've stopped dead in the middle of the block and started pacing in circles, brain waring against my heart as uneasiness grips me in its clutches. Go home or go back for her. Maybe I'll just double back to make sure she's alright, she doesn't even have to know I came back to check on her.

Turning around, I head back to Brownstone Books. Back to Silver.

I just have to hope she won't feel like I overstepped.

When I'm halfway back to the store, I run into Holly and Carmen.

"Hey, Hen!" Carmen shouts at me. "What did you think about tonight?"

"I loved it. I want all future book recommendations from you." I look behind them, hoping to see Silver coming around the corner after them, but she's not there. "Is Silver not with you?"

"No, she sent us away. She knows I'm on deadline, and Carmen is on her way to a party. We tried to stay and help, but she insisted she could lock up on her own," Holly answers.

"Right, okay, thanks. I'll see you guys next week." The churning in my gut has gotten worse. The only thing keeping it at bay was the hope the girls were there with her.

I step around them. "She's probably still cleaning or about to close up. You should be able to catch her." There's a knowing glint in Holly's eyes, but I don't have time to consider it. It's obvious she knows I'm gone for her friend.

Everything is okay—it has to be—but the sinking feeling in my gut won't go away, so I hasten my steps. I'm only a couple blocks from the store, heading towards the quieter and much less populated block the store resides on.

I round the corner of the street and stop dead in my tracks, understanding the gut feeling I had.

My blood runs cold at the sight of Silver halfway down the block, fighting off an attacker, and a fear I've only experienced one other time seizes my body before I take off like a rocket toward my girl.

Chapter 16

Silver

To say the girls gave me a thorough ribbing after Hendrix left would be an understatement, and despite all my protestations that he and I are just friends, they didn't believe me. I don't know if I believe me either.

I've been working overtime to keep the smile off my face ever since he started choking on his drink tonight. How am I supposed to keep things professional when he does things like showing up at a book club about orc smut and just rolling with it? All in the name of *support*.

I had to send him home, or I might have jumped his bones on the shop floor before I could even lock the door. He looked so earnest, it physically pained me to turn him away, a gut punch feeling that is still roiling in my gut. But it was for the best.

Right?

I dig through my tote bag, rifling through receipts and no less than thirteen different lip products in search of my keys to close the store. When I finally have them in hand, I lock both the handle and deadbolt before jiggling the door to make sure it's secure.

In college, I made the mistake of forgetting to lock the door one night when it was my turn to close. I was stressed with exams coming up, trying to keep up with all the parties I felt obligated to go to, and it was unsurprisingly one of the rare times my mom decided to pop up. Thankfully, nothing bad happened, but Pat never let me forget it, and I'm so traumatized, I still get a little spooked every time I lock up.

Giving the door one more shake for good measure, I turn around to see a man lurking by the curb, staring right at me.

My heart starts beating erratically out of my chest, and every horror story I've ever heard from women plays like a film reel through my mind.

Okay, it's no big deal... If I don't engage and just walk as quickly as possible to somewhere more populated, it'll be fine. I briefly entertain the idea of running back into the store, but I don't want him to follow me in and then block my only exit.

Keeping my keys in my hand between my knuckles, I move to walk past him, but he steps in front of me, blocking my path. He's too close for comfort, and it's making my pulse jump.

"Go back in, and give me all the money from your register."

Fuck. Fuck. Fuck.

His pallid complexion shines with sweat under the lamp light, as his imposing frame lumbers over me. I try my best to not be cowed by it, to not show the fear racing through my body in case it emboldens him further. Decades of living in New York City, and nothing like this has ever happened to me.

"We're cash free," I lie. I have no idea where it came from, but I guess I'm rolling with it. My subconscious doesn't want me to relent, even though it would be stupid not to. It would be safer to just do what he wants, but I don't want to get trapped inside with him where no one can see us. What should I do? I really need to *not* be robbed right now. Money is getting tighter and tighter as the days and renovations wear on, and even the meager amount of cash in the till counts right now.

"Then give me what you have on you." He moves to grab my bag, but my body reacts of its own accord and jerks back out of his grasp. I start to back away, moving to flee. Turning my back on him would be a mistake, but I'm not sure what other options there are, other than to run like a bat out of hell and get away from him as fast as possible. I might be able to make it. I'm smaller than him; surely, that gives me some sort of advantage, right?

Hoisting my tote higher on my shoulder, I tighten my grip around the straps and move forward, readying to sprint. He anticipates my move and grabs me by my hair, yanking me back.

A sensation like singing fire dances along my scalp from where he grabs me, but my mind moves past the pain, because now, I'm *pissed.*

I'm not a vain person, but I *love* my hair. It's been years of tender love and maintenance to get it soft and thick...and the fact that this fucker touched it has me forgetting I should be trying to get away to safety. Instead, adrenaline starts to flood my body, and I'm gearing up for a fight.

He shifts his footing to spin me around, trying to gain better access to my bag, and as he does, I wind up my right fist and land a punch squarely on his jaw.

"You bitch!" he yells in surprise, but his grip holds firm.

"Fuck, that hurt so much more than I thought it would." I shake out my sore knuckles, swelling already starting to form.

"It's about to hurt a whole lot more," he grunts as he gets a grip on my bag.

I don't know why I'm being so stubborn. I should just let him take it. He won't get very far with a bunch of measly receipts and a twenty dollar bill floating around at the bottom. But it's the principle of it all that has me fired up now. He will not get my bag or my favorite lip oil. Not on my metaphorical watch.

I wrestle to keep my grip on the bag as he hooks one of his legs between mine to throw me off balance, and it works as I stumble a step.

How is it possible no one is seeing this happen right now? Eight million people in this fucking city, and not a single one is on this block right now to help me?

I struggle to stay upright as he continues to try and trip me while he grabs the arm holding my bag and squeezes. His grip is bone crunching, and I need to switch tactics somehow, but all the self-defense classes Nan enrolled me in as a girl dissipate from my brain in the height of my panic.

"Just give it up."

I should. At this point, I should, just so I can get to safety. The adrenaline is wearing off, and the fear is setting in again when something shiny flashes in his hand. This guy has a knife, and I'm trying to defend...what? Nothing that matters, at least. In the far reaches of my mind, I realize I'll need to call a locksmith tonight to have the locks changed on the shop door because my keys are in the bag I'm about to let him have.

"Fine, take it." All the fight leaves my body, and I go a little limp, offering him my bag.

"Give me your necklace too." He motions with the knife toward the dainty gold pendant around my neck. The necklace I wear every day without fail. The one my dad gifted to me right before he died.

"No," I whisper softly, hardly audible.

I take a step back, uncomprehending what to do. He can't have this necklace, anything but the last piece of my dad I have left.

The attacker follows my retreat, latching on to both of my arms to hold me immobile, spinning me around and pinning my back to his front. The contact makes me want to vomit. He's banded his arm around my upper half in a vice grip as he snakes his knife-wielding arm up and settles the edge under the chain of my necklace.

A tear silently tracks down my cheek at what I'm about to lose.

I glimpse a tall shadow not far off in the distance, but my devastated mind can't make sense of what it is, only that it's lumbering closer and closer, faster than I even thought possible. Then, my gaze settles on eyes the color of sun soaked evergreens.

Hendrix.

He came back? For me?

The haze of resignation starts to retreat at seeing him, and it gives me the boost of strength I need to make one last ditch effort to get out of this. The attacker hasn't noticed Hendrix is here yet, and I need to deploy distraction tactics and hope to God it works.

Striking like an asp, I bring my leg up and swiftly crunch it back down on his foot, hard enough that he bends forward, taking me with him. The sudden movement makes the blade under my necklace nip the side of my neck, and I feel my pendant fall to the ground. In our crouched position, he's brought me parallel to his groin, and I sail my arm back with as much force as I can manage into his balls.

His hold finally weakens, and I push myself out of his grip and away from him just in time for Hendrix to take him to the ground like a seasoned NFL defensive tackle.

Safe.

Hendrix is here. I'm safe.

All the blood rushes to my ears, and all I can hear is a faint ringing. The adrenaline I had moments ago has fully worn off and my whole body has run cold. Vaguely, I can hear someone speaking to me as I crouch down and pick up my necklace, now broken, from the pavement.

I stare down at the floral embossing on the face—frozen, ears buzzing, buzzing, buzzing.

The last thing my dad ever gave me is broken. I can no longer feel its soothing weight against my chest, can no longer reach for it when I'm sad or confused or pensive, expecting it to have all the answers. I feel cold with it gone, or maybe that's just the air outside. I'm not sure.

The voices persist until something finally gets through to me.

"Silver!" Hendrix calls out my name, gentle yet ringing with authority.

He said my *name*.

Not another random name like he does when we play our little game. I almost forgot what it sounded like falling off his lips, and it's everything I never thought to dream of.

I want to hear it a million more times.

"I need you to call 911. Can you do that for me, Sunshine?" I like when he calls me that too.

I nod at him, but I don't say anything as I crouch down to my bag, discarded on the ground, and reach shaking hands inside for my phone.

Hendrix has the assailant down on the ground, straddling his back with the guy's face pressed to the concrete, bones crunching and both hands gripped behind his back. He's definitely not going anywhere if the flex of Hendrix's biceps is anything to go by.

When I finally get through to a first responder, I answer all their questions, and within minutes, there is a police car on the scene, handcuffing my attacker.

With Hendrix no longer detaining him, he gently walks over to me, intuiting I may need some space.

I don't. Not from him.

So, I bridge the final few steps between us.

His hands twitch like they want to touch me, check me over to make sure I'm not hurt, maybe hug me. I think I could use a hug. I'm about to step in and just take one from him, take what I *need*, what I've been *craving* ever since I told him we needed to be friends, when an officer comes over to get a statement.

I spend the next thirty minutes recounting everything that happened, filing a police report with Hendrix's steady presence at my back.

Once done, the cops get back in their vehicle and drive away with the perp handcuffed in the back seat, glaring daggers at me.

"Can I walk you home?" He looks desperate for me to say yes, like the idea of parting with me right now might kill him. But before I can say yes, he follows up with a solemn plea. "Please."

"Yes." Nothing else needs to be said.

We walk the ten minutes it takes to get to The Langham in

silence, close to one other but never quite touching.

When we approach the front doors, we both peer in and notice Tony sitting at his bench, watching a show on his phone.

"Sunshine, I—" he pauses, looking away from me, something like shame on his face. "I'm so sorry. This shouldn't have happened. I shouldn't have left you tonight." There's guilt in his eyes, and I don't understand why it's there. How could he think he's responsible for any of this?

"You only did what I *asked* you to do. You respected my boundaries," I offer in his defense.

"I should have been there, insisted I stay and help you clean up." There's something haunted in his eyes, a panicked quality to his voice. "I just...I should have been there."

He's on the edge of a spiral, and I have no idea why. His body is shaking lightly, and he's scratching at the back of his neck, rubbing his skin raw.

Stepping forward, I grab his hands and bring them down as I step forward and wrap my arms around his waist, finally stealing the hug I need, the one I suspect he needs just as much. Something to buoy us in reality.

I can feel his rapid breathing start to slow as I bury my face in his chest, listening to his heartbeat start to level out before I pull away. We're staring at each other, my stomach in my throat. The fear from the evening is starting to ebb, but I don't want him to leave, not yet.

"Will you stay with me tonight? I just...I don't want to be alone after that."

His eyes dance back and forth as he looks at me, and then I see him glance behind me to where Tony sits. Tony, his coworker.

Because he *works* here, and I'm a tenant, and this is not allowed. A fact I conveniently like to forget.

"I'm so sorry. I shouldn't have ask—"

"Yes," he cuts me off.

"But..." I glance over my shoulder, and he reads my meaning.

"It'll be fine. Let's go."

We step inside, and a smile lights up Tony's face until he takes the both of us in, dirty and scraped and a little worse for wear.

Hendrix leans towards me and says low enough that only I can hear, "Go on up. I'm going to talk to Tony quickly, and I'll meet you up there."

"Okay." I make my way over to the elevators and step into the car. He watches me and doesn't look away until the doors close.

Five minutes later, there's a knock on my door.

I swing it open, and the sight of him standing on the threshold is so reminiscent of the first time, it gives me whiplash.

We stare at each other as he steps into my apartment.

He slowly, tentatively, reaches his hand up to tuck my hair behind my ear, and I lean my head into the touch like an affectionate cat, allowing myself this one comfort after a hellish night. But when he pulls away, I notice the scrapes and blood across his knuckles.

"Does it hurt?" I grab onto his palm.

"It's fine, Sunshine. Don't worry about me."

But I do. I can't *not*.

With my hand still holding his, I lead him into my bathroom, where I keep my first aid kit.

"Sit," I command, and he obeys, slowly lowering himself down onto the closed top of my toilet seat.

This bathroom is too small for the two of us, and I need to not think about how I can feel his body heat if I'm going to effectively fix his injuries.

I reach under the cabinet and pull out the medical supplies, setting out what I'll need on the countertop. Stepping between his legs, I pull his hand back into mine, inspecting the cuts for any gravel or debris. I can feel his eyes on my face, watching *me*, not what I'm doing. Relieved when I don't find anything that needs to be extracted, I work to clean and disinfect the cuts, apply a thin layer of healing salve, and set his hand down before taking a step back.

"There. All good."

He looks at me briefly before he stands. "Why don't you hop in the shower, and I'll make you some tea?"

I don't know how to respond to this level of care, and I'm fairly certain I'm gaping like a fish, because he just smirks and leans around me to turn on the shower before he leaves me to it. There's nothing else to do but comply, and, honestly, it was the right call. Nothing could feel better than the warm water beating down on my back, washing away the horrors of the evening.

Once I'm done, I step out and change into my coziest pajamas, towel dry my hair, and head into the kitchen, where Hendrix has just finished making me a chamomile tea and a sandwich.

God, he really doesn't make this easy, does he?

I take them from him, scanning him head to toe to assure myself he's alright.

"It just dawned on me that you don't have any sleep clothes. I'm sorry. You don't have to stay."

He looks me squarely in the eyes. "I'm staying. It's as much for your comfort as it is for me to have peace of mind."

I gulp down another bite of sandwich. "Oh."

The deep timbre of his chuckle makes my body flare with warmth.

I finish my food, feeling unsteady as my thoughts drift back to how a good night was tainted by one person's actions. Then, I notice my broken necklace on the entry table by the door, and I lose it.

All composure has left as I start to cry quietly.

Hendrix wastes no time wrapping his arms around me, letting me bury my head in his chest as he holds me to him, stroking my spine in a soothing rhythm. "Do you want to tell me about it?"

I swallow thickly as I look up at him, tears hanging off my lashes.

"My dad gave it to me before he died. He was going to steal it from me, and I panicked, and nothing else mattered." A fat tear falls hot on my cheek as he reaches a hand up and brushes it away.

"You still have it. He's with you." I nod and drop my head back to his chest. "Let's get you into bed." He leads me into my bedroom, and it feels weirdly normal, natural, even. That's almost as terrifying as the rest of the evening.

Setting my drink on the side table, he peels back my covers and motions for me to get inside. When he moves to leave, I panic, shooting my arm out to stop his retreat.

"Where are you going?"

"I was going to give you space, sleep on the couch." He's so goddamn chivalrous, and while the thought of his hulking frame squished onto my tiny pink couch makes me want to smile, I don't want him to go.

"Please," I plead, desperate and needy, "stay in here with me."

Whatever he sees in my eyes is enough to convince him, because he just nods and makes his way to the other side of the bed, kicking off his shoes and getting under the covers with me.

I turn off the bedside light so he won't see the embarrassment tinting my cheeks beet red.

My bed is small, and Hendrix is a tall man, so this arrangement puts us in startlingly close proximity. I shift onto my side, facing him, to afford us more room. He stays on his back but turns his head to look over at me.

"You came back for me." It's something so innocuous to most, even he couldn't possibly realize what something like that would do to me. The girl no one came back for.

"I'll always come for you," he states, so gentle and confident.

In the darkness of my bedroom, with only the moon peeking through the curtains to bear witness, I break my own rules as I lean over to his side of the bed and press my lips against his.

The kiss is warm and tender, and it slowly fixes a part of my broken soul I previously thought irreparable. He doesn't take more than I give, and when I disconnect a few moments later, I don't fully retreat back to my side of the bed before falling asleep.

Chapter 17

Hendrix

"Mom is going to kill me if I let you do this," I plead with Maddox.

My baby brother is the textbook definition of daredevil, but those of us closest to him know he's just an idiot. A reckless, fearless, brave idiot. It's equal parts concerning and inspiring.

"What's that saying, H? Better to ask for forgiveness than permission?" He's standing at the cliff's edge, peering down into the waters below with a sort of manic excitement.

"You're an imbecile," Laurel calls out around a wheeze as she bends at the waist, camera dangling from her neck as she tries to catch her breath. We've been hiking this trail for the last couple of hours when we came upon the rocky bluff we're standing at now.

Maddox is dancing with barely contained glee, Laurel is drinking water from her canteen, and I, the eldest, am trying to figure out a way to get my youngest sibling to not listen to his inner chaos demon and step away from that crumbling ledge.

"You can tell your spinning brain to rest, big brother. I'm gonna take a dip in that pool." He points at the navy blue sparkling water at *least a hundred feet below us.*

"*How do you plan on getting back up, Maddie?*" *Laurel angles her camera toward the trees behind us.*

"*There's a path from the shore that eventually links back into this trail. I can meet you at the fork.*" *His tone suggests it should be obvious, even though none of us have ever done this hike before.*

I look at Laurel, pleading for backup, but she just shrugs as if to say, just let *him do it.*

Traitor.

I shake my head and look up to the sky, as if willing God to give me strength.

"*There's no way I can talk you out of this?*"

Maddox walks over to me and places his hands on each side of my face. "*You gotta learn to live a little, brother. You never have fun anymore. You go to work for Dad—which I know you hate—and then you come home. Wash, rinse, repeat. Your idea of a night out is going to the gym instead of coming out with us, or going on a date. You came home after college because of some fucked up deal Dad manipulated you in to, and we could all see it wasn't what you wanted. But you've stayed all these years, shrunk into this version of yourself that isn't you.*"

"*Maddie—*" *Laurel starts as Maddox finally takes his hands off my face and settles them on his hips.*

"*No, Laur, someone needs to say it.*" *He refocuses on me, and my mouth has gone bone dry as I listen to my baby brother gently scold me.* "*You have been everything* he *has expected you to be for years. When are you going to be everything* you *want to be?*"

He's staring at me with misplaced hope in his eyes.

"*It's fine, Bub. It's not a bad life.*"

The light in his eyes dims with disappointment, and I hate myself for putting it there, for giving my favorite person in the world a reason to be despondent, even for a moment. Because that's all it takes before he's back to smiling, ready to dive off the side of a mountain.

"Alright, fam, bring my backpack to the fork, will ya?" he says right before taking a running leap off the craggy rock face, arms spread wide like a hawk.

The sound of his exuberant howls reverberate off the mountainside before I hear this body crashing into the water below.

Laurel and I are waiting for him to resurface and shout so we know he's made it up, but the canyon leading down into the water is eerily quiet.

A fear colder than a glacier torpedoes through my entire body as I force my feet to carry me over to the edge. I look down but don't see my brother anywhere. A paralyzing terror seizes my body as we start to call his name, praying he's playing a prank on us or that he'll surface and be totally fine. That I'll be able to see him smile and tell him I'll start to live for me again, if he would just show us he's okay, my own version of a desperate bargain people make in churches and chapels.

When we finally spot him, he's floating upright and unconscious towards the shore. I kick into action as I grab Laurel and start to sprint down the mountain faster than I've ever run in my life, yelling out to my brother floating lifeless in a lake.

"MADDOX!"

"WE'RE COMING!"

"STAY WITH—"

"Wake up! Hendrix, please wake up!"

I startle awake to the feeling of cold sweat drenching my body, soft hands gently pushing hair off of my forehead. I want to lean into that touch, never leave the feeling of warmth it's bringing to my frozen body.

I look over and see Silver sitting next to me on her heels, worry lining her gaze.

"What do you need?"

I shake my head, unable to speak around my rapid breathing or form coherent enough thoughts to be able to figure out what I need. But I reach my hand up and grab her wrist, keeping her hand on my face. Her eyes flit back and forth over me as she continues to stroke my face. I lay there for unknown minutes, waiting for my pulse to slow, the sweat drying on my skin starting to make me feel itchy.

Once my heart settles into a normal rhythm, I'm able to focus on other details around me. The moon gilding a path through the bedroom, Silver's smooth bare legs peeking out from her cotton sleep shorts, the heat emanating from her hand as she runs her fingers through my hair at a hypnotic pace.

"Do you think I could shower?" My tone is gruff with embarrassment at her seeing me like this, vulnerable and out of my body. Weak. My father's voice filters in, harsh and unwanted. *Men don't pander to emotions, Hendrix. Get your shit together.*

She stands slowly, taking my hand and guiding me into her bathroom. She rummages around in a linen closet and pulls a towel out, setting it on the sink counter for me. When she turns to leave, I halt her with my arm blocking her path.

"Would you—would you stay with me?" I can't look at her, afraid of what I'll see if I do, but when she doesn't say anything, I glance down.

Raised eyebrows greet me, and I realize I've just asked her to stay with me when I'm about to strip naked and shower.

I rush to course correct. "Not to get in *with* me... Just stay. Talk to me like you do."

"Like what? Incessantly?" she jokes while huffing out a laugh.

A small smile curves the corners of my mouth. "Yeah, Sunshine. Something like that."

Vulnerability creeps over her expression, but she doesn't leave, instead hopping up onto the bathroom counter. When I start to take my clothes off, she turns her head to give me privacy.

After I've stepped into her shower, she starts to speak. "Sorry, all my products are pretty girly, so you're going to smell like fruit." Her voice rings out trying to cut her nervousness with humor.

"I don't mind smelling like you."

Judging by the silence, that might have been too much, but Silver is quick on her toes and picks up the conversation again.

"If you could go anywhere in the world, all expenses paid, where would you go?" She brings us to neutral territory, back to the tradition we have that feels as natural as breathing. It soothes the unrest inside me to have something that feels so familiar with her.

"Africa," I answer. "Specifically, the Serengeti in Tanzania." It was a trip my siblings and I always talked about doing together but never got to. I was always too busy with work whenever Maddox would bring it up. I still hate myself for it, not taking that vacation when I had the chance. "What about you?"

"Morocco. I want to see all the colors in the markets and try all the food and spices." She wastes no time between her answer and her next question, clearly trying to distract me. "What is your favorite controversial pizza topping?"

Scalding water beats down my back, loosening my muscles as I think through my answer. "Probably tuna."

"You're a monster." I can practically see the way her face puckers in adorable distaste.

"It's actually pretty good."

"I can't believe I'm listening to this."

We go back and forth like this for another ten minutes while I wash off the sweat and feel my body unknot from the combination of her voice and the hot water.

She leaves to give me privacy as I get out of the shower before I'm standing in her room in nothing but a towel, staring at my sweat-soaked clothes.

"I think I have a pair of Kena's old University sweats still here... They might be a little small, but you could wear those?" There's a wobble to her voice as she looks past me at her wall.

I'd prefer small over wet, so I accept her offer, and a few minutes later, I'm in gray sweats that are *definitely* too tight on me, chest bare.

Silver's gaze glides down my body slowly, but she doesn't say anything. She just pats the bed she made up with fresh sheets, and we both slip in quietly, sliding our backs against the headboard and letting the events of the night settle around us.

Her room is softly illuminated by moonlight, and I take a deep breath in before reaching out and tugging her to lay down with me, grabbing her hands in the process so they rest between us.

"Are you okay?" Her voice is gentle, tentative.

I pull her hand to my mouth and kiss her knuckles. We've slowly gotten closer these past few weeks working on the store, but this isn't something I'll ever be ready to talk about and have purposefully avoided in the past. But something about her thumb softly stroking the back of my hand makes me want to flay myself open before her.

"Two years ago, my younger brother died." Silver sucks in a nearly inaudible breath before I continue. "Both my sister and I were there, and we didn't get to him in time. My mind likes to make me relive it occasionally in a recurring nightmare."

"You don't have to talk about it if you're not comfortable."

I'm shaking my head at her before she even finishes the sentence. "No, it's okay. I...I think I *want* to." I think I *need* to.

She turns on her side, putting the hand I'm not holding under her head and giving me her undivided attention. I mimic her by flipping to my side, facing her and bringing us closer together. I get lost in her eyes, so open and warm and hypnotizing, like the riptide on the Tenerife Sea shoreline, pulling you in under its azure embrace.

"My siblings and I went on a hike one day a couple summers back. We discovered this trail we hadn't done before and decided to make a day of it. We were halfway through when Maddox spotted a cliff diving spot." My throat starts to thicken with each added detail, but I will myself to continue. "I tried—I tried to keep him from jumping, but Maddie was such a free spirit, and all the crazy things were so exciting to him. He was so...*alive*, all the time."

Moisture pools in my eyes as I think about my brother, and Silver shifts so we're only inches apart, bringing the hand under the pillow out to rest on my forearm. I look down at her hand and back up into her eyes, and she gives me a soft smile of encouragement to continue.

"He wouldn't listen, of course. You couldn't get him to do anything he didn't want to do. It drove our father crazy, his favorite pastime." The corner of my mouth quirks at the memory before quickly falling. "So, he jumped, and when I didn't hear him come back up, I knew in my gut something was wrong. Laurel and I barreled down a mountain to get to the shoreline where he was floating, unmoving, in the water."

Silver brushes an errant tear off my cheek.

"He was still alive at that point. I—" My throat feels unbelievably tight, like there are phantom hands around it, squeezing, choking me out with the intent to kill. "I hoisted him onto my shoulders to carry him as Laurel ran ahead to get our car from where we had it parked. We got him to the hospital, but his internal injuries were too severe, and he died a day later."

Silver stares at me with tears in her own eyes. For me, for what happened to Maddox, and I think I love her a little bit in this moment. I could love her a lot with more time.

"Is that why you moved here?"

A slight nod of my head confirms her curiosity. "Sorry, it's not your jilted lover theory." I try to lighten the mood.

"Kind of relieved I was wrong, actually." Silver gives me a shy smile. "So you came to New York..." she prompts.

"The silence was suffocating. We had lost this tremendous... light in our lives, snuffed out with one reckless decision that could have been stopped. I should have convinced him to not jump," I say to myself.

"It's not your fault, you know that right?"

Ignoring her comment, I brush a strand of hair back from her face. "My dad was never one for emotional...outbursts, is what he would call them, so we suffered in silence and never spoke about it beyond the funeral. Repressing every thought felt almost like relief at first, but eventually, it was like I was choking around every word I wanted to say but couldn't."

"What would you want them to know?" Her thumb strokes rhythmically against my forearm.

I take a deep breath. "That I'm sorry." My voice breaks. "I'm sorry I couldn't keep my baby brother safe. I hear his yell of excitement as he jumped *every time* I lay down to go to sleep, and it keeps me up at night. I'd tell them I'm sorry I couldn't stay, and Dad was right when he called me a coward that day. He's right to blame me. Our family is shattered because I wasn't strong enough—to stop him, to stay and take care of everyone, to fight through the anxiety clawing up my throat every time I open my eyes, wishing it had been me instead."

"Hendrix..." She says my name so gently. Do I deserve gentleness? No, but I'm too selfish to turn it away when she cups my cheek, the touch settling the turbulence in my head.

"Can I share something with you too?" Her soft voice quivers slightly.

"Please." Stark relief floods me when I had previously been feeling like a washrag wrung out and left to dry.

She takes a moment to gather her courage. "My dad died when I was eight. He, uh, had a stroke out of nowhere when he was only thirty-five. The doctors have no idea why it happened. He was the picture of health, but he was an anomaly."

I know from experience that she doesn't need condolences. Instead, I offer her the same silent support she offered me, tangling my leg between hers to give her something to ground herself to.

"My mom basically abandoned me after he died," she says off-handedly.

My body stiffens at the idea of anyone walking away from her, but I refrain from saying anything, relaxing my muscles and hoping she didn't notice.

"Dad was Mom's whole world. She was *so* wrapped up in him, she couldn't see anything else. I thought it was great when I was a kid, to be able to see my parents so in love when so many were getting divorced. But then he died, and my mom basically died with him. Carol James never wanted kids, not really. But Dad did. He wanted me more than anything in the world, and because he wanted a child, my mom convinced herself she did too. But then he died, and she said I looked too much like him, that it—" She pauses, and her eyes shift away from me. "That it hurt for her to look at me... so she dropped me off at Nan's apartment and never came back. Brought a whole new meaning to sleepovers at grandma's house." The joke falls flat around us.

I scoot closer to her, putting my spare hand on her waist and rubbing my thumb back and forth in a soothing motion. She lets loose a contented sigh that I will echo through my mind for the next week.

"All that to say, you may have noticed I tend to keep people at an arm's length." She stares at me for confirmation, and I give a slight nod and kiss her forehead that's now settled much closer to me. "I don't like to get close to people, because in my experience, they always end up leaving. Dad died, Mom abandoned me, even Nan left for Florida. Only Kena remains, and I'm always waiting for that to change. I know my hang ups can't hold people back, that's not fair, but...I don't know, a therapist once told me it was avoidant attachment, before I stopped going to appointments, another thing I couldn't commit to," she says with wry humor. "Basically, I'm broken, always waiting on a knife's edge." She looks away from me.

"You're not," I say firmly, not to assuage her belief, but because it's true. Her dad didn't choose to leave, but her mom *did*, and that left scars far deeper than I could fathom. It makes me want to hold on to her forever, to kiss all the pieces she thinks are broken and beyond repair until she realizes she may have a chip or two left by careless people, but she's still perfect to me.

The look she throws at me says she doesn't quite believe it, and I want to hunt down every person who ever made her think otherwise.

"Let me prove it then. Just don't laugh because this is embarrassing to admit." She grimaces, and I squeeze her hip in response. "Sometimes, I like to go to Central Park and read all the little plaques on the park benches. You know the ones people have dedicated to their loved ones? I don't know, there's something about them. I feel connected to people without *having* to connect to anyone when I see their declarations of love to people I'll never meet. These people had someone who loved them so much, they had to have it memorialized forever on a bar of steel for everyone to see. It makes me feel... I don't know? Linked to my humanity in a way?"

"That's not embarrassing, Silver. That's beautiful."

She fidgets, trying to crawl out of her skin at the thought of someone, anyone, perceiving her. But I've always seen her—I always will.

"Did we just...trauma bond?" she asks, clearly trying to lighten the mood.

I laugh. "I think we did, Sunshine."

"I'm sorry about your brother, Hendrix."

"I'm sorry about your parents."

She shrugs as if it's nothing, but it's not. I have the overwhelming urge to lean forward and offer her any sort of comfort I can, to selfishly take comfort I know only she can provide.

I bridge the minuscule gap between us, giving her enough time to pull away if she chooses, and press my lips to hers.

It's soft and exploring, but in seconds, it deepens to something headier. My body is begging me to take more, but my brain is telling me to chill out, to not take too much too soon. Silver is used to men who are just around for an evening, and I won't be that to her. So, I pull back, even though it just about kills me.

I don't ask her what this is or what we are to each other. We can take our time to figure that out. I just know I want to be hers.

I already am, even if she's not there yet.

She protests once I've pulled away, but she immediately lets out a huge yawn. When I look at the clock, I see we've crept past three in the morning.

We settle further into bed with the intention to sleep when Silver lets out a soft, sleepy admission. "I think I really like you."

The confession drops on my head like an anvil but lifts my heavy heart just enough that maybe I can finally get some sleep. "I really like you too, Sunshine."

When I fall asleep, it's with her hand still tucked into mine.

Chapter 18

Hendrix

I wake after five in the morning to Silver wrapped around my body like a koala bear. It's the best sleep I've gotten in years.

It's creeping closer to dawn, and I need to get up and out of her apartment before the rest of the building wakes and someone rats me out to Mr. Fairbanks. But as I look over at her, mouth slightly parted, hair mussed from sleep, her lashes fanning against the tops of her cheeks, pulling myself out of her warm bed will be harder than pulling a semi-truck with my bare hands.

In the still-quiet silence of the morning, with only muffled city sounds distant in the background, I marvel at the past twenty-four hours as Silver's soft breaths puff against my bare chest.

I almost couldn't believe it—how easy it was to look into her soft eyes, so open and willing to carry my burdens—and recount the horrors of that day. After Maddox died, Mom quietly begged me to talk to a grief counselor, but I didn't see the point in rehashing the worst day of my life to a sympathetic stranger when it wouldn't change anything. It wasn't going to bring him back, and it wouldn't make me feel any better.

Except it had—felt better—when I told Silver. An inexpressible weight had lifted off my chest as I told her, and she looked at me with understanding, not pity. She too had lost someone pivotal to her. Two people. She understood loss on a level that was different from mine, but that still changed the way she moved through the world.

Silver's eyes open slowly, bleary and unsure, her body stiffening slightly against mine, as if waking up next to someone is a foreign concept for her. She slowly looks down to where her body is plastered to mine, covers shucked down around our waists, and slowly slides her gaze upward, taking in every detail. When her gaze settles on my face, her body loosens, and a sleepy smile graces her full mouth. A mouth I'm aching to taste again.

"Good morning." She lets out the cutest yawn as she averts her eyes and removes her wrapped limbs from my body with an inaudible *sorry*.

Without her weight blanketing me, everything is suddenly much colder. I want to beg her to come back and cling to me again, press the softness of her body against the rigid planes of mine, but I don't want to crowd her while she processes whatever is currently making her mind race.

"Morning."

She looks over at me, and she looks...shy. It's a look certain to end me completely, a softer side of her I don't think anyone but me has ever seen.

"How are you feeling?" I ask at the same time as she says, "Did you sleep well?"

We both huff out a laugh as she gestures for me to go first.

"I slept fine after...well, you know." My ears flame with humiliation.

If she notices, she doesn't let on, answering my question instead. "I'm a little sore from the scuffle, but otherwise, I'm fine. Grateful, actually."

"Grateful?"

"Objectively, it fucking sucked...but you showed up." She gives me a soft smile. "I still have dad's necklace and will get it fixed after the renovations are over. The store is okay." She turns, finally seeming at ease, and burrows herself deeper under the covers. "What time is it?"

"Half past five in the morning. I should probably slip out before someone sees me."

A brief flash of disappointment crosses her features before she schools it into one of cheerful neutrality.

"Oh yeah, of course." She looks away from me.

Brick by brick, walls start going up, ones that were knocked down last night and that I have no intention of letting her erect again.

"Hey." I nudge her under the chin to look over at me. "I don't *want* to go. It's the last thing I want to do. Last night was... It meant something to me. I've never—I've never been able to open up to someone the way we did, I don't want to lose that. I want to see where this could go, if you do," I hasten to add on, suddenly feeling very vulnerable and remembering that, just a couple weeks ago, she told me we needed to remain platonic.

Her eyes bounce around my face. "I–" She takes a deep breath. "I don't know why this is so hard for me."

The sting of rejection lands swift and brutal, and I try and fail to not let it show on my face.

"No! No, *ugh*, that came out wrong," she rushes to assure me. "I've just never...dated anyone before."

"Never?" My surprise is obvious.

"Well, once in high school, but it wasn't a good experience, and I just never cared to try again." She pauses to collect her thoughts, and my heart teeters on a ledge the height of the Chrysler building. "I'm not used to this feeling." She indicates between the two of us with her hands. "This *consuming* feeling I get when I'm around you." She settles her hand on my chest, and my heart is beating a million miles a minute. There's no way she can't feel it. "But for the first time, I want more." She draws in a deep breath. "And it scares the shit out of me."

I slide my arm under the covers and hook it around her waist to pull her closer to me. Her body is soft, sinking into my hold. "I'm scared too, Sunshine. We can figure it out together, at whatever pace feels right, but I'm not going anywhere."

She seems to breathe a little easier as she reaches her hand up exploringly and brushes a lock of hair from my eyes. "Why do you call me Sunshine?"

A flush creeps up my neck and onto my cheeks, an undeniable reaction she's looking right at. I clamp my lips together, unwilling to admit this truth to her for fear it will make me sound crazy. I shake my head in denial at her.

"What? No, tell me!" I bury my face in her shoulder to avoid her stare, but she digs out my face with a hand on each stubble-coated cheek. "Tell me right now, Hamilton."

"Don't say I didn't warn you."

"Please; it's not like I'm asking you for the nuclear codes. Fess up."

"When I met you, it was the first time I felt warm in a very long time. Like the sun was shining down on me, heating my bones after a really harsh winter," I admit to her, wishing I could stuff the words back into my mouth.

Silver stares at me for a silent moment that feels like it stretches on for an eternity, saying nothing. I knew it was too much; now, I've scared her off.

"I'm sorry, that was too much. Let's pretend I said it was cause of your sunny dispos—"

Her lips collide with mine, and every thought I've ever had scatters to the wind.

"That is—" *kiss*, "the most ridiculous—" *kiss*, "and stupidly romantic—" *kiss*, "thing I've ever" *a nip on to my bottom lip*, "heard." She pulls back to look at me with a kiss-drunk look in her eyes. "Are you even real?"

The look she's giving me rockets my pulse into space as she leans in for another long, languorous kiss, sliding her tongue against my bottom lip to ask for entry I gladly give her. I tighten my hold on her waist as she moves her mouth against mine in a punishing rhythm, our tongues tangling in a way that makes my skin tighten and my dick harden.

She smirks into my mouth. "Very real, if what I'm feeling is any indication. God bless these too small sweatpants."

"You're a menace," I pant against her lips, groaning as she hooks her leg over mine and grinds against me. I grasp her thigh, bringing it even further over my lap until she's settled atop me, thighs straddling my hips.

She whimpers into my mouth at the feeling of our bodies connecting, my rigid middle against her soft center. Reaching my hand up to brush the hair out of her face, I grasp it in my fist as I pull her head back to expose her neck, peppering kisses on her collarbone and leading them up to her ear.

"This isn't very platonic," I grit out, nipping at her ear, and teasing her previous attempts to keep me at arms length.

She bears down on me harder, bringing her mouth to mine. "You don't do this with all your friends?" she teases, smiling against my lips.

"Jae tries, but he's not really my type."

"Shame, he's pretty hot." I pinch her side, making her jump and land directly on my hard length as she steadies herself with her hands on my bare chest.

Her nails scrape against my skin, and we both groan before I capture her lips with mine.

Gasping for breath, my voice is husky. "What do you need from me, Sunshine?"

She moans at the sweet nickname I've given her in such a filthy position as she he grinds against my length, desperately searching for friction.

I tug on her hair.

"*Fuck*," she sighs, and I realize my girl likes it a little rough. That knowledge goes straight to my head, making me feel out of control as I buck up into her.

"Do you need to use me, baby?" She grinds down onto me, ratcheting both of our collective pleasure higher and higher, chasing that explosive finale I'm desperate to give her. "Whatever you want me to be, whatever you need me to do, it's yours. Say the word." I suck on the patch of skin beneath her ear before she grabs my face and hauls it back to hers.

Our lips collide in a mess of tongue and teeth as she rubs against me with abandon, and I groan, swelling beneath the grey sweats, climbing to that final peak of pleasure.

I'm impossibly hard. Even with the clothing separating us, I can feel how perfectly she's enveloping me, her warmth seeping through layers of cotton, driving me mad. It's a taste of how she would feel bared to me, too much and not enough all at the same time.

It would never be enough with her when my body is screaming more, more, more.

She mewls. "I'm so close. Please, I'm going to—"

I move both of my hands to her hips, holding her down firmly on top of me to rock her body at a punishing pace. "That's it, Silver. Let me hear the pretty sounds you make when you come undone for me."

She whimpers and rocks against me, desperate and needy as pinpricks of pleasure gather at the base of my spine. I've never come like this, with such little contact, but Silver's cries of pleasure interspersed with the hot breaths puffing against my ear are about to send me right over the edge into oblivion. I lean into her, licking and sucking at her neck, and her hands grasp onto my bare back, nails digging in and providing a delicious bite of pain that makes my cock twitch.

I'm holding her hips, fingers spilling over on the top of her round ass, guiding her movements as her pleasure peaks and she unravels on top of me.

The moan that claws out of her throat is guttural and uninhibited and so sexy, I tip over the edge with her, biting her neck to muffle my groan as I spill into my pants, unable to control myself.

Sweat beads her temple when she pulls back and kisses me, lazy and unhurried, as we both fight to catch our breath.

"I wasn't planning on...that," I say, not wanting her to think I expected this.

She leans back slightly. "Do you regret it?"

I brush a rogue strand of pale blonde hair out of her eyes. "Not a fucking chance."

She gives me a disbelieving smile that has me sitting up to capture her lips again. My intention was to keep it sweet, but I easily get carried away, sweeping my tongue into her mouth on impulse, getting drunk on her taste.

She cries against my mouth before she tears herself away, and I chase after her lips like a lost man in the desert chases an oasis.

She rests her forehead against mine. "You should probably go before someone sees you."

I wrap my arms around her waist, not wanting to leave but knowing I have to. But before I do, I take a leap of faith, hoping she'll jump with me. "Can I see you this weekend?"

I can see a grain of fear behind her eyes, this bit of unknown territory she doesn't know how to navigate. But it fades the longer the question hangs in the air, replaced by something that looks a lot like determination.

"Yes." She leans down and kisses me one last time before hopping off my lap.

I pop into the bathroom to clean up and change back into my now-dry clothes from the night before.

Color stains my cheeks as I hold the ruined sweatpants in my fist. "I can wash these and bring them back to you."

A grin splits Silver's beautiful face. "No need. I'm going to sell them on the dark web. People will buy anything these days."

"You bastard!"

A shoe comes soaring towards me, but I duck, narrowly evading the house slipper careening toward my face as it flies through the still-open doorway behind me.

"What the hell?"

Jae steps out of the kitchen to my left, hands on his hips, a dramatic pout lining his mouth.

"You've been gone all night, no note. Who is she? Who are you cheating on me with?"

"You're ridiculous." I kick off my shoes by the door and head into the kitchen Jae exited before he assaulted me with a shoe.

I grab ingredients out of the fridge to make myself something to eat as my best friend hops up on the kitchen counter and crosses his arms, giving me a *very* pointed look. A *tell me everything* look. I will absolutely not be telling him everything. Some things are sacred.

"Dude, did you and Silver..." He trails off but makes a lewd gesture with his hands.

I swat at him with the spatula I'm holding. "Stop. It's not like that."

"You really like her, huh?"

I choose not to say anything, turning my back to him and face the stove.

What I feel for her doesn't feel like it can be encompassed by the word 'like'. It feels like coming home after being gone for too long, finally settled. It feels like when you're at the top of a rollercoaster, and your heart is in your throat but you're still excited for the moment you drop. It feels like fireworks over the lake on New Year's Eve, exhilarating and brimming with endless possibilities.

I nod my head instead, a small, nonverbal admission and nothing more.

I flip the omelet I made out onto a plate and hand it to Jae before starting a second one for myself. "I told her about Maddie."

The clink of fork against plate immediately halts as the reality of what I've confessed hits Jae square in the chest.

"That's...Wow. Are you okay? Was it hard for you?" he asks while setting his plate down and giving me his full attention. Jae knows me better than just about anyone, and he's the only person I ever felt semi-comfortable talking to about my brother. I couldn't talk to my family; Mom would start to cry immediately, Laurel was dealing with her own trauma surrounding being there, and Dad— well, Dad blamed me for it all. But even the truths I told to my best friend were limited, too afraid to confess that the nightmares were making sleep impossible. I stayed awake instead, sometimes for days, before my body gave in. I never told him, anyone, about how that lack of sleep almost cost me my hand while I was using a carving saw at work. It was that slip up that made me seek over-the-counter medication so I wouldn't worry my family or friends.

"Not in the way you would think. It was hard to talk about initially, but it felt right with her."

Everything feels right with her. Lapses in silence didn't feel awkward. Peppering each other with questions under the guise of a game in an effort to get to know each other didn't feel suffocating. Her in my arms, me in her bed, it all feels natural, like we've been in each other's orbit for a millennia, constantly passing each other until we were perfectly aligned in this moment in time.

I've never felt this way for anyone. I've dated in the past, had a couple more serious girlfriends and a few too many flings in my twenties, but none of them gave me the same knee-weakening feeling I get when I'm with Silver. Colors are more vibrant when she's around, life feels fuller, and I'm pretty sure her kiss could cure any ailment.

I left her only an hour ago, and I'm already desperate to get back to her, to taste her lips again. I think it's safe to say I'm going to be replaying this morning's events in my head until the day I die. The soft noises she made in my ear as I kissed up and down her neck, her head thrown back in ecstasy as she used me to bring herself to the brink—nothing could ever compare.

"What about your job? The no mingling with the tenants law that had you nervous before?" Jae's question shakes me out of the memories of Silver above me.

"I don't know. I just...I need to be near her."

Jae whistles loudly in the small confines of our shared kitchen as he resumes eating his omelet. "Does she feel the same?"

That's the million dollar question, isn't it? I knew on a base level, Silver harbored some type of feelings for me, but did they run as deep as mine? I no longer believed I was just a fling for her. No, we definitely broke through the stainless steel wall she had erected around herself, a wall that was rightfully constructed and maintained over the years. But while she says she wants to try with me, will she be able to when the rubber meets the road? Will I be run over in the process? Despite it all, I know one thing with certainty: she will always be worth any risk.

I evade his question.

"What are you doing up this early anyway?" It was only seven in the morning on a Saturday.

"I have a coffee date with a Pilates instructor, and she wanted to go after her six a.m. class. I figured I'd hit the gym after that before heading into Anarchy." He shoves the final few bites of his breakfast into his mouth.

"I'm telling Laurel you've moved on from her." I scoop egg onto my fork and bring it to my mouth right as he smacks it out of my hand.

"You wouldn't dare."

"She'll be so relieved to be rid of you."

"That's just a lie she likes to tell herself to stop thinking about me naked."

"Too far."

He nods his head. "I sensed that was maybe too far."

I chuckle as I reach to grab another fork from the drawer. Laurel and Jae would be great together if there wasn't a country between the two of them. That, and the fact that my sister seems to barely tolerate him for reasons unknown to me.

"Do you want to come to the studio later and get a new piece? I had my noon appointment bail on me, and if I don't fill the time, I'll be relegated to doing all the tourist walk-ins. If I have to do one more *live, laugh, love*, I'm going to walk into traffic."

My gut reaction is to say no, to hold on to that memory of Maddie and not have another experience like the one I shared with him on his birthday. But something about the idea feels right. I don't know if it's because I feel at home in New York, or if it's the effect Silver has had on me these last few weeks, but I find myself *wanting* to do it. I can almost hear Maddie joyously whooping in my ear at the idea. "Yeah, that would be cool."

A wide smile stretches across Jae's face and crinkles the corners of his eyes in excitement. "I know just the piece."

Chapter 19

Silver

I'm still riding the high of this morning when I step inside Brownstone Books and immediately into a disaster.

At least two inches of water is covering the floor and rising by the second in time with my panic. How the hell has this happened? The only thing that could be more detrimental to a bookstore than flooding is fire. As grateful as I am that I'm dealing with an inch or two of water as opposed to bonfire kindling, this is the absolute last thing I need on a Saturday. It's our most profitable day of the week, and I can't afford to close to deal with this.

Racing over to our stockroom to access our bathroom where I assume the water is originating from, I stop short when I see the damage to our back stock. Storage in New York is a dime a dozen, and my little shop has always severely lacked the proper space needed to house all our inventory. As a solution, we resorted to stacking on the floor—the same floor now covered in fluid.

Holding back tears, I rush into the staff bathroom and shut off the water valve before grabbing my phone and calling an emergency plumber.

Half an hour and one hastily written *"opening late"* sign on the door later, Steve the Septic Savior is finishing up his assessment.

"From what I can tell, it's a combination of your pipes being older than God and a pretty nasty blockage. All the pressure coalesced and ruptured."

Has anyone in the history of the world had the same shit poor luck as I've had with pipes lately? Did I piss off some vengeful plumbing deity?

"And how much is that going to cost me?"

Bracing for the impact of his estimate never could have prepared me for his answer.

"My estimate is somewhere around five grand." My heart sinks down to my feet, through the floor, and straight into the Earth's core, where I currently wished I was instead of here.

Five grand means depleting the rest of the money in my savings and giving up my dreams of the second floor. That's just for the cost to fix this catastrophe; it doesn't include replacing the damaged inventory, renting industrial fans to dry out the shop floor, or the potential damage caused to the floorboards.

Fuck. What brand of misplaced confidence did I have, thinking I could pull this off? I had nothing in my life I could point to to indicate I would be able to accomplish something of this magnitude, and that stupidity is going to bleed me dry.

I am Icarus, and this store is the sun burning my wings.

"Can you start today?"

"Yup, I'll just need to go grab some supplies. I can be back in around an hour."

Steve heads out as I grab a mop while wondering if it's too late to start selling feet pics online until I've come out the other end of this renovation period.

The pressure sitting on my shoulders feels so immense, I think it might crush me. I am the sole provider for Holly and Carmen's income now; this isn't just about me. It has to work out. There is no other option. People are counting on me for the first time ever. Still, I can't deny that the feeling of others relying on me makes me feel cagey, like I need to cut and run.

But my insecurity is a Hydra, and that bitch is rearing its nine heads right about now in every aspect of my life. My ability to run a store—let alone rebuild it—coupled with my fears surrounding Hendrix and this...relationship has me on pins and needles.

It's just after noon, and I haven't heard from him since he snuck out of my apartment this morning. I'm loath to admit it, but for the first time in my life, I'm anticipating when I'll see him again. The fact that I haven't heard from him yet makes me feel like maybe I shouldn't have divulged so much to him last night.

Either way, it's not what I need to focus on right now.

Maybe more than the business would come to bite me in the ass by the time we got to the re-opening in a few weeks.

If I'm even able to pull it off at all.

If one more person asks why the store is a mess, I'm going to scream.

Yes, it looks like a tornado tore through it, and yes, it looks a bit random with the mismatched shelves, mess of shipment scattered throughout, and industrial fans drying out the floorboards, but can they not see I'm teetering on the edge of a mental breakdown? I look like a frenzied hyena on the hunt for dinner, for fuck's sake—which is precisely when my stomach growls and everyone starts to look like a slice of pizza.

When the jingling of the bell above the door signals a customer, I suppress a groan. There is a special place in hell for the people who come into a store right before closing. Nevertheless, I am the proprietor of this fine business and have to try and get money out of this person before I resort to turning tricks on the corner of the block.

I twist to greet the customer and stop when I see who's in front of me.

"Hi," I squeak out.

"Hey, Sunshine." Hendrix's smile feels like freshly baked donuts, warm and sweet. I want to guzzle down a dozen of those smiles.

"What are you doing here?" He stares at me with a mix of humor and confusion. "I just mean that it's Saturday. We don't work on Saturdays."

"Can I still see you on Saturdays? Or are they reserved for some sort of pagan sacrificial ceremonies?" He's dressed in slim cut jeans and a dark green sweater, the combination doing horrendously primal things to my insides.

"That's every first Saturday, actually. I can add you to the group chat if you want to join next time."

His resulting laugh is loud and carefree and so damn sexy, I fear I may combust. Someone is going to have to roll me out of here on a stretcher, because Hendrix Wells is the most beautiful man I've ever met. He gets even sexier when he pulls a takeout bag from behind his back.

"I thought you could use some dinner."

"I could kiss you."

"You *definitely* could. I sure as hell won't stop you." He smirks.

So, I do just that. I walk right up to him, angle myself up on my tippy toes, and press my lips to his. The kiss lasts only seconds, but it has the effect of a ninety minute deep tissue massage the way all the anxiety seeps from my bones.

I settle back down on my heels and press my forehead to his firm chest as his free hand settles onto my hip, squeezing me tightly, deliciously.

"What happened in here?" His gaze darts around the store, taking in the mess and fans.

"Noticed that, did you?" Hendrix drills me with a look. "Pipe burst and flooded the store."

"Wow, you must be cursed or something," I scoff in agreement.

"What did you bring me?" I ask, nodding toward the bag.

"Chow House."

"Who told you?"

"The secrets of the Pentagon? I believe that was Nicholas Cage."

I swat his arm. "No," I laugh. "Chow House is my favorite Chinese place in the city."

He smiles softly. "It's mine too. I've been getting it since I was in college. Best sautéed green beans on the East Coast."

"You would point out the vegetable. Please tell me there's something fried in there." I lean forward, trying to peek in the bag, but he holds it out of reach.

"Be patient, and I'll tell you."

"Diabolical," I murmur, turning to move away before he hauls me back with the hand settled around my waist, placing a kiss on my forehead, lips lingering for a beat too long, making me *melt*.

"Do you want to eat here or somewhere else?"

"You overestimate my ability to make it further than a few steps with food at stake. We can eat here." I reach out with grabby hands for the bag, and he finally acquiesces by giving it to me before I lead us toward the back to the only available space for us to sit. I settle down on the floor between two stacks of freestanding shelves and start pulling out to-go containers, music from the store speakers setting the tone for our dinner.

I waste no time inhaling a spring roll at record speed, and when I look up, Hendrix stares at me with a fondness I'm not used to. It's a heady feeling that makes me feel cherished and frightened in equal measure.

I hold out the bag with the remaining roll in offering, but he shakes his head. "You have it."

"Are you sure?" Hoping he doesn't want it, I lift the roll slowly towards my mouth, praying he won't change his mind before I can demolish the second serving.

"I like watching you eat."

A slow smile spreads over my stuffed cheeks. "Pervert."

Hendrix gives me another one of his free laughs, and I think I'd do whatever, say whatever, to keep hearing the sound. His laugh—the real one—is like the wind whistling through the evergreens, like cerulean waves crashing down onto the shore, like the sun hitting your face after polar night—natural, strong and incandescently beautiful.

"I just mean I like seeing you happy. Those spring rolls were making you *very* happy. You let out this soft sigh after taking the first bite, and it was the cutest fucking thing I've ever heard."

I'm positive my face has gone beet red. "I could use a little happy today," I admit.

"Tell me about it?"

"I know it's not a big deal, and worse things could have happened, but the damage is zapping the rest of my savings. I can't fix the second floor now. I'm feeling a little morose about it." I shove the last of the spring roll in my mouth.

"It's okay to be upset," he says.

Old habits rise, and I feel the need to deflect. "This is helping, though." I point at the spread of food. "Will you tell me more about your life back in Seattle?"

He looks down at the container of beef and broccoli, and I worry I might've taken it a step too far, maybe he's still feeling too raw after last night's conversation. "I'll tell you whatever you want to know."

"Why did you move back after school? You seem to really like it here." There's an ease to the set of his shoulders now that was absent when we first met.

"I made a deal with my dad—" he uses his chopsticks to take a bite of the savory meat— "when I was eighteen and picking a college. I wanted to see what the world had to offer. I wanted to experience somewhere completely different than what I knew. But I was a kid with no way to afford tuition, so we made an agreement. I could go to college in New York, but I had to study business, and I had to move home after graduation so I could be primed to take over the family business."

"Sounds like that wasn't what you wanted?" I fish for more information, desperate to know everything about the man who has me so tied up in knots.

"That's one way of putting it. Dad values control over everything else, so I agreed to his plan just so I could have four years of freedom. The thing is, I liked the work. I liked designing something and bringing it to life with my own two hands. It just wasn't enough for him. I wanted to *create*, and he wanted me to manage the shop, take over for him. I didn't want to leave my life here, but I had made a deal and dad had always drilled into me the importance of a man's word. A few years later, Maddie died, and well, you know the rest."

"What are your siblings like?"

This brings a soft smile to his face, and I have to hold myself back from lunging forward and tackling him to the floor. This big, brawny man is so soft and gooey inside, and it's making my pulse accelerate.

"Laurel is a spitfire, always has been. She's definitely the type to punch you in the face and then read you the riot act as to why *you* deserved it."

"A woman after my own heart."

"Yeah, I figured you'd say that," he scoffs. "Maddox..." He takes a second to gather himself. "Maddox was the life of the party. There was never a dull moment when he was around. You remind me a lot of him, actually. Just so full of life, so brave."

Oh. Oh no.

My nose starts to tingle. "Brave?" Surely I didn't hear him right.

"You don't think buying up your favorite place in the world and creating a community, not knowing if it would pan out, with no guarantees for success, is brave?"

"I guess when you put it like that..." I try to joke, feeling sheepish and unable to escape his penetrating stare.

"Don't minimize what you're doing here, Sunshine. I was there at book club. I see how your friends look at you with awe and admiration. It's the same way I look at you every day." He gives me a cocksure smile. "Well, the way I look at you might be a little different than your friends." And then, he, honest to God, winks at me. Who knew a wink could feel so charged?

The song playing softly over the speakers changes then into something slow and aching, and Hendrix jumps up and extends his hand out to me.

I look up at him in confusion. "What are you doing?"

"Dance with me."

Chapter 20

Silver

My gaze darts around, glancing at the many safety hazards scattered throughout the store. "Here?"

"Yes, here. Between hundreds of books filled with romantic stories, let me give you one of your own." He keeps his hand outstretched, waiting on faith alone that I'll take it and join him.

"There are stories about murder in here too, you know." He spears me with a *don't be a smartass* glare.

I tentatively reach out, my nerves making my insides quake like tectonic plates are shifting inside my body, as he grabs ahold and lifts me from the floor. The strength of his pull, however, is more than I expected, and the trajectory has me flying up into his hard body.

"Oophfff."

A laugh rumbles out of his chest as I let my forehead fall against it and catch my breath.

"Apparently, I have a thing for smacking into your statuesque body," I mumble against his sweater.

"Statuesque?" His breath ruffles my hair.

I glance up at him now. "You know—tall, hard...imposing."

The look on his face is a mixture of humor and pure mischief. "If that's what does it for you, I'll be whatever you want me to be."

I don't know exactly when our roles reversed in this...whatever you would call what we are, but I used to be the one making him flustered, not the other way around. This simply will not do.

I trail my finger down through the valley of his chest, hook it through his belt loop, and tug. "I thought we were gonna dance, twinkle toes."

Hendrix's eyes darken as they drop down to my index finger. They linger there a beat longer than necessary, and my smile grows exponentially wider. When he looks up and sees my expression, he snorts and grabs my wandering hand.

"How about we put your hands up here?" he says as he places both of my hands around his neck.

I immediately thread my fingers through the strands at the nape of his neck, giving them a little tug, and the groan that escapes his mouth unwillingly is so delicious, I feel it deep in my core. We're playing with fire here, and I don't think either of us care if we get burned.

"You're trouble," he groans.

"Don't call me by my government name." My smile is positively wicked, and he retaliates by slowly sliding one of his large palms from the small of my waist up to press between my shoulder blades, fingering the ends of my hair like I did his. But my attention is quickly diverted by his other hand settling so low on my back, the tips of his fingers skim the top of my ass, digging in possessively.

Hendrix wastes no time tightening his hold on me, connecting our bodies with one firm push of his hand into my back. I gasp at the sudden proximity. Heat tingles up my spine from the delicious friction as he leads us in a gentle sway to the music.

Between rows of romance books and the culmination of weeks' worth of our hard work and twenty questions, Hendrix starts to sing along with the song, low and hypnotic. He's not particularly good, but I think that makes this moment even more perfect.

"–and the edges of your soul I haven't seen yet," he croons in my ear, low and gravely. It would have made my knees buckle if he hadn't been keeping such a firm hold on me as he sways us back and forth.

We're suspended in a moment of what I can only describe as peace, my face buried in his collarbone, his hovering just above my ear, breathing the lyrics into my soul, infusing his unspoken promises into every atom of my body.

Out of nowhere, the song kicks up, and Hendrix wastes no time guiding us along the uptick in melody, as if he anticipated it. Suddenly, we're flying through the room, dancing throughout the stacks and tables piled high with books, my right hand now in his as he dodges tables and industrial dryers left and right, spinning me under his arm as I laugh, wild and free. He brings us back to where we started when the song slows back to its original rhythm and settles us back into a gentle sway.

I stare up at him in wonder, both of us panting through smiles as our heart rates begin to slow. I nuzzle closer into him as the song ends, and neither of us pull away. His hand strokes the back of mine as he leans down and brushes a kiss under my ear that sends goosebumps prickling over my skin.

A soft moan escapes from my lips as I bring myself impossibly closer to him, trying to burrow myself into his skin, begging for more. I stretch up onto my toes, and he angles his body down until our noses touch, a moment of vulnerability before we dive into the deep. He searches my eyes, asking without words, and I nod my head in assent, begging him to give us what we both want, what we *need*. This connection between us sparking like a live wire.

If I think he'll give into the desire we're both feeling like a blazing inferno, I'm wrong. He brings his lips back down to my ear, tracing a path down my neck, slow and languorous like a drop of honey out of a bottle. I breathe out a sigh, angling my neck to give him better access. He smiles against my skin before softly biting down, making us both groan.

Hendrix snakes his tongue up my throat to my mouth, settling his lips against mine in the sweetest connection. I twist my arms up and around his neck once more, bringing his face to mine as he settles his palms on the top of my skirt over my hips, pushing me backward into the wall of books behind us. The shelf bites into the middle of my back, but I can't find it in me to care as Hendrix devours me. He licks into my mouth, the stubble on his chin scraping my face, making me wonder what it would feel like between my legs. The thought alone has me clenching my thighs together.

"More," I pant into his mouth. "I need more of you." I grip at his belt, but he stops my hand and pulls back an inch. Just as I think he's about to put the kibosh on this whole thing, he slowly sinks to his knees, and my brain short circuits. My day is about to get so much better.

"Why do you look stunned?" He chuckles, face inches away from where he's about to find me embarrassingly wet for him. "Are you nervous, baby?"

I muster up as much bravado as possible. "I'm simply admiring the view."

"I'll give you anything you want, Silver. All you have to do is say the word." His palms skate up each leg over my sheer tights, his warmth searing me like a brand. "Do you want to come on my hand or on my tongue?"

I nearly choke. I've imagined this very scenario, but in my wildest fantasies, I never imagined Hendrix to be quite so sure and assertive. I'm used to having to direct men in the bedroom if I wanted to get off, but something tells me that won't be the case here. Hendrix will know exactly how to handle me.

"Both." I score my hand through his dark locks.

His eyes darken as he reaches under my skirt for the banding of my tights. His fingers slip inside as he looks up at me, waiting. It takes me a second to realize he's asking for consent. "Yes," I whisper, desperate for him to continue.

He grips the edges of the nylon and slowly peels them down, exposing my thighs to the air. I kick out of my shoes and tights as he reaches for the side zipper of my skirt, and next thing I know, I'm standing in my underwear.

Hendrix sits back on his heels, breathing deeply as he takes me in, rubbing his hand back and forth over the stubble I want to feel scraping against my thighs.

"Fuck," he grits out. "I've been dreaming about these little scraps of lace you call underwear since that first day I came to your apartment. It's sick how much I've thought about it." He reaches out and runs his finger under the thin band of my pink lace thong. " Do you always wear things like this under all your colorful outfits?" He pulls the band back, snapping it onto my skin.

I shiver at his touch and the focus he has zeroed in at my center. "Pretty much," I say, shifting back and forth to help relieve some of the tension between my thighs.

The movement doesn't go unnoticed. "Didn't I tell you to be patient?" He tuts, pressing a kiss to my inner thigh, making me whimper.

"You're evil," I pant, heart pounding.

He places more soft kisses, intermixed with teasing bites to my thighs, ratcheting my anticipation higher and higher. "You won't be saying that in a few minutes."

"I'll get you back for this."

"I'm looking forward to that." The pure male arrogance in his voice is so arousing, I could slap myself for being so turned on. "But until then, I want to take my time. You don't go to a Michelin starred restaurant and not savor every bite, do you?" He sinks his teeth into my hip bone, hands cupping the back of my thighs. "Now be quiet and let me eat. The next sound out of your mouth better be my name or a moan."

Oh God. Where did he come from?

Slowly, so slowly I might scream, Hendrix pulls my underwear to the side and sees the evidence of my arousal practically dripping down my legs.

"Fuck." He parts me with his thumb, sliding the digit back and forth through my folds as a groan tears out of my throat. He pulls his finger out and sucks it into his mouth, moaning in pleasure. My eyes nearly cross at the filthy view. "Delicious."

I think I might die from the euphoria.

Hendrix grasps one of my thighs, placing it over his shoulder, then shocks the hell out of me by doing the same with my other thigh until I'm hovering in the air, his face inches away from my core.

"Perch that gorgeous ass on the shelf for me, Sunshine."

I look behind me at the recently renovated shelf and back to Hendrix. "What if I break it?" I whisper, as if anyone else could hear me.

He smirks a devil's grin at me. "Then I'll fix it. It's kinda my thing, you know."

"You're insufferable like this," I complain with no real conviction as I obey his order and settle my ass gently on the shelf, a leg on each shoulder anchoring me.

"That's my girl," he praises, and I preen under the attention, my body flushing hot all over.

"There's a lot of talking coming out of that mouth..." I squirm against his grip, trying to bridge that final gap between us.

He places a chaste kiss to each of my hip bones, forcing me to wriggle against his grasp.

"Hendrix," I whine. Never in my life have I been so worked up when I've barely even been touched. Something about his brand of torture speaks to me on a level that feels borderline religious. Somehow, he knows my body and its needs intrinsically, as if he were made for me. No one could ever compare to him if this is what his foreplay feels like.

He chuckles against my skin, mouth mere inches away from where I need him, and I've had enough. I grab his hair in my fist, pulling him away from me with monumental effort when what I really want is him closer. His pupils are blown wide, looking up at me from between my legs, a man possessed. The sight has me close to detonating.

"You have five seconds before I take matters into my own hands."

His eyes darken even further. "As much as I want to watch you touch yourself, let's table that fantasy for another time. I'm focusing on a different one right now."

Before I can protest further, he finally bridges the gap, licking a path from my hip bone straight to where I'm open and weeping for release.

Hendrix shows me no mercy as he takes a moment to stare up at me through hooded lashes, holding eye contact as he gives my clit a gentle flick of his tongue that nearly makes me come on the spot. I throw my head back in euphoria, releasing a guttural cry as he latches on to my wet flesh with his lips, sucking me into his mouth in one swift move that has all the blood in my body rushing south, pulse hammering erratically in my center.

My hand dives back into his hair as my thighs clench on each side of his head, causing him to release a groan of his own as he reaches down with one hand and squeezes the bulge in his pants. Hendrix eases off my clit in a moment of reprieve before he dives back in like a man possessed, licking a hot stripe up my center before teasing the tip of his tongue over my swollen bud.

"Fuck, fuck, fuck," I grit out through clenched teeth, sweat beginning to sheen all over my body. He doesn't relent. He grants no clemency as he devours me like I'm his last supper, worshiping at my altar on his knees.

I never understood when women got so lost in a man, they couldn't see reason. But if *this* was what they were experiencing, I could now say I didn't blame them. Hendrix was a drugging combo of caring, smart, sexy, and secretly funny. And when you take that and factor in that the man has a tongue blessed by the gods? Yeah, I could see myself getting a little stupid for him.

"Fuck, Silver." The way he growls my name into my skin makes goosebumps prickle all over my skin. "You taste like sunshine and strawberries."

I press my hands into my mouth to stifle a whimper, but they're soon ripped away. When I look down at Hendrix, he's smiling up at me. "I want to hear your sounds, sweetheart. Hands back in my hair." He guides them back through his strands. "It's driving me mad."

I give the strands a tug, and he sighs into my pussy before he's back to working me into a frenzy. Licks melt into bites that melt into sucks, intensifying my pleasure so high, my entire core is tense with the need to relieve the pressure. I start grinding my hips against his face, no longer caring if I break the shelf I'm perched on if it brings this madness to a head.

"Please," I beg, not able to form a coherent thought.

"I've got you."

I bring his head back to my center, his beard providing the most delectable scratch of friction against my inner thighs. I'm so close, it almost hurts. The pressure in my lower belly dances with the tingles lighting up my spine, waiting to explode like a firework show.

True to his word, Hendrix knows just what I need as he brings his fingers up, pausing at my opening as he waits for me to consent.

"Yes, fuck. Please."

He wastes no time working the first finger in as I moan so loudly, it reverberates through the shop floor. He tests what my body is comfortable with as he strokes his finger in and out, bringing his tongue back to my clit in a dizzying rhythm.

"You're so wet. So tight. Can I give you one more?"

His filthy words send my head into a tailspin as I nod my head so vigorously, I'm surprised I don't bash it against the shelf behind me.

He pulls out his one finger, slowly going back in with the added second, and I'm moments from cresting over that hill. My breathing is frantic, my moans a soft mewl as I beg without words for him to let me come.

When he presses his tongue to my clit, sucking it into his mouth at the same time he hooks his fingers inside me, hitting the perfect spot, I shatter. One hand flies out to the shelf next to me, the other staying in his hair as I cry out. My legs shake against his shoulders as he continues to lick me through the aftershocks of my orgasm. I'm fairly certain I blacked out for a nano second there, because my vision is spotty as I come down from the height of ecstasy.

Hendrix finally pulls back from me, but not before giving me a soft kiss to the top of my pelvis, so tender after doing such dirty things to me just seconds prior. The juxtaposition of that realization has me warm all over.

Slowly, he unhooks each leg from his shoulders, gently setting me down while making sure I'm steady enough to stand on my own. He reaches for my tights, discarded off to the side, and helps me step into them, gently guiding them up my legs until they're settled over my hips. He follows that with my skirt until I'm fully clothed again. As he stands to his full and glorious height, Hendrix leans down and gives me a soft kiss, the taste of me still coating his lips. I see him subtly adjust the bulge in his pants, and I reach out instinctively for his belt, but he steps out of my reach.

"Am I ever getting in your pants?" I quip, trying to soothe this sting of his rejection. He just gave me the most mind-blowing orgasm; the least I can do is return the favor.

"Most definitely."

"Then what's the deal? Let me return the favor." Unless he's into—I just blurt it out. "Is orgasm denial a kink of yours? Because, no judgement, but I'd like to know now before my pride takes another blow."

"Definitely not one of my kinks, trust me." He's staring down into my eyes while I try to puzzle him out.

"But you *do* have kinks? Let me guess." I start listing off the more outlandish fetishes. "Clown fetish? No, I bet it's not as exciting as that. Spanking? But that doesn't feel like you. OH! Jello." His eyes sparkle, amused by my rambling.

"Jello?" His eyebrow tips up.

"It's a real thing. You can look it up."

"Do I want to know how you know about it?"

"Probably not. But I do want to know why you won't let me touch you." I settle my hands onto my hips.

"For starters, tasting you was as much for my own enjoyment as it was for you, so stop calling it a favor that needs to be repaid. Second, I won't be like the other men who have overlooked all that you are." I start to protest, to defend the men who took the only thing I was willing to give, but he doesn't let me. "I understand that's what you wanted. I'm not saying either party was wrong, but I need you to understand something." He brings his knuckle under my chin, tipping it up so I'm forced to hold eye contact. "You are a *force*, spectacular in every sense of the word. Wildly brave and kind and far too funny for your own good. You're smart and spontaneous and open-hearted. You're the most beautiful person I've ever met, and I don't deserve you. I want to *earn* it, I want to earn *you*—your heart."

I swallow hard, holding eye contact but feeling...unworthy of his praise. How could he possibly think he doesn't deserve me?

"I know this is uncomfortable for you to hear," he carries on, "but I need you to know who you are to everyone around you. Being near you is the first time I've felt *alive* in two years. You are important. I'm in this with you. I want you so bad, it physically hurts, but I want to do right by you before we take that next step."

"Oh." God, this is so much for me to process. It isn't a bad thing, but it makes me nervous. I feel like I'm going to fuck it up.

He leans forward and kisses my forehead as my eyelids flutter closed.

"Can I take you on a date?"

My eyes pop open. "What?"

"You heard me. Let me take you on a date."

My eyes flit back and forth over his face, sincerity shining through every pore. Every time I'm with him, I feel more and more out of my element. I've yet to decide if that's a good or bad thing. I know Kena would tell me it's a good thing to be pushed out of my comfort zone, that it's where I would flourish. Maybe he's right.

"I'll go on a date with you. No need to beg."

He tips his head back on a laugh. "Oh, I'd wager there's plenty of begging in my future."

My cheeks flame at the implication, but I don't deny anything. We start to clean up the shop, Hendrix picking up the dinner off the floor and me straightening up the tables and shelves. We intermittently sneak glances at each other that last a little longer than necessary and always end with one of us asking a question to break the tension.

When everything's settled, Hendrix holds his hand out to me for the second time tonight, and this time, I don't hesitate to take it. I see the breath he was holding release. "Let's get ice cream while I walk you home."

"Are you going to get a grandpa flavor? How many AARP mailers do you get weekly?"

"Rum raisin sounds good."

"I'll corrupt you yet."

"I don't doubt it, Sunshine."

Chapter 21

Hendrix

"It's massively under baked—"

Paul Hollywood fondles the inside of a loaf of bread while chastising some poor amateur baker through the speakers on my phone. I get an hour each day for lunch, and this is how I've been spending them lately, legs kicked up on supply boxes, sketch pad propped against my thighs, charcoal pencil in hand.

My thoughts oscillate between the piece I'm drawing and Silver writhing against my shoulders, gasps of pleasure falling from her beautiful mouth. It's safe to say I've been less than productive and sporting a semi every day over the past week. We've had a repeat of last weekend nearly every night this week while working in the bookstore, and it has made our progress...less than impressive.

I stare down at the varying shades of gray that make up the design I've been working on. It's a light wood grain, four leg table with intricate floral designs running up and down the legs. Each one is carved with vines wrapping around different flowers. It's an heirloom piece, something to be passed down from generation to generation.

These are the designs my dad hated. It all comes down to what's quick and efficient, any ounce of creativity sucked right out of a project. I was a robot producing carbon copies of big box store furniture when I worked for him.

What the hell is the point of doing custom builds if you aren't going to actually *customize* anything to the client? If I had my own shop—I catch myself. There is no point in dwelling on something that isn't a possibility, I have no capital and no clients. But if I let myself daydream, I could admit I don't hate the thought of that path, could easily see myself at a work table, sawing and shaping before coming home to Silver with sawdust snowing out of my hair. I'd shower the wood shavings off before cooking us dinner, and we'd spend the rest of the night on the couch—a book in her hand with her legs across my lap, while I trace designs against her skin until she's too distracted by my touch to read anymore.

A knock on the door jolts me out of my fantasies and has me sitting upright. Before I can answer the door myself, Mr. Fairbanks steps through, looking around the room with a sneer, drooping jowls making his expression even more severe.

"Hello, sir," I greet him.

He takes in my discarded notebook, array of charcoal pencils, and the frantic bakers fighting for their loaves of bread on the tiny screen of my phone.

"Hard at work, I see," he condemns.

"I'm on my lunch break."

He heaves out a dramatic sigh, indicating his annoyance over not being able to reprimand me, though I'm sure he'll find his moment sooner or later. Maybe the former, if I can't get my feelings where Silver is concerned under control.

"It's been brought to my attention that certain members of staff are being too friendly with some of the tenants."

Sooner it is, then.

"As far as I know, Tony always acts above board with the residents of the building, though I did see him and Mr. Harris chatting in the lobby the other day while they drank their morning coffee. Do you think they're organizing some sort of cabal?" Antagonizing him is probably not the wisest course of action, but I can't help it. I'm feeling more myself these days than I have in a very long time, and I'll be damned if I let him ruin my good mood.

Fairbanks levels me with a withering glare. "I informed you upon employment that there would be no—"

"Are you accusing me of something, sir?" I stand so I can meet him eye to eye.

He shrinks away from me ever so slightly, but he seems to catch himself, remembering that he's the one with the power in our dynamic.

"I'm just here to *remind* you of the consequences of such breach in our terms of employment. Fraternization with tenants will be met with immediate dismissal."

"I haven't forgotten."

"The walls have eyes and ears, Mr. Wells. You'd do well to remember that in the future." Then, he departs, leaving the stench of Drakkar Noir floating through the air behind him.

I almost feel guilty lying. I did tell him he had nothing to worry about in this area when he hired me. I was being truthful then. I *didn't* intend to fall for Silver, actively avoided it in the beginning, but it happened, and I'm too far gone to do anything about it now.

For all intents and purposes, I'm hers.

And no job is going to stand in the way of that.

However, it did make me wonder who's spreading gossip and what they may have seen. Did someone see me leaving Silver's apartment a couple weeks ago? I had taken every precaution, and the only person around when I came into the building with Silver was Tony. But he wouldn't say anything. Tony liked his stories and idle chit chat, but he cared about everyone, and felt like they were his own family. He would never do anything to hurt them in any way.

Either way, it didn't matter. The only way I'll stop seeing her is if she told me it's what she wanted, even if it killed me.

But until then, it's clear I need to find a different job before I get fired. It's crazy how the thought of that doesn't send me into a crisis like it would have a couple months ago. Pre-Silver, this job was my lifeline, my ticket to staying in New York, and I'm not sure when it happened, but now, *she* was. She came in and flipped me inside out, forcing me to show her my tender, pulverized insides, and I survived, was better for it even.

There are thousands of businesses throughout the thirteen miles that encompass Manhattan. I'll have to find something to tie me over until I figure out what I really want to do, develop a more permanent plan now that the situation with The Langham was a bit fraught. I don't want to have to hide what I feel when I'm around Silver. I want to be able to wake up next to her, to bring her her favorite coffee in the mornings, to *not* sneak out in the dark hours of the morning. After all she's been through, she deserves to know that she's my priority.

Two years ago, Maddox told me I needed to learn to live life the way I wanted, and I think I finally understand. I ran away and found my home again, here, with my friends and a woman I was falling for. This is where I want to be, where I want to build a life. It's high time I figure out a plan for it—my own plan, no one else's. No more wandering around aimlessly, adrift on an unpredictable wind, or living according to someone else's whims. If Silver can be brave enough to risk everything she has to save the store, I can be brave too.

I pull out my phone, feeling the urge to talk to her.

> **Hendrix**
> So I've been thinking...

Silver responds almost immediately, and it brings a smile to my face.

> **Sunshine**
> Sounds dangerous. Are you wearing safety gear?

> **Hendrix**
> Hilarious. Do you have plans tonight?

> **Sunshine**
> There's an evening squirrel watching club I was thinking of attending in Central Park.
>
> But I could be convinced otherwise.

> **Hendrix**
> I'll pick you up at the store.

> **Sunshine**
> Do I get to know what we're doing?

> **Hendrix**
> No.

> **Sunshine**
> How am I supposed to tell every person I know where I am in the chance you turn out to be a murderer?

> **Hendrix**
> You don't. It's going to make the documentary that comes in ten years fascinating.

> **Sunshine**
> The perfect crime. No one would suspect you.

> **Hendrix**
> I'll see you soon, Sunshine.

A few hours later, I step through the doorway of Brownstone Books to find Carmen dusting the shelves.

"Christ, I forgot how hot you are," she states boldly, drawing a chuckle out of me.

"Thank you." I look around for a head of bright blonde hair and sea-foam green eyes, but I don't see Silver anywhere.

"No, seriously, it's no wonder why Sil won't stop talking about you." Her gaze admires me openly, and I start to squirm at being so baldly checked out.

"Oh? She talks about me?" I know it's pathetic to fish for intel, but any sort of outside confirmation that this insane buzzing in my chest is reciprocated is nice.

"Totally!" She bounces around the store, wiping down shelves and tables as she goes. "It's always Hendrix this, Hendrix that." She stops abruptly and puts a hand to her chest in dramatic reenactment. "Hendrix and I fixed this floorboard last night. Hendrix thought I should paint the shelves yellow. Hendrix is a fantastic kisser. Yada, yada, yada."

I cough into my hand. "She told you we kissed?"

A devious smile lights her face. "No, but you just did."

With perfect timing, Silver finally emerges from the back office. The sight of her immediately wipes away all coherent thought. She's wearing tight fitting jeans that hug her in the most sinful way, and a pink checkerboard sweater that ties at her chest but leaves a triangle of stomach exposed. Her hair is half pulled back, tendrils framing her face, offsetting the cherry earrings dangling from her lobes. She looks so cute, I don't know how I'm going to survive the night.

"What are you guys talking about?" Silver eyes Carmen skeptically.

"Nothing," I say, knowing she wouldn't want our business openly discussed like her employee seems inclined to do. "Are you ready?"

She nods and looks at Carmen. "Don't forget to lock up, and if I go missing or get murdered, point them in his direction." She hooks her thumb at me.

"Oh, I bet something gets murdered tonight..."

We both stare at Carmen, speechless, as she starts to cackle like a deranged demon.

Silver looks over at me. "And you thought I had no filter."

I usher her out the front door, leading us out into the crisp, late October air. The leaves on the trees lining the block are slowly starting to shift from green to a mix of yellows and orange as we make our way down the street.

"She scares me a bit."

Silver laughs, and it's bright and lovely. I want to bottle the sound and have it with me for a rainy day.

"So, where to, Romeo?"

We've reached the end of the block, her just a step ahead of me, when I grab her hand and whip her around, tugging her into me. I quickly lean down and capture her lips between mine. Surprise ebbs into a soft sigh as her body melts into mine. When I pull away, she's leaning forward, trying to chase after my mouth.

I settle my forehead against hers. "I've been dreaming of doing that all day."

"Call me Walt Disney then, cause I just made your dreams come true."

"You're ridiculous," I huff against her lips.

"I think you like that about me."

"More than you know. Now, let's go, *Walt*. There's romance to be had." I grab her hand, leading her towards the subway, the sound of her laughter trilling behind me like wind chimes.

Chapter 22

Silver

At twenty-eight years old, I'm on the very first legitimate date of my life. And I'm...nervous. As a teenager, I went on casual hang outs in the park with a group of people, but I don't really consider that a date. But this? What we're doing here tonight is most definitely a date.

Hendrix and I walk down the block hand in hand, passing by brick inlaid townhomes, tiny cafés, and boutiques, and I absently think we must look like the picture of domesticity. The people we're passing would never know I have a serious case of the bubble guts because the man clutching my hand and steering me around the city to take me out is so perfect, I have a hard time believing he's real.

When I spotted him in the shop tonight, my heart stopped, and my stomach did a back handspring so sharp, it would make an Olympic gymnast envious. He was standing there, talking to Carmen, open and friendly, looking so handsome, I couldn't get my heart to stop racing. It should be illegal for him to look that good in jeans, a white tee, and an oversized leather jacket. That was distinctly a very normal outfit as far as menswear goes, and yet he looked like he'd just stepped off a movie set—golden skin gleaming under the shop lights, full mouth smiling, hair perfectly tousled in a way that made me want to rake my hands through it like I had so many other times the past week. I hesitated to make myself known just so I could openly admire him.

But it isn't just my attraction to him that makes my chest ache.

It's his vulnerability with me, the way he's opened up over the past couple months and allowed me to see behind the curtain. It's how quick he is to pick up on my jokes and lob them right back at me, how I feel safer with him than anyone else. It's every time he shows up after working an eight hour shift to help me and never complains. He is kind, and selfless, and steadfast and funny and so sexy, my bones ache for him.

It was dizzying. Terrifying. I didn't want it to ever stop.

I was starting to have a vague understanding of how my mom must have felt for my dad, and that was a hard pill to swallow, giving her any kind of leniency over abandoning me in the wake of her heartbreak. *Our* heartbreak. It made me uncomfortable, thinking about it.

"What's wrong?" He lumbers over me, but his hold on me is gentle.

"Nothing." The look he gives me is assessing. "I promise."

He takes a beat to respond. "Come on, we gotta hop on the train."

We rush over to the subway station, dodging the rush of after-work traffic, and the whole time, Hendrix never lets go of my hand, creating a path for me through the throngs of people trying to get above ground and out of the station.

"Are you going to tell me where we're going now?" I grip his hand tighter.

"You're not one for surprises, are you?"

"I don't think anyone's ever surprised me with anything before." The unknown variables that always accompanied a surprise stressed me out, so I did my best to avoid them at all costs, mitigating any potential disappointment.

He finds us a spot to rest on the platform, caging me between his arms and a wall while we wait for the next train to arrive. Faint music floats from down the tracks, a musician playing a well-known hip-hop song on an electric violin.

Until you, I think. *I'm having a lot of firsts with you.*

A second later, a packed train pulls up, and we're whisked uptown. The subway crawls along the track, screeching metal against metal on every turn, jostling us around. Hendrix places my arms around his middle before pinning my body between his arms and the closed door, keeping me steady on my feet.

When he signals we've made it to our stop, I notice we've come all the way up to Washington Heights, a neighborhood in the northwest section of the city.

I give him an inquisitive look, but he just tugs me by my hand. "Let's go."

We exit the subway and walk for a couple blocks, passing a corner bodega with a grey shop cat sitting outside, a few chain eateries, and a deli with couple centenarians at a table outside playing a round of cards, before we stop in front of a place called Mimi's Bakery.

"Did you bring me all the way uptown for pastries?" I'm perplexed. "I mean, I'm not mad about it, but we do have plenty of bakeries closer to us."

"This is stop *one* of your personalized New York City donut tour." He is clearly very proud of himself for the idea.

"You're joking."

"Not even a little."

"But—but you hate donuts..." My voice trails off.

"But I like *you*."

I hold back the squeal that wants to burst out of me, acting unaffected by his words. "Yes, well...I'm very likable."

He chuckles as he ushers me inside the building, and we get in line to order. The bakery is very unassuming but has a vintage sort of charm, the kind where you feel like you've been transported into a southern grandma's kitchen. The walls are a buttercream yellow with white trim, varying shades of blue accenting throughout while antique frames in need of a good dusting are scattered around haphazardly.

"The rules are as follows—"

"Ah, now you're starting to sound like you again."

"Cute." I laugh as he continues. "We have this booklet I made." He pulls a tiny leather bound notebook out of his jacket pocket, and when he opens it, I can see he's labeled the top page with our first stop at Mimi's and has categories for rating. "By the end of the night, we'll have rated and found your favorite donut place in Manhattan."

"Wow, you sure know how to impress the ladies, don't you, Haskell?"

"As long as I'm impressing *you*, Saskia."

The line shifts forward, and we're suddenly face to face with a dark skinned woman with kind eyes. Her bright white smile greets us, happiness etched into every well-worn line on her face.

I glance down and see her name tag reads Mimi. "Is this your place?" I ask.

She beams. "For thirty-seven years. What can I get for you two today?"

"Do you have a recommendation?"

After inquiring about any allergies, she suggests the key lime pie donut and wraps one up for me. "What about you, sugar?" She gives Hendrix a flirtatious smile. I can't even blame her—he has that effect on me too.

"Just a coffee for me, please. Black, no cream or sugar."

"He has an aversion to joy," I quip.

"If that were true, I wouldn't be here with you, would I?" He knows that line was smooth as hell, based on the smug look on his face as he bends down and kisses my neck.

Mimi gives me a *you're in trouble* look. "You better watch out for that one with a tongue like that."

Oh, Mimi, you have no *idea.*

After saying thank you, we make our way to a table at the front against the window. Hendrix pulls out my seat for me in a feat of chivalry I've yet to experience in life before he takes the chair opposite me, setting his scoring book on the table between us.

"Alright, the categories are as follows..."

"It's such a turn on when you go all Type A on me." I bite my lip for extra humor, but he fixates on my mouth instead, not catching the joke.

"Whatever does it for you." Leaning back in his chair, he wraps his hands around his coffee cup as he nods toward my donut. "What are you waiting for?"

He rattles off the categories for judging as I pick up the

confection and bring it to my mouth. My teeth cut through a toasted meringue layer and pillowy soft dough before settling into the tart, key lime center. Flavor explodes along my tastebuds from the combination of smooth subtle sweetness cut with the sharpness of the lime curd. A sigh escapes my nose, and I drop my head down into my free palm as I try to process how sinful this tastes.

"That good?"

I take another bite before I respond by holding it out to him. "I know you're not a sweets guy, but you have to try this. It would be a crime not to. Do it for Mimi. Do it for me."

Without hesitation, he leans forward, grabbing onto my wrist and bringing the donut to his mouth while maintaining full eye contact. When he pulls away slightly, I notice a bit of cream gathered at the corner of his mouth and, without thinking, I bring my thumb up, brushing it off before I bring the digit up to my mouth to taste.

His eyes darken, staring intently at my mouth, and a slow, wide smile stretches around the finger in my mouth. A look that can only be described as devious settles on his face. "Second best thing I've ever tasted."

I blush furiously. "So bold, Mr. Wells. I've been a bad influence on you."

He harrumphs in my direction. "Come on, pretty girl. Finish that one off. We've got more stops to hit."

The excitement that jolts through my body at his words is equivalent to being thrown into an electric fence. I don't know if it's the sugar high or Hendrix calling me pretty, but my body feels like a live wire. I may not have much experience in the dating department, but I can't imagine it gets any better than this.

Three stops, one hazelnut crunch, one strawberry rhubarb, and one maple bacon donut later, we're walking to our final stop on the Lower East Side. According to Hendrix, he saved the best for last, but if you ask me, each stop has been perfect, especially all the moments in between.

While waiting for a train in Times Square, we stumbled upon a performer who had dozens of electronic plushies scattered around him, dancing and gyrating to electric house music. Hendrix groaned when I grabbed his arm, forcing him to dance with me and a harem of creepy stuffed animals, but judging by the carefree smile on his face, I'd wager he secretly liked it.

As we arrive at our final destination, I see him sneaking glances at me every few seconds. At first, I think it's because he wants to look at me, but it's happening more often than is normal. It's almost...anticipatory.

"Do I have something on my f–" and then, I see it.

Our last stop on the Manhattan donut tour, in all its neon-signed splendor, is called *Glory Holes*. A shop that specializes in donut holes. Their honest to God slogan is, *'put us in your hole"*. It's marketing genius at its finest.

"No way." I start jumping up and down, cackling my excitement. "How did I not know this existed?"

Hendrix is laughing at my obvious joy over an inappropriately named bakery. "I think it's fairly new."

"This is the greatest day of my life." I beam up at him.

I'm suddenly overcome by a feeling of absolute happiness. Hendrix has seen so many pieces of me and hasn't balked. I've been so many different versions of myself in his presence—struggling business owner, fearless karaoke starlet, broken and traumatized, raunchy and irreverent, and he's embraced each one, encouraged every facet of me and who I am, who I could be.

He smiles down at me softly, brushing a tendril of hair out of my face before leaning forward and whispering against my lips, "I'm glad, baby." A shiver skates up my spine at the endearment. Leaning forward, he kisses me gently, like it's the most natural thing in the world—and it feels like it might be.

"Can we go get some glory holes now?" I whisper against his mouth.

He laughs and places his hand on my lower back, pushing me towards the open door. It's a small space, only big enough to hold maybe three to four people in line, with a counter top made of wood behind glass pastry cases. Inside the cases are various flavors to choose from, and when we make it to the front of the line, we order one of each to try.

With a box of each hole in hand, we make our way to a small park nearby to sit on a bench and eat the last donuts I'll be enjoying for a long while. And when I say long while, I mean three weeks maximum.

The mini spherical delights are delicious, and I even get Hendrix to have a couple with me as we discuss ratings and rankings.

"As much as I love the depraved marketing strategy of Glory Holes, Mimi's is still hands down the best. I think I might have to move uptown just to be close to it," I say.

"I'll go get it for you whenever you want."

"Don't make promises you can't keep, Hen. I think you're underestimating how often I might want it."

"I'm fully aware of your sweet tooth. I'll go get you the donuts."

"Mhmmm," I moan as I bite into another one.

Hendrix is fiddling around in his jacket pocket for something as I polish off the last two pieces, a glimmer of gold catching in the street light.

"I almost forgot, but I have this for you." He sounds nervous, and when I look over at what he's holding, my breath catches.

Dangling from his hand is my gold necklace, not broken but whole. I set it on my entry table that night to take care of after handling the store renovations. Then, the plumbing repairs happened, and my necklace took a backseat. I hadn't given it another thought, prioritizing everything else over my need to have it fixed.

"What—"

He stops me. "I hope you don't mind, but I took it to have it repaired. The jeweler was able to replace just a couple of the links on the chain, so it's mostly still the same necklace your dad gifted to you."

I am absolutely speechless, like I cannot get a single word out of my mouth. If I had any more glory holes left, you could fit at least five easily in my mouth by how far my jaw has unhinged.

"I'm sorry if I overstepped–*oomph*!"

I launch myself at him, arms wrapping like a vise around his neck.

"Thank you," I breathe into his neck as his arms wrap around my waist, gripping me to his broad chest.

My heart is pounding out of my chest at the feeling consuming every cell in my body. He knows what this necklace means to me, and to have it repaired for me—to ensure the broken links were switched out and it stayed the same chain my father gifted to me—it makes the muscle in my chest constrict and swell with gratitude as I grip him tighter.

"You're welcome, Sunshine," he huffs into my hair.

We stay like that for a minute, an hour, a year. I don't know how long it's been; I don't ever want it to end. But as his hands start to rub up and down my back in a comforting gesture, my body starts to warm all over, an ache starting to build in my core.

"Hendrix..." I say.

"Hmmm?" Slow, languid movements tease up and down my spine.

I pull back ever so slightly so I'm aligned with his ear. "Take me home. Now."

Chapter 23

Silver

I don't know what sort of cosmic fate I've pleased in a past life for the stroke of good luck, but as it turns out, Hendrix's place is not very far from the park we're in. But the fifteen minute walk is going to feel like an eternity with the way I'm feeling right now. Thank God Hendrix had the wherewithal to secure my pendant around my neck before we took off, because I am not thinking clearly.

I need to get my hands on him, my mouth on him. I need to feel his skin against mine, sweat soaked and warm. I just need... *him*. With me, around me, inside me. I'll burn up from this wanting if I don't get it soon. We've been dancing around each other for months now, and this craving inside me is like a dam ready to burst open. Water has already been slipping through my seams for weeks, making my once-sturdy foundation start to crumble at my feet. All because of him.

"Are we there yet?" I whine, impatience lacing my tone as we wait for the light to change.

I can feel the rumble of a laugh in Hendrix's chest, pressed against my back as the arm wrapped around my waist pulls me closer into him. I can feel it echo throughout my entire body, charting a course from the top of my head all the way down to my toes, curling within my shoes, making me ache.

"Impatience is sexy on you," he rumbles into my ear, giving it a light nip that shoots straight to my core and has me dancing on the balls of my feet to keep going. Judging by the groan he lets out and the semi I can feel against my backside, I'd say he's starting to feel a little restless too. I press further back into him, and he hisses, "Cruel woman."

The signal finally changes, and I'm off like a light. I don't even know where I'm going. I'm just trusting my Spidey-senses will guide me in the direction of his apartment.

"You're the one who's been edging us for the last week," I huff.

"Slow down, sweetheart," he laughs, catching up to me and hauling me back into his chest, nuzzling his bearded face into the crook of my neck. Tingles crop up all over my skin from the friction of his stubble. "We'll be there soon, and once we get there, I'm not letting you out of my bed for *hours*. I want to smell you on my sheets for weeks."

I twist around in his grip, bringing his lips to mine and coaxing his lips open with my tongue. He grants me entry instantly, and I devour him, or he devours me—it's hard to tell with my lust clouding my senses.

Groaning, he pulls away an inch, his breaths panting. "We need to stop, or I'm going to take you right here."

I nip at his lower lip. "Seems as good a place as any."

He growls, "The first time I have you isn't going to be up

against a dirty wall in The Village with college kids mulling about. They don't get the privilege of seeing you when you're being fucked the way you deserve for the first time in your life. They don't get to see these pretty eyes blown wide, skin flushed, or hear the sounds you make when you're coming on my cock. That's for me. Only me."

I have to admit, the territorial bullshit does wonders for me.

"That isn't helping matters." I shift on unsteady legs, breath fanning against his mouth.

"Say it."

I know what he's asking of me, what he wants me to confirm so he knows I'm aware of the magnitude of these feelings, what they could mean. This won't be a one night thing, it won't be something I can forget and move on from.

"Only for you." My words are whisper soft as I gaze into his golden green eyes.

He releases a small breath of relief, barely perceptible. "Thank you." I don't know if he's thanking me or some higher power, but it doesn't matter much to me at the moment.

"We are close, though, right?" There's a neediness to my voice I'm only vaguely embarrassed by.

"Oh, I'd say we're both definitely close."

I swat at his arm. "To your *place*, you perv."

He grabs my hand before I bring it back down to my side and kisses the back of my knuckles. "Next block over, Sunshine. I'm ready for you to ruin me for all other women."

Even the thought of him with other women has my hackles rising, a new feeling for me, and it surprises me that it's not an unwelcome one.

When he tugs me along after him, a wicked grin on his face, I think he might be the one to ruin me.

We barely make it through the door before I'm on him, pushing him so his back is flush against the front door and I'm sealing my lips to his in a desperate kiss.

Hendrix's tongue plunges into my mouth setting my body on fire, I meet him stroke for stroke as his hand dives into my hair, cupping the side of my neck to keep me in place.

I don't know how I have ever lived without this. Any kiss I've ever had before him was inconsequential, paling in comparison to how being with Hendrix makes me feel. Sensation is sharper, colors are brighter, and the flutters in my stomach turn into a full on swarm. I feel like I can't breathe, simultaneously feeling like this is the only thing keeping me grounded, tethered to this Earth and unburdened, like nothing bad could touch me as long as he's with me.

His hands are wandering a lazy path from my neck down my sides until they settle on my ass, eliciting a groan from both of us as he palms each cheek before reaching under my thighs to hoist me up around his waist. I wrap myself around him with little to no effort and bring my mouth to his neck, sucking on the spot where his pulse hammers against my tongue. Smiling against his skin, I bite down on the same spot I had been licking, and he groans, dropping his head into my shoulder.

"Doing alright?" I pull his ear between my teeth.

I decide at this moment to make it my mission to drive him as crazy tonight as he's done to me over the last week. I want him absolutely out of his mind, so blissed out, he doesn't know up from down for days.

I can feel his hard length behind the fly of his jeans, holding me up so I'm just barely grazing the top of his erection. So slowly, he doesn't notice, I shift slightly downward, rolling my core over the tip of his cock, rocking back and forth as well as I can in this position. He grunts, gripping my ass to stay my movements, holding me firmly against his body.

He brings his face in front of mine. "Are you trying to kill me?"

"Set me down." I drop a brief peck to his mouth.

He slowly lowers me to the ground, my body dragging down his in a delicious descent of friction. When he sets me on my feet, I don't stop my trajectory, slowly sinking to my knees and looking up at him from my position on the floor.

"So that's a yes to killing me then." He looks like he's in pain, and I revel in every moment, knowing I'm the one making him feel this way, that I drive him as crazy as he does me.

"Maybe just mild torture." I grin and reach for his belt buckle.

He stops my hand. "You don't have to do this."

I can see in his eyes how desperately he wants it. He's trying to be noble, like he has been for weeks, and it makes me fall a little more each time. But I'm done with him being a valiant knight. I want him depraved. I want to see him unleash and lose control, in me—in us.

"You've been taking care of me every day for a week." I loosen his belt buckle, unbuttoning his pants.

"That doesn't mean you o–" his words catch as I grab onto the bulge in his pants, "–owe me this. *Fuck.*"

"I'll stop if you want me to," he squeezes his eyes closed, as if seeing me on my knees before him hurts, "but you've been taking care of me for a week, and it's been *so* good. But I'm going crazy not knowing what you taste like, feel like. Can I?"

"Christ," He gives me a look that says *are you insane* before he nods his consent.

A devilish grin ignites across my face as I unzip the fly and pull the denim down his legs until he's able to toe out of them. I finger the edges of his briefs, pants discarded off to the side, before I reach my hand in gently to grab ahold of him. The grunt he emits when I finally make contact with him has my own panties dampening beneath my clothes.

I give him one firm tug before I remove my hand so I can pull his briefs down and bring him out fully. "Holy shit," it's almost vulgar how perfect he is.

His cock juts up, leaking with pre-cum, and I have to resist the urge not to lick my lips at the sight.

"If you keep staring at me like that, I'm going to come before this even starts," his eyes are dark as onyx, and there's a sheen of perspiration lining his brow from the effort of holding back.

"Well, we can't have that, can we?" Another firm tug as I inch closer and closer.

Bringing my mouth within an inch of his cock, I give it a teasing puff of air that makes him twitch in my hand. It earns me a deep sigh, and when I look up at Hendrix, every visible muscle in his body is pulled taut with restraint, eyes laser focused on me. It's a heady look, addicting to be the sole focus of his attention.

Without breaking eye contact, I run my tongue in a teasing caress around the head before I suck the tip into my mouth.

"*Fuck!*" He throws his head back so quickly, it hits the door behind him, but I don't stop my ministrations to check if he's alright.

I swirl my tongue around the crown before taking in another inch, my hand holding him steady at the base. Hendrix mutters incoherent curses as he reaches around to cup the back of my head gently while I draw him further into my mouth, cheeks hollowing, until he's as far as I can get him to go.

"You have no idea how beautiful you look with your mouth full of me." He affectionately rubs the base of my head.

I'm suddenly too hot for the amount of clothing I have on, boiling from his words and my actions. I pull back quickly and pull my sweater over my head, letting the cool air of the room temper my skin, my nipples peaking under the black lace of my bra.

"Your turn." I wink and bring him back to my lips, licking from base to tip before pulling him back into my mouth.

Hendrix's breathing notches imperceptibly higher as I bob my head up and down on his length. He follows my order to take off his shirt, and I feast my eyes with a golden torso dusted with light patches of dark hair. I notice the dark lines of a tattoo emerging out of the left side of his briefs, but curiosity will have to wait.

I relax my mouth to take him deeper until he hits the back of my throat, causing him to yell out and pull my head off him with a squelching *pop*.

I look up at him, sitting back on my heels, lips swollen and wet. "Why did you stop me?"

"The first time I come inside you will be inside your pretty pussy. I was seconds away from exploding." I smile up at him, this curious look of devastation on his face. "You have no idea what you do to me, Silver."

"Tell me." I bet it's the same as what he does to me.

He shakes his head but pulls me up to my feet, keeping a hold of me so I don't lose balance. Then, he brings his mouth down to mine and *shows* me what I do to him. His kiss tells me I drive him out of his mind, that this connection is so much more than physical desire. His body aches for me, yes, but his mind does too. This infallible feeling I get when he's touching me is because he understands me more than anyone ever has, he sees me for all that I am, and he wants me more for it. He wants all my broken, tired, happy, successful, stressed, angry, and joyous moments. Because they're mine, and he wants me. All of me.

"More," I mumble against his mouth before he grabs my hand and leads us into his bedroom.

Chapter 24

Silver

We're standing in his bedroom, but I can't take in any details, unable to focus on anything but him. There would be time later to look around and see how he lives, but right now, I want to crawl into his skin and live there forever.

He reaches out a broad hand and undoes the button of my jeans, helping me shuck them down my legs until I'm standing in just my bra and panties, black lace with small floral appliqués adorning the material. Hendrix reaches a hand out, grazing my hardened nipples through the material with the back of his knuckles, and then reaches behind my back, unclasping my bra and dropping it to the floor at our feet.

He breathes out heavily. "You're exquisite."

I blush, feeling shy by the compliment, exposed and free at the same time during a moment so intimate. This is far from my first time with a man, but it is the first time I have feelings attached, heightening every sensation on a cardinal level.

He groans. "Fuck. The flush is trailing down to your tits."

He grips his hard length, giving it two firm jerks. "Get on the bed, Sunshine."

I hasten to obey, practically flinging myself onto the duvet and watching him take off his briefs until he's standing fully nude before me. I go to sit up, but he stops me with a hand to my chest, lightly pushing me back.

"Lay down and open for me. It's my turn."

Fuck. Fuck. Fuck.

Hendrix kneels on the floor before me, grabs behind my knees, and pulls me to the very edge of the bed in one swift tug. He runs a finger along the lace of my thong, making me whine impatiently as he sucks in a breath, realizing how wet I already am.

"Did sucking my cock turn you on, Silver?" There's a distinct note of triumph in his voice.

"Yes," I gasp as he pulls the fabric to the side and runs his thumb through my slick core before plunging the digit inside me. My back arches off the bed slightly, and I fist the sheets, grappling for any kind of hold on reality, when he leans forward and flicks his tongue against my clit. "Shit. God, that's so good."

I cry out as he removes his thumb and works two fingers inside me, paying careful attention to my swollen bud with his mouth, working me up, getting me ready for him. The sensations zipping around my body, lighting me up like a Christmas tree, are almost too much to handle.

"Never need another dessert when I have the best one right here." He licks a hot stripe up my center. "So sweet, so fucking good."

I grab his hair as I ride his face, hips undulating, all thoughts on the man between my legs.

"So goo—*ah!*" I scream, back bowing, as a sneaky orgasm bursts out of me, making my whole body shake with tremors as he continues to soak up my arousal, not letting a single drop go to waste.

I'm slowly coming down from euphoria, legs quivering as I pull his head off my center. "Fuck me, please. *I need you.*" It's desperate and vulnerable, but it's honest, and he sees it then. I understand what this is and how it's about to change everything.

"Jae has condoms in his bathroom. Let me go get one." He moves to get up, but I pull him back to me, not wanting him to leave.

"I have an IUD, and I've never...I've never slept with anyone without one. I was tested after my last encounter—" I couldn't exactly call it a relationship, "and I was good." I trust him with my heart and my body, and the thought of there being anything between us right now is near unbearable.

"I'm clear too, but I don't mind using one."

I grab his face with both hands and look him in his beautiful eyes. "I want to *feel* you, Hendrix, with nothing between us."

"Are you sure?" His gaze pings back and forth on my face.

I draw him down to kiss me instead, adjusting so we're both fully on the bed and he's hovering above me. I can feel his cock resting on my thigh and reach down to grab it, rubbing it back and forth over my clit and we both moan into each other's mouths from the sensation.

"Please," I mewl.

And that seems to be enough, because Hendrix reaches between us to line himself up with my opening, looking in my eyes once more for consent that I give freely.

Leaning down, he brushes a kiss against my mouth and sinks

himself inside me inch by torturous inch. I cry out against his mouth at the sensation, stretching around him with the most delectable amount of pressure. He gives me a moment to adjust to the size and feel of him. Within seconds, I shift, begging him with my body to move.

Settling a warm palm against my hip, Hendrix drops his head into the space between my neck and shoulder. "Give me a minute." He takes a slow inhale. "You feel so perfect, I need a second."

I don't listen as I draw my nails down his back to his ass, needing to feel him moving inside me, to feel his strong thighs fucking into me until I can't remember my name.

I bite his earlobe. "Fuck me so I can't walk tomorrow."

"Give me a second," he grits out. "You're strangling my cock, Sunshine. Gripping me so goddamn tight, I can't breathe."

"I believe in you."

He huffs out a laugh and sits up, slightly starting to move, slow at first, setting a steady pace that is quickly working me up. The pressure of him filling me, stretching me wide, is going to drive me to madness. I grab my breasts, needing to hold on to something, and I give my nipples a pinch, ratcheting my pleasure up higher and higher from the extra bite. Hendrix's eyes ping back and forth between the rough treatment of my nipples and his cock sinking in and out of me, like he can't quite decide where to keep his focus.

But Hendrix is a multi-tasker; he leans forward, his thrusts going slightly out of rhythm as he takes one of my nipples in his mouth, biting down, mixing in a slight burst of pain that swiftly ebbs into satisfaction as he sucks at the tender bud.

When he picks up his pace, my walls loosen further, taking more of him as he grips my knees, pushing them even further into the bed, opening me for him.

"*Fuck,*" he growls. "So pliant for me, so tight and wet. I feel like I'm going out of my mind. I must be dreaming, the way you feel wrapped around me can't be real. It's too good."

I constrict around him at the words falling off his lips. I've dreamt of this so many times over the past few months, and none of my wildest fantasies could compare to him in real life.

His thrusts grow vigorous as pounds into me, hands now grasping onto my hips to help move me back and forth along his length. I'm getting close, can feel the edges of my orgasm fluttering along my spine, making my walls contract. He feels it too, based on the way he's clenching his jaw, trying to hold off until I'm ready to join him. I'm almost there, desperately wanting to come while also never wanting this to end.

"You're close, aren't you, baby?"

"Y-yes," I stutter, grabbing onto his back and digging my nails into his back so hard it would definitely leave marks. "Your cock feels so good. Nothing's ever felt this good."

He pulls out to the tip and thrusts back in with one, rough motion, hitting that perfect spot deep inside. I scream out, back bowing off the bed, and eyes rolling back as my hands grapple for purchase on his inked biceps. "Fuck, right there, yes!" He repeats the motion, holding onto my hips as he beats into my pussy, making sure to drag his pelvis against my clit on every plunge, making my legs start to tremble.

"That's my girl." He growls so loudly, the walls practically shake. "My cock was made for you." *Thrust.* "That's why it's never felt like this before." *Thrust.* "Just like your perfect cunt was made for me." *Thrust. Thrust. Thrust.* "Where do you want me?"

"Inside me. Come inside me," I pant out through cries of pleasure, meeting his thrusts with ones of my own, driving him wild.

One more rough plunge, and the orgasm tears through me, shocking my body with volts of electricity. Hendrix follows me a second later, emptying inside me as he groans out his release. My whole being feels like it's alive with explosives detonating throughout my body when Hendrix softly drops onto me, the weight of his body tethering me back to this planet.

We're both breathing heavily, catching our breath when he pulls back, immediately making me crave his warmth again. But he's adjusting so he can kiss me, and it sends a flight of butterflies rampant through my stomach. Would that ever stop, or would I always feel this way around him?

He slowly pulls out of me, watching our bodies unjoin with laser focus as I stay splayed open on the bed. Lifting me up and carrying me into his adjoining bathroom, he sets me on the counter, shifting around to turn on the tap to the shower.

When he looks back to me, he crowds into my space like he needs to be as close to me as possible. "How are you feeling?"

It makes me smile, being taken care of in the aftermath of sex. I never wanted it before, didn't realize I would need it now, but Hendrix did. Everything he does draws me in deeper and deeper.

"I'm perfect," I assure him, settling a kiss on his chest as I hop off the counter and drag him into the shower. "I hope you have an extra shirt for me to sleep in."

"I do. But you won't be needing it."

If this is what relationships feel like, I'm starting to think I could get on board, as long as it always led me into his arms.

Chapter 25

Hendrix

I wake to soft snores trilling lightly in my ear.

Silver and I fell asleep shortly after our shower last night, thoroughly wrecked from sex so unbelievable, we had to do it again in the shower to make sure it wasn't a fluke—for science. Then again in the middle of the night, when we were pulled toward each other like magnets, bodies connecting lazily until we writhed against each other, racing to that final pinnacle. Then, she kissed me softly, and we fell back asleep, tangled in each other.

But the more I lay here, watching her chest rise and fall, a light buzzing of fear bubbles to the surface. I don't want her to feel pressured into this—into us. I want her to choose to be here, in this with me. She could wake up in five minutes and decide she had satiated a curiosity and wanted to move on. Everything said and done last night could be chalked up to being caught up in a moment. Maybe it's my own insecurities rising, or maybe there's merit to it. I know in my bones what she is to me, but am I the same to her?

Fuck, I hope so.

I'm desperate with that hope, and last night only solidified what I already knew: I'm in love with her, so painstakingly in love with her that everything in life would now pale in comparison to the magnitude of what I feel for her.

She was incandescent, bright and blinding like a star, too great for this world to contain. In every survival class our parents made us take as kids, they would always say if you got lost to look for the brightest star to guide you home. Silver is my North Star, guiding me with her light even when I couldn't see I was in the dark. I would follow her anywhere, go on any adventure, if she would have me. Because that's what every day with her has been: an adventure.

I was finally *living*, not just existing, for the first time in years. Maybe ever.

Silver moves next to me, shifting to snuggle deeper into my chest, draping her leg over the top of my thigh. "You're surprisingly comfortable for someone who's hard as a brick wall," she mumbles into my bare skin before placing a soft kiss to my chest, never opening her eyes.

The small brush of her lips makes my cock twitch behind my sweats, and I urge it to lay low, to give her some space. I hum in response and rub my thumb softly over where it's now settled against her spine. She sighs, and a delicate smile curls her mouth at the corners as I stroke a lazy pattern up and down her vertebrae.

Silver stirs against me, bringing her hand up and placing it on my stomach, then settles. I tell my body to calm down; she's just getting comfortable, and there's no reason to get turned on. Until she does it again, fingers trailing even lower on my stomach, rubbing against me like a cat. Only this time she doesn't still, she keeps up her teasing, making my breath hitch as the tips of her fingers slip into my sweatpants just enough to lightly graze under the band of my briefs. I clench my jaw, letting her take the lead, seeing what happens in the early morning hours of the day.

Silver dives her hand deeper under my clothes until her fingers toy with the tip of my cock, and I suck in a sharp breath.

"Sunshine…" I don't know if I'm admonishing her or begging her to keep going.

"Hmmm?" She fully grabs me now, giving me a teasing tug.

My hips jolt upwards off the bed as I groan, and I grab her bare hip, squeezing onto her to keep me grounded, or else I might float away on a cloud of bliss.

She keeps up her teasing, bringing her hand to my tip and using the pre-cum beading at the end to lubricate my shaft, getting me worked up and wet. Then, she sits up, my hand falling from where I clutched her, and swings a leg over so she's straddling me. My NYU t-shirt she wore to bed hangs loose on her frame, pooling at the apex of her thighs.

Reaching both hands between us, Silver grabs my pants and starts to tug. I lift my hips to give her space to shuck them down far enough so I can kick them off the rest of the way. I know where this is leading, but I want to hear her say it. I need to hear her words.

"Silver?" I sit up on my elbow and catch her eyes. Is she okay this morning? Is this what she really wants, or a deflection from how she's feeling?

"I've never woken up next to someone after sex before. I've never *wanted* to." She shifts her body so she's hovering over my cock now, and I can feel the warmth of her blanketing me.

She brings me between her folds, rubbing me through them so

I can feel how wet she is for me.

"Fuck. I'm trying to stay focused on what you're saying, sweetheart, but you're making it really hard," I groan at the feeling of her coating me, my shaft slick with our combined arousal as she rocks back and forth, soft, breathy moans falling from her lips.

We must paint such a picture, her in my lap, sheets tangled around us, sweat glistening against our skin as she leans forward and brings her forehead to mine. Silver reaches down and lines me up, lifting on her knees to put distance between the middle of our bodies.

"I *wanted* to wake up next to you," she says and sinks down onto my cock until I'm fully sheathed inside her tight heat. We both shudder from the unmatched euphoria of being joined like this. "I felt...*peace*, waking up in your arms."

I sit up and band my arms around her body in a vice grip, telling her without words that I don't ever want to let go. She starts to rock against me, and I glide my mouth down her neck, lightly sucking and nipping at the flesh.

She starts to lift off me, only to bring herself back down over and over again. She cries out at the friction of her clit hitting my pubic bone, helping bring her that much closer to the release we both crave.

"It's too good." A husky admission when her voice is still groggy from sleep.

I piston my hips up into her. "The way you're gripping me is driving me insane."

She curls her body against mine, chest to chest, arms snaking around my neck, not allowing a single inch of space between us as we bring our bodies together, too lost for any more words.

Pulling my hand from around her waist, I trail my palm up her torso, over her breast to settle it around her neck. Goosebumps materialize over her skin in the wake of my touch. I pull her in for a kiss, tongue licking into her mouth before I pull back and look deeply into her sea-foam eyes, hair wild around her face.

"Open," I command.

The inherent trust she puts in me as she opens her mouth without hesitation is almost enough for me to finish. My hand coasts from its home on her neck, up to her jaw, gently cupping before I move on to trace her lips with my fingers.

I dip my index and middle fingers inside her mouth. *"Suck."* Her eyes blaze and she immediately complies, sucking on them with enthusiasm, making my cock jerk inside of her. We both groan. "Perfect. You're so fucking perfect."

She's writhing, fucking herself onto me as I pull my fingers out of her mouth.

"*Fuck*," she whines in my ear. "More, I need more of you. Fuck me—*fill me*," she pleads.

"I think I like it when you beg." Silver tugs hard on my hair in retaliation, but doesn't stop her movements.

I'm gripping her hip with my other hand, helping her move against me as I glide my free hand, soaked with her spit, down her back until it's settled on her ass. I press my fingers against the tight ring of muscle at her backside—barely breaching, and adding just enough pressure to add to her pleasure as I bite down on her neck once more, pounding in and out of her tight, wet heat.

She explodes around me in an instant, her walls contracting around my cock so viscerally, I follow her orgasm with my own, roaring out in pleasure. I pump into her slowly as we ride out our releases, still clinging to each other, neither one of us ready to let go.

We stay locked together like that for an unknown amount of time, and only when the sweat on our bodies starts to dry and cool our skin do we reluctantly disentangle ourselves. But neither of us moves very far, laying back down on my bed, my arm around her and her head resting on my chest, content in our silence.

She starts lightly tracing my newest tattoo, the one that spans from the top of my thigh, over my hip, and onto my torso. "A phoenix," she states, taking in all its intricate lines—the tail that curls down my hip to the wings that stretch high above its head and onto my side. "It's beautiful."

I place a kiss on her nose. "Do you have to work today?"

Please say no. Stay with me all day. We don't have to do anything. I just want to be around you.

She shakes her head. "I'm meeting Kena later at Brooklyn Flea. He needs a lot of things for a project and I promised to go with him."

I try not to be disappointed. I see her all the time because of the arrangement with the store, but going a day without her after what we just did feels wrong.

She props her chin on my stomach and looks over at me, hair wild around her like a crown of gold. "Will you come with me?"

My insides crack, fizzle, and pop. I bring my hand up to cup her neck, fingers scoring through her hair to rub at her scalp. She sighs and closes her eyes. "Yeah, baby, I'll come with you."

"You must be ingesting too many fumes from all the cabs if you think I'm paying that price," Kena shouts at a vendor.

We arrived ten minutes ago to find him haggling with a

salesman selling antique wardrobe chests. We stood back to watch as he wore the man down harder than tires on a racecar. When he noticed us standing fifteen paces away, watching slack jawed, he came bounding over, a gleaming smile stretched across his face as he threw his arms around us both.

"Did the hot maintenance man finally *nail you to the wall*?" He leaned in, whispering loudly, before she swatted him on the arm, blushing furiously, sneaking a shy glance over at me to see if I had heard. I pretended I didn't.

"I've got a list of things I need to get for the Park Ave project. What are we finding for you, Sil?

"My list will have to wait until later." She tells him about the incident at the store and how it means everything unnecessary will have to wait. He asks about the second floor, knowing that was what she was most excited for, and tries to soothe her when he sees the disappointment written on Silver's face. "It's okay. These things happen." She waves him off with a smile. "Where should we go first?"

The Brooklyn Flea is a maze of tents and tables hocking anything from jewelry to vintage clothes to home décor of all kinds. We weave our way under the Brooklyn Bridge, where most of the stalls reside, when Kena pulls me into one with him, leaving Silver in a different section close by, looking at frames.

"I've been here for an hour, scoping out the wares ahead of time, and I saw this dining room hutch that's perfect for my client." He's speaking animatedly, gesticulating wildly with his hands. "But the seller isn't budging on the price. He's this real hard ass man's man, you know?"

"And?"

He stops abruptly, putting a hand on my chest before quickly removing it with a soft 'oh my', shaking his head out of a daze. "Keep up, brother wife. This is important."

"You didn't explain anything?"

"Context clues! I need you, a big burly man who looks like he knows how to hold a hammer, to come help me get this guy down on a price."

"Okay, how do you want me to do that?"

"You'll have to freestyle. I'm sure you'll be fine."

"You're always throwing me into uncomfortable situations where I'm put on the spot," I huff.

"Don't act like singing 'What Dreams Are Made Of' in front of a crowd wasn't a transformative experience for you. I was there." He grabs my arm, pulling me in the direction he wants me to go. "Silver! I'm stealing your boyfriend for a minute."

Pink creeps into her cheeks at the use of the term 'boyfriend', but she doesn't correct him. "Okay! But be gentle with him. He's delicate."

"We both know that's not true." I shoot her a suggestive wink, further deepening her blush.

Kena gasps next to me, clutching his pearls. Literally—he's wearing a pearl necklace.

We head about two hundred feet in the opposite direction of where we left Silver, and each step away from her has me aching to run back, but I also want to get on Kena's good side since he's her best friend.

Walking up to the antiques vendor, I see what Kena was talking about. This guy looks more likely to be a butcher for the mafia than he does a furniture salesman.

"I already told you my price is final." His New York accent is thick, and his ire is directed fully onto my friend.

"I understand, Vinny. I just brought my contractor over to take a look. I want to make sure it'll fit in the space I'll use it for."

Kena nudges me, and I start walking around the mahogany cabinet with filigree embossing. It was a nice piece of furniture, tall and sturdy, but nothing crazy. I make a big show of opening the doors, tapping around the inside, bending down and checking the fluted styling on the legs. Then I see the price, and I realize our friend Vinny here is a scam artist.

I stand in front of Kena. "He's charging four grand for that?"

"I know, it's insane. I'm trying to get him down to three." Kena shoots daggers at Vinny over my shoulder.

"I could make that for you."

His head whips in my direction. "Come again?"

"I mean, this is kind of what I do. My family owns a furniture design business back in Seattle. I grew up doing this." I don't need to go into the specifics of the family drama behind it all, but I would be damned if he got taken advantage of like this.

"How much would that cost you?" Oh, he's serious. Part of me thought he wouldn't take me up on it, and I didn't want to hope for more than what I've already been given recently, afraid to jinx my good luck.

"Materials would probably cost a few hundred. With labor, we could round it out to a grand?"

"Hey!" Vinny yells, finally catching on to what we're discussing.

"I'll give you two grand." He sticks out his hand to shake on it.

I shake my head. "That's too much."

"Let's make it two and a half. Know your worth."

And goddamn, if there isn't something inspirational about

that. Something that makes my chest flutter uneasily. It couldn't really be that simple could it?

"I'll get you some sketches by the end of next week?" I slip my hand into his and shake.

"That's perfect."

We turn and head back to where we left Silver, Vinny shouting a trail of expletives as he chases after us. We weave through stall after stall until I see her, head thrown back in laughter at something the person next to her is saying as they rifle through boxes of tchotchkes. I stop and stare, struck stupid by how beautiful she is like this, carefree, with sunshine pouring down over her skin, making her glow.

Kena clears his throat, and when I turn, he's looking at me, looking at his best friend with a knowing smile.

"She's beautiful, isn't she?"

I want to tell him I love her, that I'll do everything in my power to make sure she feels that love and security every day. But I don't want to tell him before I tell her. "To put it mildly, yes, she's the most beautiful person I've ever met."

His grin stretches wider.

She looks over then, having spotted us, and jogs over. But instead of directing her attention to Kena like I think she will, she comes to me, face alight with happiness, and rests her free hand on my stomach.

"You have to come see this." She starts to drag me towards the table she was standing at. "They have mini figurines of celebrities, and look!" She reaches down and grabs a miniature Paul Hollywood, searing demonic blue stare and all. "I'm gonna get him for the bedside table."

I throw my head back and laugh. "For mine or yours?"

"We can work out a joint custody agreement."

I can't help myself—she's just so fucking adorable, I'll die if I don't kiss her. Leaning down, I brush my lips against hers lightly, testing how she feels about public displays of affection. But she leans into me, deepening the kiss in a way that signals I need to pull back now, or this is about to get very inappropriate for a flea market.

She pouts as I retreat but reaches her hand out to wipe her lip balm off my mouth with the pad of her thumb. The move is so familiar and intimate at the same time. I plant a kiss on her forehead, resting my hand on her back as I pull away and look at the employee working the stall. "We'll take one Hollywood."

Chapter 26

Silver

It's been four weeks of near perfect bliss.

Four weeks of Hendrix taking me on dates, unbelievable nights lost in each other's bodies, and my personal favorite—waking up next to him. Every time I opened my eyes to see him asleep next to me, chest rising and falling peacefully, I felt the fears and anxieties settle within me. I never want to sleep alone again.

During the day, I work at the bookstore, still yet to be given a new name but with new floorboards, thanks to the damage, and Hendrix works at The Langham. At night, he meets me to finish up the last few things we have to do before the soft reopening, and we almost always get distracted. Sometimes, it's just talking to each other, discovering new things to fall for, and sometimes, we're distracted by other, more tantalizing things... Either way, the store is just *nearly* there.

Today is the only day I have off before the big day on Saturday, and I'm trying my best to actually relax some, but my body feels like it's twisted up in knots.

I've been running on autopilot for weeks now, working to get everything done and avoiding thinking about what happens when it's actually finished. Namely, the scope of work I'll have to do just to keep the shop afloat so we all keep our jobs and I don't let everyone down. All the responsibility falls to my shoulders. But as the philosophers say, I made my bed, or some bullshit to that effect.

For the last week, we've been getting word out about the re-opening so we can have a good turnout, mostly by hanging up fliers in cafes and on street lamps around the city. But it's hard to really market yourself when things still feel incomplete. Holly and Carmen have been hounding me to decide on a new name for the store, but it feels like too big of a decision, too much pressure, and it's psyching me out. Nothing *feels* right. A new name will set the tone for who we are, who *I* am. I'm terrified I'm going to get it wrong before it has a chance to go right. Or maybe that's my avoidant attachment rising to the surface. Almost like when you find a stray animal and don't want to give it a name, because then you'll love it too much before having to give it up.

And the cherry on top of the chaos sundae that is my reckless decisions: I've been trying to bring the store into this century by upgrading all of our tech—new phones, point of sale systems, and website—but getting appointments has been a struggle. I've managed to get the POS systems installed, and we've been uploading inventory and training on it before Saturday comes, but the phone and website still aren't done. It's looking like I won't be able to get someone out until after the party.

Convincing myself it's not a big deal, that it won't make or break our success, has been hard when there's a small, persistent voice in the back of my head, screaming, *not enough. Your efforts are not enough. You* are not *enough*. That voice sounds disturbingly like my mother.

But then there's another voice, one that comes in quietly at first, tentative and unsure before it rises in volume, louder than the other, telling me I *can* do this. That voice...it sounds a little like me. It's me with a choir of my friends behind me, echoing my words. That's what is keeping me going. The money has run out, my body is tired, and it's not going to be perfect, but I'm happy. I'm *proud*— even while I'm scared of screwing it all up. I've lived my life keeping everything an arm's length away from my heart, not committing to anything or anyone, but the store changed that in an instant. It's mine, for better or worse.

But today is my day off, and I've been ordered by pretty much everyone to rest and recharge, since the rest of the week would be so hectic. So far, I have not listened to their advice. In my defense, my apartment is a wreck and in serious need of a deep clean. I'd been spending most of my time either at the store or at Hendrix's, and as a result, my place has fallen to the wayside. I now have a pile of laundry taller than The Statue of Liberty that I have to tackle in the tenant laundry room today.

I put on my headphones and click play on my latest audiobook, a dark romance, to keep me company as I dart around my modest apartment and get my life sorted out. Clear mind, clear life—or whatever all the lifestyle gurus keep trying to convince me of when I'm doom scrolling at night.

Two hours, a sink full of dishes, a spotless bathroom, and a pristine bedroom later, I'm sorting my mammoth-sized pile of laundry into different categories, when my phone rings, pausing my audiobook. My heart leaps, hoping it's Hendrix so I can hear his voice. I don't know when I became a person who looks forward to hearing from a man, but every time he texts me, and I see the picture of me force-feeding him a churro, my own face stuffed full, my heart does a little dance.

I race to the other side of the room to retrieve my phone, expecting to see Hendrix's exasperated smile looking down at my chipmunk cheeks. Instead, my stomach drops.

A charcoal background with the word *Mom* lights up the screen.

I stare at the phone until it goes silent once more, screen darkening to black, my face a blurry reflection in the glass with a frown marring my mouth.

A few seconds later, a voicemail notification pops onto the screen. My body reacts instinctively, opening my phone and deleting the message. Whatever she has to say, I'm not interested.

Why haven't I blocked her? Why does the thought make me queasy?

I reopen my audiobook app and hit play again, letting the narrator's voice sweep me away as I grab my laundry and head down to the basement.

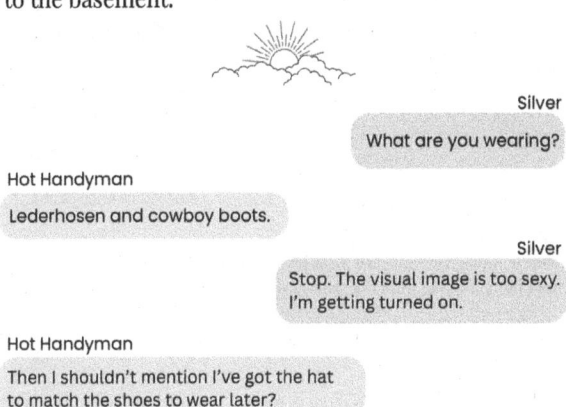

Silver
What are you wearing?

Hot Handyman
Lederhosen and cowboy boots.

Silver
Stop. The visual image is too sexy. I'm getting turned on.

Hot Handyman
Then I shouldn't mention I've got the hat to match the shoes to wear later?

> **Silver**
> Now you're just teasing me.

> **Hot Handyman**
> I'd never joke about your pleasure, Sunshine.

Well. Now I actually *am* a little flustered.

I've been in the building basement, doing laundry, for an hour now, and not a single person has come in here. Logically, I know I could go back upstairs, wait out the cycle, and come back down, but I just...I don't want to be in there right now. After the phone call came in, I needed to put some distance between myself and the place where my good day collapsed, at least for now.

> **Silver**
> What are you doing?

> **Hot Handyman**
> Snaking a drain in 9F.

> **Silver**
> I know another drain you could snake.

> **Hot Handyman**
> Are you trying to give me a semi next to sweet old Mrs. Reinbeck?

> **Silver**
> I don't kink shame.

> **Hot Handyman**
> You're insane.

> **Silver**
> Do you have a full day?

> **Hot Handyman**
> This is my last scheduled work order. I'll just hang around until my shift is up.

> **Silver**
> Or...

> **Hot Handyman**
> Why does that 'or' make me nervous?

> **Silver**
> You could come hang out with me in the laundry room.

> **Hot Handyman**
> I don't know if that's a great idea, since I'm not actually supposed to talk to you.

> **Silver**
> Seems a moot point when you were screaming my name last night.

> **Hot Handyman**
> Fuck.

> **Silver**
> C'mon. Break the rules and come hang out with me. I'll behave.

> **Hot Handyman**
> Somehow, I doubt that's true.
>
> I'll be there in 15 minutes.

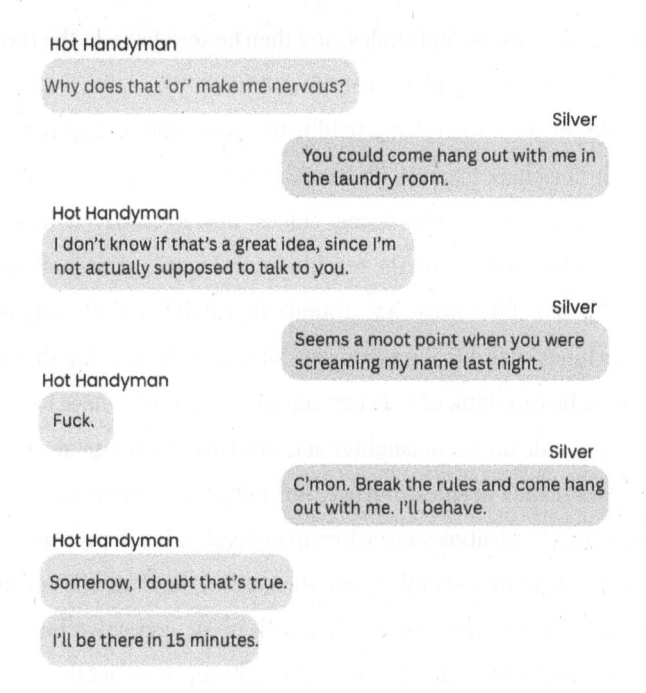

I'm giggling as I put a finished load in the dryer then replace the now-empty washer with another load of colors.

This room is far from luxurious. If even a single light went out, it would be quite creepy in here, with its low ceilings, dark stone walls, and singular metal table in the middle of the small room—not to mention the ominous chill from the lack of a radiator. As we creep further into November, it gets more and more drafty down here.

The door creaks open, and my heart jumps, but as I turn around, my heart sinks when I see Mrs. Evans walk in, wicker laundry basket in hand. She gives me a derisive sneer as she ambles toward an open machine, taking her time transferring her clothes. I pray to whoever will listen that she doesn't linger.

The door creaks open for the second time in minutes, and both me and Mrs. Evans look to the door to see Hendrix stepping through. He sees me and smiles, and then he sees Joyce in the room and freezes for a second, unsure of what to do.

He coughs into his hand to hide his smile, nodding his head at us both. "Just here to check on some...things."

"No one cares," Mrs. Evans chides, now aggressively tossing the last of her clothes into the machine and slamming the door shut.

Hendrix starts tinkering around with random objects, tapping on machines with his hammer, checking coils behind the dryers, anything he can think of to bring validity to his story. I have to turn around to hide my silent laughter at his lackluster attempt at a ruse.

Mrs. Evans decides to leave, but not before eyeing my outfit head to toe, her features screwing up in disgust. I inch my way over towards where he's standing, and the second the door clicks shut, I'm throwing my arms around his neck in an aggressive hug, his strong arms winding around my waist and squeezing tightly.

"I missed you too," he huffs into my neck.

I pull back and kiss him sweetly before untangling myself. He leans with his back on one of the unused machines, and I hop on the metal folding table across from it so we're facing each other.

"Everything okay?"

"Yeah." My voice comes out too high, and his stare says he's unconvinced.

"You never have to hide from me. I want all of you, good and bad. There's nothing you can say that will scare me away from you, Sunshine. I'm not going anywhere."

I suck in a deep breath. "My mom called...just before I came down here."

He doesn't miss a beat, concern etched onto his handsome face. "Did you talk to her?"

"No. I just stood there, screened the call, then deleted the voicemail." I look down at where my hands rest in my lap, fingers picking at my cuticles. "I feel like a coward."

"Look at me." His voice is gentle but rings with authority. "Choosing yourself over someone who hurt you beyond compare is not cowardice—it's bravery. You don't owe her a conversation or a place in your life. She forfeited that a long time ago. It's okay to not want to let her in again. You get to choose."

He always knows what to say to set me at ease, and it was terrifying how much I was coming to rely on him. But I just...I trust him. Intrinsically. Everything in my being tells me I can count on him in every way.

"You're kind of the best. Did you know that?" I smile, feeling my shoulders loosen and my body start to relax.

"What do you need?" he asks, always putting me first.

"Just you, I think."

His smile is so bright, it blinds me.

"I do believe I was promised lederhosen, though." I pout, pointing at his work pants and t-shirt.

"You don't think this is sexy?"

It definitely was. The casual blue collar worker vibe was definitely doing things for me, but I had a bit to commit to. I reach my foot out, grazing it along his thigh. "It's fine. I was just looking forward to making you yodel for me." My foot brushes against the crotch of his pants, and he yelps at the unexpected contact, grabbing my ankle. "Yeah, like that." I wink.

"I knew you wouldn't behave," he laughs, rubbing circles around my ankle before releasing me.

"Where would the fun in that be?" I hop off the table and prowl towards him, slipping my hands around his waist and resting my chin on his chest, peering up at him.

"You're shameless, using those eyes against me like that." He leans down, brushing an almost-kiss against the tip of my nose.

I leap up and capture his mouth with mine, and he falls into the pull with me, deepening the kiss before pulling away abruptly.

"We can't. I'm at work, and this," he motions between our two bodies, "is forbidden."

"Yeah, that just makes it hotter," I laugh.

He weighs his decision—indulge in something a little illicit with me, or take the safe road.

"Mrs. Evans could come back. She's just looking for a reason to get me fired," he says half-heartedly, looking at the door.

"There's still fifteen minutes on the spin cycle. Seems like plenty of time to me," I shrug, a challenge clear in my voice. "But if you don't think you can d–"

Then, he's lifting me off the floor and setting me on the table, spreading my legs and slotting his hips between them, hands grasping my waist and pulling me tightly into his body. His lips take mine in a punishing kiss, tongue sweeping against the seam of my mouth, and I open for him instantly, tongues grappling for dominance as the taste of him drives my pleasure higher.

Hendrix reaches down to the waistband of my pants but pauses, pulling back. "What are these?" He looks down at my rainbow argyle pajama pants.

"It's *laundry day*," I scoff. No one should be judged for their outfit choice on laundry day. We're down to bare bones in the closet.

He shrugs, accepting it for what it is, and pulls at the drawstring. I lean back a bit to give him room to slip his hand under the waistband. He stills, sucking in a harsh breath.

"Why aren't you wearing panties, sweetheart?" He runs his finger through my folds to find me already wet and ready for him. I'm always ready for him.

"Like I said, it's laundry day." I throw my head back on a sigh as he rubs back and forth, paying close attention to my clit, and I cry out as he applies more pressure.

He leans forward, growling into my ear, "You aren't playing fair." Then, he spears me with two fingers, my whole body lurching forward, chasing more, seeking his touch.

I'm writhing into his hand now, fucking myself on his fingers while the palm of his hand applies steady pressure to my clit, driving me out of my mind. I reach for Hendrix, licking his bottom lip before moving to his neck, sucking on the skin beneath his ear. His answering groan and the hardness I feel against my thigh tells me everything I need to know.

"More," I gasp. "*Please.*"

The desperate plea seems to break him, because he pulls his hand out of my pants rapidly, lifts me off the table, and turns me so I'm standing facing the washing machine. He places his palm between my shoulder blades and presses me to lean over the top of the machine before shucking my pants off completely. I'm shifting back and forth, desperately seeking friction, as the sound of his zipper descending fills the room, drowning out the machines.

I jump when I feel the head of his cock rub against my center, spreading my arousal along his shaft in preparation. I know this isn't going to be sweet. It's going to be fast and filthy. He lifts one of my legs, hooking his arm under the back of my knee and opening me for him. I find myself leaning forward to give him the best unobstructed angle.

"You like the thrill of maybe getting caught, baby?" Back and forth, he fucks through my folds, driving me mad, aching for him to fill me.

"Please," I whine.

He slowly rocks into me an inch, giving me what I want but not nearly enough at the same time. I try to press back, but he holds me in place, controlling the rhythm. I bury my head into my arm as he feeds me another inch. It's the most delicious torment, one I don't know how he's surviving.

"Hendrix..." I try my best to sound stern.

"Hmmm?" Another inch.

"I swear, if you don't fu–" He slams all the way to the hilt, and the sensation is so acute, my eyes cross.

"Always so impatient." He doesn't give me a second to recover as he pulls back and rams into me from behind, making us both groan in pleasure. The feeling of him stretching me wide, dragging in and out, is the most intoxicating feeling. I want to be drunk on it for the rest of my life.

"Is this what you wanted? To be ridden hard in the laundry room when anyone could walk in?" One arm is still under my knee, the other curling up between my breasts, holding me against his chest as his hand settles around my throat.

My eyes roll back in my head as his cock nudges that place inside that drives me out of my mind. "Yes," I stammer, completely lost to the carnality of what he's doing.

In and out, he pounds into me, grunting in my ear, taking as much pleasure as he gives. It's the single most erotic experience of my life.

Distantly, I can hear the elevator bell chime. We both clock it but are too lost in our bliss to care.

"Touch yourself, Silver," he commands, applying pressure to the hand around my throat, making me clench around him. "If I could have my way, I would fuck you like this for the rest of time, but we've only got a few minutes left on that machine, and no one but me is allowed to see you like this."

I gasp, fireworks popping at the base of my spine and shooting out across my skin like a web. We're both close, and Hendrix clutches my leg tightly in an effort to hold himself back to make sure I come first. I reach one of my hands down between my legs, groaning loudly as I start to circle my swollen bud, tightening around his shaft.

"*Fuck*. You have to be quiet, Sunshine." He growls in my ear.

"Faster." I twist my head around and take his lips with mine.

He pounds into me with the speed of a man possessed as I rub myself, feeling the orgasm dance up my core, making everything pulsate.

"So. Fucking. Perfect." He enunciates each word with a punishing thrust, and it sets me off.

I come with a guttural cry, prompting Hendrix to cover my mouth with his hand as my core flutters wildly around him, spurring on his own release. He pumps into me until the last of his orgasm subsides, his strong tattooed arms bracketing my body. My legs are still shaking and then go limp all together. If it wasn't for Hendrix holding me up, I would be boneless on the floor. He leans forward, resting his chest against my back, settling my raised leg slowly down on and holding me softly to him, chin resting on my shoulder as we catch our breath.

He pulls out of me with a wince, the aftershocks of our

orgasms making the movement hyper-sensitive. He helps me pull up my pajama pants and fixes himself before he spins me and rests his head against my forehead.

"How are you real?" He hums, full mouth an inch away from mine.

I tip up to brush my lips against his, a barely-there touch of our mouths, when the buzzer for the washer goes off, startling us apart and making us laugh.

"Wanna watch baking show reruns and order pizza tonight?" I ask.

He's about to answer when the door to the laundry room opens, and Mrs. Evans swaggers in, looking between us with accusation in her eyes. I can't tell if we've been caught, or if that's her typical *I despise you* stare.

"I unclogged that filter, so you should be okay to use that dryer," Hendrix says to me in an overexaggerated tone.

I look at him, confused, for a minute before he nudges his head in the other direction, and I catch on. "Great. Thank you."

He squeezes my hand quickly while Joyce looks away before Hendrix slips out the door.

No sooner is he gone that I get a text from him.

> Hot Handyman
> Yes to tonight, but if you start lusting after Paul Hollywood again, we're changing the show.

I smile down at my phone.

> Silver
> Boooooo.

Chapter 27

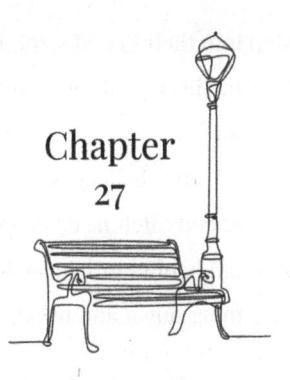

Hendrix

"No, we absolutely cannot put *War and Peace* next to an alien romance titled *War and Tease*."

I came to the bookstore during my lunch break to bring Silver lunch, almost positive she hasn't eaten today, but it would seem I have entered into the middle of a duel of literary proportions. It's the day before the re-opening, and emotions are high. Silver is visibly stressed, even if she acts like everything is fine.

"Why not?" Carmen huffs.

"Well, for starters, they're different genres," Silver volleys back, throwing her hands up.

"That sounds like discrimination, boss lady. Maybe the person who's buying Tolstoy is going through something, and they look over and see a seven foot tall alien with a ten pack of abs next to it and think, you know what—*this* is what's going to fix me."

Silver has gone silent, but I can see a subtle twitch in her left eye and decide now is the best time to intervene.

"I think Tolstoy would prefer being shelved next to the

minotaur smut." I step into their line of sight, making my presence known, and something in Silver's pale eyes softens before crinkling at the corners with humor.

"What do you know?" She challenges.

"Lots of things. I've been catching up on my reading since book club. Wouldn't want to fall behind or be caught unaware...again." I sidle up next to her, leaning down and brushing a kiss against her temple.

"See! Even Hendrix agrees with me."

Silver turns to me. "No more sex for you if you take her side."

"Hey! That's sexual coercion." Carmen settles her hands on her hips, shaking her head. "You are out of control today."

She steps away, probably to go shelve the two books together anyway, when Silver turns to me. "What are you doing here? Shouldn't you be at work?"

I hold up the lunch I picked up on my way over. "I'm on lunch, and now, so are you."

She looks from me to the bag, contemplating. "I don't have time."

"Ten minutes. That's all I'm asking, and then you can go right back to checking things off your sticky notes." I wave the bag of take out under her nose, and she sways on her feet to chase after the smell.

"How do you know I have sticky notes?"

"Because they've been littered throughout the store for weeks. I found one in my shoe the other day. Don't forget to follow up with the graphic designer doing the website."

She grabs a fresh sheet and scribbles the reminder down.

"Sit with me, eat some food. Carmen can handle things while

you're resting."

She still looks uncertain, but the smell of the double cheeseburger with fried onions wafting from the bag has her waffling on her decision.

"Or I can pick up whatever task you need done while you sit down and have lunch," I offer.

"No," she says quickly. "Sit with me."

A few moments later, we find ourselves sitting on the small bench under the shop window, watching people pass by while Silver demolishes the food I brought her. She allowed the business one day to close and get the store ready with final touches for tomorrow, and plenty of people walking past are checking out the commotion, wondering why the windows are suddenly papered shut. Every time they do, Silver invites them to the event tomorrow as I sit back, bursting with pride. After the last person walks off, she shoves a couple fries into her mouth and turns to see me smiling at her.

"What?" she says around a mouthful of potato.

"Nothing. It's just cute how excited you get telling people."

"Well, I have to. This place needs to be a success."

"I don't think that's it." She raises an eyebrow at me. "I'm sure that's part of it, but I think there's a much bigger piece of you that wants it for you too, to prove to yourself you could stick to something."

"Maybe." She looks down at her lap.

I worry I've said the wrong thing, or that maybe I've pushed her too far into her thoughts. She takes the final bite of her burger and comes to stand, scrunching the wrapper in her hands.

"Sunshine, I—"

She cuts me off. "It's fine. I need to get back though." She leans down, and I rest my hands on the backs of her thighs as she places a soft kiss on my lips. "Thank you for lunch," she mumbles against my mouth.

"I'll come back after work."

"*You* have done enough for this place." She runs her hands through the hair at the nape of my neck. "The girls and I are gonna be here late getting everything ready, and then I'm going to try and sleep so I can be rested for the long day ahead. Something tells me if you're around, I *won't* be resting."

The smile I give her is wolfish. "I'll see you in the morning then."

As much as it pains me to give her the space, it's obvious she's feeling overwhelmed. Even with as far as we've made it in terms of being open with each other, she's leaning on old habits right now, feeling like she needs to do this part alone.

She turns to walk back into the store, but I grab her wrist, spinning her around and bringing my mouth down on top of hers. Instantly, her body melts into mine, and the rest of the world fades away for a moment in time. When I pull away, it's only to look in her eyes, to infuse her with this surety that I have in her, in us.

But she keeps her eyes closed, breathing me in slowly before walking back into her shop and getting back to work.

My walk back to The Langham leaves me feeling unsettled, and when I enter the building, I immediately feel a sense of wrongness settling in the air. I look at Tony, who has a concerned expression on his face, before seeing Mrs. Evans step out of Fairbank's office. The look she gives me is smug, self-congratulatory, and I know whatever is about to happen won't be pleasant.

Mr. Fairbanks pops out of his office a moment later, fingers motioning for me to come forward. "My office. Now."

This could really only be about one thing, and it's time to face the consequences of my inevitable choice—there was no choice, falling in love with Silver was inevitable.

I trail into his office after him and wait for him to speak.

"Do you know why I've called you in here?"

"To chat about the latest episode of The Real Housewives?" He does seem the type.

"No," he sputters and straightens the lapels of his jacket. "It has been brought to my attention that you have breached the terms of your employment."

"Ah."

He's taken aback by my unruffled demeanor. "I've been informed by a concerned tenant that you have been cavorting with a resident of the building. Do you deny engaging in an inappropriate relationship?" I don't think he wants to know just how inappropriate I've been.

"I don't," I say plainly.

I don't think he heard my admission, as his gaze flicks to the lobby, and I know he's thinking about Mrs. Evans. "There has been talk of you being too friendly with Ms. James, and even claims that someone with your features was seen leaving the building well before any scheduled shift you may have had."

"I understand."

"The same concerned tenant claims to have seen you around town with Ms. James, and at this point, there have been too many instances for me to ignore such brazen disregard for the rules."

They could have seen us anywhere—at Get Nailed while getting supplies for the shop, at that Italian restaurant off Cornelia Street, on a walk around Central Park to see the leaves change as she showed me some of her favorites bench plaques. The fact that we were being watched makes my skin crawl.

"I'm afraid I must relieve you of your position." His dismissal pulls me out of my thoughts.

I should feel panic at his words. A few months ago, I certainly would have, but instead, I feel a strange sort of calm settle over me. This was never supposed to be what I'd do forever. It was a means to an end, even if that end was nowhere on the horizon. The end of this job no longer feels like an end to New York like it had when I'd first arrived from Seattle. No, this is my home. I can feel it deep in my core. I felt that way when I was here in my early twenties, and I can still feel it now. It was always going to be this city. It was always going to be Silver.

Home was here before her. Home is here *with* her.

I was always meant to end up in this very place, tool bag in hand, knocking on the door of the woman who would flip me inside out, and help me become the version of myself that I liked. I could feel in my bones that I would have found my way to her even if I hadn't left after college. I don't know who we would've been back then, but I still would have been hers, in every version of this life.

"Do you have nothing to say for yourself?" My *former* boss pulls me out of my thoughts.

"No, sir. The termination is fair, if not unavoidable." He's at a loss for words. "I'll grab my few things and be on my way. Thank you for the opportunity—it gave me a second chance with the woman of my dreams."

Fairbanks doesn't know I met and fumbled my first chance encounter with Silver that very first day the world tipped on its axis, pitching us toward each other and spinning my plans out of control. The fact that she lives here and awarded me a do-over was pure fate.

"I'm sure I'll be seeing you around because, well, because my girlfriend lives here." Fuck, that feels good to say out loud. I reach my hand out to shake his, and he reluctantly grips mine back. "I hope it won't be awkward." Giving his hand one final shake, I make my way out of his office.

I quickly gather the few things I had in my office storeroom, shoving my sketchbook of designs, the one specifically housing the mock ups for Kena's hutch, into the bag of clothes I stored there for a quick change.

I walk through the lobby, Tony giving me a salute, but I laugh and pull him into a hug. "I'll see you soon Tony."

Mrs. Evans is lurking in the corner. "I warned you to stay away from that girl. I told you I would make you sorry."

I face her head on. "I'm not. Sorry, that is."

She scoffs derisively in my direction. "I tried to warn you. She's a tramp, nothing but trouble. You're just one of many—"

I bridge the few feet standing between us, and she yields a step. "If you can't see her for what and who she is, then I feel bad for you. But you don't deserve her. Hell, I probably don't either. But the difference is, I get to try every day, and you'll be here, trying to make everyone around you miserable when the only person you're hurting is yourself, Joyce. I would wish you peace, but quite frankly, I hope you stub your toe on the corner of your bed every day for the way you've treated her." Mrs. Evans goes to argue, and I can sense Tony to our right trying not to laugh. "But I'll see you soon. I suggest you be nicer the next time you see my girl, or I might have to let Fairbanks know about that stolen—what was it again, Tony?"

"Scotch." Mirth lines his answer.

"Ah, yes. Scotch."

I don't wait for a response before I step out of the building into the crisp mid-November air and head towards my apartment. I want to go back to the store and help, but I know Silver will question why I'm there, not at work. I don't want to tell her I lost my job the night before the biggest day of her life. She doesn't need that distraction right now.

I spend the rest of my free afternoon finishing up the sketches I have for Kena before shooting some pictures over to the number he gave me. The money I make from this one project will help to sustain me for at least a month, so I want to make sure I get it right for him.

The rest of the night slogs by while I do the most menial tasks to stay busy, wishing I was at the bookstore. I debate shooting Silver a quick text to check in, make sure she and the girls don't need anything, but decide against it, not wanting to distract her.

I do a quick home workout to pass the rest of the evening, shower, then hop in bed so I can be up early tomorrow to pick up coffee and breakfast for everyone.

Before I know it, sleep takes me under, and I fall into a dream about a beautiful girl with hair the color of the moon and eyes as bright as the sea.

I shoot out of bed to a loud trilling that abruptly stops.

Reaching over and grabbing my phone, I note two things. First, it's three in the morning, and second, there are two missed calls from my mom.

That can't be right.

The ringing picks up again, the bright light and shrill sound splitting my head in two.

"Mom?" My voice is hoarse with sleep as I answer the phone.

Sobbing runs through the line and straight to my heart, waking me up faster than a bucket of cold water over my head.

"What's wrong? Are you okay?"

"It's—" Sobs wrack her body, making it impossible for her to speak. "It's Laurel, sweetie."

My heart stops cold in my chest.

"She's in the hospital." *I can't feel my toes.* "She was in an accident. It's bad, the doctor said... Hen, please get here."

All the trauma from losing my brother comes rushing to the surface like a tidal wave, drowning out everything and crushing me with terror. My body goes completely numb, and my mind drains, painfully blank.

"I'm coming," I say before she tells me the hospital and we hang up.

Panic starts to claw its way up my throat, choking me on all my regrets. I left on bad terms. I've barely spoken to her or the rest of my family since I left. What kind of brother does that? What if she dies, and I never get to tell her I love her again, or that she was the reason I stayed in Seattle as long as I did after Maddox died? I would live the rest of my life in penitence.

I don't have a single thought in my head other than my little sister lying still in a hospital bed. That thought alone spurs me into action, scrambling for my wallet and a hoodie, not even stopping to change out of my sweatpants. I run out the door and hail a cab to the airport, purchasing a flight on my phone before slipping the device into my pants. I'm too distracted in my terrified state to notice when it falls back out onto the taxi seat, before throwing myself out the door and onto the first plane out to Seattle.

Chapter 28

Silver

This day will end with me sick and bent over the toilet bowl.

I arrive at the store earlier than the girls so I can take it all in and make sure everything is ready, ensuring no Post-It was missed in the making of this store. It's still driving me mad that some things aren't complete, namely the phone lines, website, and a little thing called a new store name. But I am trying to make peace with the idea that this was a physical reopening; I could always do a digital rebrand in a few weeks once everything is ironed out and running smoothly. The renovation was about drawing in new customers and starting to turn a profit—the rest could come later.

At least that was what everyone has been telling me so my eye would stop twitching.

The store is nearly unrecognizable. Gone are the decades old warm toned and bowing bookshelves filled with unsold titles. The floor is no longer creaking, and the walls are a sad, time yellowed beige no more. Instead, Hendrix and I managed to create something both bold and timeless.

With the new flooring, we sanded down the area tables, staining them with a more neutral shade that complimented the pale sage green of the walls. All the shelves are now a brilliant white, helping to offset books on the shelves instead of feeling lost. I finished off the place with bold floral rugs in shades of pale pink, lavender, and green, accenting the free space on the wall behind the counter with a gallery of vintage gold frames. One day, I would fix the stairs and transform the second floor, just not anytime soon. I need to get out of the financial hole I buried myself in first.

I'm lighting a candle, tying balloons around the shop, and setting up some beverages for patrons when the front door opens, letting in a cold snap of wind.

"Sorry, we aren't open for another hour. Please come ba–"

"The place looks great, Silly."

Every ounce of blood leaves my body as I stand frozen, unable to turn around, to face her.

"Don't call me that," I gasp out on a breath that barely escapes my body.

"Silver, please." There's a desperation in her tone that has no right to be there. She *left*. She *chose* this reaction.

I turn to her and finally look at the face I haven't seen in years by *her* own volition. She's no longer the mother I remember; she's older now, with grey hairs littered throughout her blonde strands, deeper lines around her eyes. Her face is beautiful—it makes me mad, and she flinches back at whatever it is she sees on mine. Maybe it's the anger or the resemblance to my father that affects her so much. I don't know. I don't particularly care.

"What are you doing here?"

"I–I wanted to support you."

I scoff. "Since when?"

The silence is deafening. She's had two decades to support me, and she never showed up. Not for recitals or holidays or birthdays. She wasn't there when I got my first period, or when I lost my virginity and was confused. She's never met my best friend or come to our graduations or took us trick-or-treating. She's had twenty years of opportunities and chose herself every single time. So why show up now, for this?

"I know there's some bad blood between us–"

"That's one way to describe abandoning your child," I murmur under my breath.

Hendrix words from earlier in the week float to the forefront of my mind. *Choosing yourself over someone who hurt you beyond compare is not cowardice. It's bravery.*

"–but I was just hoping we could put that behind us." Her tone is soft, like she's trying to gentle parent me into forgiveness. It feels manipulative.

My vision starts to spot, and I'm battling anger and devastation in equal measures. I decide to focus on the anger, choosing to ignore the latter, as I snap.

"You talk about what you did as if you ruined my favorite sweater! You dropped me off at Nan's *a week* after Dad died and never came back. I waited for you, for months–*years*–and you never showed. All I got was a half-assed birthday card and a phone call whenever you could be bothered to remember. And now you come here, *uninvited*, on the biggest day of my life, to what? Ask for a do-over?"

She has the good sense to look sheepish. "You wouldn't answer my calls. What was I supposed to do?" Apparently, all sense has flown out the building.

"Take the fucking hint!"

"Silly, please. We can fix this," she urges. So desperate, and for what? I don't understand this sudden need to reclaim her motherhood.

"*You* don't get to call me that. That was Dad's name for me. Remember him? Because he wouldn't recognize you." She jerks back as if I've slapped her. My hand comes to rest on the necklace he gave me before he died, and it gives me a strange sort of comfort, holding on to it like it's imbuing me with his strength.

Tears threaten to spill, but I refuse to give in to that vulnerability, to show her how badly she's hurt me for the last twenty years.

"Why are you really here?" I ask.

"I have something for you."

"I don't want it."

"You get that stubbornness from your dad, you know." She huffs a laugh that makes me grind my teeth.

"Good."

The silence permeating the room is suffocating, and the woman trying to masquerade as my mother shifts back and forth, clearly weighing a decision before deciding to drop a nuclear bomb on the last dregs of our fractured relationship.

"I'm getting remarried." The words echo through my mind, pin balling around and banging against my skull. I wish I could say it stopped there, but that would have been a mercy. "Paul wanted me to try and mend our relationship. He wants to meet you."

"Well, if *Paul* wants it." I let the unspoken words hang in the air. Paul may want to meet me, but if he wasn't suggesting it, would she have ever even showed up here?

"He's got two young kids and wants them to know you too." My stomach sinks, and a painful pricking starts behind my eyes. I don't think that's the good news she thinks it is. All I hear is there *are* kids she's willing to raise and nurture, just not me. It stings more than salt on a festering wound.

"I want you to leave. Please."

"Silver–" She moves to take a step towards me.

"No!" I shout, stopping her with a upheld hand. "You don't get to show up here after twenty years and try to upend my life! I do not owe you anything when you have given me *nothing*. I stopped waiting for you to show up, stopped waiting for *anyone* to show up for me because of you and your choices. I have spent years feeling unlovable, squeezing myself into a fun and agreeable mould, keeping everyone at arm's length because I was afraid they would all just leave like you did. So forgive me if I don't feel inclined to accommodate you now."

The tears finally fall, and I roughly wipe them away with the back of my hands.

"Please, just go."

She stares at me, face unreadable, before she rifles around in her bag, pulling out a cream envelope and handing it out to me. When I make no move to take it from her, she walks toward the cash wrap and sets it down on the smooth wood surface before heading towards the entrance.

She turns back when she's at the front door, pausing with her hand on the new brass fixture. "I loved him, you know, your dad. Probably too much." And that love poisoned everything in the end. She spares me one last glance, as if she's memorizing my face, cataloging all the ways it might change in the future, how it might look like hers. A future she won't see.

And you didn't love me enough, I think as she walks out the door and out of my life.

I rest my hands against the table in front of me, taking a deep breath in, and start to cry. And cry. And cry. I cry until my lungs ache and my eyes burn from exertion, and when it seems there's no moisture in my body left to release, I reach for my phone and dial the one person whose voice I need to hear most, whose presence will tether me back to Earth and make me feel like everything will be alright.

But the phone just rings and rings and rings before taking me to an automated voicemail.

I pull the phone from my ear, disappointed but knowing I'll see him soon enough. He'll wrap his strong arms around me and tell me he's proud of me in his deep baritone, and everything will be okay after that.

Because he's the sure thing I never expected.

"Jesus Christ. Maybe I would've updated this shit hole years ago if I knew it would make this much of a difference." I sent Pat an email inviting her to the reopening if she was still in town, hoping she would be able to come and see her place was in good hands.

"Do you like it?"

"Do you?" she asks.

I scan the room, seeing people of all ages and walks of life moseying around, books in hand, smiles on their faces. I also see Hendrix everywhere. He's in every paint stroke, perfect shelf alignment, and beam of crown molding—even though he's still not here.

I turn to Pat and nod. "I don't think I realized how much this place meant to me until the threat of losing it happened. I'll owe you forever for letting me do this."

"You owe me nothing as long as the checks clear," she jokes, even as her face is set in a look of severe stoicism.

"Thank you for coming."

"Honey, nothing could keep me away." She grabs my hand, which is a bit of a shock to the system, because Pat has never been affectionate. "I've watched you grow up here over the last ten years. It feels right that it belongs to you." She pats my cheek and walks away.

We've been open for a couple hours, and I've never seen the store so busy.

It would seem the combined efforts of the reno plus all the word of mouth advertising we've been doing really paid off. The opening is a success, and I can't relish the feeling because my mind is too distracted, alternating between the encounter with my mom and Hendrix's absence.

I tried calling him again, and it went straight to voicemail instead of ringing. I'm trying not to let it bother me, but on the cusp of the ordeal with my mom, I'm feeling a little tender.

Thankfully, I have no time to ruminate on any of it for too long, because the store is slammed. Holly, Carmen, and I have been fielding customers left and right while trying to keep the place tidy as much as possible. I've noticed a few familiar faces, some of the people from book club, Dax from Respect the Drip stopped by to bring us coffee, Carmen's fuck boy ex who Holly chased off with a particularly thick copy of *A Clash of Kings*. Even Simon and Isla stopped by. Everything is going smoothly.

Warm arms slide around my waist from behind, and for a moment I breathe in a deep sigh of relief before I realize the scent is wrong, the build much smaller. I twist in Kena's arms to see him beaming down at me, Julien standing just off to his right holding flowers. I try my best to muster up a smile, but it feels fake, even to me, and my best friend is immediately concerned.

"Julien, my love, could you go get me a drink?" Julien takes the request for what it is, a hint to get lost for a few minutes. "Okay, what's wrong?"

I tell him everything. How my mom showed up and dropped an anvil on my head. How I tried to call Hendrix because he's the only one I wanted to talk to about it. How he didn't answer and hasn't since. How he isn't here when he said he would be.

I look at my best friend with defeat in my posture and can tell he's at a loss for words. I don't need to tell him all the muck this is dredging up for me. Abandonment claws at my throat, digging in like a starved wolf, my misery its meal. I'm drowning, lost in a sea of regret and sorrow, no life vest in sight.

"He could still show up," he offers in encouragement.

"Maybe." We both know he's not coming. He would have been here by now or given any kind of indication he was running late, but he hasn't. He's been radio silent since he left the shop yesterday, after I was acting weird and stand-offish and not my normally bubbly self at lunch. Is that what happened? He peeled back enough of my layers to get to my tender underbelly, didn't like what he saw, and decided to cut and run?

"Everything will be okay," Kena tries to assure me.

"I've gotta go. The store's busy." I give him a quick kiss on the cheek. "Thank you for coming."

I'm inverting in on myself, building my walls back up brick by brick because it's the only defense mechanism I know.

Hours have gone by, and the day was a whopping success. I fake celebration with the girls as we clean up, tossing out cups and straightening shelves. I close out the till, and it's the highest sales day we've had in years.

There's a large part of me that's proud, but the numbness that's spread through my body hours ago isn't allowing me to fully enjoy the success.

When the girls and I gather outside to lock up, I give them each a hug. "Thank you for all your hard work, and for pushing me towards this."

They exchange a glance. "We actually got you a gift," Carmen says.

She reaches into her bag and pulls out a small box, handing it to me. I lift the lid, and a bark of laughter launches from my throat. It's the most genuine slice of joy I've had today as I pull out a pink ceramic mug that reads *World's Sexiest Boss*. A tear escapes my eye, and I'm lucky I can pass it off as tears of laughter when really, I'm so overwhelmed, and this small kind gesture sets me off for some reason.

"This is the best. Thank you."

We say goodbye before going our separate ways, and I'm left with spiraling thoughts again. It's still early in the evening, but I can't wait to get in bed and be enveloped by darkness and the oblivion of sleep.

As I walk into the building a few minutes later, I make one last desperate decision—one last ditch effort to make sense of this.

"Hey Tony, have you seen Hendrix?"

Tony scratches the back of his neck. "He was fired yesterday... He didn't tell you?"

Fired? Why wouldn't he tell me that? Did he blame me for it, is that way he was a no show today?

"Umm, no, but thanks anyway." I turn, walking quickly to the elevators, and when I step on and the doors close, I crumble.

I can't hold it in anymore. The tears pour out of me in rivulets for the second time today, because he didn't show up when I needed him most. He's spent weeks, months demolishing my walls, smoothing over my rough edges, and making me feel shiny and new—making me feel *loved*—only to not show up on the day I needed him the most, when he *promised* he would be here.

Years of bottled up trauma comes rushing over me like an avalanche of despair, burying me under a suffocating reality: I never should have allowed myself to get attached, to rely on him.

I somehow make it through my front door, not remembering the steps I took to get here, fall into my too empty bed where I habitually reach for a body that isn't there, and cry myself to sleep.

Chapter 29

Hendrix

To my luck, the first flight out of JFK direct to Seattle was boarding by the time I made it to the airport. I ran a mad dash through security and got to my gate right before they closed the doors. Once I was seated and we were in the air, the adrenaline I was surviving on up until that point abruptly wore off, and I fell asleep immediately.

I was grateful for it, though, since it kept my mind from spinning to worst case scenarios. But now that I was back on the West Coast and in a cab straight to the hospital, all the *what ifs* were running rampant.

Mom said Laurel was in a bad accident. It was vague, but there was enough panic in her voice to scare me into action. She could be in surgery right now. What if she was in a coma? Fuck, she could be paralyzed. The thought of my wonderfully stubborn and headstrong sister lying prone in a hospital bed makes me physically ill, and the shaking of the car as it rolls over the highway isn't helping the rising nausea churning inside my gut.

After what feels like an eternity, we roll up to the hospital, and the wheels have barely stopped turning before I throw myself out the door into the bustling emergency room. The place is packed full of people. Nurses are flying around, charts in hand, family members pacing the waiting room, biting their nails down to the quick, all while announcements are being made over the speakers. It's an overwhelming, sensory overload nightmare cloaked as a health facility.

I scan the room but don't see my parents anywhere before quickly walking to the front desk, sidestepping an anxious kid with the zoomies.

"I'm looking for Laurel Wells' room, please," I pant out of breath.

The woman at reception barely spares me an upward glance. "Relation?"

"I'm her brother." She types something into her computer, nails clicking against the keyboard, ratcheting my anxiety up higher the longer she doesn't tell me anything. "Is she—is she okay?"

"I can't disclose that information."

I am seconds away from running through the halls of this ER to search every room until I find my sister, to let her know I am here, that I'm sorry I hadn't gotten here sooner.

Please let me be here on time *this time*. An image of my brother's body floating face up in a lake flashes through my mind, reminding me of the day I *didn't* make it in time.

"She's in room 3410–" I'm already sprinting down the hallway in search of her room, barely pausing long enough to check the directional signs hanging on the wall telling me I need to go up.

I dart up two flights of stairs and tumble out onto the third floor hallway, hanging a right, passing room after room bringing me closer. My chest is heaving from the cardio and anxiety fueling my every movement this morning when I notice I'm one door away.

Room 3410 is just up ahead on my left. I pick up my pace, steeling myself for the worst before bursting through the door to find—what?

"What the hell are you doing here?" Laurel half-shouts around a heaping spoonful of chocolate pudding.

Laurel—who's sitting up in a hospital bed with wires coming out of her arm, with bruising and swelling covering her face. She has a leg and an arm both in castings but otherwise, she's fine. Not dead, paralyzed or in a coma.

The pressure on my chest eases infinitesimally as tears fill my eyes.

"Did I hit my head harder than I thought, and now I'm hallucinating my oaf of a big brother standing before me?"

"Laur..."

"Quick, if you're really Hendrix and not a mirage, tell me what priceless family heirloom I broke when we were kids." She's painfully serious as she holds my stare with raised brows.

"You broke half of grandma's vintage dining set when you were eight." That set had been passed down through multiple generations before she toppled too hard into the cabinet and sent half the pieces falling—then tried to blame it on me and Maddox before eventually fessing up to Mom.

She tries to adjust herself in bed but winces as pain coasts along her body. I rush over to help her, fussing over the pillows to help them hold her up higher.

"Why are you here, Hen?"

"Isn't that obvious?" I grab her hand.

"Not really. You live across the country."

"Mom called me in the middle of the night, sobbing hysterically, saying you'd been in an accident and that it was bad. I wasn't really thinking after that. I just...got here as fast as I could. All I–" my voice breaks around the words, "all I could see was Maddie. I needed to be sure you were okay." Nothing more needs to be said. She knows as well as I do the permanent scars that day left on us.

"I appreciate you for coming, but I'm okay. I'm just a little banged up." She smiles at me, trying to ease the tension written all over my face.

"That's clearly not true." I nod at her broken and wrapped body.

Before she can reply, my mother pushes into the room carrying a tray of food. "I got you a plate of your favorite breakfa—oh!" Mom gasps when she sees me, nearly dropping the tray. Tears immediately well up in her eyes, a twin mirror to my own.

"Hi, Mom." I stand and grab the food from her, setting it on the table next to my sister so I can wrap her up in a hug. She silently sobs against me, her shoulders shaking, and I squeeze her tighter.

"What are you doing here?" My whole body tenses at the sound of my dad's voice coming in through the door.

"So many warm greetings this morning," I mumble, turning to face my father. "Dad." I give him a clipped nod.

"You've got some nerve showing up here like this after leaving the way you did."

"I don't think this is the best time to do this," Mom says, trying to mitigate the rising conflict my dad seems hellbent on seeing through.

"Mom called me. I'm here. There's nothing more to say." My voice is clipped as I try to keep my cool in front of the man whose judgment I can feel burning a hole in my temple. It's a complicated thing to dread someone's presence while also still feeling like the kid who always begged for his approval. I love my Dad, but that love often felt like trying to hug a cactus.

"The first call you've answered in months. Isn't that lucky?" The blow lands exactly how he intended it to, swift and to the gut. And the worst part is, I can't even refute it. He's right. I've been a horrible son, screening calls and never calling back. At first, it was because I desperately needed the space, but then it was because I never thought to. I got caught up in living life the way I wanted to, in a way that made me truly happy for the first time in my life.

I stay silent, trying my hardest to not give him the reaction I know he wants. He's itching for a fight, never the first to back down, and I feel my hackles rise as I feel him staring at my back. But he just won't let it go.

"I guess it's fitting that you're here, since you were the cause of the accident, after all." My whole body goes ramrod straight.

What is he talking about?

"Dad. Don't," Laurel pleads.

But the thing about my dad is, he always has to have the upper hand. He's always had it over me, and that's part of what took me away from here.

"You don't want him to know that the only reason you were even in the car was because you were going to follow in his footsteps and run off to New York?"

My eyes dart over to Laurel, and she's looking pointedly down at her lap. "Laurel?"

"I had a red-eye. I was on my way to the airport," she whispers, still refusing eye contact.

"Why?" My voice is gentle.

"Because you put it in her head that she could run away from this family too."

I never take my eyes off my sister's face as dad's words land, and she flinches in her hospital bed. Something about watching my normally larger-than-life spitfire of a sister, sheltering away from my father's harsh words, is all it takes for me to finally snap.

"Or maybe she needed to get away from you."

"Excuse me?" His tone is filled with ice shards that cut through the room, sending an instant chill around the fluorescently lit space.

"I was just coming to visit you." Laurel tries to dispel the tension, but I've already been sent down this path, and all the feelings I've been burying around my father for years have finally come to a head.

I rise out of my seat and face my dad. "You've never been a warm man, and I convinced myself that was okay because you were never cruel. But since Maddox died–"

"Don't say his name." Anger seeps from his tone, but underneath it, I also hear a chord of grief.

"–since Maddie died you've become…callous and cold. Before I left, nothing I did was right and I was a constant failure to you. You would berate me over every little thing. Punishing me for the accident. As if I wasn't punishing myself enough over it. I know it's my fault he's gone, I know that! I'm sor–" I choke on a cry, "I'm sorry. He would still be here if I had been stronger, and I'll live with that for the rest of my life." I can hear my mom and sister softly crying behind me.

"So the answer is to just leave? I thought I raised you to be tougher stock than that," Dad admonishes.

"I was dying here!" Everyone in the cramped hospital room goes stock still at the admission I lay at their feet. Even my dad's fury seems to abate a fraction in the face of my words. "I—" I choke back the tears I'm trying hard not to release in front of the man who will only see it as weakness. If I start, I won't stop, and I need to get this out. "Maddie tried to get me to see it. He begged me before he died to start living my life for me and I didn't understand. I didn't realize it then—that I was just going through the motions. It wasn't until I met..." I trail off, thinking of Silver, and a small smile creeps onto my face.

"Well, I'm so sorry that being with your family is such a burden," my dad sneers.

"Jonah," my mother admonishes, but my dad won't even acknowledge anyone else is in the room but me.

"That." I point an accusing finger at him. "That right there is the problem. You're so goddamn stubborn. Your pride is a monster that fills up every room, allowing no space for me to feel anything or grow in a way *I* want to. You won't allow it. How am I supposed to have an open conversation with you when your gut instinct is to repress *everything* you feel?"

That infamous pride rears its ugly head now. "No one's forcing you to be here."

I can hear my mom suck in a breath as Laurel's monitors beep behind me.

I wish Silver was here with me. She would probably be telling off my dad in fine form, and it would make my mom adore her, make Laurel want to be her best friend, and it would make me love her even more. I miss the steadying feeling I get just by being around her. I want to hear her raspy laugh floating through the air as we fix the store up for the opening.

The opening...which is today. And I'm on the other side of the country.

"Fuck!" I shout, frantically reaching into my pockets in search of my phone, but I can't find it anywhere. *"No. No. No."* My phone isn't here. I must have left it in the cab, and the terror I felt over Laurel's condition kept me from noticing until now.

"Honey? What's wrong?" There's concern in Mom's voice after my outburst.

"I...I lost my phone, and—" I glance at the clock on the wall, noting that with the flight and the time zone change, Silver would have already opened the store, and I wasn't there with her. My heart sinks into my stomach, and I feel sick, knowing I've let her down on the day it mattered most for me to show up, to show her she's *more* than worthy of the love she thinks she's incapable of.

I sink down into the chair next to Laurel's bed and drop my head into my hands.

"I should be there." Renewed nausea churns in my gut.

My mom crouches down to face me at eye level. "Where?"

"Silver's store opening. I should be there, and I'm not. She's... *everything*, and she needs me today. I'm not there, and she doesn't know why. I can't tell her why."

Understanding dawns on their faces as they realize exactly who Silver must be to me.

"I left my phone in the car but I can go get it," Mom offers, but I'm already shaking my head.

"I don't know her number by heart yet, and the store's phones aren't working either. There's no way to tell her what happened."

Silence permeates the room, no one knowing what to say at my obvious distress. "Will you tell us about her?" Mom asks, clearly wanting intel on the woman who flipped my world upside down.

It draws the tiniest of smiles out of me. I start by telling them about how she spilled her coffee on me that first day we met, how the scent now reminds me of her. I tell them how it shocked the hell out of me to discover that she was a tenant of the building I worked at and how I had to fix up her apartment and loved every day more and more. How the thought of not seeing her daily made me feel panicky, and I offered to help her repair her store just to stay close to her. I tell them about how each day, I felt myself slowly come back to life, one smile, one question, one repaired floorboard at a time. I told them about our first date and the ones after, about how she is kind, compassionate, whip smart, and funny as hell. About how hard she's worked to build the community she always craved, despite her fears, and how that bravery made me feel fearless too. I told them how I had never felt more myself around anyone before, how I was able to open up to her like I had been doing it my whole life. Every day felt like the greatest adventure with Silver, one I prayed to any god that would listen would still be the case after today.

And when I ran out of things to say, because our story was still new and unfurling, I looked up to find both my mom and my sister with tears streaming down their faces.

"I didn't realize," my mom says, choking back tears, "how much you were deteriorating here, how much you blamed yourself for something that wasn't your fault. I didn't realize until just now, listening to you talk about her. Your whole face just came to life before our eyes. I can't remember the last time I saw that look on your face. Long before we lost your brother, at least."

I placed my hand on my mom's arm. "It's okay, Mom. We were all lost in our own grief."

She's shaking her head in refusal, but it's true.

We all died a little the day we lost Maddox. That part of us was gone forever; we would never be the same, but we could find new versions of ourselves, find the adventure he craved and live it for him, for us. It's what he would want. What he begged of me that day, right before we lost him...it took me a while to figure it out, but I did. I like to think he's rolling his eyes at me from the beyond for having my head shoved up my ass for this long.

"So what are you still doing here then?" Laurel asks, wiping tears from her face.

"What do you mean?"

"You have to go back to New York, to tell her what happened. Like right now." She motions with her hands to shoo me out the door.

"Laurel, I can't leave. Look at you."

"I know. It's hard to believe I can look this good after a car accident." She makes a show of inspecting her nails, the picture of elegance in a hospital gown.

Dad snorts from the door in a rare display of humanity; I almost forgot he was here.

"Be serious. I can't leave you like this."

"You can and you will," Mom chimes in. "You love this girl." A fact, not a question. I nod my head in an affirmation she didn't need. "Then it's settled. You need to get back to New York now, explain to her what happened, make a grand gesture. Whatever it takes. Don't let my daughter-in-law go without a fight."

"Mom, it's only been a few months," I say to deflect against what I'm really feeling as butterflies take flight in my stomach, thinking about Silver being mine forever.

"A mother always knows." She winks.

"Seriously, Hen, my doctor said she would probably discharge me by tomorrow morning anyway. I'm okay. You did right by me by showing up. Go do right by your girl."

Moisture builds along my lashes as I stand from my chair and bend down to kiss my sister on her head. "I love you."

"Yuck. Love has made you mushy and soft." She pushes me away and towards Mom, who I wrap in a tight hug.

"I'll call *you* next time, I promise. I'm sorry." I deepen my squeeze.

"I know you will."

I'm walking back towards the door when I see my dad standing guard next to it, arms crossed and face unforgiving.

"Leaving again?" he asks, even though he already knows the answer.

I nod. "You always taught me to be a man of my word didn't you?" His jaw tightens at the brief mention of how he raised me being thrown in his face. "If you want to talk," I pause, wondering if I'm putting myself out there for nothing, "try to fix this...rift, then you know where to find me. But it's your decision now."

I give my mother and sister one last look, one smile I hope conveys everything I'm feeling—that I love them, that I'm in a good place. They don't need to worry about me; I will call them as soon as I can.

I tap on the frame of the doorway and make my way back out into the cold Seattle air, hop in a taxi, and make my way back to the airport for the second time today.

Only this time, I'm going back home.

When I make it to the store, no one is there.

I knew it was a long shot with the time difference and six hour flight, but I had to try in the hopes Silver might still be here, cleaning up after what I know was a wildly successful day.

So, I beeline home, flying through the front door fast enough that it puts Jae on full alert. He jumps off the couch and brandishes his dinnerware as a weapon in case I'm an intruder.

When he sees it's me, he relaxes. "Dude, what the hell? Where have you been?"

"Seattle." I head toward my room, Jae trailing behind me.

"What? Why were you in Seattle?"

"Laurel was in a car accident." I start stripping, desperate to change out of the clothes I've been wearing for the last eighteen hours, give or take.

"What? Is she okay? What happened? Hendrix!"

"Huh?"

"Is Laurel okay?" His eyes have gone frantic, and his chest rises and falls in rapid succession.

"Shit, yes. I'm sorry. I didn't mean to scare you. She's banged up and has some broken bones, but she's fine. The doctor is going to release her in the morning."

He drops down on my bed, relieved. "So why are you acting so...turbulent?"

The image of Silver setting up the shop, excited for the big day, waiting for me to walk through the shop doors holding her favorite coffee, flits through my mind. Then her face falling when that moment never came. I failed her and I have to make it right—will do anything to make sure she knows I am her safe harbor.

"I need your help." My brain runs a million miles a minute, trying to figure out how to pull off what I need to do.

"Whatever you need, brother." He places an arm on my shoulder, sensing the gravity of the moment, and I quickly recount the events of the last

"Can you DM Kena? It's not too late, and there's a chance he'll see the message. I need to get his number again so I can call him from your phone. And then we need to call Sam. We're going to need him for this too."

"I have Kena's number," Jae states proudly.

"Really?" I would be less shocked but the one time we all hung out, Jae spent ninety percent of his night with a bachelorette party instead of us.

"Yeah, I asked him to send me the recording of your performance. You enthusiastically singing, "What Dreams Are Made Of, is going to be the song that plays as I enter mine and Laurel's wedding." He unlocks his phone and hands it to me.

"I'm looking forward to watching Laurel string you up by your balls for even suggesting that." I scroll through his list of contacts, finding Kena's name and pressing call.

The phone rings twice before the line connects, and the voice on the other end starts yelling when I tell him who it is. When Kena stops, I plead, "I know. Which is why I need your help."

Chapter 30

Silver

By the time five am rolls around, I've gotten a collective two hours of sleep.

I've spent the whole night tossing and turning, intermittently waking up and remembering the day before, either my mother or Hendrix at the forefront of my mind each and every time I startled awake..

Eventually, I toss back the covers and get out of bed, needing to just...move. I don't know. I just need to be anywhere but here, where all I do is think of him.

I can see him standing in my kitchen as I make us lunch. Hendrix on a ladder in my room, pants fitting him so perfectly, it was impossible not to ogle. Hendrix standing in my living room, offering to help me with the store and me stupidly agreeing to it.

After quickly washing my face and brushing my teeth, I change into leggings and an oversized cable knit sweater, before I head out the door and start walking.

The air is colder this morning than it was yesterday, and I

welcome the bite it gives to my skin, waking me up a little more with each step. I have no direction but away from my apartment as my feet pound the pavement.

The city is still quiet, not quite abuzz with activity yet, but I wish it was. I left my phone and earbuds at home in the hope that the city would distract me from the relentless thoughts swirling in my head. So far, I have been unsuccessful in that mission.

I stop by one of the food carts on the sidewalk hawking stale pasties and burnt coffee to get myself a cup, forgetting I didn't bring anything with me. When I say as much, apologizing to the owner, he takes pity on me and sends me off with a drip coffee and a donut that tastes like ash in my mouth.

I walk for miles as I watch the city wake up—cafés putting out their shop signs, joggers on their morning runs, food carts setting up for the day. Around and around, people run about to their next destination without noticing me. I am one in roughly eight million, inconsequential to everyone around me. Buildings a thousand feet high all bursting out of the ground around me making it very easy to feel small–insignificant.

I weave in and out of the streets of Midtown, passing through Times Square and all its bright Jumbotron screens, easily walking around the minimal number of people who would have a reason to be here this early on a Sunday morning. It's almost eerie, seeing this part of town so quiet.

Before I know it, my aimless wandering has dropped me off at Central Park South, and it seems kind of poetic to me that I would wind up here, the place I always came to when I was feeling alone in a city full of people. I would torture myself by reading all the bench plaques engraved with tributes and words of love and admiration for people I'll never meet but who meant the world to someone somewhere.

I thought I was starting to understand that kind of love for another person, to actually let it in and feel it for the first time in my life, but I guess I was wrong.

I slowly pass bench after bench as I walk around the southern portion of Central Park, working my way higher and higher.

To my wife Delia, for making every day an adventure.

For our parents, who sat on this bench every Sunday and played the crossword together.

Celia, James, and a love that transcended it all.

For Miley, who loves to bask in the sun on this very hill. You saved me, baby pup.

On and on, the confessions of love go as I wind through the lush walking paths of the park, reading every single one with tears threatening to spill.

I walk, fingers grazing against engraved steel plaques until my heart can't take it anymore, my knees crumbling beneath me. I catch myself on the arm rest of the closest bench, sit down, and finally let them fall.

I have no idea how much time has passed. Minutes, hours, years—it could be any, and I wouldn't be surprised.

I miss my dad, and I wonder what he would have made of all

of this—of me. I wonder who I would have been if my childhood wasn't ripped away from me. Would I have liked who I was—who I would have become? Would I have ever met Kena, or been as close to Nan as I am? How many different paths could my life have taken if the experiences of my youth didn't bring me down the one that led me to a park bench on a Sunday morning? More silent tears spill because I don't know the answers, and I've never been good with uncertainty, always preferring the road that led to the destination I could predict. At this point, I am one giant tear, and I don't know how there are any left. Every emotion that I've bottled up over the last twenty years, breaking through the dam, drowning everything out.

A gentle hand settles on my shoulder, startling me. When I look up, it's to find the kind eyes of my nan staring back at me, Kena standing just behind her.

"What—" I get out one word before the tears start anew.

Nan sits down next to me, Kena taking up the other side. She pats my leg and grabs my hand, bringing it into her lap. "I thought I might find you here."

"How did you get here?" Baffled is the only word to express what I'm feeling right now.

"Something called Uber? Creepy business, if you ask me, telling people it's okay to ride in cars with strangers."

I choke on a laugh that bubbles up my throat. "I meant in New York, Nan."

"Well, Bear, I think it's obvious I took a plane."

Kena finally interjects. "I called her yesterday and told her she might want to come in."

"Ah, yes. My sweet boy said my best girl might need me."

"How did you find me here—in the park, I mean?" I could have been anywhere.

"You used to always want to see the Balto statue when you were a little girl. When you weren't at home this morning, and didn't answer our calls, I figured this would be the best place to start."

I look up at my surroundings, and there he is, the magnificent Balto in all his burnished glory. I didn't even realize this is where I settled when I stopped walking and crumpled.

"Why didn't you tell me about the reopening party?" Nan settles a wrinkled hand on my knee.

I wipe under my eyes with the back of my sleeve, and look toward Balto. "You hate flying. I didn't want to put you through that for a small party."

"You're downplaying it," Kena says. "You've spent months working toward that *small party*." His subtle irritation puts me on edge and I can feel the urge to assuage him, rush to the surface, but Nan interrupts before I can.

"Tell me what's going on, Bear."

Old habits nip at my heels, begging them to dig in, to not worry my family with the heartache that's plaguing me. But another part of me, the part that Hendrix dug out of the muck, is pleading with me to let them in—to let them see the mess I've been hiding behind easy smiles and professional deflection skills.

Brave. Hendrix once told me I was brave, and while even recounting the memory of that conversation makes my heart cave in on itself—I feel the urge to prove him right.

For the first time in my life, I open up and tell her everything, spilling my guts out onto the pavement at our feet.

The scent of coffee floats through the air, filling my senses as I tell Nan how Hendrix and I met. How I thought I had lost my shot, only for him to be dumped on my doorstep, a tool belt slung low around his waist. I admit to my fear of commitment, thinking everyone would just leave me in the end, but tell her how he showed up every day at six on the dot, ready to help me with coffee in hand. My eyes drift around the park, now more alive with people, and I laugh when I give her examples of some of the ridiculous questions we'd ask during our endless rounds of twenty questions. Tears form when I tell her about our first kiss, how it scared me so acutely, I needed to pull away from him, but he kept showing up, kept proving to me he cared. Nan gasps and puts a hand to her mouth when I tell her about the attack, how Hendrix made me feel safe just by being there, and in that moment I knew things would be okay. Everything changed after that, and despite my fear—I let him in—started to crave the sound of his voice, the steadying weight of his touch. I recount the weeks following our first date, how he made being in a relationship with him feel fundamental, how he eased my fears and made me feel like I was something to be cherished.

I swallow, looking down at my feet when I tell her how Mom showed up, uninvited, to the store before opening day, and it brought back every feeling I've had since I was eight. Worthless, a burden, never good enough for anything or anyone. But Hendrix never made me feel that way, and I just wanted to hear his voice. All I needed was to hear his deep honeyed voice telling me it would be okay, and that he was on his way. But he never answered, and then he never showed.

I don't tell them how I've felt hollow ever since, like a large chunk of me is missing where my heart should be. My gaze darts around the park, not wanting to look at them after stripping bare, wishing I could stuff all the words back inside my mouth.

"Something's not making sense to me," Nan says, brow furrowed.

"What do you mean?"

"Well, it's just the picture you painted of this man of yours... It doesn't add up with him not showing up for you yesterday."

"I was thinking the same thing," Kena chimes in.

"Tell that to his voicemail," I mutter.

"No, but really," Kena starts. "I've seen him with you. That man is in love with you. The way he talked about you when we were at the Brooklyn Flea made that *very* obvious."

My heart skips a beat at his words, at the hope that blooms and then withers in my chest.

"Do you really think, after everything he's done to show you he cares for you, he would just up and leave with no notice?" Nan asks, though she knows my answer.

"I didn't think so, but he didn't show and hasn't called. What else am I supposed to assume?"

"I think you shouldn't assume at all."

"Nan, be realistic," I scoff. What else am I supposed to think after yesterday?

"Honey, I know life dealt you a bad hand when you were a kid, but you have to realize there are people who would go to the ends of the Earth for you. Hendrix sounds like one of them."

"Thank God someone said it!" Kena throws his hands in the air.

"What's happening?"

Kena cups my hand in his, resting them on his lap. "You are my best friend, and I would do anything for you. But I know there's a part of you that you have always kept hidden away."

My body locks up tighter than a vault, ashamed by his observation and the truth behind it.

"I know it's a defense mechanism you developed after your mom left, I understand. Even when it's me, your best friend, you still feel the need to hide and put on a brave face. And that's okay. I know you've let me in more than anyone else before. But sweetie, you started to let those walls down for Hendrix after a few weeks. You felt safe enough to let him see behind the curtain of the fabricated version of you the world sees. That kind of connection doesn't happen to everyone. I know you're scared, but don't you think that's something worth fighting for?"

"What if—" I pause, my words breaking off at the thoughts swirling in my head.

"Say it. Don't hide from the pain," Nan encourages.

I take a deep, shuddering inhale. "What if I'm not enough?" I'm shaking my head as new tears form in my eyes. "I don't think I could survive it. Not from him."

Kena moves to kneel in front of me so I'm now looking down into his warm face. "Do you honestly think he thinks that?"

I shrug.

Nan cuts in, her tone resolute. "I need you to listen to me now and hear what I'm about to say to you. I don't know where you got this idea that you're not enough, but it's a lie you're using to keep yourself from being truly happy. You're running scared. But the unavoidable truth is—every time you give a piece of yourself to someone, you run the risk of being hurt, but that doesn't mean love will only end in pain. You have to realize the people around you want to show up for you, love you, if you'd only let them close enough. I would have been on the first flight out to be at your opening, threat of probable death be damned."

I let out a shuddering breath. "I'm scared. What if he wakes up one day and decides to leave?"

"Ah, my girl, that's the silver lining of it all, isn't it? When you allow yourself to be brave, to do the thing that scares you most, only then will you really learn who you are. We have to choose to risk our hearts every day to truly know what it is to love and be loved. To *live*. Sometimes, it doesn't work out, and we learn valuable lessons, but sometimes, it works so perfectly, we don't know how we survived without it. There's no point to this floating rock in the sky without love."

Nan might have a point. I was just having a hard time grasping it while my heart was in tatters.

"So tell me, *who are you*, Silver James?"

Chapter 31

Silver

Who are you?

I've been mulling over Nan's words since I had to leave her and Kena to come open the store. As I walk up to the shop, every thought leaves my body when I see the door slightly ajar.

I know I locked up last night.

My irrational brain supplies every worst case scenario, and the one leading the charge is the attacker from all those weeks ago coming back for revenge. I would never recover financially or emotionally if the store was robbed.

I slowly approach the door, pushing it open, peeking my head in and smelling sawdust and something chemical. When I step inside, my body comes to a full and complete stop so abrupt, I nearly drop the second coffee I picked up on my way over with money Nan gave me to get food because I looked *peaky*.

Hendrix is here.

Hendrix is here?

And he's on the second floor? Staining the banister?

Question after question swirls around in my mind like a tornado. Where the hell has he been? How is he up there when the staircase is broken? Why are there tarps covering my shelves? Why is there sawdust on the floor? And why on Earth does he look so goddamn delicious?

"What are you doing?" The words come out of my mouth without me even realizing it.

Hendrix whips his head down to me and smiles, but his gloriously beautiful grin fades as he takes in the look on my face, the dark circles that are no doubt under my eyes. Slowly, he sets down his staining rag and bucket and makes his way down the stairs. I brace myself for the areas I know are broken, waiting for them to creak and snap and send Hendrix tumbling down. But with every step down the stairs, there's silence, the boards are quiet beneath his feet until he's stopped in front of me.

"Sunshine, I—" he starts, but I quickly interrupt.

"Where the hell have you been, Hendrix?"

Out of nowhere, there's a crash upstairs before I see Sam and Jae's heads pop up, both men looking sheepish, and brandishing their own staining supplies.

"Sorry." Sam starts to canter down the steps with Jae on his heels. "Let us just get out of here before you start laying into him."

"Try to avoid his pretty face when you start swinging, Silver," Jae says as he claps Hendrix on the shoulder.

I watch them smoothly exit the store, and when I turn back, I realize Hendrix never took his eyes off me, the gold striations blazing brighter than the rest with a look of determination.

He goes to reach for me, but I step out of his hold, and his hands and face fall. "There's nothing I could do or say to make this right."

"Try." My voice cracks on the word, desperate for him to fight for me.

"I'm so sorry, Sunshine. I broke a promise to you when I wasn't here for you yesterday, to see you get everything you've been working so hard towards. And I know you." He risks a step towards me. "I know your instincts are telling you to put up your walls again. I don't have a right to ask, but if you need those walls to feel safer, I'm begging you to let me stand inside them with you."

My breath hitches, and I stare up into the face of the man I've spent months slowly falling for.

"Why weren't you here?" An errant tear charts a path down my face before Hendrix reaches his hand up to brush it away. I lean into his touch automatically, breathing him in, missing him even though he's right in front of me.

His face falls slightly. "I was in Seattle."

My head jerks out of his palm, and his hand lingers in the air, expecting me to fill it again before dropping down to his side. "What? Why?"

He wouldn't go to Seattle out of nowhere, and he certainly wouldn't go and not tell me about it. So why hadn't he?

"My mom called me early yesterday morning. Laurel was in a car accident."

A gasp falls from my lips, and on instinct, I'm reaching for him. "Is she okay? Are you okay?"

His breathing levels out a little when he looks down to where my hands grip his shirt. "She's okay. Mom called me in a panic, and I didn't think. Every fear I had from Maddox's accident came flooding to the surface, so I ran to the airport and hopped on the first flight out. I lost my phone and couldn't get a message to you. I came back last night and came straight here, but you had already gone home. So, I'm here," he indicates to the staircase behind him, "grand gesturing."

"We need to get you back to Seattle, then. You should be with Laurel, with your family."

Hendrix's face falls.

"Do you not—" His voice goes hoarse, and he looks down into my eyes, pleading with me. "Please forgive me. Don't push me away. I can't..." A single tear drops from his eye. "I can't do this without you. Everything has meaning again because of you." His hands tentatively settle on my waist. "I don't deserve it, but I want it, *need* it. I need you and your light every day. My world was gray before you came barreling into me, throwing it into technicolor. *Please*."

I step toward him, and he holds his breath as I reach out a hand and cup his jaw, wiping the tear from his cheek. "I just meant you should be with them. I know what getting that call must have done to you. Being back home might bring you more comfort. I'll be here when you get back. I promise."

He turns his cheek, kissing my palm. "Laurel is fine; she practically shoved me out of the door with her crutches to come tell you what happened. I'm exactly where I am supposed to be." He leans his head down so it's resting against mine. "My place with you is where I *need* to be." He breathes me in and I inch my body a little closer. "I told you once I would always come back for you. I'm sorry I was a little late." He places a gentle kiss against my brow.

"It's okay—"

"No, I should have found a way to tell you what happened. I should have been here." There's desperation lining his handsome face. I feel a certainty burning in my chest that he never would have missed the re-opening for anything less than an absolute emergency. And it's so easy to forgive him when he's looking at me so earnestly, so easy to remember all we've gone through together that led us here. Everything has always felt easy with him—natural.

Something worth fighting for.

"You were." He looks at me quizzically, not understanding. "You *were* here, in every paint stroke, in every floorboard replaced, in every perfect shelf—you were here. You have *been* here, every day for months. I felt you everywhere yesterday, I couldn't escape it—couldn't escape *you*. I don't ever want to."

"I don't deserve you," he says, looking at me like I'm some sort of miracle.

I smile at him, and I feel lighter than I ever have. "I think we deserve each other."

We both stand there, breathing each other in, content in the quiet.

"Tell me about how the day went?"

I start with Carol James showing up.

Hendrix jerks back. "Your mom was here?"

I quickly tell him everything that happened yesterday morning, his face morphing from shock to outrage to sadness on my behalf.

"How do you feel about it all?"

"Upset...but also proud? For standing up for myself." The pride in his eyes warms me from my head down to my toes. "She left some sort of note, though. I haven't been able to bring myself to read it."

"Do you want to do it now?"

I shake my head. Whatever she had to say, she waited years to do it. A little more time in blissful ignorance wouldn't hurt.

I smile softly at him. "I'd rather you tell me how you broke into my store and what you've been doing in here."

"I didn't break in," he says, abashed as he rubs the back of his neck. "I called Kena, who got me in contact with Holly, who let me in last night."

"Kena knew you were here?"

He nods in confirmation. I guess that explains my best friend's vehemence earlier this morning. The whole time, he knew Hendrix was here waiting for me.

"I wanted to do a grand gesture to apologize for missing the store reopening and enlisted the help of Sam and Jae so we could finish on time. The staircase and the second floor landing are safe to use. I was just finishing up the staining so it matched the floors when you came in."

I reach out and grab his face, stroking my thumb back and forth across his cheekbones, amazed, but not surprised that he would do this for me. He's been showing me from the very beginning, waiting for me to catch up, and I'm finally starting to believe that I'm worth it. He is the lighthouse guiding my ship home, because that's what I feel when I'm with him—I'm home.

"Where did you get all the supplies to do this overnight?" I redirect.

"I may have had Sam call every hardware store in a twenty mile radius until I got all the materials I'd need."

"Can I go up and see it?" I whisper in a way that belies my excitement.

He grabs my hand and pulls me towards the stairs, tugging me once we reach the base, as if he can sense my reluctance to climb them. "Come on, Sunshine. I promise it's safe. I won't let anything hurt you."

And he's right. Not a single step creaks or moves beneath my step. They've all been rebuilt with structural integrity that feels poetic on a personal level. Somehow, the stairs were a metaphor for how I felt inside—broken and unusable. But this store, this new direction I have in life, is the renovated version of me. When we've reached the top, my eyes line with tears for what feels like the hundredth time today.

I never realized how lovely it could be up here. It's only about a third of the size as the lower level and hangs over the back section of the store. The low ceilings up here lend to its cozy feeling, and I note Hendrix installed sconces along the wall to bring a warmth to the space.

"It's perfect." I choke slightly on the words, unable to express my gratitude. "Thank you."

Hendrix comes up to me then, wrapping his arms around my waist, turning me so we're looking over the banister onto the shop floor. I settle my head back on his shoulder and take in the view from up here, truly appreciating how far the space has come.

How far I've come.

"Look at what we built," I remark.

Hendrix shakes his head. "Look at what *you* built. This was all you, Silver. Your vision, your determination, your dream. You did this all on your own." He leans down and places a soft kiss to my neck, the scruff of his beard making goosebumps break out over my skin. "I've also got some designs I want you to look over."

"Designs?"

"Yeah, uh..." He's nervous about something. "I've been working on some pieces for up here, small tables and chairs I could build if you liked them. You mentioned wanting to turn this floor into a place where people could come read and write, as well as hosting events up here, and I just thought..." He huffs a breath against the back of my head. "Of course, if you wanted to thrift some furniture instead, the Brooklyn Flea had some coo-"

I cut him off by twisting in his hold, throwing my arms around his neck and crashing my lips to his. His surprise quickly ebbs as his warm lips move against mine slowly. Kissing him is like feeling that first ray of sun after a week of cold rain. I wanted to revel in this warmth forever.

I reluctantly pull back just an inch, fingers playing with the hair at the nape of his neck. I gaze into the eyes that have come to feel like home to me and leap. "I love you."

And then, I burst into tears.

He holds me through it, whispering words of love and affirmation against my head as I feel every vulnerable emotion under the sun. Fear, happiness, anxiety, hope, joy—they all feel like the heaviest and lightest weight on my shoulders. He never eases his grip on me. He tells me I'll never be alone as long as he lives, that he loves my courage and resilience, that he loves that I can always find a joke in any situation, that I can't sing for shit, and that doing menial tasks with me feels like an adventure he wants to go on every day.

When I'm finally done crying, he looks me in the eyes. "I love you too, Sunshine."

And it's the most beautiful thing I've ever heard.

Two weeks later...

"You don't have to read it. You can just throw it away, and no one will blame you."

Hendrix and I sit on the loveseat upstairs in the bookstore, staring down at the letter my mom left for me. I've been looking at the cream envelope for ten minutes already, trying to muster up the courage to open it and see what's inside.

There's a part of me that doesn't want to care, and then there's a part of me that knows I'll always wonder if I don't see what's inside. It's the latter that has me reaching for it now.

Hendrix places a steadying hand on my knee to help ease my nerves as I slot the tip of my finger under the corner flap to open the note.

I take a deep breath before pulling the contents of the envelope out. It seems she put a lot of things in here, the first being a save the date to her wedding that I promptly set aside. The next is a handwritten letter. It's short, to the point, and lacks any sort of familiarity.

> Your father and I started a savings account for you when you were born. I continued to pay into it when I could throughout the years after his passing and thought it was time for me to give it to you. Do whatever you want with it. Paul and I hope to see you at the wedding.
>
> Best, Mom

Best.

Not love. Not sincerely. Not even a warm regards. It doesn't sting the way I think it would have a couple weeks ago.

I reach behind the *heartfelt* letter for the third and final component to her interruption in my life, pulling out a thin slip of paper—a check to be exact. For fifteen thousand dollars. I drop it like it just caught fire in my hand and burned me.

"Unbelievable," I mumble.

I look to Hendrix, my steady rock against the crashing waves. He's been stroking my leg in a soothing motion since I brought him up here to do this, never wavering in his support of whatever I choose.

"Talk to me."

"She's trying to bribe me. Her future husband wants me at their wedding, and this is how she thinks she can accomplish that. If I take her money, I'll feel obligated to go." It's hard to keep the bitterness out of my voice. For as much as I've worked through the dynamic between myself and my mom in the last couple weeks, I can't say I'm fully at peace with it. I don't think I ever will be—my new therapist told me it was a perfectly normal reaction to all I had been through. I was still figuring it out.

"It could be helpful after you depleted your reserves," Hendrix points out. I know he's right, suggesting it to make sure I weigh all my options.

I reach down to pick the check up off the floor and extend it towards him. "If anyone deserves it, it's you."

"That's ridiculous." He pushes it away from himself like it's riddled with the bubonic plague.

"I'm serious. You did so much physical labor on this place and deserve to be compensated for it. Let me pay you." I lean forward to try and shove the check in the pocket of his hoodie.

"Absolutely not." He grabs my arm, stopping me from forcing the check onto his person as he grabs me by the waist with his other arm, swinging my body over to straddle his, effectively shutting me up.

I wiggle in his lap, eliciting a groan from deep in the back of his throat. To make matters worse—for him—I lean forward to pepper kisses along his obscenely perfect jawline.

When I reach his ear, I lean forward. "Please let me use my mom's guilt money to pay you." A delicate bite to his ear has him clenching his teeth.

His firm hands are on my shoulders, pushing me so there's a respectable amount of space between us. I hate it. I want to burrow under his hoodie and stay there forever. It's crazy what being happy and in love does to a woman.

I pout, and he appeases me by giving my lips a quick peck before holding me away again.

"I helped you because I wanted to be near you every second of every day. I never had any intention of taking money from you, and I didn't need help with a portfolio. I already had an extensive one. So no, I will not be taking the money. I don't need it." He smirks with the arrogance of a man who knows what he's capable of.

Getting let go from The Langham actually turned out to be a blessing in disguise, because Hendrix now has all the free time in the world to work on custom builds Kena has been commissioning. He was so impressed with the design Hendrix turned in a couple weeks ago, he wanted to have his very own hot carpenter on speed dial.

"So, if you don't take the money... Oh my god. I'm Richard Gere in Pretty Woman, and you're Julia Roberts. You're my paid for whore."

"I have no clue what you're talking about, but I'll be whatever you want me to be."

I lean forward, bringing my face close to his. "Great answer," I murmur against his mouth before capturing his lips in a soft kiss. The soft kisses have become my favorite—unhurried, tender, and always with the promise of more.

"I think I want to donate the money to the library."

The look in Hendrix's eyes is enough to make me melt into the floor. His gaze is intense but gentle, beaming with pride. "I love you." A soft smile crinkles the corners of his eyes.

I'll never get tired of hearing it. I have no clue how I've made it this far before realizing I needed it, this connection. I think I was always just waiting for him. I could have never felt this magnitude of emotion for someone else, an electromagnetic wave so potent and visceral, there would only be one outcome. Cosmic, kismet, fate, magic—whatever you wanted to call it, it was us, and it was perfect.

"I love you too, Herschel."

The laugh that bursts from Hendrix's mouth as he tips his head back is bright and boisterous. It's the loveliest sound I've ever heard, my favorite drug.

He surges forward and kisses me full on the mouth. All earlier traces of gentleness are gone, replaced with something bordering on feral. Not that I'm complaining—I'm still straddling his lap, meeting his tongue stroke for stroke, and it's suddenly feeling too hot on this cozy second floor. The store has only been open for a few minutes, and we haven't had any customers stop by yet, so I decide to lean into the recklessness a little longer.

I start to grind down on him, rocking my hips back and forth, drawing a growl from his mouth.

"Don't start something you can't finish, Summer."

"Hopefully, one of us finishes," I quip, shoving my fingers into his thick chocolate strands and giving them a rough tug.

I've just shoved my hands up under the hem of his hoodie when the bell to the front door dings, alerting me to customers.

I pop up off his lap and look down at the noticeable bulge with a smirk. "Might want to wait a moment before coming downstairs."

I can hear the newcomers chatting excitedly to each other about a new thriller they've been hunting for. I lean down and give my boyfriend one last kiss before I make my way downstairs. This place was the first thing I ever committed to, the first major decision I made for myself that felt right.

It was home.

Halfway down the stairs, I glance back at Hendrix and realize I have *two* homes now.

I hit the landing and smile at the group of shoppers. "Hey guys! Welcome to Silver Linings Bookshop. Let me know if you need anything."

Epilogue

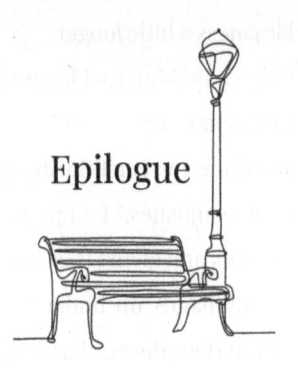

Silver

One Year Later—

"The only reason you got me out of bed this early on the *Lord's Day* is because you bribed me with donuts," I grumble around a mouthful of fluffy, maple bacon greatness.

"Suddenly religious?" Hendrix chuckles.

"When you interrupt a *very* good dream to insist we go on a walk at ungodly hours, yes." This time, I reach into the box from Mimi's and pull out a white chocolate glazed with matcha cream filling. I take a *too* big bite and moan at the sweet, slightly herbal flavor.

"A very good dream, huh?" Hendrix leans down, whispering in my ear. "What was I doing to you in this dream?"

"Who says you were even there?" I tease and then jump when he pinches my side.

I dart out of his grasp before he can do it again, but he chases after me, grabbing me by the waist and lifting me in the air. "Hey! Donuts! Precious cargo here. Have some respect," I would slap at his arms, but my hands are currently occupied by fried dough.

Hendrix slowly settles me onto the ground, chuckling in my ear in a way that still makes my body flush with heat, even a year later. He hasn't let go of me yet; instead, he grips me tighter, burying his face into the crook of my neck and placing a gentle kiss there.

"So soft and warm," he sighs into me.

"You're the one who insisted we go on a walk on the coldest day of the week," I say, snuggling back into him. "Even Central Park is empty."

We arrived at the park twenty minutes ago after we took the train uptown to pick up Mimi's and coffee. It's become a monthly ritual whenever I take a Sunday off from the store, and it's one of my favorite things we do together. It's like we're reliving our first date over and over.

The day I found Hendrix at Silver Linings, we spent so much time talking long into the evening, nothing holding us back. It's the closest I've ever felt to someone in my life. And when we FaceTimed with Laurel to check in on her, she practically launched out of her hospital bed in excitement. Since then, she and I have become thick as thieves, much to Hendrix's dismay.

There's something to be said for finding your person, the one who compliments your life, who makes everything about it fuller and brighter. I used to never think this kind of love was possible for me, too scarred from my past to consider it. I never believed I deserved it, not until Hendrix showed me his love didn't have to be earned—that it was freely given unconditionally. Understanding that has created a domino effect of sorts, spilling over into all my other relationships.

"Yeah, but if it was warm, you wouldn't let me hold you like I am now," Hendrix says, pulling me out of my internal musing.

He's not wrong. I hate the heat; the last thing I want is to cuddle when it's ninety-five degrees out. Air conditioning remains, to this day, the world's greatest achievement, and you can't convince me otherwise.

We walk the winding path through The Rambles, a densely wooded area within the park, spotting various birds as we walk south. By the time we exit, the sun has peeked out from behind the clouds, and the light layer of frost over all the grass has melted. We spot a few tourists on pedi-cab rides, some early morning runners, but it's otherwise still pretty empty for a weekend morning.

We're looping around the southern half of the park when Hendrix stops me. "Why don't we sit down so you can finish your donuts?"

"This is why I love you." I plop down on the bench he ushers me toward, facing a small pond and bridge with skyscrapers peeking over the treetops at our backs, setting the box of confections in my lap and flipping open the lid.

"Maybe one day, you'll look at me the way you look at a box of donuts." He sounds exasperated, but when I look up, he's smiling at me fondly.

"Let's not get our hopes up." I pat his thigh in a placating gesture, and he tosses his head back on a laugh. "Do you want any?" I point at the baked goods.

How I ended up with a man who doesn't like sweets is beyond me, but he doesn't decline like I think he will. Instead, he leans forward and hooks his knuckles under my chin, bringing my face up to meet him in a kiss. His tongue coaxes my lips open, and I moan into his mouth as his tongue tangles with mine.

He pulls back slightly, breaking the kiss, eyes dark, staring down at my swollen mouth. "Delicious."

"I think I've been a bad influence on you," I mutter, turning slightly to face him.

"Mhmm, probably."

I scoff in mock affront and playfully swat at his arm. He stops me before I make contact, wrapping his hand around my wrist, bringing it to his mouth, and placing a kiss there.

"This one looks new," Hendrix notes.

"Hmmm?" I hum in question, having just taken a sip of my coffee.

"This plaque... It looks new."

He always reads them with me now, knowing how much they've meant to me over the years.

I turn to read the one attached to the bench we're sitting on.

Twenty questions will never be enough for us, Sunshine.
How about a lifetime?

Tears well in my eyes, and when I turn to look at Hendrix, he's in front of me, down on one knee.

"Oh my God." I bring a hand to my mouth.

"Silver James, from the moment you barreled into me like a bat out of hell, spilling coffee on my shoes, I knew I was done for," I choke around a laugh. "You have shown me the sun and brought me back to life when I didn't realize I was withering away in the dark. You are the most miraculous, resilient, *outrageous* person I've ever met, and I've loved you from the moment I saw your eyes light up at a store called *Get Nailed*. You make every room brighter and every day with you is an adventure I want to go on for the rest of my life. People write about the love I feel for you, the type of love I hope I show you every day."

A silent tear tracks down his face, and I brush it away with my thumb. "I've called you a lot of names over the past year, but the one I dream of calling you is wife." He reaches into his coat now, pulling out a small, pink velvet box, opening it to reveal the most ethereal ring I've ever seen. "Will you marry me? Spend the rest of our lives writing the best love story of all?"

I launch myself off the bench, throwing my donuts to the pigeons, and wrap my arms around Hendrix. I start peppering him with kisses—so many, he probably can't breathe. In between each one, there's a word: *yes, yes, yes*.

I'm sitting on his bent knee when I pull back, staring into eyes that look like the sun breaking through redwood trees. I cup his jaw in my palm. "I never dared to dream for you. I thought love had abandoned me a long time ago, but you made me hope. I grew up thinking love was a burden, too heavy for me to want to carry, but loving you is the easiest thing I've ever done. So, yes. In every lifetime, in every universe, yes."

I don't know who moves first, him or me, but our lips connect in a soul melding kiss. It's not wild or fervent. It's ineffable. It's devotion, raw and beautiful and us.

We pull apart, only an inch of space remaining between us as Hendrix slips the ring onto my finger, a perfect fit.

"You launched your precious donuts to the sky, Sunshine," he laughs, grabbing my hand and settling us back on the bench.

I look at where they connect, the ring sparkling on my finger bracketed by his, and sigh a breath of pure contentment at the rightness of this moment, of us.

"That's okay. We can get more the next time we come to sit on *our* bench."

Acknowledgements

They say it takes a village...well get ready, because mine is really more of a kingdom:

First, I have to thank Lauren L'Heureux, my ultimate girl's girl and boss bitch inspiration. I never thought this day would come, but you always did. For YEARS you never let me give up on myself. You never let me entertain a moment in which I wasn't able to accomplish this and you have never failed to make sure I know that my dreams were important to you too. This book is greatly here because of your constant and undying support and love. Thank you for always pushing me, for asking at every lunch or dinner date "what's going on with the book", and for never ever giving up on me or letting me give up on myself. I love you.

To my unhinged girlies, Carla, Naty and Jen. You three came into my life when I felt adrift and anchored me. From nights out at Back Pocket, movie nights in pajamas, random coffee dates, walks through bookstores and book club meetings, your presence kept me afloat. Thank you for all the wake up and write texts, the evening check ins, the unconditional support, and the embarrassing amount of handholding . You cheered me on at every milestone, and never wavered in support. You are the friends I always dreamt of having.

To the many authors who have encouraged me along this journey. Buckle up, it's a long one. To Nicole Rubino, having your constant support before you ever even read a sample of my writing meant the world to me. Thank you for always lending your ear, for helping me work through ideas, for daily "are we writing today" texts, all the dark romance recs and for letting me read your books early. I don't think this book would be what it is without you always being willing to listen and help me work through every thought that pops into my brain. To Lana Ferguson, for naming the book, and for being the first person to read a majority of it when it was only halfway done. You assured me it's good, and maybe one day I'll believe you. Until then I say thank you for the encouragement, for being willing to help whenever I needed it and for the canon Hendrix and Jae romance. To Kate Golden for all the random check ins, voice memos and writing sprints, sometimes you kept me going when I most needed it. Your passion for writing always found me and inspired me just in time. You were the first person to ever finish a book I wrote, maybe one day that'll be something to brag about! To Sophie H Morgan, my angel across the pond. Our 30 minute long barrage of voice memos talking about anything from books to our dreams, kept me company on many walks and mornings getting ready for work. You've been a confidant and friend and I can't wait to one day cuddle you and Molly. And lastly, to Scarlett St Clair who always took the time to chat with and encourage me on this journey. Thank you for being someone to look up to in this industry, and for always staying true to yourself. You are an inspiration to many, but especially to me.

To Wendy and Aurea. You guys transcend coworkers. For years, you listened to me ramble about characters and ideas, laughed with me, and helped me outline when we should have been working. And to Mako, my newest coworker turned friend who brings me untold joy every day. Gyrating plushies is your legacy, you absolute icon.

To Katie—your often aggressive words of encouragement helped me get past any reluctance I had to give this dream a try. I'll be forever grateful for every time you let me self-deprecate and lovingly threatened to block me if I kept talking badly about myself. Looks like I proved myself wrong after all. Please keep showering me with your brand of unique aggressive love and support. I'll always need it.

To Natalie, who popped into my life by chance and who helped a struggling writer get off the ground by making edits I couldn't even begin to conceive on my own. You lent a hand out of the kindness of your heart and I'm so happy I gained a friend out of it. Thank you for every time you talked me down from a spiral, and for seeing my characters exactly how I wanted them to be seen. I can't imagine life without you now and I don't want to. Our brain cells have merged and there's no going back, you're stuck with me now.

To my Mom who must have strength and fortitude in droves to raise a child just like her husband. And to my dad for always telling me I'm the bravest person he knows. I hope I did you proud and I hope you never read this book. To Meagan who is my biggest cheerleader in everything and my #1 fan and to Matt who's always there to keep me humble. You're both big old softies and I'm not sorry I'm the hottest of us. Save the best for last and all that. To Sarah for being my book buddy, and for doing anything to encourage this path for me, I hope you like this one enough to give it a GR rating. To Ashley for your gentle support and for always encouraging me to be my authentic self. And last but not least, to Lincoln and Rowan, for the unparalleled amount of joy you bring us every day. You two are the greatest gifts our family has ever known.

To Laura Rose. We've been friends since I had no eyebrows and you took your makeup off with alcohol. And if our friendship could survive that disaster, it can survive anything. I love you more than words and am blessed that you're my ride or die. Thank you for believing in me through every era of my life and for taking my author photos—you made me feel like the badass you always tell me I am.

Thank you to my Beta Readers/friends Ada & Abbey. Your love for this genre is unparalleled and I'm so lucky you were the first eyes to ever read this in its entirety. Thank you for your hard work and attention to detail. Your comments on the doc kept a perpetual smile on my face and made me realize that letting other people read my books might not be so bad. And for all the encouragement and cheerleading post feedback. I owe you both so much.

To my nutritionist Jennifer and therapist Monica. Thank you for always listening to me ramble, and for helping me get my life on track, I know I did a lot of heavy lifting but you spotted me the whole way. I'm so encouraged by the forces of nature you both are.

To the people I met through a crazy app who have become so dear to me. Thank you Laura Heath for checking in with me even when you've got a million things going at once, you're an inspiration on all accounts. To Korina, for being the world's best hype woman. No one goes harder for authors than you do and you've been cheering me on far longer than I allowed myself the title. To Vanessa, for saving me when I couldn't figure out how to format this book to save my life. And to everyone I've met over the last five years being in this community. Reading connects us all, and that's kinda beautiful.

To my editor Alexa (@thefictionfix). I'm floored by how brilliant you are. Thank you for taking something so precious to me, handling it with care and polishing it up to a dazzling shine. Get ready for book two.

To my cover designer Brenna (@brennajonesdesign) for creating a beautiful cover and wrap. Thank you for your attention to detail and all the time you spent creating my first ever book cover.

And finally to Miley. My steadfast companion every day for the last 14 ½ years. Thank you for sitting by my side as I wrote this book for over 3 years and for keeping me tethered to this world in a way only a pup can. You are my sunshine.

Connect with Violet

Instagram: @thevioletpage
TikTok: @thevioletpage